D0802857

Books by Eileen Wilks

TEMPTING DANGER
MORTAL DANGER
BLOOD LINES
NIGHT SEASON
MORTAL SINS
BLOOD MAGIC
BLOOD CHALLENGE
DEATH MAGIC
MORTAL TIES
RITUAL MAGIC
UNBINDING
MIND MAGIC
DRAGON SPAWN

Anthologies

CHARMED
(with Jayne Ann Krentz writing as Jayne Castle,
Julie Beard, and Lori Foster)

LOVER BEWARE
(with Christine Feehan, Katherine Sutcliffe, and Fiona Brand)

CRAVINGS
(with Laurell K. Hamilton, MaryJanice Davidson,
and Rebecca York)

ON THE PROWL
(with Patricia Briggs, Karen Chance, and Sunny)

INKED
(with Karen Chance, Marjorie M. Liu, and Yasmine Galenorn)

TIED WITH A BOW
(with Lora Leigh, Virginia Kantra, and Kimberly Frost)

Specials

ORIGINALLY HUMAN
INHUMAN
HUMAN NATURE
HUMAN ERROR

DRAGON SPAWN

EILEEN WILKS

BERKLEY SENSATION
New York

BERKLEY SENSATION
Published by Berkley
An imprint of Penguin Random House LLC
375 Hudson Street, New York, New York 10014

Copyright © 2016 by Eileen Wilks
Excerpt from *Dragon Blood* by Eileen Wilks copyright © 2016 by Eileen Wilks
Penguin Random House supports copyright. Copyright fuels creativity, encourages
diverse voices, promotes free speech, and creates a vibrant culture. Thank you for buying
an authorized edition of this book and for complying with copyright laws by not
reproducing, scanning, or distributing any part of it in any form without permission.
You are supporting writers and allowing Penguin Random House to continue to
publish books for every reader.

BERKLEY and BERKLEY SENSATION are registered trademarks and the B colophon is
a trademark of Penguin Random House LLC.

ISBN: 9780451488039

First Edition: December 2016

Printed in the United States of America
1 3 5 7 9 10 8 6 4 2

Cover art by Tony Mauro
Cover design by Katie Anderson

PROLOGUE

~~

THE sunlight glittered on ocean waves, the air sparkled with sorcéri, and the baby he held was asleep. Sure, the beach was crowded and it would take a while to get to the front of the line. The snow cone stand was doing a brisk business. But all in all, Cullen Seabourne was having a good day . . . until the two gigglers got in line behind him.

Both were blond. Both wore bikinis. Cullen had nothing against blonds or bikinis; he enjoyed looking at female bodies and had developed a particular fondness for blond hair. Cynna's hair was blond. So was Ryder's. But both his wife and his baby had hair much shorter than the polished curls on the short girl or the ironed hair on the tall one.

But then, they hadn't come to the beach to get their hair wet, had they?

"She's absolutely adorable!" the taller one cried. "How old is she?"

Cullen wasn't about to argue with clear and irrefutable fact, but he was sadly aware of what would come next. Both his nose and experience warned him of that. He shifted the hand on Ryder's back, making sure his wedding ring showed. It probably wouldn't help. "Nine months."

"I just love babies!" The short one beamed up at him without paying any attention to the baby Cullen was holding. "And there's nothing sexier than a man holding a baby."

Her taller friend chimed in. "That is so true. I'm Meghan. What's her name? And yours?"

"Ryder. And Cullen."

"What a pretty name! Hers, I mean. Is she yours?"

"Yes." The pleasure that filled him at being able to give that simple answer had only grown deeper with time. It mellowed him enough to give them another chance to back out gracefully. "Not mine alone, of course. My *wife's* hair is the same lovely color. Do either of you have children?"

The short one giggled. Her friend struck a pose, running a hand along her torso suggestively. "Oh, come on. Do I look like I've had children?"

"No, but I hesitated to mention the size of your breasts. Don't worry. They'll get larger when you're nursing." He turned his back on them while their mouths still hung open. A second later, they both decided they didn't want a snow cone after all, and went in search of better prey.

The woman in front of him—a roly-poly, dark-skinned matron of an age that made him think the three children she was shepherding through the line were grandkids—let out a loud laugh. "If you're tired of women climbing all over you, why you wearing that little Speedo? Man as pretty as you don't need to show off what he's got."

"What, you think I'm asking for it? Isn't that what some people say if a woman wears anything more revealing than a burka?"

"I like you," she announced. "What's your name?"

"Cullen. What's yours?"

"Sarah Winstead."

He and Sarah talked about babies and raising children while they waited their turns for snow cones. They were almost at the head of the line when the trouble started.

There were three of them—two with brown hair, one blond. All young, male, and very fit. Early twenties, he thought, which was surely old enough to know better, but it seemed no one had taught them how to behave in public. They wore swim trunks—red, green, orange. One of them had a brand-new tattoo of the Confederate flag on his left bicep. The skin was red and puffy still.

There were three people on the other side of the trouble, too: a man in jeans and a San Diego Padres T-shirt; a woman in a pretty green hijab, long sleeves, and a maxi skirt; and a beautiful dark-eyed boy about four years old.

The line had stayed pretty constant behind him. There were a lot of kids, mostly with moms, a small knot of teens, an older couple holding hands. Cullen hadn't been paying attention to them, not consciously. But he never completely shut off awareness of his surroundings when he was out in public. Not unless he had someone he trusted to watch his back, and he could count on one hand the people he trusted that much. So when the three fit young men decided to cut in front of the small family, he noticed. He didn't do anything. Best to avoid trouble when you could, and it wasn't his job to make the humans around him behave. But he noticed.

The father objected. The young man with the new tattoo told him to go back to his country if he didn't like it here. Cullen stopped listening to Sarah and stepped out of the line so he could see what was going on—using both kinds of vision.

Pretty the sorcéri might be, but they were also distracting. He usually kept his Sight tamped down this close to those magic-churning waves—though "tamped down" wasn't a good descriptor for the process, which was more a matter of his level of attention. When he listened to music, he didn't stop seeing what was around him. He just stopped noticing it. Same with his two types of vision.

Neither trio gave off the glow of magic. Good. That kept things simple. He flipped the mental switch that kept him from noticing magic as much.

The father informed the young man that he was already in his own country. He was an American, born and raised here.

That set off all three of the young men. "Dirty terrorist" was one of the terms they used. "Raghead" was another. The one in orange swim trunks told the woman he bet she'd be real pretty in a bikini and outlined an hourglass shape with his hands.

The father flushed with anger. "Leave my wife alone! Leave her be!"

"Make us!"

"Shut up, raghead!"

"Yeah, make us!"

"Hey," Sarah said. "You, there! You cut that out." Another person—also female, one of the teenagers—objected, too. But these young men weren't likely to listen to those who weren't able to enforce their objections.

They didn't. "Shut the fuck up!" one yelled, and from another: "Mind your own business, Granny."

"Sarah," Cullen said, "would you mind holding Ryder for a few minutes?"

"Now, you just calm down. The cops—"

"Aren't here right now. I am, and I don't like bullies. Would you take Ryder?"

Sarah sighed, but accepted the baby.

"Thanks."

Cullen walked toward trouble. "Hey!" he called out. "I need to explain something to you boys."

Confederate Flag scowled. "Who you calling a boy?"

"Well, you don't look like girls. If you're transitioning, I have to say the drugs don't seem to be working."

That just confused them. Cullen stopped far enough away to give himself room to move, but close enough to make his challenge clear. The fumes from all the alcohol the three had consumed made him wrinkle his nose. He hated the smell of alcoholic sweat. "Everyone else might want to step back a bit. Yes, like that, very good. Now, boys—or whatever you are—here's what you need to know. You're rude, crude, and not very smart, so I'll make this simple. Go away. It would be better if you apologized first, but I'll settle for you leaving."

"Oh, the queer wants us to leave!" That came from the one in green trunks. This struck his fellows as hilarious, so he made a kissy face at Cullen.

Cullen rolled his eyes. "Two more things you need to know. First, someone has probably called the police by now. That make you ready to clear out? No? Then I'd better warn you that I'm not a good enough fighter to be sure I won't break anything. Benedict could take you three down without inflicting any real damage, but I'm not Benedict." He shook his head sadly. "I might break a bone or two. I'll try not to, but it could happen. Best if you just leave."

Orange Trunks called him an Arab lover. Green Trunks, having discovered what he considered an insult, was sticking with it. He wanted Cullen to "kiss my ass, fag." Confederate Flag used a word Cullen hadn't heard used in public in years—a word that he applied to Sarah, along with a couple more choice terms implying that Cullen knew Sarah in the biblical sense. That word just really pissed Cullen off.

"One more thing," he said. "Your dicks are really, really small. So small I bet you have trouble finding them when you need to pee, and when you—"

Confederate Flag threw the first punch. Cullen swayed to one side, letting the man's roundhouse swing pull him off balance. He leaned over and snapped out one foot. It connected with Green Trunks's stomach just as the man rushed him. As that one crumpled, Cullen spun, avoiding a blow from Orange Trunks, and bitch-slapped Confederate Flag once with his left hand and Orange Trunks twice with his right.

Orange Trunks toppled like a small tree. Confederate Flag staggered but didn't lose his footing, so Cullen kicked him in the stomach, too. Then he looked at the three men on the ground. Green Trunks was throwing up. No blood, so that was good. Confederate Flag was curled tightly around his gut, moaning. Orange Trunks might be unconscious.

The whole thing might have taken ten seconds.

Cullen had spoken truly. He wasn't a top fighter, not among his own people. He was dancer, though . . . among other things. And he was unusually fast, even for his people. "Damn. I hope I didn't break his neck," he muttered, and went to check.

Not a broken neck, Cullen determined with relief when he squatted next to the unconscious young man in orange swim trunks. The boy would wake up with one hell of a case of whiplash, but he would wake up. "Someone's called the cops, right? We need an ambulance, too."

No one answered, but then, it was noisy. One of the kids who'd been in line was crying. The father was saying something to his wife, the teens were exclaiming, and almost everyone else was making some kind of racket.

The breeze brought Cullen a familiar scent. He looked up with a smile. "Hey, there."

A few feet away, an amazon in a hot pink bikini accepted Ryder from Sarah. Her short, choppy hair was a shade warmer than platinum. Her sunglasses and tote were apple green; the tote was the size of a small suitcase and carried a diaper bag, among other things. Many other things. It was slung over one shoulder. A lovely shoulder, in Cullen's opinion—strong and shapely, like her thighs and calves.

What people noticed first about her, though, was her skin. The arabesques and runes covering most of it were so finely drawn and intricate they might have been spider-spun rather than tattooed—and indeed, Cynna's ink hadn't been applied with a needle.

That's what he saw with his regular vision. To the Sight, she was ablaze with magic. Some of it followed the paths laid down by her tattoos, but not all. Nowhere near all.

Cynna was flanked by three men, two of them tall and buff. They paid Cullen not the slightest attention, which was as it should be. They were her guards, not his. She didn't much like having guards every time she left Clanhome, but she wasn't stupid about it. You never knew when a dworg might pop out of a gate.

The third man was short. Very short. Also ugly, with a face as compelling in its way as a peacock's spread tail or a head-on collision. He wore baggy swim trunks in a Hawaiian print and a disapproving scowl. "If you were gonna fight, you might have waited for me."

"There were only three of them," Cullen said apologetically.

Cynna shook her head. "I can't take you anywhere, can I?"

"Now, that's exactly wrong. You can take me anytime, anywhere. Not that beach sex is a personal favorite of mine. The sand gets—"

"Shut up, Cullen."

He grinned and rose. Confederate Flag was stirring. Cullen told the boy to stay down.

"Want me to make sure of that?" the ugly man asked.

"Thanks, Max. Don't hit him unless you have to. The cops will surely . . . ah, here comes one now."

The first cop to arrive had to be a rookie, as he looked about thirteen. But he was sensible enough; he immediately summoned an ambulance and told everyone to hold on— they were all talking at him at once—and that he'd hear them out, but one at a time. Unfortunately, he started with what he thought were the victims.

Confederate Flag—who turned out to be named Marvin—wasn't a very good liar, but he tried. By then Green Trunks had stopped throwing up and was eager to agree with everything Marvin said about how it was all Cullen's doing, which caused everyone else to start talking at the cop again. Before the rookie could get them straightened out, one of the beach EMTs arrived. Orange Trunks had woken up, but he did not look well. The EMT thought his jaw was broken. Then the rookie's partner arrived. She was twenty years older, twenty pounds heavier, and not in the mood for nonsense.

Cullen took note of all this somewhat absently, being more interested in keeping Ryder happy while Cynna obtained the much-delayed snow cone. She'd just returned with it when the older cop came up to Cullen. "Name?"

"Cullen Seabourne."

"You don't seem to have any ID on you." Her disparaging glance made it clear what she thought of his swimwear.

"It's in my wife's tote. Here, sugar"—that was to Ryder, who was chewing madly on his finger—"this will be better than Daddy's finger." He removed the digit, replacing it with tutti-frutti shaved ice. "No, you don't get to hold it yourself, but you can hold it along with me." Ryder wanted to do everything herself these days, including things that were dangerous, impossible, or both.

Cynna had retrieved Cullen's wallet and held it out. "Do you need to see my ID, too?"

"Did you witness the incident?"

"No, I arrived right afterwards with Max, Joe, and Sean."

Max, Joe, and Sean were right there. Joe and Sean had the sense to say nothing. Not Max. "Nice boobs." He leered up at the officer.

"See the uniform, Max?" Cynna said. "That means she's a cop, which means she can arrest your ass."

"Hey, it's a compliment!"

"We've had this talk before."

"Did I ask if she wanted to fuck? I did not. I just compli-mented her, which is no more than common courtesy. If she did want to fuck, that would be great, but I didn't ask, so there's no need to get your . . ."

Cullen stopped listening. He'd caught a glimpse of a face he recognized. Or thought he did.

The crowd around them shifted. He got a second, better look at the man's face—and handed Ryder and the snow cone to Cynna and took off running.

ONE

~

"**YOU** did what?" Lily shook her head. "Bad move, Cullen. Cops get excited when you take off running while they're questioning you."

"It would have been worth it if I'd caught him."

Maybe. Or maybe it would have been disastrous. "If it was really the guy who gave you those shields—"

"It was."

Cullen was wearing his stubborn face. Stubborn looked good on him. So did anger, arrogance, vexation, or intense focus, which were the expressions she saw most often on a face whose beauty could cause strangers to stop and stare. She tended to forget that. Mostly he just looked like Cullen to her. "Did you see his magic, then? If he was a sorcerer—"

"I didn't look. There were a lot of sorcéri around, so I'd tuned out on the Sight—and then he was gone, vanished in the crowd. But he saw me, too." He frowned. "I bet he locked his power down so I wouldn't see it."

"Can sorcerers do that?" Lily asked, startled.

"Adepts could, back in the old days. Some mages, too."

"You only got a glimpse of him," Benedict observed from his spot on the couch. "That's a lot of certainty from one glimpse."

"Two glimpses," Cullen said, "and I've spent enough time resurrecting what memories he left me of our encounter. I know what he looks like."

Roughly two years ago, a friend of Cullen's had arranged a meeting between him and another sorcerer. Cullen came away from that meeting with the strongest mental shields on the planet, memories that had been tampered with, and a burning desire to find the man again. So far, he'd failed.

Benedict leaned forward, curious. "His first name was Michael, wasn't it? What was his last name? I've forgotten."

"Maybe because he didn't use one. Damned sorcerers," he muttered, sublimely unaware of any irony. "Secretive as hell, every one of 'em."

Lily snorted. "Shouldn't you say, 'every one of us'?"

"Whatever." Cullen brooded a moment. "I'm going to find him."

Lily knew why Cullen wanted to find the mysterious Michael. He was convinced the man had the Codex Arcana—aka The Book of All Magic. She just wasn't sure that was a good idea.

It did seem like the Codex was or had recently been on Earth, based on the Great Bitch's efforts to find it—for which she'd needed Lily. The idea had been to wipe clean Lily's mind and imprint a copy of the Codex on that nice, blank slate, a process that apparently only worked if the target brain belonged to a sensitive. Lately their enemy had been more interested in killing Lily than capturing her, which made Lily think the Codex wasn't here anymore. But if she was wrong—if Cullen did find the Codex—it would change so much. Some of it for the better, sure. Who knew what kind of powerful spells such a book might hold? None of them could use adept-level spells, but Cullen was almost as good at magic as he thought he was. He'd undoubtedly be able to make use of some of them . . . if the Great Bitch gave him time to learn them.

She wouldn't. They were already targets. If they held the Codex, she'd throw everything she had at them, all at once.

Probably the issue wouldn't arise. Probably Cullen had just caught a glimpse of some guy who looked like Michael, but wasn't him. Why would this mysterious sorcerer show up here? And even if Cullen was right—about whom he'd seen and about Michael having the Codex—the man would go *poof* now that he'd been spotted. He'd vanished successfully before.

"Did you get his scent?" That was Rule, speaking from the kitchen. They'd gone for a mostly open floor plan on this floor, but from where she sat, the study and stairwell blocked her view of the kitchen.

"He was too far away and I don't have your nose. Not that I could recognize his scent, as the son of a bitch didn't leave me a memory of what he smells like."

"Son of a bitch" was a major lupi epithet. Cullen held a grudge. "Are you out on bail?" she asked.

"Of course not. It isn't against the law to interrupt a cop by running away. It just takes some explaining. Are those cookies done?" He stood abruptly and started for the kitchen.

Lily stayed put in the oversize chair that used to comprise one-third of all the furniture she owned and absently stroked the pile of orange fur draped across her lap. Dirty Harry purred loudly. She smiled. There was just something about petting a purring cat . . .

"You think he really saw that sorcerer?" Benedict asked.

Lily snorted. "Cullen's always certain. He isn't always right."

"True." Benedict fell into a thoughtful silence.

Silent was the default state for Rule's big brother.

Sometimes he overdid it, but today it felt restful. Lily wasn't feeling terribly chatty, either, though it was good to have company. It was really good to be home.

Home meant a lot more than it used to. Twenty-two months ago, it had been just her and Dirty Harry. Now she was married. Back then she'd been a homicide detective with the San Diego PD. Now she was a Special Agent with Unit 12 of the FBI. Back then, home had been a tiny apartment. That's how she'd thought of her place, anyway—as home— and it had possessed the basic elements: familiarity, her bed, and a front door key she paid for. One she could turn in the lock to shut out the rest of the world.

Then she'd met Rule and the mate bond hit. That bond had given them no choice; they had to be together. It had made more sense to share Rule's apartment in a high-rise than to try to fit him into her place. Harry had hated it there, though he'd mellowed a bit when Rule's son, Toby, joined them. Harry adored Toby. But they'd given up that apartment, thanks to the war the rest of the world didn't know about, and moved to Nokolai Clanhome to stay with Rule's father, Isen. Isen's house was spacious and comfortable, but it had never felt like home. It wasn't hers.

This place was hers. Hers and Rule's.

Admittedly, in terms of dollars, he'd put way more into it than she had, but the only way they'd ever be financial equals would be if he lost most of his wealth. She wasn't crazy enough to wish for that. Her new goal was to stop defining the "equal" in "equal partners" in terms of dollars. She wasn't there yet, but she was working on it. And it was true that some of the whopping price tag for their place was his to shoulder, since the land and the guard barracks were necessary because of his position as Leidolf Rho. Even so, he'd put more into the house than she had, because he'd paid for all of the renovations. She'd contributed little except opinions.

Turned out she had plenty of those.

Twenty-two months ago she'd have said she didn't care what her place looked like as long as it wasn't cluttered, but once forced to contemplate backsplashes, closets, and lighting, she found she did have likes and dislikes. Fortunately, some of them coincided with Rule's. Some, but not all. Who could have guessed that a man who loved contemporary design would have such a fixation on wood?

Compromise was the name of the game in marriage. Their bedroom was not sheathed in dark, heavy wood paneling, thank God. But covering one wall in scraps of reclaimed wood—which he insisted on calling an art installation—had turned out well. Rule hadn't gotten the open shelving he wanted in the kitchen, either. Trendy, sure, but way too cluttered for her. Why did people want to see all their stuff all the time? But she'd caved on the ceiling. Paneling a ceiling sounded weird, but Rule really wanted it, so she'd gone along. She was glad of that now. The honey-colored wood looked fantastic overhead.

This house was nothing like her old apartment, and not just because it was so large and upscale. It had only one of the elements she'd once believed made up home—her bed, the one she shared with Rule. But she wasn't paying for the place all by herself, and it wasn't familiar. Not yet. They'd only been in the master suite for a couple weeks when they took off for Washington, D.C., and they'd been back from that trip for less than twenty-four hours. Yesterday was the first time she'd seen the finished second floor . . . finished except for furniture, that is, and when was she going to find time to shop for that? Or the rest of the stuff the place needed. And it didn't matter who had a key to the front door, not when everyone and his brother felt free to drop in.

One reason they'd bought this house was because of the land that came with it. Rule needed to be able to house the Leidolf guards he'd brought from that clan's territory on the East Coast. Those guards had a barracks of their own, but Rule was their Rho. Lupi need contact with their Rho.

They also have a limited sense of privacy and no grasp of the concept of alone time.

And yet the moment she and Rule walked in the door again yesterday, something inside her had relaxed. Home. She was home again after more than two months on the other side of the country. She glanced at the wall separating her from the kitchen. She was hoping that being home would relax something in Rule, too. She didn't think he'd had the nightmare last night, but she wasn't sure.

Dirty Harry lifted his head. He stared intently at nothing in that disconcerting way he had. Then he leaped down and headed for the French doors, one of which was open. Places to go and things to do, apparently.

A muffled thud from the kitchen interrupted her thoughts. Since it was accompanied by Cullen's triumphant "Ha!" she didn't spring to her feet. She did call out a warning not to break anything.

"Just Cullen," Rule said, "though I don't think he's badly broken. Here, make yourself useful."

Cullen appeared carrying two mugs of coffee, trailed by a young woman with a bonfire of curls caught up on top of her head and serious black-rimmed glasses. She held a plate of cookies.

"Here you go," Cullen said, handing one of the mugs to Lily.

She accepted it and made a come-along gesture with her other hand. "Come closer with those cookies, Arjenie."

The front door slammed open and ninety pounds of ten-year-old boy came racing in. "Hi, Dad! Hi, Lily! Damn, I'm hungry. I hope—" A pause. "Oh, shit."

Cullen burst out laughing. Lily kicked his calf. "Sorry," he said, grinning. "But that was a perfect double fault."

Toby flushed, mortified. And not, Lily knew, because he'd cursed. Because he'd been *wrong*.

When they came home from their prolonged stay on the

other side of the country, they'd found a couple of changes in Rule's son. Even before First Change, lupi tended to have more muscle mass than humans, so they weighed more than their appearance suggested. So while Toby was heavier than many ten-year-old boys, his growth spurt had him looking like a string bean. An undernourished string bean. Lily knew about growth spurts, but how could he have grown so much in only two months? Rule had assured her it wasn't that sudden. She just hadn't noticed how fast he was growing until they were separated for a couple months. Any day now, she thought glumly, he'd be looking down at her.

The other change had been in his language.

"Mark it," Rule said, emerging from the kitchen with a tray. The tray held three more mugs of coffee, a glass of juice, an apple, and a second plate of cookies. "Quietly, please. Cynna's putting Ryder down for a nap upstairs."

Toby brightened. "Can I—"

"After your homework's done, if Ryder's awake and they're still here."

Toby grimaced and dragged himself into the kitchen, where the Chalkboard of Doom awaited—aka the place where he had to tally his infractions.

"What's the big deal?" Cullen asked. "So he said a couple bad words."

Rule put the tray on the table. "He's not allowed to use curse words until he's older."

Cullen's eyebrows lifted. "How very human of you. I don't see it, myself. Why is 'shit' more objectionable when a kid says it than when an adult does?"

"That's roughly what Tom Erdquist says. Tom allows his son to curse, and Mark is Toby's agemate and a good friend." Rule took his coffee from the tray and sat beside Lily. "It's not surprising Toby picked up the habit."

"What's the problem?"

"The problem is that it is a habit."

"Yes, and . . . ?"

Lily shook her head. "Come on, Cullen. Think. What do you lupi value more than anything?"

"Children," he said promptly.

"What character trait?"

He frowned, bit into one of his pilfered cookies, and chewed. Just as Toby came back into the room, he spoke. "Ah. Control. A habit is by definition not behavior under conscious control. You don't object to Toby cursing. You object to it being a habit."

Rule nodded.

Toby grabbed the apple and plunked down on the big hassock. "I didn't think it was a habit. Dad said that if I was right, I wouldn't have any problem not cussing for a week."

Benedict's eyebrows lifted. "And you agreed?"

"He didn't ask me to agree. He told me that if I didn't cuss for a week, he'd lift his ban."

Arjenie nodded. "Sounds reasonable. How many marks on the chalkboard now?"

The boy sighed. "Six."

None of them pointed out that he'd only been tallying his use of bad words since late yesterday. Clearly he was aware of that.

"I don't get it," Toby said, taking a man-sized bite out of the apple. Toby was allowed to have sweets after he came home from classes as long as he ate a healthy snack first. Growing human boys burn through a lot of calories. Growing lupus boys eat like sumo wrestlers. "Why do I keep forgetting? I remember not to cuss around Grandpa."

"Are you wanting an answer from me?" Rule asked. "Or would you rather discover the reason yourself?"

He thought that over. "Myself," he said, and took another big bite.

That was another, more subtle change, but Lily had spotted this one as it emerged over the last few months, so it didn't come as such a shock. Toby was beginning to seek his own answers.

"What's the situation on the homework front?" she asked.

"Just some geometry. We're supposed to read the next chapter in *Huckleberry Finn*, but I already finished the book, so that doesn't count."

"What about that paper on Nokolai history? How's it coming?"

He shot her a quick glance. "I guess I forgot about that."

She had to smile. Toby was so bad at lying. For the next few minutes they talked about his paper—how far along he was (not very) and what he needed to do next.

Such a paper wouldn't have been assigned had Toby still been in public school, nor would he have been allowed to write it. Clan history was not made available to the wider public. Plus Lily didn't think fifth-graders were usually tasked with writing research papers. She sure hadn't been.

The war had changed things. As far as the State of California was concerned, the boy was being homeschooled now. So were most of Nokolai's youngsters. Until last year most lupi kids had gone to public schools before First Change, but the increased threat from the Great Enemy made that unsafe. At first Nokolai had only had one full-time teacher for their daughters and the boys not old enough to be sequestered at *terra tradis*. Now they had four plus a bevy of volunteers.

It was expensive. Everything about war was, she supposed. Nokolai was wealthy enough to pay its teachers, but it stretched the clan's budget, and most of the other clans simply didn't have the resources. Leidolf, for example. Rule had made lupi history by becoming the first of his people ever to be heir to one clan—Nokolai—and Rho of another—Leidolf. Two-mantled, they called him. His second clan was a lot poorer than Nokolai. He worried about the Leidolf kids, who couldn't all be brought to that clanhome.

That might change. Once Cullen and Cynna worked out the problems involved in mass production of the Triple M . . . "If you'd like me to look over your outline when you get it roughed in," she told Toby, "I'd be glad to."

"I bet you're good at outlines."

"Outlines are a type of list. I am the queen of lists."

He grinned and stood. "Can I take the cookies with me?"

"Just a sec." Lily grabbed one from the plate, thought about it, and grabbed a second cookie—chocolate chip, warm from the oven. Rule made great cookies. "Now you can."

As Toby left with the remaining cookies to wrestle with homework, Cullen was saying, ". . . what you have in mind. You decide whether we're going big and rich, or small and hungry?"

"Big," Rule said unhesitatingly. "If we wanted small and hungry, we'd set up our own manufacturing firm. Have you made progress with the matrices?"

Cullen looked smug. "That was just a matter of finding the right cleansing parameters for the crystals. I tried several, but the full-moon cleanse will work best. A couple other techniques are just as good, but they require casters with specialized knowledge. Any halfway competent coven can do a full-moon cleanse, so keeping a good supply flow should be simple and cost-effective. We've run some tests and confirmed that heavy silk offers sufficient insulation when shipping the cleansed crystals to the main production facility. Overnight shipping, that is. Given the constant fluctuation in magic levels—"

"Cullen," Lily broke in, "are you saying it's a done deal? The Triple M works?"

A voice spoke darkly from the second floor. "He better not be." Cynna started down the stairs. "Dammit, Cullen, you promised—"

"You're here, aren't you? I said I wouldn't tell them without you—"

"I was upstairs!"

"And I didn't. Ryder's asleep?"

"At last." Cynna sighed. "Weaning is hell."

The question of how long to breast-feed had obsessed Cynna until Ryder began teething in earnest and she decided "to hell with the so-called experts. I like my nipples. I want to keep them." Ryder was nine months old and eating solid food. Also occasional nonfood items, but so far she hadn't poisoned herself. According to any number of experienced moms, Cynna said, that was the best you could hope for once they started crawling.

"She's still cranky about it?" Arjenie asked sympathetically.

"Pissed as hell every nap time. Not so much at night, for some reason, but at nap time . . ." Cynna sighed and joined Cullen on the couch. "I've probably warped her for life. She seemed so ready to be weaned right up until I did it."

Cullen put an arm around her shoulders. "Teeth," he said firmly.

"Too true. And I guess babies all survive weaning, but I wonder if anyone has done a study of the mom survival rate."

"Not that weaning isn't important," Lily said, "but . . . the Triple M? Have you two figured out how to mass-produce it or not?"

A smile spread over Cullen's face. "Yeah. We have."

Triple M stood for Magical Mystery Machine, which was what they'd started calling the device Cullen had been working on that was intended to soak up free-floating magic. They called it that because—to Cullen's deep and abiding frustration—he had no idea why it worked. The black dragon had agreed to teach him how to fix the array in exchange for a favor. He had not agreed to explain anything.

Still, learning how to make the device work without the unfortunate side effects had done a lot to help Cullen get over his anger at the black dragon. Two months ago, Sam

had put him in sleep and carried him off to keep him from
getting involved in dragon affairs. In Sam's mind, that had
been a kindness. Dragons were secretive by nature, but
some secrets they would kill to protect.

The demand for something like the Triple M was huge.
Ambient magic levels had been increasing ever since the
Turning, and tech did not coexist well with magic. The dragons did a great job of soaking up excess magic, but it was a
big world and there were only twenty-four dragons. Then
there were magic surges. Those were a concern even in areas
that had a dragon. Once in a while nodes didn't just leak,
they discharged—and those magical discharges packed a
wallop.

Cullen had made a single device that worked. The next
step had been figuring out how to produce it in commercial
quantities. Cullen and Cynna had worked on that together
while Lily and Rule were in North Carolina. Mass production on the scale of phones or computers wasn't possible;
the device was too labor-intensive, and much of that labor
required trained spellcasters. But they now believed they'd
worked out how to produce the Triple M in sufficient num-
bers to bring in a corporate partner.

That's what they talked about now. Rule had definite
ideas about how to handle it, thank God. None of the rest
of them had a clue, but Rule would make sure they got a
good deal. Nokolai held the rights to the Triple M, but for
now, much of the profit would go into the joint war chest,
which all the clans could draw from for war expenses.

Maybe Leidolf would be able to house all its children
and pay an adequate number of teachers soon.

"Speaking of celebrations," Benedict said, looping an
arm around Arjenie, who'd settled beside him on the couch,
"we have some news, too."

Rule went as suddenly still as he did on a hunt. "We? As
in, both of you?"

Benedict nodded, his stoic face softening into a smile so

vulnerable it made Lily's breath catch and her heart hitch. Her eyes flew to Rule and caught him looking at her, his eyes bright with something that looked very like how the sudden prickle in her chest felt.

Arjenie—the opposite of stoic—wiggled in delight. "A week ago! It happened a week ago, but we wanted to tell you in person, not over the phone."

"Hot damn!" Cynna cried.

TWO

~

THEIR congratulations woke Ryder, who set up a noncongratulatory wail. Cynna winced. "My turn," Cullen said, standing. Before he reached the stairs, though, Toby appeared at the top of them, carrying the baby, who was chewing madly on Toby's knuckles. "She woke up," he said unnecessarily. "Can I—"

Rule was grinning. "This one time, yes, if it's okay with Cynna and Cullen."

"Bring her on down," Cullen said. "We're celebrating."

"We need champagne," Rule announced. "I'll get it. Cullen, you can get the glasses." The two men started for the kitchen.

"Fruit juice for me," Arjenie called after them as Toby came down the stairs, cradling Ryder.

Most of the things that would mark Toby as other than human wouldn't show up until he hit puberty and First Change initiated him into the two-natured world, but a few were innate. Ten-year-old boys typically didn't consider taking care of a baby a treat, even if it did let them postpone homework. Toby did.

"What are we celebrating?" he asked as he held a chocolate chip cookie up to Ryder.

"Half it," Cynna said quickly. "She doesn't need the whole thing."

The boy did that and repeated his question.

Arjenie beamed. "In about thirty-seven weeks, you're going to have a new baby cousin."

Toby whooped. Ryder looked up from her cookie, startled, then decided to make happy noises like everyone else.

And she *was* happy for her friends, Lily assured herself. How could she not be? Their joy was contagious and took nothing away from her. She'd accustomed herself to the idea of not having children herself. She had Toby, didn't she? And this would be a terrible time to turn up pregnant, in the middle of the war . . . Arjenie could stay safe at Clanhome. Lily couldn't.

"Thirty-seven weeks," Lily said. "That's a hair over nine months, so . . . next April?"

"March thirtieth," Arjenie said as proudly as if she'd planned it for that day on purpose. "We haven't told my family yet. I want to tell them in person, but Benedict worries about traveling with things so unsettled, so we're still discussing that. Can you see anything yet?"

"See—oh, you mean, is the baby's mind, uh, present?" Interesting question. "It doesn't seem like there'd be anything yet for me to sense, but who knows? I'll check." Lily gave the coiled sense in her middle a nudge. It unfurled easily, reaching out . . . she shook her head. "Sorry, but no. Your mind is a nice, fuzzy yellow, though. Kind of like a round, fuzzy banana." The texture meant that Lily could mindspeak Arjenie if she wanted, which was cool. She couldn't reach slick minds. Curious, she checked out Benedict with her new sense. "And Benedict's mind is green and furry. Most lupi minds feel like that. Like short-haired avocados."

Arjenie burst out laughing.

"How about me?" Cynna said. "What does my mind look like?"

"It's not exactly seeing." Her mindsense was more like a weird combination of vision and the tactile way she'd always responded to magic. "But you're kind of like a kiwi, only mossy." The color was a surprise. Most minds looked/felt like glowing fruit to her—many with texture, some without it. Human minds were usually a yellow fruit, however, not green. Green was the lupi color. Maybe that had something to do with Cynna being a Rhej? But the presence of texture pleased Lily. She could mindspeak her friend. "Mossy and glowing. You're a glowing, mossy kiwi."

Cynna's eyebrows lifted. "I'm radioactive?"

"Minds always glow."

"I thought I'd be able to feel you sensing my mind," Cynna said. "I've got shields, too. Not like Cullen's, but still—shouldn't I feel something?"

"Probably not unless I actually mindspeak you." Carefully Lily touched that glowing, mossy mind and sent a pulse along her mindsense. Her lips moved as she did. She couldn't mindspeak clearly without that physical cue, but she didn't have to speak out loud anymore. *So how does it feel?*

Cynna's eyes widened. "Weird. Like when Sam does it, only not. Your mind voice is . . . it sounds like you."

Lily heard Cynna's response both ways—with her ears and her mindsense. She was getting used to that.

"Can you do two of us at once?" Arjenie asked.

She shook her head. "I can barely do one person most of the time."

"Do it some more," Cynna said, leaning forward. "Tell me when you're going to try my bike. You'll love it, Lily."

Off-roading was Cynna and Cullen's new couple

thing—something they did together, without Ryder. Cynna
had ridden a motorcycle before, back in her wild child days,
but dirt bikes were new to her. She was a passionate convert.
*I think my time as a traffic cop ruined me for appreciating
motorcycles*, she sent.

"But dirt bikes are different. No roads, so no road burn.
No cars to smash into you."

That conjured one of those memories Lily tried to keep
packed away. *At least you wear a helmet.*

"I'm not an idiot."

Rule returned carrying two bottles of champagne. "Only
one of you seems to be talking. I hope that means Lily's
doing her talking differently."

"I'm showing off," Lily admitted.

Cullen followed Rule, carrying the champagne flutes—
the empties in one hand, one with orange juice in the other.
He handed the juice to Arjenie. "The Mother's blessings
on you."

Arjenie flushed with pleasure. "And on you."

"Is that a Wiccan saying?" Lily asked. Curious, she
released her touch on Cynna's mind to reach for Cullen's.
"Huh. Cullen's mind is not what I expected."

Cullen raised his brows. "I would have thought my shields
would make me invisible to your mindsense."

"No, but you're really faint. The glow is faint, but you're
there. Only you're slick as black ice."

Cullen smirked and held out a flute for Rule to fill. "I
already knew that. How about now?"

The slickness suddenly sprouted fuzz. She slid her mindsense over it . . . fuzzy on top, icy underneath. She sent a
pulse along her mindsense and laid words into the fuzzy-ice
mind. *What did you do?*

"Opened the shield that blocks mindspeech. Cynna's right.
You do sound like yourself when you mindspeak. I wonder if
that means my brain processes what I receive through my
auditory cortex?"

"Seems like it would be routed through the language center. Or are they the same thing?"

"Not at all. The language centers—there are two, Broca's area and Wernicke's area—are in—"

"Never mind," she said hastily before he could go into detail. Rule was holding out a champagne flute. She accepted it. "We'll talk about all that later. Right now we need to celebrate." No doubt they'd talk about it whether she wanted to or not. Cullen was extremely interested in her new ability. They'd discussed it twice while Lily was on the other side of the country, but with recently renewed paranoia, neither wanted to say too much on the phone. "Congratulations!" She lifted her glass in salute.

Cullen handed a brimming flute to Cynna. "You seemed surprised by what you sensed."

"I thought your shields would make you invisible to my mindsense the way Tom Weng is."

"You mean the way he was," Cynna said. "Dead people get the past tense." She closed her eyes and took a sip. "My first grown-up drink in well over a year. First I was pregnant, then nursing . . . it's only right it should be champagne."

"I'm not sure Weng is dead," Lily said.

"What?" Cynna stared. "If the fireball didn't get him when the helicopter blew up, the fall would have."

"His body was never found. All the others were."

A silence fell. It was the children, she knew. The bodies of three children had been found in the wreckage along with those of two adults. They'd been identified through dental records, as the bodies were too badly burned for any other sort of recognition: Sharon Plummer, forty-two. One of the conspirators. Frederick South, thirty-one. The pilot. Adrian Farquhar, fifteen. A farseer or clairvoyant. Susan Thompson, thirteen. A Finder. Amanda Craig, twelve. Telepath.

To turn their minds from that ugliness, Lily returned to her original topic. "Plus we know he can levitate."

Cullen cocked his head. "That was only for a few feet,

though. Big difference between levitating fifteen feet and levitating a couple hundred feet up—and doing it fast enough to stay ahead of a fireball."

Exactly what Rule kept pointing out. "I didn't say I knew he was alive. Just that it's possible. Given the way all records about him vanished after—"

"Which could have been done at any time," Rule said, entering the room. "Perhaps we could postpone that argument, Lily. This time is for Benedict and Arjenie." He'd filled flutes for himself and Cullen, but there was still one empty flute.

"Is that for me?" Toby asked. The baby he held had gnawed her way through most of the half cookie she gripped in one determined fist, in the process smearing drooly cookie-stuff on Toby's shirt.

"Of course," Rule said. "Though you'll need to set Ryder down."

Of course? Lily looked at him, startled.

Rule poured an inch of fizzing golden liquid into the last flute. He glanced at Lily, his eyes smiling. Amused. "It's not as if he can develop alcoholism."

True, but giving even a little alcohol to a ten-year-old boy was wrong. She knew people did that in Europe, at least with wine, but this was America and . . . and what difference did that make? But just because Toby couldn't develop alcoholism . . . and he couldn't. Soon after he entered puberty, First Change would hit. After that, his body wouldn't let him get so much as a buzz. But didn't alcohol affect the developing brain? The younger someone started drinking, the greater the chances of him or her becoming an alcoholic.

Which Toby could not do. And she was arguing with Rule in her head and he was winning. How annoying.

Rule's phone beeped. He pulled it out, checked the screen, and frowned. "Mike tells me company is coming."

"Who?"

"Mateo Ortez. He wishes to speak with his Rho."

She shook her head. "I don't recognize the name."

"Oddly enough, neither do I."

"Leidolf's a big clan. You can't expect to remember every name yet." The Leidolf mantle had come to Rule only a year ago, and unexpectedly. Before that, Leidolf and Nokolai had been enemies—not quite at war, but perpetually close to it.

Rule frowned and raised his voice slightly. "Sean."

The French doors at the back of the house opened and the guard stationed there looked in. Sean looked a bit like a grown-up Opie—red hair and a round, freckled face. "Yes?"

"Who is Mateo Ortiz?"

"He's Leo's son. Leo Freeman."

"I've met Leo. I don't recall meeting Mateo."

"He's been out of the country, I think. Mike could tell you more."

Mike was acting as Rule's second because José hadn't finished regrowing his leg. Mike's own leg was back to normal now that he'd had the bone surgically straightened. "Mike isn't here. You are. I'm asking you."

Sean sighed and darted a glance at Cullen, then at Benedict. "Mateo is high dominant."

THREE

HELL, Rule thought. High dominants were rare—extremely rare in most clans, slightly less so in Leidolf. Few of them lived very far into adulthood. Usually they became lone wolves, and most lone wolves led short, miserable lives. A high dominant literally could not submit, even to his Rho. The mantle did not command him.

After a long pause, Rule turned to Benedict. "It seems I'll be dealing with a private Leidolf matter in a few minutes. I'm afraid I have to ask—"

But Benedict was already on his feet. "Come on, Seabourne. We're taking a walk."

"Me, too, I suppose?" Arjenie said, and stood.

Cullen bent and scooped up his cookie-smeared daughter. "How far? And shall we take Toby?"

"Dad?" Toby's face was tense. Worried.

He smiled reassurance. "Go with the others, please. Perhaps you could show them the kestrel nest you found." It was in the abandoned orchard north of the house, far enough to make it clear Nokolai ears wouldn't overhear whatever Mateo had come here to say.

"I'll stay here," Cynna said. When Rule looked at her, she grimaced. "I'm not being stubborn. At least I don't think so. I have a feeling I should stay."

Rule hoped she was wrong. Normal rules didn't apply to Rhejes, a fact Cynna enjoyed taking advantage of at times. He'd prefer this be one of those times, rather than a prompt she'd received from the Lady.

The moment Cullen left with Ryder and Toby, Lily asked Sean, "How long has this guy been out of the country?"

"Several years."

"Since he became an adult?" Lily persisted.

"I, uh . . ."

"Sean." Rule looked at him. "Answer."

The man grimaced. "Yes. Leo got him away right after the *gens compleo*."

The *gens compleo* was the coming-of-age ceremony when a young lupus was brought fully into the mantle. "How many years ago was that?"

"Five, I think. Something like that."

"You were there?"

Sean nodded unhappily.

"I take it the mantle accepted Mateo, and Victor didn't kill him for failing to submit." Both of which astonished Rule. Leidolf's previous Rho, Victor Frey, had been a high dominant himself. He'd also been a narcissistic control freak who tolerated no whiff of dissent. "But how and why?"

Sean shrugged. "I don't know why Victor let him live. It's not like Victor ever explained himself. Maybe it's just that Leidolf doesn't see high dominants the way other clans do. That's what I've always heard, anyway—that the other clans kill their high dominants because their mantles won't accept them. Is that true?"

"Not exactly. If a young lupus is unable to accept the authority of the mantle, it usually means that the mantle can't accept him. Not won't, but can't, so he either becomes a lone wolf or is killed. There have been exceptions. A friend of mine from Cynyr comes to mind, but he was—" Rule broke off, frowning. A car had pulled up out front. He heard the motor shut off, the door close . . .

Lily was frowning, too. "I guess Ortiz was out of the country when all the clan members submitted to you, but shouldn't Alex have told you about him?"

"Yes." Alex had some explaining to do. "Sean, you may answer the door."

Sean started for the door. A second later, the doorbell rang.

"What are you going to do?" Lily asked.

"Meet Mateo Ortiz."

"Yes, but—"

"I don't know," he said curtly. Knowing what she wanted to ask, and hating the worry in her eyes. Worry he'd seen there too often lately, though his *nadia* was under the fond illusion she'd kept it to herself. Dammit, so what if he'd had a few bad dreams? That didn't mean he was falling apart.

He didn't want to kill this man. If duty allowed, he wouldn't. But duty could be a right monster at times.

Sean announced their visitor and Rule stood. "Let him come in."

The man who entered was built short and square, as if he'd started out taller but had somehow been compressed into a shorter, broader version. Even his head had a squared-off look beneath close-cropped black hair. He wore old jeans with scuffed boots, a new brown T-shirt, and a small gold cross. His skin was warm and dark, his features a blend of mestizo and African. That came as no surprise. Mateo's name was Spanish, suggesting that his mother was Mexican or Latin American, and his father would be considered black by the human culture.

Mateo stopped several paces into the room. His eyes were very dark, heavily fringed with lashes. "You are Rule Turner?"

The mantle in Rule's gut stirred. It recognized this man. More than recognized—there was a draw, a sense that . . . ah. Yes. That explained some things. Rule nodded. "I am. This is my mate, Lily Yu"—he indicated her with a gesture—"and the Nokolai Rhej."

Mateo bent his head slightly in Lily's general direction, then at Cynna. "I am honored to meet a Chosen and a Rhej." His voice was deep and musical, the accent an odd but pleasant blend of Southern and Spanish.

Lily had risen to her feet. "I prefer to be called Lily, and I don't know if I'm glad to meet you or not. If what Sean told us is accurate, you didn't come here to submit to your Rho."

"No." Those dark eyes shifted back to Rule. He stood very stiff and erect. "*Rho meus—voco y provoco!*"

"Shit," Cynna said.

"What did he say?" Lily demanded. "What did he just say?"

Rule kept his feelings out of his voice. "He issued formal Challenge."

"Shit," Lily said.

A few minutes later, they were all sitting at the kitchen table.

Lily had not thought that asking Mateo to join them for coffee was an appropriate response. Mateo hadn't, either, but after a pause he'd accepted—then balked when they reached the kitchen and Rule told him to have a seat. Rule had given him an annoyed glance as he pulled out his own chair. "I am your Rho. You may be determined to take my life—or to end your own, I'm not sure which—but you owe me courtesy."

The young man had chosen a chair on the other side of the table from Rule. He looked ready to leap up and defend himself at any moment, but at least he was seated.

"Where have you been living?" Rule asked.

"Guatemala. My mother's people are Guatemalan."

"You've been there since the *gens compleo*? Thank you, Sean," he added when Sean set a steaming mug in front of him. He hadn't yet found a houseman or cook, so he'd asked Sean to make them a fresh pot of coffee. Normally he took care of such things himself, but at the moment he was being Rho.

Mateo nodded.

Sean distributed the other cups, managing to set down Cynna's and Lily's at the same time—a tricky matter of precedence there, with both a Rhej and a Chosen to serve—then Mateo's. "Whose idea was this Challenge?"

Mateo's voice remained level. "I have Challenged. The Challenge was witnessed by others, even by a Rhej. Not our Rhej, perhaps, but a Rhej. You haven't given formal response. You cannot—"

"*Clueo et accipio*," Rule said. *I am named and accept.* Not that he wanted to, but the pup was right about that much. He had no choice. "Did the idea to Challenge originate with you?"

No response, other than a slight increase in the young man's heart rate.

"I didn't think so. You're not suicidal. Willing to die, perhaps, and weary of having to live apart from clan, but not truly suicidal. You can have no personal complaint of me, only what you've been told."

"I have heard enough." Mateo leaned forward, his eyes blazing. "You do not put the clan first. Of all that may be asked of a Rho, that is the most fundamental—to put the clan first. And you have failed."

Mateo's body language was a more direct challenge than his words. He reeked of *seku*, too. Rule's lip lifted at that stink of dominance and aggression. Without conscious intention, he pulled on the mantle. "Sit back."

It had no effect. "You can't force me to—"

"You can't be so ignorant you are unaware of what your body is saying. You are high dominant." If he'd had any

doubt, the mantle's response—and Mateo's lack of it—
confirmed that. "You must know, better than most, how to
keep from issuing challenge with every move you make.
Unless you wish to be schooled in manners right now, you
will sit back."

Mateo's lip lifted, too. "Let us go outside now and see
who is schooled! I have Challenged. You have accepted.
What more is needed?"

Rule wanted to. He didn't intend to, but he wanted to
leap on that insolent pup and teach him—

"Mateo." That was Lily, using her just-the-facts voice.
"How old are you?"

The young man blinked . . . and sat back. "Thirty-two,
Chosen."

"Call me Lily. How many Challenges have you personally witnessed?"

"Only one, but I know of others, and—"

"You know how Victor Frey responded to Challenges.
You don't know how Rule responds. You don't know Rule
at all. You're offended because you think he isn't taking
you seriously, but he is not Victor Frey. Adjust your expec-
tations."

Mateo drew in a deep breath. Held it. Let it out again. "If
you are not simply playing with me, why are we sitting here,
chatting?" He made the last word sound vaguely obscene.

Rule had himself back under control. Mostly. "It is traditional for a Rho to seek to understand why a Challenge
has been issued. Sometimes matters can be settled short of
death."

"Victor never—" That much came out, but he stopped
himself, darting a glance at Lily. "But you are not Victor.
Very well. You would know why? Because you risk your life!
Over and over, you have risked yourself, yet you have no heir.
Alex acts as your Lu Nuncio, but he does not carry the heir's
portion of the mantle. You have not invested the *heres valos*
in him or in anyone. You endanger the *mantle*."

Rule's eyebrows lifted. "You would amend this risk by killing me?"

"If you die in honorable Challenge, the Lady will see that the mantle goes where it should."

Rule stared. "That's nonsense."

Mateo's chin lifted. "The Challenge is holy to the Lady. When Arturo of Deroso Challenged his Rho back in the time of troubles—"

"His Rho killed him," Rule finished dryly.

"So some say. Others say that Arturo was killed through treachery before the Challenge." Mateo shrugged. "We do not know for certain. Those memories were lost along with the clan's mantle when the Inquisition killed the Deroso Rho and his sons. But had Arturo met his Rho in proper Challenge before the Spanish authorities acted, the clan might have survived. The Lady would have moved to mantle to one in a collateral line who was unknown to the human authorities. She cannot act to preserve a mantle when a Rho is killed outside Challenge, but—"

"The *Santo Desafío* heresy," Cynna said suddenly. "That's what he's talking about. Lord, I didn't think anyone even knew about that these days!"

Lily frowned. "The what?"

"*Santo Desafío*. Holy Challenge. You know that whole trial by combat thing that everyone believed back in the Middle Ages?" Cynna gestured vaguely, perhaps to indicate swordplay. "The idea was that God would finger the bad guy by letting the other guy kill him. That worked about as well as drowning women to find out if they were witches, but people were really into it back then. You can see why some lupi bought into it, only with the Lady doing the fingering instead of God. They claimed that the Challenge was sacred to the Lady—which is not what the memories teach—and that during Challenge she controlled the mantle directly and would determine where it went. Not a surprise that lupi who believed this were big on Challenges, especially when a new

Rho took over. Got to make sure the mantle went where she wanted. But *Santo Desafío* pretty much died out after the Spanish clans were destroyed. They'd been its biggest proponents."

"I never heard of this *Santo Desafío*," Rule said.

"It's not a part of the Nokolai memories," she said, "because *Santo Desafío* didn't take root in our clan, but it's in some of the shared memories. Back then, the Rhos tried to tell everyone that the mantles didn't work that way, and the Rhejes called it heresy, but you know how it is. People believe what they want to."

"Why heresy?" Lily asked.

"It was a form of Lady worship, and that's forbidden."

Mateo scowled. "I am Catholic. I worship God, not the Lady, but I know she is present in the Challenge, that it is sacred to her and—"

"I'm Catholic, too," Cynna interrupted, "*and* a holder of the memories, and I'm telling you that you're wrong."

"With all respect"—Mateo sounded more condescending than respectful—"you are a Rhej, but not my Rhej. What Nokolai knows is not the same as what Leidolf knows."

"So what's the bottom line?" Lily demanded. "You think the Lady can keep the mantle from being lost if Rule is killed in Challenge?"

"Certainly. Such knowledge has been suppressed by the Rhos for obvious reasons. I do not criticize. Such suppression may have served a purpose I am unaware of. But if you stop to think about it, it is obvious the Lady would not allow a mantle to be lost."

Cynna rolled her eyes. "And the Spanish clans? Were their mantles lost because she was taking a nap?"

"But those Rhos were not killed in Challenge, when she—"

"But you don't know that she can control the mantles in Challenge," Cynna persisted. "You're assuming that based on some idiotic mishmash of medieval theology and—"

"*Dios Mio*—she *gave* us the Challenge! I do not know

why Rhejes are so reluctant to credit the Lady's power. Perhaps the long suppression of female authority in the human culture makes it difficult for you to see clearly, but it is obvious from—"

Rule didn't hear the rest. The outside voices were drowned out by one that didn't involve his ears. One that could not be mistaken for any other. A voice as precise as crystal, as cold as the vastness between stars.

Rule Turner. Lily Yu is correct about Tom Weng. He survived the explosion of the helicopter and is almost certainly still alive. You and she are owed an explanation. If you come to my lair now, I will tender it.

"—does not convince you, the Lady's own words when she spoke of—" Mateo broke off and was on his feet in a flash. "What is it?"

Rule had risen from the table. So had Lily. Clearly Sam had spoken to her as well. They exchanged a glance, confirming that. "Your pardon," Rule said, "but Lily and I must go now."

Anger tightened the young man's mouth. "You take my Challenge lightly."

"No," Lily said, "but you've been preempted by a dragon."

FOUR

~~

THEY didn't leave that very minute. Rule sent Mateo to the guard barracks and called Alex Thibidoux, his Lu Nuncio for Leidolf. Alex didn't answer, so Rule called his father— or rather, his Rho. They were the same person, but when Rule addressed Isen as his Rho instead of his father, he spoke differently. It was weird, but it worked for them. Isen was Rho of Rule's birth clan, Nokolai; he had to know about the Challenge since there was a chance he'd lose his heir.

While he did that, Lily spoke with Cynna, then arranged for the car to be brought around and for the guards who'd follow them in another car.

Follow, not accompany. Not this time.

Dragons guard their secrets well. They'd clouded the minds of an entire world to protect one in particular, and what Sam wanted to tell them might be connected to it, since it was about Tom Weng. As far as Lily knew, she and Rule were the only nondragons privy to the forbidden knowledge. They needed to keep it that way.

Alex didn't answer. Rule made another call, this time to Alex's second. "Alex has gone for a run," Rule told her when he disconnected. "He'll call when he returns and Changes back."

Lily nodded. "Cynna's fetching everyone who went to look at the kestrel nest. When she gets back, she'll call the Leidolf Rhej."

"I need to speak with the Rhej as well, and I want to tell Toby myself about—"

"She won't tell Toby about the Challenge, and she wants you to hold off on talking to the Leidolf Rhej. She said this *Santo Desafío* stuff is Rhej business."

Rule grimaced but nodded. "Let's go."

He gave her a sharp look when he saw his car waiting out front sans driver or guards, who were in the nondescript Toyota. She held out his keys. "We might need to talk about . . . things. Also, this way we can stop along the way and make out if we want to."

A grin flashed across his face. Rule always looked gorgeous, but it was his grin that made her heart stumble. It lit up his face, wiping away troubles and years, worry and calculation, a grin as open as a boy's—and as full of mischief. "We could do that anyway if you weren't so prudish."

"I thought lupi considered it rude to indulge around others." She hadn't seen that grin much lately. She grinned back and dropped the keys in his hand. "It's been a while, hasn't it?"

"Clearly I'm doing something wrong if you've already forgotten—"

"Driving, Rule." She rolled her eyes, opened the passenger door, and slid in. "I meant that it's been a while since you drove yourself."

"Ah. I thought you were referring to—"

She closed the door, still grinning.

Rule got a call before they were halfway down the long

driveway. Not from Alex, but from Lily's cousin Freddy. Leidolf's finances had been a mess when Rule inherited that mantle. They still were, but for different reasons. Recent events had cost Leidolf a lot of money, and while the president had promised to reimburse them, governmental wheels turn slowly. They'd get the funds eventually, but for now Rule was shuffling money around madly.

Freddy specialized in currency trading, one of the riskier forms of speculation. Done right, you could increase your investment quickly—if you were lucky. Rule had been using him to try to build Leidolf's capital quickly, but had had to cut back because of what he called "Leidolf's current lack of liquidity." Apparently Freddie had some deal that needed quick action and thought Rule might want to increase his investment. Lily didn't listen long, her understanding of the conversation quickly smothered by terms like "trade price response," "resistance level," "LIFFE," and "pegging."

Her interest lapsed, too. She glanced at her watch.

The Dragon Accords allowed dragons to lair almost anywhere they wished, though the way this was accomplished varied among the countries who were parties to the Accords. Here in the United States, that meant anywhere on public land, with exceptions for places like the White House and military bases, with subsidies paid to local and state entities whose land was claimed by a dragon. They could lair on private land, too, but the property had to be seized through public domain. That took time; most of the dragons hadn't wanted to wait.

Sam's lair included several acres around the den he'd dug into the low mountain next to the Sweetwater Reservoir. It would take about forty-five minutes to get there. Lily didn't know the straight-line distance, but she thought it was too far for her to mindspeak anyone but a dragon or another sensitive.

Not for Sam. The black dragon could mindspeak across thirty miles as easily as thirty feet. Or thirty inches. He could mindspeak across the entire continent if he needed to, which ought to have been impossible. Earth and rock blocked mind magic, and the curvature of the planet put a great deal of earth and rock between San Diego and the East Coast. Plus the sheer amount of power it would take to reach that far boggled her brain.

But Sam could do it. He hadn't—not with her, that is, not while she was on the other side of the country. She hadn't expected him to. When she and Rule first headed to D.C., she'd been on a precarious cusp in the development of her mindsense, and contact with Sam's mind would have tipped her the wrong way. Once she'd passed through that cusp, he probably hadn't seen the point in expending so much power.

Now that she was back, though, she'd expected to hear from him. He'd spent a good deal of time training her. Surely he'd want to see what she could do. In the privacy of her own thoughts, she admitted that she'd been looking forward to showing him. That was probably dumb. The black dragon didn't exactly subscribe to modern notions about the value of positive feedback. She hadn't expected Rule to be summoned as well, or for Sam to confirm her suspicion about Tom Weng. That was not good news.

Forty-five minutes. That was time enough to do some thinking . . . but not about Tom Weng and whatever Sam wanted to tell them. They'd learn that once they arrived. No, she had a more pressing concern. The Challenge, and the possibility—no, probability—that Rule would have to kill that intense young man with high ideals and screwed-up notions. Formal Challenges were fought to the death. Oh, the challenger could submit, which would stop the fight. But Mateo was incapable of submitting.

There was always the chance that Mateo would kill Rule instead. She didn't put that risk very high. Rule had experience and training that Mateo lacked. Rule had been trained by the best—his brother, Benedict. Benedict was considered the top fighter of his generation, maybe the best for several generations. Having seen Benedict in action, Lily leaned toward "several generations."

Rule wasn't Benedict, but he was good. Very good. Most lupi fought primarily by instinct while in wolf form. That made sense; the wolf's instincts were strong and allowed them to react instantly. The very best fighters learned how to use the man's greater tactical knowledge without losing the wolf's instinctive advantages. That blending took years to develop, however. Mateo simply wasn't old enough to do it. Rule was.

And that's how they'd fight, of course. As wolves. Lowercase *c* challenges were sometimes fought on two feet, but not formal Challenges. The law didn't take note of wolves fighting to the death, but it paid keen attention if men did.

That was both good and bad. Good because Rule was probably better than Mateo in wolf form. Bad because it meant Lily couldn't step in as an officer of the law and put a stop to this incredibly stupid, destructive—

"You're quiet," Rule said.

"Thinking."

"You can't kidnap him."

Huh. Interesting idea. "That would be illegal."

"Lily . . ."

"You don't want to kill him. There has to be some way to keep that from happening." Something other than kidnapping Mateo, which, in addition to being illegal, would be really hard to pull off. "Even if you delegated the Challenge to Alex, it would only change the casting for this event." Someone would still end up dead. Someone would still be forced to kill.

And Rule didn't need that, dammit. He already had nightmares.

"I can't delegate to Alex," Rule said patiently. "Either

the Rho or his heir must fight when a formal Challenge is issued. There are a couple of exceptions, but they apply only in very unusual circumstances."

"I thought the Lu Nuncio could answer a Challenge."

"No, the heir can. Normally the heir is also Lu Nuncio, but as Mateo pointed out, I've no heir."

"For good reason."

"Good from my standpoint, yes. Good for Leidolf?" He shrugged. "The pup is right about my not putting the clan first when it comes to naming an heir."

"You can't tell him why."

"He's undoubtedly guessed part of it," Rule said dryly. "I'm averse to being assassinated."

When the previous Leidolf Rho died and Rule inherited the full mantle, he'd decided not to invest the heir's portion of the mantle in any of the handful of clan who had enough founder's blood to carry it. Leidolf and Nokolai had been enemies a long time. If Rule had an heir, he could count on receiving repeated Challenges from those who didn't appreciate having their clan led by one brought up by the enemy. Outright assassination had been a strong possibility, too. But no Leidolf wanted Rule dead if that would mean losing the mantle.

There had been another, even more vital reason not to name an heir. Toby.

Last year Rule had seen signs that his son was at high risk for developing what lupi called the wild cancer—a deadly malignancy that could strike at only two times in a lupus's life: old age or First Change. According to Cullen, there was one way to keep the wild cancer from occurring after a young lupus Changed for the first time. If Toby were invested with some portion of a mantle soon after First Change, the mantle would reinforce his pattern and keep the wild cancer from manifesting. But this was a deep, dark secret of Cullen's former clan, Etorri. Rule had given Cullen his word he would not reveal Etorri's secret.

"I meant about Toby," she said. "You can't tell him about Toby because you gave your word to Cullen."

"No." He was silent a moment. "I wonder if Mateo knows he could carry the mantle?"

"What? You mean he could be Rho?"

"Possibly. Probably. When the mantle recognized him, I felt . . . not a pull. Call it a sense of affinity. He has founder's blood."

"Then this is more of a takeover attempt than some screwed-up idealism."

"Not necessarily. He smelled utterly honest when he spoke of his belief that the Lady could move the mantle where she wanted during a Challenge."

Lily snorted. "Move it to him, he means."

"Perhaps. But while Alex failed notably to tell me about Mateo, it's hard to believe he would have withheld that information if he'd known that Mateo carried founder's blood. If Alex doesn't know, it's possible Mateo doesn't, either."

"How could they not know? Surely Leidolf keeps records like Nokolai does."

"Founder's blood isn't simply a matter of ancestry. That's part of it, but not everyone who can trace his lineage back to the clan's founder carries founder's blood. Mateo's father, Leo, doesn't have it. Not enough for the mantle to notice, at least."

"That doesn't make sense. If Mateo has founder's blood, his father must."

"I don't know why it's true, but it is. I had enough of the Leidolf founder's blood for Victor to force the heir's portion of that mantle on me. But my brother, who is descended from the same runaway Leidolf daughter as I am, doesn't seem to have any of that founder's blood."

"None? But that . . . maybe the Leidolf mantle just couldn't recognize it because Benedict's Nokolai, so even though he's got a bit of Leidolf blood, it didn't . . ." She stopped. Frowned. "It's hard to say what I mean when I don't know what I'm talking about."

He didn't laugh. Quite. But he snorted.

"All right, all right. I accept that you can tell whether or not someone carries founder's blood, and Mateo does, but he might not know it."

"Victor knew. That's why he didn't kill Mateo. Why the mantle was able to accept him, too, even without his submission. I don't fully understand that, but I haven't dealt with a high dominant since becoming Rho."

Lily drummed her fingers on her thigh. "Why didn't anyone tell you about Mateo? At first, yeah, I can see them not saying anything. They didn't trust you. But that's changed."

"I suspect Mateo is well liked. They expected me to kill him once I learned of his existence. They may have been right."

She sighed. "I wish he'd just go away again. I can't find a best-case scenario here. They're all ugly."

"Best case would be for him to withdraw the Challenge."

"He can do that?"

"Of course. That's one reason I invited him to stay at the barracks. He'll hear from other Leidolf with a different perspective. Unfortunately, he strikes me as the stubborn sort. I suspect it will take more than a day to wean him from his notions about the Lady and the Challenge."

"Can't you put off fighting the Challenge? Give him time to figure out that he's wrong?"

"I'm afraid not. Except in exceptional circumstances, a Rho must answer a formal Challenge within twenty-four hours."

"You already answered."

"Not that kind of answer." He glanced at his watch. "Dammit, Alex still hasn't returned my call. I need to know who put Mateo up to this."

"You're sure someone did."

"I asked. He was careful not to answer."

"I noticed." Lupi mostly didn't lie to their Rho. There wasn't much point when he could smell the lie. "His father is the obvious suspect."

"Leo is probably the one who filled his head with this holy Challenge nonsense. That doesn't mean he's the one who manipulated Mateo into making this Challenge. I wish Cynna—" He cut himself off, tapping his fingers on the steering wheel.

"She'll let us know what she learns."

"Probably. Her focus will be different from mine, however. As it should be," he admitted. "Any hint of Lady worship has to be stopped right away."

To Lily's mind, there was often a hint of worship—or more—in the way lupi regarded the one who'd made them, but Rule wouldn't agree. Maybe the line between reverent service and worship was clear to him. It was damn near invisible to her, but she knew it was vital that they not worship their Lady. The long explanation involved ideas she couldn't wrap her mind around. Beings who'd existed since before the Big Bang? Who'd hung around from the previous cycle to help out, only to find that the rules were different this time around? Surely that was more myth than reality.

But the short version seemed to be true: worship could wrap a godhead around its object, and Old Ones who assumed a godhead tended to go insane. The last part was confirmed by experience. The Lady refused to be worshipped and she was sane. The lupi's Great Enemy liked worship just fine and she was one crazy bitch. So yes, it was important not to worship the Lady. "Can't the Leidolf Rhej just tell Mateo not to Challenge because he's wrong about this *Santo Desafío* deal?"

"No. Not unless the Lady speaks to her about it, which

is highly unlikely. A Rhej's authority—ah." He took out his phone, which she hadn't heard. He probably had it on vibrate. "Alex at last."

Lily didn't listen. There had to be some way to stop this Challenge from proceeding, but she couldn't come up with one. She understood why Rule had accepted Mateo's Challenge—at least, she understood as well as a human could. The Challenge wasn't simply tradition. It was both sacrosanct and necessary, given the top-down, autocratic nature of lupi governance . . . which was also necessary, much as that bugged Lily. Lupi needed the mantles and a clear hierarchy, with someone at the top. They also needed a way to remove the top person if he kept making bad decisions.

So the Challenge was necessary, but it was also really stupid. Victor had been a terrible Rho, but although he'd been Challenged multiple times, he'd remained in charge of Leidolf until the wild cancer took him out. Rule was a damn good Rho, and now here was this young man with a head full of mystical nonsense who might legally kill him.

Though it was more likely he'd just force Rule to do the killing.

". . . all right. Let me know what you find out," Rule said. A pause. "No, but it will be sometime tomorrow. Yes. I'll let you know what I decide about your status after the Challenge." He disconnected.

"Is Alex in trouble?"

"He withheld information from me about the very existence of a clan member."

"When you said you'd decide about his status later . . . are you thinking of removing him as Lu Nuncio?"

"A Lu Nuncio's primary duty to his Rho is honesty. None of his other duties can be discharged honorably without that."

Okay, that sounded bad for Alex. "But who else could you—"

"I haven't decided, Lily. Leave it for now, please. I'm wondering why Sam summoned us instead of simply mind-speaking us."

She let him change the subject. It was his decision, after all. "Privacy, I guess. Whatever he has to say, it goes beyond just telling us that Weng's alive. He already did that. And he likes for us to speak out loud when we respond to him. At home, people could overhear us."

"They might overhear me, but you don't have to vocalize now when you mindspeak."

"Responding to Sam's mindspeech is a totally different experience from mindspeaking someone myself. I'm riding on his wave, you might say, which . . . but I'll skip the description. I still have to move my lips."

"Which may not be sufficiently private for whatever Sam intends to tell us. Speaking of Weng's survival . . ." He quirked an eyebrow at her. "You haven't said, 'I told you so.'"

"Well, that spoils things. It's no fun to say it once you point that out. And anyway . . ." She grimaced. "I'd rather not be right this time."

"Weng is probably going to cause trouble at some point," he agreed, slowing for the turnoff onto a gravel road marked by a sign warning that the area was restricted. "Did you tell the men to stay on this side of the inner fence?"

"And to stay in their car." This was not exactly the first time Lily had made this trip. She'd been coming every week for months, and both she and the guards knew the rules. The area between the first fence and the inner fence wasn't truly part of Sam's lair, being where pigs and cattle were released periodically—part of his payment for soak-ing up magic, per the Accords. He did not like people wan-dering around in his larder. Trespassers might not be eaten, but they were strongly discouraged.

They proceeded down the bumpy gravel road about fifty yards, stopping at a simple gate. Lily got out. The sign on the gate was large, its message delivered in all caps: DRAGON LAIR. DO NOT ENTER. U.S. AND STATE LAW SUSPENDED BEYOND BARRIER.

FIVE

~

THE trickiest part of the negotiations that ended in the Dragon Accords had been the dragons' refusal to submit to human law, which they considered capricious, absurd, and quite inapplicable to themselves. They had agreed to follow certain basic rules—no eating people, pets, or livestock, for example. But in a dragon's lair, all bets were off. A dragon cannot conceive of his lair being subject to any authority except his own.

Or her own. That's what Lily was thinking about as she dragged the gate open so Rule could drive through. There was exactly one female dragon . . . and until last year, she'd been a he, just like the rest.

As far as Lily knew, she and Rule were the only two people who were aware of Mika's sex change. Well, and Grandmother, but Grandmother was outside all the rules. The rest of the world knew that Mika was female and a new mother—and had forgotten that they used to refer to the red dragon as "he."

And that was one half of the dragons' big secret. They were all male until they decided to become female.

It was a crazy, convoluted system of reproduction, complicated by instinct and hormones. A mother dragon would not tolerate having a male dragon anywhere near her clutch, plus she reverted to a more primitive state after laying their eggs. She was still capable of logic, but not much interested in it, and she lost the ability to use mind magic.

That was a major problem. Baby dragons had to be named when they first hatched. Not named the way human babies were, but given the first syllable of what would be their true names through mind magic. This naming kept their minds from closing up forever.

And that was the other half of the dragons' big secret. It was why Mika had kidnapped Lily: to mindspeak and name her babies as they were born. An efondi, the brownies called her. Normally that role was filled by another female dragon, but at the moment there weren't any female dragons except Mika.

Sam had conspired with Mika and the brownies to kidnap Lily. She'd forgiven him for that; the need had been great. She slid back in the car and closed the door. "Have you gotten over being mad at Sam?"

"His secrecy and manipulation nearly cost your life. I understand why he did it. I respect his reasons. I will probably still be angry a decade from now."

A breeze blew across her mindsense. That's what it felt like, anyway, a touch so light it was no more than a hint of movement. So she was expecting it when an icy mental voice spoke.

Your anger is justified, but as you have concluded, it is largely irrelevant to today's conversation. Lily Yu, you have not reached for my mind. Do so now.

"Okay," Lily said. Now was her chance to show off for the teacher, however little praise she was apt to receive. She gave the glowy stuff curled up in her middle a nudge. Slowly it uncoiled . . . then shot out like a metal filing pulled to a strong magnet.

Mika's mind had been compelling to Lily's new sense. Fascinating. Lava-mind, she'd called it, for what she sensed had reminded her of magma, dark-crusted on top and seething with heat below. Of course, Mika had been in a primitive mind at the time. She expected Sam's mind to be different, but still compelling.

Turned out she had vastly underestimated the difference between a young dragon like Mika and one who counted his life in millennia.

Sam's mind was stars and night and crystal. Black crystal. If the void between stars turned to ice, it would look/feel like this, its facets gleaming with the light of a thousand distant suns . . . texture, yes, and beyond compelling, both in itself and because of what she dimly sensed below the crystalline surface, depths and layers and complexity beyond her grasp, hints of movement darkly illumined by what lay at the core of that mind.

Power. Vast and pure and burning, like a star gone nova.

The darkness spoke. *You need to return.*

And she was back in her body—had she left it or just forgotten she had a body?—her mindsense curled up tightly once more. She winced at the ungodly glare of the sun. "Ow," she said, her eyes tearing in spite of herself. "Ow and damn. I haven't had a headache like this since—"

"What did he do?" Rule demanded. "What did he do to you?"

"He didn't do anything." She blinked the dampness away. Already the pain was diminishing, folding itself away layer by layer. "It's just what he is. His mind . . . ice and fire. Too much power."

You are human, the black dragon agreed. *Both your mind and your brain have adapted well, considering your inherent limitations. However, it will be best if I handle speech between us. I suggest you do not attempt to contact my mind again.*

"Yeah, I can see that." She could also see that Rule was way too ready to be angry with Sam. "It's not his fault, Rule, no more than it's the sun's fault that we can't stare at it for long without going blind."

"Mmm," he said, a nonanswer that annoyed her.

He put the car in gear and drove through the gate. She got out again to close it. As she climbed back in the car, she felt that breeze brush across her mindsense again.

Lily Yu, you were correct in thinking I would wish to examine your progress. We have limited time for that. I will address you privately for this. Attempt to respond clearly without vocalizing.

"Ah—Sam's going to talk to me, teacher to student, for a minute."

Rule nodded. "He told me."

You have chosen an interesting metaphor for your experience of the mindsense.

It wasn't a metaphor. Well, thinking of minds as various kinds of fruit was a metaphor, but what she actually experienced when she used her mindsense wasn't.

You err. Your brain is unable to process this sense directly. It has no physical analog and your brain is, to borrow a human term, wired for physicality. The first time you fully experienced your mindsense, your mind created a metaphor or template for the experience which is now your reality, shaping both your perception of the sense and the way you are able to use it. I expected this. I had some concern that you would select one of the more restrictive metaphors. I am pleased with the one you chose, which combines the tactile with the visual.

Lily blinked. *You don't experience your mindsense that way?*

Very faint, a whiff of amusement. *No. Should you encounter other beings with mindsense, you will find that they do*

*not, either. Elves who develop it, for example, experience it
through purely visual metaphors.*

She didn't see how you could use the mindsense to conduct mindspeech if you only "saw" with it.

*You are correct. Even elven adepts are not proficient at
mindspeech. Their metaphor for the sense limits them. I
now wish to examine your present skill level and we have
little time. Open your mindsense.*

When she'd done that before, it had shot straight for
Sam. This time she was prepared, and she'd had enough
practice using it near Mika to know it was a matter of focus
and, well, metaphor. Instead of simply nudging her mindsense so it would unfurl, she imagined it already spread out
around her like a mist.

It was hard, way harder than it had been with Mika. She
couldn't fail to sense Sam's mind when he was this close,
but she could—with effort—refrain from "staring" at him.
Was it her mindsense that found the dark splendor of Sam's
mind so riveting? Or her mind?

Now mindspeak Rule Turner.

That was even harder. To mindspeak, she had to abandon the mist metaphor and concentrate her new sense on
Rule's mind. She groaned and did her best.

It went on like that even after Rule stopped the car and
they got out to walk the last bit. Sam waxed downright
sarcastic about her inability to walk and maintain control
of her mindsense at the same time.

But she tried. When she stumbled, Rule slid an arm
around her waist.

By the time they stopped on the flat sand of Sam's landing pad outside the dark opening in the mountain's side, she
was exhausted. Her head didn't hurt, though. She considered that a triumph.

The black dragon was nowhere in sight. She exchanged
a glance with Rule.

You may allow your sense to rest now. Come under earth.

Lily wasn't fond of caves. Rule hated them—at least, he hated the tight, narrow, twisty ones. She squeezed his hand. "Sam won't be someplace we'd consider cramped. He wouldn't fit."

He sighed. "True." But he paused on the way in. "I don't remember this." He laid a hand on the tall outcrop of boldly striated stone that formed part of the arched entry. "It's lovely. I'm surprised I didn't notice it before."

"It just showed up one day, but not exactly the way it looks now. He's been . . ." She struggled for a word. "Grooming it? Doing something, anyway, that brings out the markings and subtly changes the shape." Dragon notions of decorating didn't involve obviously sculpted rock. The one Rule rested his hand on looked as if it had been there for eons, slowly shaped by wind and weather rather than a dragon.

His eyebrows rose. "It showed up? That's a lot of rock to tote around, even for Sam."

"Maybe he magicked it up from under the earth. Who knows? He wouldn't explain."

"*Quelle surprise,*" Rule murmured as he went in. Rule liked to use French for sarcasm.

Lily had been in the "under earth" part of Sam's lair many times, but only as far as the outer chamber, where she'd spent many a dreary hour staring at a candle flame. It was dim here, but not dark. Sam was a large dragon; his entry was correspondingly large and let in plenty of light. The floor was packed sand, like his landing pad, and equally lacking in dragons.

There were two tunnels leading deeper into the mountain. Both gaped darkly when they first entered the chamber, then the one on the left was lit with a pale, directionless light. Not mage light, not the way Lily had always seen it—as small, glowing balls. This light seemed to come from nowhere and everywhere.

"Now he's just showing off," Lily said as she and Rule headed for the softly glowing tunnel.

It smelled like dragon there—not an unpleasant scent, sort of a mix of hot metal and spice. To her nose, anyway. She'd never know just what dragons smelled like to Rule. She glanced at him. He looked easy, relaxed. Why did she think he was wound tight?

Maybe she was imagining things. She slid her hand in his anyway.

The tunnel was downright spacious, wider across than the living room of Lily's old apartment and with a much higher ceiling, which would put it between cozy and cramped for the black dragon. It twisted around some, and here and there outcroppings of crystal glittered in the pervasive light. The floor was smooth enough, but slightly gritty.

It led down. Quite a ways down, which bugged her. How could Sam mindspeak her through all that earth and rock? And read her mind, and watch her perform for him . . . and why didn't the earth and rock block his mind from her?

Because it didn't. Even with her mindsense coiled up inside her, she was aware of Sam's mind—not in a direct way, but as a tantalizing presence. Earth and rock hadn't blocked Mika's mind from her, either. Which made no sense. It sure blocked other minds—

You do not yet know enough for an explanation to be useful, Sam told her.

She hated it when he said that.

At last the tunnel opened out into another chamber. This one was not empty. The walls here were mostly smooth, with craggy outcroppings. It was less spacious than the chamber above, but the ceiling was every bit as high. Coils of dragon filled about two-thirds of the space—coils as black as night in the directionless light, though she knew they would be iridescent in sunshine. Sam's head was raised a couple dozen feet on that long, muscular neck. Yellow eyes glowed down at them.

He wasn't alone.

Shocked, Lily stopped dead. "Grandmother! You're wearing jeans!"

SIX

THE indomitable old woman sat, regally erect, on a red cushion near one of the coils of dragon. She wore a black silk shirt and Nikes with the unprecedented jeans. One thin eyebrow lifted. "You criticize my apparel?"

"I wouldn't dream of it. I've just never . . . I didn't think you owned any jeans."

"They are suitable for some occasions. Sit. We will have tea."

Occasions such as being flown here on dragon back? Lily hadn't seen a car.

There were two additional cushions. Also a tea set. Not Grandmother's good set, but the everyday one. She and Rule exchanged a glance, then took their places on the extra cushions. Might as well. It seldom did any good to argue with Grandmother.

"Madame Yu." Rule inclined his head. "It's good to see you again."

"You are angry with me. This is foolish, but I overlook it. You have been through a difficult time."

"I am wondering why I was summoned here for tea. The timing was not convenient."

"You are not stupid enough to think that is why you are here." She lifted the teapot, poured a cup, and handed it to him.

Apparently they weren't undergoing the full tea ceremony this time. Grateful for small blessings, Lily accepted her cup with a murmur of thanks. The tea steamed gently in spite of the lack of any visible heat source. Other than the dragon, that is.

Lily couldn't resist opening her mindsense just a wee bit, though she'd have to be really careful this close to Sam. This was the first time she'd seen Grandmother since acquiring the new sense, and she was intensely curious about what Grandmother's mind . . .

A second later she blinked, disoriented, having had her mindsense swept right back inside her as tidily as a housewife might clean up crumbs on the floor.

"You were right, Sun." Grandmother was addressing the black dragon. She always called him by the name she was used to, the one she'd used over three hundred years ago. She took a sip of her own tea, her black eyes gleaming. "Curiosity overcame her. Do not use your mindsense this close to Sun, child."

Had it been Sam who tidied away her mindsense? Or Grandmother? Grandmother didn't have mindspeech, but she did have at least one type of mind magic. Did that mean she had some form of a mindsense, too? "How do you experience it?" she blurted.

"Not as you do. We will not discuss this now. Now you will learn about dragon spawn."

About what? "I thought Sam was going to tell us—"

The tea will give you something to do with your mouth other than interrupt. Sam's mental voice bit like winter. *Drink it.*

Lily opened her mouth. Closed it. And took another sip of tea.

The tea is Li Lei's contribution. She is not, however, the reason you are here. I have brought you under earth, where I possess additional defenses against intrusion, in order to fully secure our conversation. At least one of the other dragons would feel compelled to attempt to stop me from revealing what I am about to tell you. He should not pry into my actions in my territory, but his thinking on this topic is muddy. I do not wish to kill him, so it is best he remains unaware of what I do until it is too late to stop me.

More secrets that dragons would kill to keep? Lily scowled. "And what's to stop him from killing us when—"

He is illogical on this topic, not childish. He will not violate our customs out of pique. This matter is secret for reasons of grief and shame rather than survival.

Grief and shame? That jolted Lily. It was weird to think of any strong emotion in connection with that chill mental voice, but especially shame. Though when she thought of the nova at the core of Sam's mind . . . oh, but she'd been wrong, she suddenly realized, her eyes widening with revelation. At the heart of the black dragon lay power, but not that alone. Power . . . and passion.

She glanced at Grandmother. With an effort, she managed not to send her mindsense out to ask Grandmother questions she knew very well the old woman would not answer.

"To what customs do you refer?" Rule asked.

Those concerning Lily Yu's status among dragons. As her mate, you partake of that status to a degree. Be aware that "status" has different referents for dragons than it does for lupi or humans. We are not a social species.

"What are these referents?"

I advise you to hold your questions until I am finished, as I will not answer them now. You are both aware of what happens to dragon young if there is no efondi present at their hatching. Their minds quickly become impermeable to magic, rendering them unable to communicate or receive communication. You are unaware of the results of this condition.

Human infants, if deprived of the early experience of bonding, may fail to thrive. If they survive, as adults they may exhibit excessive impulsivity and anger, possess limited empathy, and be unable to form the kind of emotional attachments considered healthy in humans. Your term for this condition is sociopathy. Mind-dark hatchlings also exhibit pathologies, including self-mutilation and other acts of self-destruction, an inability to self-govern, and behaviors which suggest psychosis.

Psychotic dragons. That was a terrible thing to contemplate. "You believe these, um, pathologies arise for the same reason that humans become sociopaths? That failure-to-bond thing?"

Because I am unable to observe the minds of the mind-dark, I cannot trace the pathologies directly and can only form reasoned hypotheses about the root cause or causes. With that caveat, I can say that the lack of such a bond appears to be the determining factor.

We did not always understand this. For many thousands of years, we believed that the inability to communicate was, in and of itself, sufficient to cause madness.

Throughout, Sam's mental voice remained as cuttingly cold as ever . . . until that last sentence, about which hung the wispiest fog of emotion.

Horror. That was part of the fog, and not surprising once she thought about it. Madness would seem the most horrific condition possible to a dragon, so terrible that even Sam could not completely cleanse the emotion from his thoughts. And blended with the horror a faint, sad mist . . . sorrow. Old sorrow, so very old . . .

Botched hatchings—those unattended by an efondi— are extremely rare. You may have a false perception of the likelihood of such occurrences due to recent events. The brownies, zealous in protecting our privacy, did not tell you why Mika underwent her third birth when she did.

"They didn't explain, no." By "third birth," Sam meant the change from male to female. The brownies said that dragons had three births: one when the eggs were laid; one when they hatched; and one when they changed from male to female. Apparently changing back to male after the kids were grown—which they generally did—didn't count as a birth.

It seems rash to you. Mika lacked a female dragon to act as efondi, relying instead upon a human for whom mindspeech remained merely a potential until almost the last moment. I will tell you what the brownies did not. We can undergo the change to female at any age once we reach physical maturity, but the older we are, the longer the change takes, for we do not attempt it until we reach that point in our cycle. It would have been another three years before the second youngest of us could have completed such a change; none of the rest were even close.

Mika was unable to forestall his change that long, even with our assistance. It had already been delayed much longer than is normal due to our sojourn in Dis. Dis is not a good place to raise young.

"You mean that the change to female isn't voluntary?" Lily asked. "She didn't have a choice? I mean he didn't. You said 'his change.'"

We use the pronoun pertinent to the sex at the time referenced. You, however, might do well to consistently refer to Mika as she. Such misassigned gender offers no insult to a dragon, and human memory is poor. It would be unfortunate if you were to refer to Mika as "he" when speaking to other humans.

He hadn't answered her question.

Nor will I. I have told you this much so you will understand

*why Mika underwent his third birth even though there was no
female dragon to serve as efondi.*

"Did you know that I would reach that cusp when I did?
Or did you make it happen when it did?"

*I had some control over how quickly your nascent abil-
ity became active. A degree of speed was necessary, given
the deadline imposed by Mika's condition. Too much speed
endangered your mind. Balancing these needs was a tricky
and interesting problem.*

Rule growled. He shouldn't have been able to achieve
such a wolfish growl in his current form, but he'd done it
before.

*Rule Turner believes I risked you. This is true in one
sense, but not as he means it. It is impossible to eliminate
risk. My duty as your tutor was to minimize it. I fulfilled
that duty although it meant uncomfortably close timing.*

Rule was not placated. "You didn't speak of risk when
you offered to train Lily in mindspeech."

*She is adult. She is aware that all actions involve risk. We
are diverging from the information I need to impart. I ask
you again to withhold your questions until I am finished.*

*The instinct to change to female is cyclic in nature. As
we grow older, that cycle grows longer and, in a general
way, more readily controlled. It never disappears, however, and can be triggered by . . . I will say by external
events, although that is a gross simplification of a complex
cascade. Fortunately, this is rare. When it does occur,
there has usually been another dragon, currently female,
who could serve as efondi. Not, however, every time. Unattended hatchings have occurred. Over a period of time
longer than your recorded history, we have tried many
ways to alleviate the condition of our mind-dark offspring.
Nothing worked. We always ended up having to kill those
who survived beyond the first few decades. We are . . .*
Sam's pause was brief. In a less precise speaker, it would

have gone unnoticed . . . *highly averse to killing our young, however damaged, yet it seemed all the mercy we could offer, and their suffering was clear. It has been our custom to do so jointly, so that the burden did not fall on only one or two of us.*

A time came when I could no longer accept this. I devised a possible solution—imperfect, yet I judged it preferable. It took me some time to master the magic involved, but I had time. Such hatchings do not occur often. I was ready when, roughly seven hundred years ago, a clutch of hatchlings emerged from second birth without the presence of an efondi. After some discussion, the other dragons agreed to attempt my solution.

We turned them into humans.

"You—" Lily shut her mouth on the stupid thing she'd been about to say. Clearly such a transformation was possible. Three hundred years ago, Sam had turned her grandmother into a dragon—then at some point, turned her back into a human.

It is important to note that, by "human," I refer to their physicality. Obviously we could do nothing about their mental states. They remained mind-dark, and we were unsure how their innate natures would be translated by their transformed brains. Our hope was that their needs would be sufficiently human to be met by normal human parenting. We believed that, at a minimum, they would acquire speech and thus not be trapped in permanent isolation.

We called our altered young Lóng Luăn.

Lily translated aloud for Rule. "Dragon spawn."

Yes. They were placed with a handful of human families in a remote village in the territory of the dragon who'd birthed them. At first the transformation seemed to work as we'd hoped. Their mother reported to the rest of us occasionally; none of them displayed early signs of psychosis or self-destruction. They learned auditory speech easily and seemed to relate to the world realistically. She did observe behavior which distressed their human caretakers, but some traits which are considered mildly sociopathic in humans are normal for dragon young. She believed these behaviors were a reflection of their innate natures and not a serious problem.

She was wrong. The spawn were not mildly sociopathic. They were psychopaths.

Lily's breath hissed in.

"I don't understand the difference," Rule said.

Lily had done some reading on the subject once she realized how many of the Great Bitch's agents seemed to be psychopaths or sociopaths. The current thinking was that psychopaths and sociopaths both suffered from antisocial personality disorder, which was now the official term for both conditions. In practical terms, however, there was a difference. "Sociopaths can form emotional bonds, though usually not healthy ones. The opinions of others matter, though often not in a healthy way. Psychopaths don't give a shit what we think. We aren't real to them."

"I see. You use the term in the human sense, Sam?" Rule asked.

I use it to indicate a complete lack of empathy and conscience stemming from the inability to grasp the reality of other sentient minds. The spawn had no concept of right and wrong. For each of them, there was only one real person in existence, one "I" who was the center of the moral universe. Each spawn considered his wants and needs the definition of good; whatever displeased him was evil. What others wanted was irrelevant unless they could enforce their will.

It was several years before their mother was forced to acknowledge their true state and reported more fully to the rest of us. I was prepared for her revelation, having monitored them myself, albeit infrequently and with great circumspection. All dragons are territorial; she was rabidly so, and my intrusion into her territory would have rendered her extremely uncooperative, had she been aware of it.

This proved to have been a mistake on my part.

I suggested that the spawn should be killed. She would not consider it, nor would most of the others. I expected this. The spawn were troublesome and hard on the humans in their village, but most felt that the occasional death of a human did not warrant killing our offspring. I then proposed that we make sure they received no magical instruction. Their mother agreed to this, as did the others. The spawn would never use mind magic, but they were powerful and possessed what, in humans, is called the Sight.

Oh, shit. The ability to see magic was the definition of sorcery. It was extremely rare in humans. Not so with dragons.

"They were powerful sorcerers," Rule said. "And they were psychopaths."

You perceive the problem.

"Adepts?" Lily ventured.

No, nor were they able to become so. While adepts may become mad, the mad cannot become adepts.

She blinked and tried to sort that out.

However, high-level mages are capable of causing a great deal of trouble. Moreover, I was unable to predict their actions or the potential results of those actions. Their magic, like that of true dragons, acts on the patterns in such a way as to render them extremely difficult to read. So while our concern was theoretical rather than empirical, we believed that, given magical training, one or more of them would establish themselves as despots or demigods. We strongly disliked such an outcome.

We did not know they would be able to reproduce.

Lily frowned. "But if you made them physically identical to humans, you had to guess it would be possible."

We had altered the vasa deferentia while they were prepubescent so that sperm were unable to enter the seminal stream. However, they were capable of consciously directed healing, an ability that dragons do not develop until they are fully adult—a process of one or two centuries. Their mother knew they had developed this ability. She did not inform the rest of us, and it did not occur to me or to the others that the spawn's magical abilities might mature on a human time frame rather than draconic. We assumed they would die long before they were able to direct their healing.

This was appallingly lazy thinking. Hypotheses are tested; assumptions often remain unnoticed and go unchallenged. We did not check on the maturation of their healing and so didn't realize they had discovered the tampering to their vasa deferentia and healed it.

By the time the last of the original dragon spawn died, they'd had thirty-two offspring. Most of those offspring inherited varying degrees of magical ability; all were mind-dark. The subsequent generation, however, was substantially less powerful, and less than half of them were mind-dark. The number displaying clear psychopathic—

"Wait a minute," Lily said. "You let them go right on having kids?"

Given their ability to heal and their determination to breed, we were unable to do otherwise unless we killed them. My solution had proven far more imperfect than we'd hoped, but they didn't suffer as much as earlier mind-dark offspring. It was clear that the passage of time and thinning of their blood would eliminate the problem. We did not want to kill our young or their descendants.

Lily couldn't say he was wrong. No sane parent wanted to kill their young.

Rule spoke. "You mentioned the spawn's determination to breed. That was significant, I think?"

Yes. Several of us had visited them by this time, so they were aware that we considered them flawed.

"I thought their mother didn't allow you to enter her—" Rule broke off when Lily elbowed him in the ribs. He gave her a quizzical glance.

She shook her head. She'd explain later, but she thought Sam referred to parental visits. The brownies had told her about those. The father of a dragon hatchling was allowed limited visitation rights by the mother, but these were never spoken of. Dragons considered parentage extremely private.

Sam continued as if there had been no interruption. *Conversation between us and the spawn was indirect. We could not mindspeak them, so we had to use a human intermediary. Yet they knew the basics of their history. They understood that their lack of mind magic would have left them unable to communicate had they remained dragons; they did not consider this sufficient reason to condemn them to a human existence, however. They fervently wished to be returned to their natural state, to be full dragons. The very nature of their other flaw—the psychopathy—rendered it invisible to them, and so they created their own explanation for our actions. A creation myth.*

Like human psychopaths, they considered empathy and emotional attachment weaknesses. In their mythos, they were the perfected beings, and we exiled them to ignorance and humanity because we recognized their superiority. Logically we should have killed them, but our own weakness prevented it. It is a tidy syllogism. If you ignore their basic misunderstanding of the nature of weakness, the logic is consistent.

Grandmother snorted but didn't comment. Not out loud, anyway.

They passed this mythos on to their offspring, who in turn passed it to theirs, somewhat embellished.

"For how many generations?" Lily asked softly.

The mythos persisted past the point that any of them were readily distinguishable from pure humans. By the time we left for Dis, the draconic heritage of those descended from the spawn had become so diluted that only rigorous study could detect it. None were wholly mind-dark, although they remained unGifted in mind magic; none possessed enough magical power to pose a significant threat to the human culture; and the percentage of psychopathy among them was only slightly higher than in the general population.

A startling thought occurred to her. "Am I—"

Grandmother gave Lily a look. "Think. The spawn had no mind magic. You do."

Li Lei is correct. Your heritage is magical, not genetic. Through all the generations we observed, the spawn's descendants remained incapable of any form of mind magic. You are not descended from them.

"I'm wondering," Rule said slowly, "how this connects to the reason you brought us here. To Tom Weng."

Your surmise is correct. He is a dragon spawn.

For a long moment none of them spoke. Rule broke the silence. "And he's working for the Great Bitch."

So he informed Lily Yu, although I suspect he considers himself her ally rather than her subordinate.

"Cousin," Lily said suddenly. "Weng called me cousin, which must refer to my magical heritage and his genetic heritage. That was right after he flew or floated or whatever— which is dragon magic, isn't it?" Dragons used their wings to fly, but various experts had determined that wings alone couldn't lift such large bodies. "Plus he's a sorcerer, he sure acted like a psychopath, and I couldn't sense his mind at all, which suggests he's mind-dark. That adds up to a dragon spawn, according to your description. Not a descendent of spawn, but the real thing."

You are correct. All the evidence—which includes the results of tests Mika has made and shared with me—indicates that he is a true dragon spawn, like that first generation. This should be impossible. There have been no botched hatchings in over seven hundred years, and all the spawn from that hatching have long since died. This is why—DOWN!

It didn't occur to Lily to disobey. She hit the ground. Rule landed on top of her.

The earth jumped. The mountain groaned. And Sam *moved.*

That much dragon shouldn't be able to move that fast. Coils of dragon unwound like thread from a spool as he shot off down the tunnel. If she and Rule hadn't been flat already, they'd have been flattened.

For a long moment, nothing happened. Lily's heart pounded as her body urged her to fight or flee or do something, anything, other than lie there. She turned her head to check on Grandmother.

Li Lei Yu lay flat on the floor like her, although without a couple hundred pounds of lupus sprawled on top to protect her from all the nothing that was going on. She muttered something in Chinese that Lily didn't catch, then said more clearly, "It would be useful to question him." Then she grimaced, mouthed what might have been a curse, and sat up. After a brief, frowning pause, she rose to her feet with more grace than a woman her age was entitled to.

Lily poked Rule. "Off." After a moment he complied and they both stood.

"Were you addressing Sam, Madame?" Rule asked, pulling out his phone.

"Hush." She tipped her head, her gaze distant.

Lily translated Grandmother's earlier comment for Rule, who was trying to call out on his phone. Unsuccessfully, to judge by his expression. "I don't know who she wanted to question, but if that earthquake—"

Grandmother snorted. "Do not be foolish. That was not an earthquake." She continued to frown, aiming it at the still-glowing tunnel. "I doubt it is blocked. Sun went through it. As to whether it is safe . . ." She shrugged and started walking. "We shall find out. It is most unsatisfactory to remain here."

Lily followed. Rule didn't. He put his phone up, said, "I need to know about the men," and took off running. By the time Lily and Grandmother entered the tunnel, he'd vanished around the nearest bend.

"Did one of the other dragons make the ground shake?"

Lily persisted, avoiding the obvious term for "shaking ground" since Grandmother had objected to it. "Is that who Sam went after? He thought one of them might—"

"Not a dragon. A missile."

"A *what?*"

"I am not familiar with military terms, but Sun referred to it as a missile. He is not often imprecise in his speech."

"No, but—but we would have heard it. There would have been a huge explosion, not just that little groan."

"I assume Sun's defenses account for the lack of noise, although it is possible he suppressed the shockwave himself. A plane fired it at us."

"Someone in a plane fired a missile at a dragon's lair. At the *black dragon's* lair." Was there even a word for that level of stupidity? And who had missiles sitting around to use in such a complex form of suicide?

And that wasn't the most critical question. What kind of missile had it been? Not nuclear, she thought—hoped— since they were all still alive. But undoubtedly destructive, only for how wide a radius? Their guards weren't at the lair, but they weren't far from it. "Grandmother, ask Sam if—"

"Sam is busy. He has gone after the plane. I advised him to preserve the pilot for questioning. I am not sure he will, however, once he has extracted what he wishes to know from the man's mind." She shook her head. "He is *extremely* angry."

SEVEN

No one would expect a winged creature to catch up to a jet—no one who hadn't seen one outpace jets in the past, that is. Whatever allowed dragons to fly let them move ungodly fast when they were motivated.

Sam was sure as hell motivated.

The two women tramped up the long tunnel in silence for a few moments. Then Grandmother sighed. "*Zhēn kěxí.*"

Roughly translated, that meant "what a pity," which applied to all sorts of things at the moment. "Pardon?"

"The pilot destroyed his plane before Sun could."

"I don't suppose the pilot ejected first?"

"No."

Dammit. Lily scowled at the floor of the endless tunnel. "Did Sam get any information from his mind before he died?"

"He was in the process of doing so when the pilot blew his plane up."

"Why is Sam talking to you? Only to you, I mean." Lily couldn't mindspeak more than one person at a time, but Sam did it all the time.

"He is doing several things at once. He is well able to do so, of course, but why add unnecessary chores to the list? He tells me, I tell you."

"What else is he doing?"

"Checking the patterns. Checking his defenses. Keeping the other missile from exploding. Speaking with some foolish general. The plane—"

"Other missile?" Lily said sharply.

"You interrupt," Grandmother said sternly. "The plane was of the U.S. Air Force. He wishes the general to explain how one of his planes came to shoot missiles at us. The general does not believe him." She sniffed contemptuously.

The plane's origin was important, but Lily knew the difference between important and urgent. "What other missile?"

"I do not badger him with questions when he is busy."

She considered that for two heartbeats, then took off at a run—only to see Rule running back to her as she rounded the nearest bend. They both called out at the same moment.

"There's a missile—"

"There's a missile—"

They both broke off. "Sam is keeping it from exploding," Lily said, stopping.

Rule stopped beside her. "I'm relieved to hear that, since it's embedded in the rock about thirty feet above the entrance."

She digested that briefly. "The men?" she asked.

"They felt the blast, but took no harm from it. Sean came to check on us. I sent him back to the car. The only thing that seems damaged is the mountain itself. Sam's landing pad is a mess. Pieces of mountain fell on it, and the peak looks like a stone-eating giant chomped on it."

She whistled. "I don't know anything about missiles. You?"

He shook his head. "I'm guessing they were both aimed at the entrance. Sam or his defenses deflected the one that took out the peak. He may have deflected the other one, too, but not enough, so he did something to keep it from exploding."

"Someone really meant to take him out."

From around the bend behind them came Grandmother's voice. "Only if they are idiots." She was speaking Chinese again. The way she kept falling into that language told Lily she was more agitated than she seemed. As she came into view, she went on in English, "The world is full of idiots, so that is possible, but Sun was in no real danger. They did not use nuclear weapons."

Lily's eyebrows lifted. "It takes a nuclear bomb to pose a real danger to Sam? One of those missiles took out the top of the mountain."

"It did not harm Sun." Having disposed of that argument, she looked at Rule. "Your men are not harmed?"

"They're fine," Rule said. "Madame Yu, perhaps we should stay away from the outer chamber. There's an unexploded missile only thirty feet or so—"

She snorted and kept going.

After a pause in which Grandmother disappeared around another bend in the tunnel, Lily said, "I guess we're safe enough. Sam left Grandmother here, after all."

He huffed. It was the wolf's way of showing amusement. "Meaning he'd gamble with your life and mine, but not hers?"

Rule's eyes were too dark. The black wasn't spreading, so he was in control, but his wolf wanted out. She slid her hand in his. "He'd calculate the odds differently with her than with us."

"True."

They started walking again, this time together. Lily began, "The thing I don't understand—"

"Only one thing?"

"—is what Grandmother is doing here."

"You didn't ask her?"

"She was repeating some of what Sam told her. That seemed more urgent." She told him what little Grandmother had shared, ending with, "I don't know how much Sam learned before the plane blew up. It was an Air Force plane, by the way."

"It almost had to be, didn't it? That kind of weaponry isn't available to private individuals."

They left the tunnel for the entrance chamber. It looked entirely undamaged. "Do you think we missed an Air Force plant? One of Smith's followers who decided to act on his own?" She referred to the NSA bureaucrat who'd put together a nice little cabal with big, patriotic plans. Supposedly they were all either dead or jailed, but . . .

"I suppose it's possible, but I don't see how this advances any of that group's goals."

"I don't see what it accomplishes, period."

Grandmother was standing on the landing pad just outside the entrance to the under-earth portion of Sam's lair. Apparently she'd heard them, for she responded. "It is a distraction. It is also an insult, but I believe the primary motive was to distract us."

"A pair of missiles is certainly distracting," Rule agreed. "Especially the one that hasn't exploded. I find myself quite distracted by that one."

Grandmother sniffed.

Stepping out into the bright July sunshine had Lily blinking. She looked around. Here at last was evidence of an explosion. Debris was scattered on the formerly pristine sand of Sam's landing pad—rocks, mostly, but dirt and twigs and leaves, too. Some of the rocks deserved to be called boulders. "I'm going to call this in," she said, reaching for her phone. "Sam might need help with that general." She checked the time. Four twenty here meant it was seven twenty in D.C., so she called Croft's cell phone. That way she'd catch him whether he was working late, on his way home, or already there.

"What general?" Rule asked.

"A foolish man," Grandmother said, "who argued with Sun. He seemed to think it was Sam's fault the plane exploded. Sam is supplying motivation for him to look into the situation."

Lily wasn't sure she wanted to know what kind of motivation Sam was supplying, but her busy brain supplied some disquieting possibilities anyway while she waited for her boss to pick up.

Her boss was supposed to be Ruben Brooks. Ruben was a precog with uncannily accurate hunches, and he'd been in charge of Unit 12 the whole time Lily had been an agent. But Ruben had been part of the fallout from the events in and around D.C. two months ago . . . not because he'd done anything wrong, but because he'd been outed as a lupus. Half the women in the country might crush on Rule, but the nation as a whole wasn't ready to see a werewolf in charge of a critical element of law enforcement. Or so the politicians had concluded—those that weren't simply screaming that lupi couldn't be in law enforcement at all. Technically Ruben was still with the Unit, but he wasn't running it anymore. Martin Croft was.

Lily liked Croft. He was canny and capable. But he wasn't Ruben.

He also wasn't answering. When his phone went to voice mail, she frowned and left a terse message. She had an emergency number, but it was more for mobilizing resources than for letting her boss know that the black dragon was busy motivating an Air Force general.

Rule was on the phone, too, pacing along the landing pad as he spoke—to his father, she realized after a moment. He looked like he wanted to do his pacing on four legs instead of two. Grandmother just looked annoyed. Not by Rule, probably, but who knew?

"What were the missiles supposed to distract us from?" Lily asked.

"Quiet. I am thinking."

Rule told his father "*t'eius ven*" and slid his phone back in his pocket. "You didn't reach Martin?"

She shook her head. "If he doesn't call back pretty quick, I'll—"

"I have decided," Grandmother announced, "to finish Sun's explanation."

"And answer our questions?" Lily asked.

"That will depend on what you ask. Sun had almost finished when those missiles interrupted him. He will be busy for a time, perhaps up until he needs to leave—if he still wishes to leave. That, I do not know."

"Leave?" Rule repeated, startled. "Where?"

"Hush. Sun has told you of the past. I will speak of recent events. The dragons were unaware of the Great Enemy's hand in the assault on Mika's lair because the presence of a dragon spawn hid . . . I will say, hid her fingerprints. This failure concerned Sun and the other dragons, so they arranged to study the traces left by Tom Weng's magic. This was a lengthy proceeding. They could not enter Mika's territory, so they had to borrow other eyes, and the traces were very faint. They . . . *tcha!* It is difficult to explain, but there is a nothingness about the spawn. A void. They are identified in the patterns and in their magic by what is missing, not by what is present. Lily, did you touch Tom Weng?"

She shook her head. "If you mean did I touch his magic, then no. He was barefoot when he kicked me in the head, but my hair kept our skin from touching."

"Had you touched him, your Gift would have registered this void. I do not know what it would feel like to you."

"Well . . . I couldn't sense him with my mindsense. It wasn't as if he was shielded, either. He just wasn't there."

"Perhaps that is similar to what Sun and the others found. Something which was not there. This examination is how they assured themselves that Tom Weng is, indeed, a dragon spawn. Having confirmed this, Sun decided he would speak with you, then leave Earth to investigate the odd fact of Tom Weng's existence. He may still do so. I do not know."

"Leave?" Rule's eyebrows shot up. "Where—and how? There's only one gate on the planet, and it isn't big enough for a dragon."

"I will not speak of his destination or his means of crossing the realms. If he wishes you to know these things, he will tell you later."

"That's why you're here!" Lily felt an absurd degree of relief to have at least one question answered. "He wants you to monitor his territory, right? Not that I know what that means, but you did it for him before. But why leave Earth? What does he expect to learn?"

"If it is impossible that any dragon spawn have been born in this realm for over seven hundred years, then either Tom Weng is over seven hundred years old or he was not born here."

"Then there *are* more dragons elsewhere?"

"I do not speak of this."

Lily knew it was pointless to argue when Grandmother spoke that firmly. She did it anyway. "But if there are more dragons elsewhere, then there could be more of these spawn. Dragons lay several eggs at a time, right? So we need to know if—dammit." Her phone had broken out into the "Stars and Stripes," which meant someone had called her official number and the call had been routed to her cell. It wouldn't be Croft, dammit, who she needed to talk to. He'd call her cell directly.

But it was still official, so she answered. "Special Agent Yu."

"This is Ackleford," said a hard, familiar voice. "I need you here, stat."

Derwin Ackleford was the SAC—the Special Agent in

Charge—for the Bureau's San Diego office. He was a pain in the ass and a first-class law enforcement officer. He was *not* Lily's boss. "Can't. I've got a situation here that—"

"Yeah? Well, we've got a situation, too. The FBI Headquarters in D.C. has been bombed."

EIGHT

~

THEIR suite's sitting room wasn't large, but it was pretty with bright colors. Amanda liked bright colors. She liked hotels, too. Until the last year—well, it had only been a couple months here, but it had been a year for her. She didn't understand that, so she didn't think about it. But until the Mistress saved her from the dragon's fire, the only hotels she'd stayed in had been cheap and no fun at all, plus she'd usually been with Sharon. Sharon had had way too many rules: Stay quiet. Don't call room service. Eat oatmeal or eggs for breakfast, not pizza. Bedtime at nine o'clock.

Sharon was dead. Amanda had felt a little squish of sorry about that later on, when she thought about it. At the time she'd been too glad she hadn't burned up in the helicopter to think about Sharon, who had. So had Adrian, Susan, and Bethany, although Amanda was the only one who knew it had been Bethany's body the FBI found in the wreckage, not hers. Mr. Weng had changed the records to fool them. But once she did think about Sharon burning up, she was sorry. That surprised her. Sharon had been such a bossy old prig. But Sharon hadn't disliked Amanda the way most people did—at least, not all the time. She'd been a little afraid of Amanda, but everyone was who knew what she could do.

With one exception. Maybe. "This is a nice room," she said, snuggled comfortably against the man who thought he was in charge of her now.

"Very pleasant," he agreed. "Now hush, my dear, and let me listen." He stroked her hair.

Amanda listened to the first part of the news bulletin, but they were saying the same things as all the others. *Apparent terrorist attack*, blah blah, *FBI Headquarters*, blah blah blah. She thought about the man with her. He touched her a lot. People mostly didn't touch Amanda. She'd decided she liked it, as long as he didn't start wanting sex or something. She was never going to do sex. She'd told him so, and he'd nodded as if he accepted that, which he ought to. They had the same Mistress. But the Mistress had told Amanda not to be upset if he did do sex sometimes—with other people, that is. Grown-up women. He was just a man, and men were simple creatures. It wasn't really his fault if he couldn't attain true purity.

But she couldn't tell for sure what he wanted, which was weird and kind of fascinating. She couldn't read Robert Friar's thoughts at all because of the shields the Mistress had given him. "You could pet my hair some more," she suggested.

"I have your permission, do I?" He sounded amused. Mr. Friar sounded amused a lot, mostly for reasons she couldn't figure out. "Go get your brush and I'll brush it for you. You like that, I think."

She bounced to her feet, but before she got halfway to the door of her bedroom, she stopped as a thrill went through her. *She* was here.

Slowly she turned. "You've done well, Robert." The voice was hers. The words, the very intention to speak, were not.

He bowed. "Thank you. Amanda has been most helpful."

"She's a good girl."

Deep inside, Amanda wriggled with happiness. The Mistress approved of her.

She spoke some more with Amanda's mouth. Amanda stopped listening. It was like there were two parts to her brain—one that heard the Mistress's words and repeated them and another, the part where she lived, that could listen in or not. Vaguely she knew the Mistress was talking about "contingencies" and a lot more she didn't understand.

She didn't have to. The Mistress had Mr. Friar for the grown-up stuff. She needed Amanda for the things only Amanda could do . . . well, Amanda didn't do them all by herself, but the Mistress couldn't do them without her. Telepaths were rare. Hard to find and hard to make, even for the Mistress, because human minds usually burned out when Gifted with telepathy, and Amanda was a telepath-plus. She could do stuff regular telepaths couldn't. And *she* hadn't burned out.

The process of awakening and deepening her Gift had affected her, though. The Mistress had explained about that. Amanda's body would grow up, but inside she'd remain a child. *Her* little girl. How cool was that? She got to be big like a grown-up without having to become one.

She was special. The Mistress needed her. *She* couldn't be here in person because of some ancient rules she had to obey . . . though not for much longer. Right now, though, the Mistress needed Amanda to give Mr. Friar his orders, and to put orders in the minds of others. Orders they wouldn't remember.

Amanda liked that part of her job. Mr. Friar teased her sometimes, but in a friendly way, saying she sure liked telling people what to do. She just giggled. She did like it. Once in a while the Mistress let her play with the ordered people and have them do silly things. Not often, but once in a while, just for fun. That was a reward for being a good girl and working hard. The work *was* hard, too, even with the Mistress helping. Amanda could put orders in the head of anyone who'd taken one of Mr. Weng's pills, but she couldn't do it the right way. She couldn't remember everything, but she didn't have to. The Mistress always told her what to do, step by step.

But Amanda knew the play wasn't the important part. The important part was stopping the Mistress's enemies, people who wanted to keep her from fixing things here on Earth.

That boggled Amanda's brain. How could anyone who'd had even the tiniest taste of the Mistress's sweetness want to keep her away from Earth? It made no sense. Even bad people ought to want her.

They haven't the advantage you have, little one, said a Voice deep inside.

The moment Amanda heard that Voice, she stopped hearing the outside conversation. Everything in her stilled, hoping desperately for more.

Sweet child, the Voice said lovingly. *Try to understand. They don't know My thoughts. They don't know Me. In truth, some of them don't wish to, and for them . . .* A sigh, as vast and sad as the ocean. *Death is the only mercy I can offer those who refuse Me. But for others, there is hope. Hope for so many in this troubled and suffering world. You are important in bringing that hope into the world, Amanda.*

Joy bloomed inside her.

Be a good girl.

I will.

Do as Mr. Friar tells you.

I will. She didn't even mind—not much anyway. Mr. Friar treated her okay.

The Voice was silent then, but the Mistress was still with her. Still close.

Mr. Friar was talking. ". . . long for that. For the moment you enter your rightful domain." He didn't sound amused now. His voice throbbed in a way that made the pit of her stomach feel funny, kind of like it did when she went in a real fast elevator.

"It won't be long now, Robert," she heard her mouth say. "My allies will open the path for me once we have some of those troublesome lupi out of the way. And her, of course."

Mr. Friar's mouth turned up in a way that didn't seem like a smile, though it should have. "Lily Yu."

"Yes. She really can't be allowed to interfere with Me anymore. I will enjoy destroying her a little more than perhaps I ought to."

Then she giggled, or maybe Amanda did that herself. The Mistress's happiness made her feel so good.

NINE

~

5:07 p.m. PDT

"**STAND** by? What the hell does that mean?" Lily glared at the rumpled man sitting at a messy desk in a cluttered office in the FBI's San Diego office.

"You need your ears cleaned, Special Agent?" Ackleford snarled back.

There was a reason Ackleford's subordinates called him The Big A, and the "A" had nothing to do with his surname. On his best days, the man was difficult and foul-mouthed. This was not one of his good days. "'Stand by' means park your ass here and wait. Maybe you'll find out what the hell it's for, maybe you won't. I sure as hell don't know."

"I've got a pissed-off dragon whose lair was attacked by an Air Force pilot flying an Air Force plane shooting Air Force munitions at—"

"If the fucking director of the FBI says that you and every other fucking Unit 12 agent are to stand by at the nearest field office, that's what you fucking do."

Lily stared. Gathering all Unit 12 agents into the field offices made sense—if you wanted to be sure the bad guys could locate their targets. "I know the director's new. I didn't know he was an idiot."

Ackleford snorted. "Maybe it's not all about you."

Maybe not. They didn't know that magic had been used in the explosion. They didn't know much of anything yet, not even who'd been in the building when it went boom. Rumors abounded—including one that the bomb had been planted in the sub-basement that housed Unit 12.

Croft hadn't answered his phone. Ida hadn't, either— Lily had tried calling her on the way here. She didn't have a private number for the others she might have called, like Jenny in Files, or Amos Baxter, or . . . Lily swallowed and locked it down again. "Hard to see how they got a bomb into the building without using magic."

"We don't know shit yet, including who was in the building." Ackleford's voice was as hard as ever. His eyes weren't. "Quit jumping to conclusions and go bother Webster or someone and let me get some work done."

At least she'd heard from Deborah, Ruben's wife, so she knew Ruben was okay. He was at what was left of FBI Headquarters now, but he'd been at home when he was hit with a sudden, overwhelming premonition and called the director and Martin Croft.

Croft, at least, had listened. He'd intended to evacuate Unit 12. Deborah didn't know if he'd succeeded. "If you hear anything—"

"I'll let you know."

6:27 p.m. PDT

"Thank you, General. If you'd give me Colonel Abram's number so I can . . ." Lily scribbled down the name and phone number of the colonel who'd been stuck with this hot potato of an investigation. As she did, her phone pinged.

Incoming text. "Yes," she said patiently to the irate general. "I understand. But I lack the authority to, ah, penalize a dragon for . . . they are arrogant, yes. I'm afraid I have to go now. Thank you, sir," she said firmly, and managed to disconnect before the man could repeat the same tirade he'd been on since she called.

Lily had a desk at the FBI's San Diego field office. It resided in an office a bit larger than her new closet. Once in a while she even used that desk. Not often, because in addition to being tiny and windowless, her office was in the ATF section of the building, and ATF and the Bureau didn't get along. But it was a place to sit while she made phone calls . . . and waited.

The text was from Rule: *Sam's not leaving. Didn't explain much. Call when you can.*

She called. He immediately asked about Martin Croft.

"No word yet, other than what Ida told me." After hearing from Ida, Lily had texted Rule that Ida had made it out with the rest of the Unit 12 personnel. Everyone but Martin Croft. *He came out of his office on the run and told us to get out*, Ida had said. *Drop everything and get out. We did. He didn't.*

"Why the hell didn't Martin evacuate?"

"Procedures," she said bitterly.

The Federal Bureau of Investigation employed about thirty thousand people. Nearly a thousand of those people worked at its Headquarters—fewer at night, thank God, but there'd still been around three hundred people present at 7:06 P.M. As with any bureaucracy, there are Procedures to Be Followed. Technically, any Unit 12 agent had the authority to order any building evacuated, including FBI Headquarters . . . but there were those Procedures.

"Meaning?" Rule prompted her.

"Croft didn't explain to Ida. He didn't have time. But she thinks he was trying to get the rest of the building evacuated. He had the authority to order that, but to claim that authority he would have had to present his credentials to the most senior person present. Turns out that person was the assistant director."

"Shit. Conroy Pine."

"Exactly."

There was a reason Ruben had called Croft and the director, but not the assistant director.

Conroy Pine was a career man, not a political appointee. He was respected if not liked by the rank-and-file, being hardworking, honest, and fiercely protective of the Bureau's reputation. But Pine hated Ruben. Before the Turning, he'd been part of the denier crowd, convinced that magic didn't even exist—and if magic didn't exist, then Ruben Brooks and everyone in Unit 12 were either charlatans or deluded. Pine's worldview hadn't survived the influx of magic that accompanied the Turning, but he still despised Ruben; he seemed to blame magic and those who used it for the mental cataclysm he'd endured when forced to accept reality.

"Conroy Pine doesn't hate Martin as much as he does Ruben," Rule said, "but he wouldn't evacuate the building just because Martin asked him to."

"And he sure wouldn't accept the authority of anyone from Unit 12 to order an evacuation unless they followed the sacred procedures." Lily drew a deep breath, trying to clear out some of the bitterness. "So what did Sam tell you?"

"Not much. He did say that the pilot who fired those missiles was under a 'strong and well-wrought compulsion.' The compulsion made it difficult for Sam to access the pilot's mind in the short time he had before the man destroyed himself along with his plane. But Sam believes the magic used to implant the compulsion carried *her* taint."

"Shit."

"Yes. That's about all that Sam learned about the pilot, other than his name, if that helps. Avery Jenkins."

"I got that much from the general—General

MacDonald, the one Sam spoke with. The plane was from his command."

"Is he a fool?"

"So Grandmother says, and I never argue with Grandmother." Especially when she was so clearly right. How did such a bloated bag of wind ever rise to be a general anyway? "He, ah, has begun an investigation."

"I feel like there should be ironic quotation marks around the word 'investigation.'"

"That would be because he's a waste of oxygen. But it did occur to him to learn the pilot's name, which he graciously shared with me." A whiff of amusement ghosted through her. "I also found out how Sam goes about motivating an Air Force general."

"Ah?"

"He wouldn't let any planes operate until the general cooperated."

"How in the world could he do that?"

"I don't know. They wouldn't budge, though. None of the planes would move an inch until the general agreed to cooperate. Listen, I should probably call the colonel who's in charge of the Air Force end of the investigation—"

"I've one more thing to tell you. I'll be quick. Sam told me he wasn't leaving because he's very concerned about some development in the patterns."

"Something other than FBI Headquarters being turned into rubble?"

"Yes."

She rubbed her forehead. "Something that seems more important to him than looking for . . . uh, Weng's ancestors."

"Yes. He wouldn't tell me more, said he didn't have time to translate what he perceived into terms I would think I understood. 'The illusion of understanding'—his words— was likely to lead me further astray than if he had said nothing."

"Sounds like him."

"Yes." Rule's voice was bone dry. "Then he told me to go away. He's gone under-earth to better inspect those patterns. I'm driving Madame Yu home now—"

"Grandmother's with you?"

"She seems to be napping. I'll join you as soon as I drop her off."

"No. I mean . . . I want you to, but I think Toby needs you to be home with him." She hadn't forgotten what was happening tomorrow. She hadn't had time to think about it, to come up with a way to stop the stupid Challenge from happening, but she hadn't forgotten. She huffed out a breath. "I'm doing this wrong. It's your decision, but I think you should be with Toby."

"I'm not going to let that pup kill me, Lily."

"I know that." She almost knew it, anyway. Things could go wrong. Things did go wrong sometimes. "Toby probably knows that, too, but—"

"But he's ten years old." A sigh. "You're right. I'll see you when I see you, *nadia. T'eius ven.*"

"Good hunting," that meant. Or "Go with the Lady." She'd take either one right now. "I love you," she said. "I'll keep you posted as much as I can."

7:48 p.m. PDT

"I wish I could tell you something, Arjenie," Lily said. "I don't know much more than what's on the news."

"I shouldn't have called. It's just so hard, waiting."

"Yeah. Waiting sucks." Arjenie Fox was an FBI researcher. She worked at home these days—home being Clanhome, where she lived with Rule's brother, Benedict—but she used to work at Headquarters. Research ran shifts around the clock, and Arjenie knew people who'd been in that building.

Lily had seen the same images as everyone else in the country. FBI Headquarters was more rubble than building.

They were still digging through the debris, hoping for survivors—and had pulled out a few, so there was hope. There was still hope.

"I should have called you," Lily said. "Sorry. When I talked to Cynna, I asked her to pass on what I'd heard—"

"She did. She said you'd heard that some of the researchers evacuated with Unit 12?"

"Yeah. It's not confirmed yet, but that's what Ida told me. Texted me, I should say. It was a group text and she asked us not to respond. She was using someone else's phone."

"And that's all you know. I shouldn't have pestered you."

"Don't worry about it. It's not like I'm doing anything productive right now. I've made some calls on, um, another case . . ." Which might be related. She didn't see how the attack on Sam's lair could be tied into the bombing at Headquarters, but she didn't have a lot of faith in coincidence. "But that's about it. Mostly I'm sitting on my ass. If I knew why the director wanted us to . . . Yes?" she said to the woman who'd appeared in the door to her tiny office.

"Ackleford wants you right away."

Was there news? "I've got to go," she told Arjenie. "Ackleford wants something."

"That charmer. Hang in there, Lily. Oh—Benedict wants to know if you've eaten."

Trust a lupus to have his priorities straight. "Not yet. Someone's bound to order pizza at some point." No one wanted to go home, though they weren't accomplishing much. "I've got to go, Arjenie."

Ackleford did not have news for her. He had a phone call. "Director Parks wants to talk to you. He's on my line—or some secretary is, waiting for you to show up. I'll put it on speaker."

Why hadn't the director called her cell? With the building a pile of rubble, everything was disrupted, but Ruben had her number and he was there. Lily remembered tact and didn't ask. Ackleford had already put the call on speaker. "Special Agent Yu here," she said, sitting in one of the worn visitors' chairs facing Ackleford's desk.

"Please stand by for the director, Special Agent," said a crisp female voice.

She'd been standing by for three hours now. She didn't point this out. More tact.

Franklin Parks was the brand-spanking-new head of the FBI, having been appointed just two weeks ago when the previous director retired suddenly. They were calling it retirement anyway, though most people figured he'd been forced out. Lily had mixed feelings about that. The previous director had screwed up during the crisis two months ago, but until then he'd done okay. At least they'd known what to expect with him. This new guy, Franklin Parks, was an unknown quantity. He was well connected politically, of course—political appointees always were—and he did have some law enforcement experience. He'd been a federal prosecutor before running off to Congress to join the other clowns in that circus, where he'd served for eleven years before being tapped for the director's job.

Rule—who paid attention to congressional critters—said that Franklin Parks leaned conservative but wasn't an ideologue. A subtle man, Rule said. Ambitious, but not a publicity hound. That was good, but Lily wasn't sure—

A pleasant tenor voice interrupted her train of thought. "Special Agent Yu? Franklin Parks here."

"Yes, sir," she said.

"You'll want to know about your boss, Martin Croft. They found him. He's not in good shape, but he's alive and is being transported to the hospital. I can't . . ." Lily missed the next few words, so swamped by relief she couldn't focus. Good thing she was already sitting down. ". . . was in Conroy's office, or what used to be his office. I'm sorry to say that Conroy didn't make it."

She'd been right. Croft must have headed for Conroy Pine's office, trying to get the building evacuated, but they'd both run out of time. At least Croft was still breathing . . . Lily didn't say any of the things going through her mind about that. "Thank you for letting me know, sir."

"I'm glad I could give halfway good news to one person today. It's a hell of a day. One hell of a day. But I didn't call you just to tell you about your boss. I need some recommendations from you. Even if he makes it, Croft will be recovering for a long time. I need someone in charge now."

That was easy. "Ruben Brooks, sir. He knows the Unit inside and out. I know Congress won't like it—or some of them won't—but in an emergency, you use what you have. Luckily for us, he's the best anyway."

"That's out. You know the man and like him. I understand that, but he's compromised. You must see that. Or perhaps you aren't aware that he knew about the bombing ahead of time?"

She stared across the desk at a grim and silent Ackleford, too shocked to respond at first. "Yes, sir," she managed. "I did know that. He had a premonition—"

"Maybe that's what it was. Can't be sure, so I can't put him in charge. What about you?"

She was still struggling with the idea that this man suspected Ruben. Did he not know about Ruben's Gift? "Uh—no, sir, I didn't have a premonition. About Mr. Brooks—"

"I'm talking about you taking over while Croft's out, Special Agent."

"No!" That came out way too strong. She moderated her voice. "Thank you, but no. I'm good at my job. I would not be good at running the Unit. That's a different skill set, Director."

"Hmm. We'll see. In the meantime, who've we got who can tell me if magic was used in the bombing? You could, I assume."

"Yes, sir, eventually, but I'd have to touch everything to see if I felt any magic on it. That might be . . . impractical. It would certainly be slow. I recommend we ask Cullen Seabourne." Which Ruben could have told him, if the idiot Parks hadn't decided to distrust him. "He's consulted for us plenty of times. He'd have to fly out, but that only takes about five hours if you get a nonstop. Seabourne's good. He'd be able to tell faster and more definitively than anyone else if magic was involved."

At least Parks made decisions fast. He asked two more questions, then told her to "get Seabourne to agree," to give his secretary Seabourne's contact info, and said that he'd arrange transport. "A military jet, I think. They're fast, and whoever did this can't tamper with one of them."

Except that had happened a few hours ago—though it was the pilot, not the plane, which had been tampered with. When she tried to tell him about that, he cut her off, reminded her to send that information about Seabourne to his secretary—"your SAC has the number"—and ended the call.

Lily shook her head, simmering. "I can't believe he thinks Ruben had something to do with the bombing."

"He doesn't."

"He just said he did."

Ackleford gave her a pitying look. "You've led a sheltered life, Yu. Sheltered from the kind of political shit most of us have to deal with. Parks isn't an idiot. He doesn't think that Brooks is responsible for anything except making him look bad."

"I don't see—"

"The top precog in the country told Parks to evacuate Headquarters, and what does Parks do? Blows him off. Now Headquarters is mostly rubble and a hell of a lot of people are dead or injured. Parks has to act like he's suspicious of Brooks. Otherwise, how's he going to explain why he didn't act on Brooks's warning?"

"That's . . . 'slimy' doesn't go far enough. Slimy the way death magic is slimy."

"That's politics."

"Only if you're a filthy ass-wipe."

Ackleford nodded. "You're catching on. That's why he told you about Croft right off. Why he dangled the prospect of putting you in charge. You've got a rep and the press loves you. Hell, you're up for a goddamn Citizen's Award. Parks wants you on his side. Now go away and do what he said. Call Seabourne and text the ass-wipe's secretary."

She stood, so angry she was nearly shaking. If FBI Director Franklin Parks thought he could plant the blame for any of this on Ruben—

"And don't say what you're thinking to anyone else in this office. People repeat shit. Even good people."

10:15 p.m. PDT

"This just in," said the professionally crisp voice issuing from the laptop's speakers.

Lily had moved to the conference room, which held whiteboards with two lists of names—one of the confirmed dead and one for those still missing. Someone had fulfilled Lily's prophecy by ordering pizza. Someone else had brought their laptop into the room so they could listen to one of the news sites while they pieced together what they could. They weren't really working. They didn't have enough data, and none of them were officially tasked with the investigation. But they had to do something.

Fielding was trying to get Lily to say that magic had definitely been involved—as if she knew!—when something in the newscaster's voice caught her attention. Lily turned to look at the small laptop as if that would help her hear better.

"We are receiving reports of a major explosion in the Hebei Province of China, near Beijing," the news anchor said.

"This may have been a nuclear explosion. I repeat—there may have been a nuclear explosion near the Chinese capital."

11:55 p.m. PDT

Lily watched the laptop intently, along with everyone else in the field office. The president had interrupted regular programming to speak to the country about the war that had just been averted. She spoke of "the great grief the American people feel for the lives lost" and praised the Chinese government for "listening to the wisdom of our dragon friends."

There had been three dragons in China. Now there were two.

Lily kept thinking of what Grandmother had said about the bomb dropped on Sam's lair: "Sun was in no real danger. They did not use nuclear weapons."

Someone in China had.

The bomb had come from China's own arsenal, not from the United States—a fact the remaining two dragons had made clear to the Chinese authorities before they could push their version of the big red button. Unofficial estimates put the size of the bomb at 100 kilotons. Not the biggest sonofabitch around, but big enough.

The bomb hadn't hit the capital itself. The dragon who'd called himself Fa Deng had laired in a relatively unpopulated portion of the mountains east of Beijing, so initial casualties were low—low for such a calamitous event, that is. The dead probably numbered in the hundreds, with thousands of injured. Fallout was another story. Beijing lay in the direct path experts expected the fallout to be carried. The city and its environs were in chaos as eleven and a half million people all tried to leave at once.

Lily watched and listened, but the president didn't really have much to say. She wanted everyone to stay calm.

Lily snorted. That was going to happen. Maybe if . . . oh. *Oh!* She pushed to her feet, looking up.

"What is it?" someone asked.

"Don't you hear it?" But when she looked around, blinking moisture from her eyes, it was clear they didn't. How could they not? This wasn't mindspeech. It was audible, and she knew what it was. No one who'd ever heard this could mistake it for anything else.

It was, of all people, Ackleford who suddenly whispered, "My God." And he, too, looked up, his face stricken.

"Come out," Lily said to the rest, hurrying toward the door. "Come outside. You don't want to miss this."

She didn't wait to see if they followed. They did, though. And that's how the entire complement of the FBI's San Diego Field Office came to be among those who heard it when every one of the world's dragons rose into the sky . . . and sang. Sang for their lost comrade or brother, enemy or friend, parent or child—for he might have been any of these things to one or more of them. Sang for the dragon that humans had known as Fa Deng.

Some of them later denied having wept.

TEN

~

RULE was explaining the purpose of the Shadow Unit to
the man who wanted to kill him when he felt Lily drawing
near. He cut the explanation short. "Our chief allies are the
dragons, but the gnomes and brownies are with us as well.
And that's all I can say tonight. Lily is nearly home."

His guest nodded gravely and stood. "Thank you for
your time. I—" He broke off, startled. "You have a cat?"

Seventeen pounds of marmalade-furred ferocity had
stalked into the room. The cat gave Rule an imperious look
and yowled. Rule wasn't sure what he was being ordered to
do. Get rid of Mateo perhaps? "Dirty Harry had already
claimed Lily when I met her. After some negotiation, he
and I achieved détente. He's since adopted my son."

"I see." Mateo's expression suggested he didn't, not at
all. "He doesn't seem bothered by our scent. Cats usually
run from me."

"Harry considers himself quite capable of keeping us in
line."

Mateo shook his head, baffled. "I should go before Lily arrives. She's upset about the Challenge."

"She's my mate." Rule wanted to point out that it was odd that the Lady would have Chosen a mate for him if she wanted him dead. He restrained himself. Mateo was bright enough to draw that conclusion himself, and like most people, he preferred his own conclusions to those handed him by others.

The two of them exchanged a few more polite words, then Mateo left, escorted by Barnaby and Dirty Harry, who'd decided he preferred to be outside. Rule sighed with relief when the door closed. Being around Mateo was a strain. His wolf wanted—needed—the young man to either fight or submit.

Submission wasn't going to happen. The fight almost certainly would.

Mateo had shown up around midnight, escorted by Barnaby. It was all very well to offer a clansman hospitality, but allowing the young man to wander around alone would be foolish. Rule didn't think Mateo would suddenly decide to opt for assassination rather than honorable battle, but he didn't care to bet his life on that.

Mateo had asked with formal courtesy if Rule would speak with him. He had some questions. Rule had, of course, agreed. It's always good to know your opponent, and it seemed that's what they were to be to each other.

Mateo's questions had mainly been about *her*—the Great Bitch, the enemy their people had been created to fight and did not name. Her, and the war currently under way. It seemed that his clansmen had been trying to persuade him to drop his Challenge. They hadn't succeeded, but they had raised questions in his mind. Maybe the dragonsong had as well. No one could listen to that unmoved. Or maybe he'd simply added things up and come to a disturbing total. Mateo was stubborn, not stupid, and the middle of a war

with their greatest enemy was a decidedly awkward time for
Rule to be killed.

Rule had allowed Mateo to ask whatever he wished, but
he'd directed the conversation subtly so he could have some
of his questions answered, too. He'd confirmed that the
young Leidolf was thoughtful rather than impulsive, but
like a lot of people, he confused impulsivity with reckless-
ness. And he *was* reckless, innately so, not just with the
insouciance of youth. Not that he realized this.

Rule did. How could he not, given who his father was?
Isen was capable of truly appalling gambles—they uplifted
him in a way no amount of sanity ever would—but he knew
himself well and penned in his risk-taking with logic.
Mateo created pens for himself, too, but they were built
more from ethical timber than reason. He was driven by the
need to behave with the highest ethical and moral stan-
dards. He and Rule had talked about that, about the difference between ethics and morals. Mateo had an unusually
good grasp of it for one only a few years into adulthood.

He did not exceed his age in every respect, however. He
assumed that having a deeply moral reason for an action
would result in a good outcome. In other words, once he
was sure his own motives were good, he freed his reckless-
ness to do whatever damn fool thing had gripped his
imagination.

The *Santo Desafío* nonsense had a strong grip on him.
And yet Mateo had so much promise. If only Rule had
more time . . .

He felt Lily pull up in front of the house, heard her car
door shut, followed by Dirty Harry's loud greeting. And
grimaced.

He wanted, needed, to see her, hold her, draw her scent
in. He didn't much want to talk with her, knowing what
they'd be talking about. Death. War. War and death, and
didn't the two go together? *A small, limp body, still warm,
the big brown eyes open and staring . . .*

"Goddammit," he muttered. He was sick of his bloody, unsubtle unconscious.

Two months ago, Rule had led the brownies in defending their home. One of them had ridden his back, acting as his communications officer. Dilly. At first Rule hadn't even realized the little brownie was shot. They'd come under fire and Rule had been creased by a bullet, but it hadn't knocked him out. He'd been able to run, to get away. He hadn't known Dilly was hurt until he stopped. He'd run again then, raced as fast as he could to the brownie healer . . . but Dilly had died in his arms before they reached her, his passing unnoted.

Brownies look like children. They took advantage of that, too, sneaky little buggers that they were, but Dilly hadn't been a child, dammit. He'd had a wife, a husband, and two children with a third on the way. Rule knew that, but his stupid bloody unconscious couldn't seem to grasp the fact. No doubt that was why this death, out of all of them, haunted him.

Knowing where the nightmare came from didn't do any good. It came anyway. He was damned if he was going to let it start visiting when he was awake, though. It wasn't as if—

The door opened. His beloved's sweet voice snapped, "What are you doing still up?" She stood just inside the door holding seventeen pounds of purring, battle-scarred tomcat—an intimacy Harry permitted only her and Toby. Anyone else who tried to pick the cat up was going to bleed. "Dammit, Rule, I told you to go on to bed."

"Ah, yes, and naturally you've every right to expect that I'll do as you bid me."

They glared at each other from across the room. After a moment Rule made a spinning gesture with one hand. "Stop. Rewind. Let's try that again, without the sniping. Neither of us is really mad at the other."

"Actually," she said, coming into the room so she could

deposit Harry, her laptop, and her purse on the couch, "I am mad. At least I want to be. Mad is easier than scared, and in way too few hours an idiot is going to try to kill you."

Harry gave her an indignant look and leaped off the couch. Cats considered it a matter of honor never to stay where they've been put. He yowled.

Lily frowned at him. "You've been fed."

Harry yowled again.

"Not by you," Rule translated.

She shook her head, but headed for the kitchen. "Why aren't you guarding Toby?"

Rule assumed that was directed at the cat, not him; Harry usually spent the first part of the night with his boy. He followed Lily into the kitchen. "Harry's been restless tonight. Not surprising, given how tense everyone has been."

She bent and shook kibble into Harry's bowl. The cat sauntered over and took a desultory bite. He wasn't hungry; he simply wanted the proprieties to be observed. She straightened. "I wish you'd gone to bed, gotten some rest."

"I don't need as much sleep as you do." Which she knew very well. "And I don't sleep as well when you aren't with me."

Her mouth quirked into a line that hit somewhere between wry and unhappy. "You just aren't going to let me stay mad for no good reason, are you?"

"You've reason to rage." He went to her, took the kibble container from her and set it on the counter, and touched her cheek. "Around three hundred reasons, last I heard, though they didn't have a full tally of the dead and injured when I turned off the news. I'm not the cause of your anger, *nadia*, but if you really need a target for it, I can say something obnoxious. How's this? Don't worry your pretty little head about me, darling. What's for supper?"

She snorted and wrapped her arms around him, resting her head on his shoulder. "Want some kibble?"

"Not just now, thank you." And at last, as he wrapped his arms around her and her warmth and scent began to sink into him, some of his tension began to unknot. He felt her body relaxing, too. He no longer knew how much of that easing was the mate bond and how much was simply love. Both were real. For a few moments they just held each other, letting two kinds of magic soothe them. "I should have been with you," he murmured.

"Nope," she said muzzily, her voice muffled by his shirt. "You should have been right where you were, with Toby. How is he?"

"Asleep. He's more worried about the dragons than me, I think." Toby was still young enough to think his father invincible. On one level the boy knew that wasn't true, but deep down he didn't think his father could die. Rule understood that. Deep down, he didn't believe Isen could, either. "Thankfully, he was already asleep when the news about the Chinese bomb came on. He missed the whole will-they-bomb-us hysteria."

"Thank God. Have you heard anything from Sam about the bombing?"

"Nothing factual. I heard him sing."

"That was . . ." Clearly at a loss for words, she didn't speak for a moment. "Dragonsong. It's so large."

He nodded, knowing what she meant. "I heard the other dragons rose and sang, too."

"They were singing for him. For Fa Deng." She sighed and straightened, one hand moving to rest on his at her hip. Absently she ran her finger over the gold band he now wore. "The Chinese bombing has to be connected to the missiles shot at Sam's lair. I'm trying not to jump to conclusions, but how could they not be connected? But the bombing at Headquarters . . . is that a bona fide coincidence, or is it connected, too?"

"Sam didn't leave. Perhaps we'll be able to get some answers from him tomorrow."

"You mean today." Her expression darkened. "I haven't had room in my head for a spare thought, much less enough of them to come up with a way to stop that idiotic Challenge. Unless you managed to talk Mateo out of—"

"I'm afraid not."

She scowled.

"Any word on Martin?"

"I'm sorry—I should've texted you. I heard from Ida just as I was leaving. Croft made it through the initial surgery and is critical but stable. The 'stable' part is probably thanks to Sherry's coven. Their healer is skilled but not powerful, so Sherry's got her entire coven there, feeding him juice."

That was probably as good as they could expect right now. Rule had spoken with Ruben; he knew how badly Martin was hurt. "Anything else I should know sooner rather than later?"

"I don't know. Yes, probably. I can't remember who you know and who you don't."

He ran a hand down her back, where every muscle was tight again. "Just tell me."

"Jen, that little freckled clerk—I think you met her. She's confirmed dead. So is Bennet. Rob Bennet. He had photos of his wife and kids all over his office. And Po from Research . . . Research is in the sub-basement, but when the Unit evacuated, they did, too, even without an official order. But Po was on break. He'd gone to see a girl in HR he was sweet on. HR usually goes home at five, but for some reason she was working late. She's dead, too. So are at least two others in HR. They've got the bodies, but haven't officially ID'd them yet."

"Human Resources is on the third floor?"

"Yes. That's where one of the explosions went off, which seems weird. Why target Human Resources? Then there's Arianne Rice—you know her, right? Dark, chubby, a laugh like a jackhammer. Sixteen years on the job. She was still alive when they pulled her out, but she died on the way to the hospital. Rutger—damn, I can't remember his first name. Round little guy . . ."

They spilled out of her—name after name, many with a quick biographical note attached. Death after death. He held her, marveling at her memory, at how she stood up beneath the weight of naming her dead. Because they were all hers, even if she'd only nodded at some in passing and had actively disliked others. They were of her other clan, the one he wasn't part of.

Finally she wound down. "I've missed some. I know I have. Seventy-nine have been confirmed dead, meaning they've officially ID'd the bodies, but . . . anyway, there were three hundred and two people in the building at seven o'clock. They're pretty firm on that. Everyone from Unit Twelve except Croft got out, plus four out of five from Research, which left two hundred ninety-two present at the time of the explosions. Another fifty-two managed to evac afterwards, most with only minor injuries. The cleaning crew, Rule. Every one of them got out, which seems like some kind of miracle. And fifteen—no, sixteen—are still alive after being pulled out of the rubble injured. So that's a hundred forty-nine unaccounted for."

Most, if not all, of those hundred and forty-nine were dead. They both knew that. It would take time to find all the bodies. What remained of the building wasn't stable; those hoping to rescue or recover remains would have to work slowly and cautiously. "You refer to explosions, not bombs. The newscasters keep talking about bombs."

She shrugged. "It might have been traditional explosives, but I don't see how the perp or perps got them into the building. I'm leaning towards magic of some kind. We don't know of a spell, Gift, or magical construct that does this kind of damage, but there's a lot we don't know. Cullen's on his way . . ." She paused, glanced at her watch. "God, it's two A.M. I didn't realize . . . Cullen should be at the site by now. The director found him an Air Force jet for transport. I told you about that, didn't I?"

"Cullen did." He had called Rule shortly after speaking with Lily.

"He didn't even bitch about interrupting his work when I asked him to go."

Because Cullen loved Lily, too. Not the way Rule did, nor the way he loved Cynna . . . who was also grieving. Cynna had been with the FBI for years before motherhood and becoming Rhej forced her to quit. "He told me that Ruben would meet him at the base where his jet landed. He was glad of that. He felt he'd get better information from Ruben than from, ah, some of the others."

She snorted. "Like that ass-wipe they've got in charge of the Bureau now."

His eyebrows lifted. "Franklin Parks is an ass-wipe?"

"He didn't listen to Ruben's warning. And okay, there's some excuse for that. Most precogs aren't all that accurate. Ruben is, but Parks never worked with him, so I guess I can see why he didn't take Ruben's word about evacuating. But he was wrong, and you know how he's handling that? By trying to shift blame onto Ruben!"

Rule's eyebrows shot up. "What? How?"

"He called Ruben 'compromised.' Said he couldn't put Ruben back in charge of the Unit because he'd known about the bombing ahead of time. As if that made him part of some conspiracy."

"When did he say this?"

"I told you. Texted you anyway. It was when the director called and told me about Croft being found. I texted you as soon as I could."

"You said you'd had word on high that Martin was alive but badly injured. You didn't say you'd spoken with the director."

"Oh." She rubbed her forehead. "Sorry. He called me on Ackleford's line. Supposedly he wanted to tell me about

Croft and ask my advice for who to put in charge of the Unit, but since he didn't listen to my advice, I'm thinking Ackleford was right. He's trying to cover his ass." She grimaced. "Here's something else I didn't tell you. He suggested he might put *me* in charge of the Unit."

Rule's eyebrows shot up. "He's not completely incompetent, then."

She stared at him, incredulous. "Have we met?"

"You like being in charge and you're good at it. You usually take charge whether or not anyone makes it official."

"Of an investigation, yes! That's a whole different skill set from running the whole damn Unit—which I would hate doing, in addition to being bad at it. Parks has Ruben right there. He could do a whole helluva lot better than me, or anyone else."

"Did you tell him that?"

"Sure. I was polite," she insisted. "I know how to do that. I was raised on polite."

"True. So who's running the Unit?"

"No one," she said bitterly. "We're way down on Parks's list of priorities, I guess. And I know things are a shambles right now, but Parks seems to be trying to run this investigation himself. That doesn't leave him time to do the things he's supposed to do, like make sure someone's running the Unit. Speaking of units, have you talked to Ruben about the other one?"

"Yes—on the phone, and Sam passed on a message later. The Shadow Unit is on high alert. Come on." Using the arm around her waist, he urged her toward their bedroom at the back of the house. "I may not need much sleep, but I need some. You do, too." She was still too wired for it, but he could help with that. "Will you shower tonight or in the morning?"

"Tonight. I need to wind down."

"Good. I'll join you."

"I'm planning on a quick shower."

"I can be quick."

She gave him a suspicious look that had nothing to do with his ability to shower quickly. His *nadia* thought he had something other than cleanliness in mind.

She was right.

So was he. By the time they crawled between the sheets, clean and exhausted, neither of them had trouble falling asleep.

A banshee howl woke him. With it, an electric wrongness. Violation.

Rule was on his feet and racing for the stairs before his head finished processing what the noise was. Harry. That was Dirty Harry's war cry.

Harry's yowling cut off. A thud, followed by another cry. Toby.

Rule flew up the stairs at top speed. He hit the door to Toby's room without taking time to open it—a spinning kick did that—and skidded to a stop.

Moonlight painted the room in silver and shadow, a room filled with the clutter of a boy's life. There were no clothes on the floor; the grandmother who'd raised Toby until last year could not abide that form of untidiness, and Lily had continued her training. But neither was the floor clear. A toppled pile of books here, a soccer ball there, three shoes, a board game, the skateboard that was supposed to be in the garage . . . a puddle of orange fur, limp and motionless. A length of white sheet, bright against the dark wood floor. It had been dragged halfway off the bed.

The empty bed.

ELEVEN

~

"I swear, Rule—I didn't see, hear, or smell a thing. I don't know how anyone got in. I—"

Rule chopped a hand down, cutting Manny off. "Crane."

The tall man was naked, having been four-footed a moment ago. He reported crisply, his gaze lowered. "No scents near the house that don't belong."

"Check the roof."

Crane took off. Rule stayed where he was, on the front porch, utterly still. Fighting a battle none could see, though his men sensed it. Smelled it. He held a volcano inside, tamped down by nothing but will.

"Ricky. Precisely where were you when—" He broke off. Over a dozen men and two wolves were streaming toward them through the darkness. The rest of the guards. Good.

"Toby's been taken. Form up in squads," he ordered, his gaze snapping to his acting second, who kept his eyes carefully averted. "Mike. Two squads are to make an immediate search of the grounds, half of each squad in wolf form.

A third squad, to include Barnaby"—who had the best nose—"will Change and go to Toby's room. I smelled two intruders there. They're to locate and memorize those scents, then report to me."

"Rule." Lily came out of the house while Mike gave quick instructions. She wore one of his T-shirts and carried a cabinet door that someone had ripped off its hinges. On that flat surface lay Dirty Harry's motionless body. "Harry's still alive. Send someone to Nettie with him, stat."

Anger threatened to spew out, lava-hot. Toby was gone. Taken, he had no doubt about that. And she was worried about the cat?

Lily stopped in front of him, her eyes dark and steady on his. She could do that, could look right at him, without inflaming him. He didn't understand that. He was glad it was so, but he didn't understand it. "Harry's mine. He's just a cat, but he's mine. And whoever did this, however they did it—Dirty Harry saw them."

"Harry's communication skills are limited, and since neither of us can lift that knowledge out of his—"

"Sam can."

Hell. She was right, and he hadn't thought of it. Besides, Harry had been injured trying to protect Toby. Rule owed him care.

He wasn't thinking straight. "Mason—" He stopped. Another wolf had just arrived, this one with half a leg missing. José. He must have Changed to that form so he could move better, but he'd still been slowed by the infirmity. José was Nokolai. He'd get into Nokolai Clanhome faster than the others. "Mason, José—take Harry to Nettie at Nokolai Clanhome. Hurry. Toby's life may depend on keeping Harry alive."

Within seconds, José and Mason were racing for the Toyota that Rule kept for the guards' use, with Mason carrying Harry on his makeshift stretcher. "Lily." Rule turned to her, about to tell her to look for Toby with her mindsense.

And stopped. She'd anticipated him. Her face wore the distant look he'd grown to recognize.

A few seconds later, her gaze snapped back into focus. "Sam is coming."

"Dammit, you aren't supposed to mindspeak Sam! You didn't fall over this time, but—"

"I didn't mindspeak him. I sort of tapped him on the shoulder. He established the connection."

"Fine," he snapped. "Now use your mindsense to look for Toby and his abductors instead of—"

"I already did. That's why I stayed upstairs longer than you. Toby isn't anywhere in my range, and the only minds I found nearby are lupi. Whoever grabbed him left as instantly as they arrived."

"It wasn't a gate. Gates don't work that way." But something had . . . and none of this was Lily's fault. She didn't deserve to catch the spillover from his rage. He looked away. "I'm not—I didn't mean . . ."

"I know." She reached for his hand and squeezed.

The volcano didn't go away. It still seethed inside him, still threatened his control. Yet he felt steadier, better able to fight it back. "It's *her*," he told Lily. "She's got Toby."

"That seems possible."

"More than possible. I *know*. The mantles recognized the taint of her magic. And I . . ." He paused, scowling. "One of the intruders was someone I know or have met. The scent was familiar. I can't place it, dammit, but it's a scent I've encountered before."

"Maybe you should Change so you can get a better read on—"

"Rule Turner." That voice was newly familiar.

Rule spun, his lip lifting in a silent snarl at the interruption. Mateo stood in front of the other men, his eyes raised to meet Rule's. Staring at him. "I am sorry about your boy. I will help if I can. But I need to know if the Challenge will be—"

Rule leaped.

Mateo's surprise lasted only the blink of an eye, but it was enough. Rule twisted as he jumped so that his kick landed squarely in the man's chest, knocking him back several feet. Mateo turned his stagger into a roll, but he didn't stay down, rising to his feet—

"Grab him! Stop him!" Lily cried.

Two of the men latched on to Mateo. Mateo landed a solid blow on Robin's jaw, but the other man was Mike, and Mateo's punch had left him open. Mike didn't waste the opportunity. Four seconds later, Mateo lay facedown on the ground, one arm lifted at a painful angle, with Mike atop him.

Rule watched, fists clenched, every muscle tight, as his body fought to be freed from the damnable restraint of his mind. He wasn't supposed to Change. He remembered that, but not why. Not supposed to Change and leap onto that upstart who kept staring at him, not supposed to rip out his throat—

"What do I do with him?" Mike asked.

Lily answered before Rule could get his mind to supply words. "Knock him out, tie him up—I don't care. Just keep him away from Rule." Then she came to Rule and put a hand on his shoulder. "That wasn't a Challenge, Rule. Stupid, yes, it was deeply stupid, staring at you that way. But Mateo wasn't challenging you. He's already done that."

With a shuddering breath, reason returned. Mostly. Enough that he remembered why he shouldn't Change. He didn't dare. His wolf was not interested in control. In that form he'd be all rage, and he had to be able to *think*. Rage wouldn't find Toby . . .

Find. Oh, yes. "Cynna," he said. "She can Find Toby." He reached for his phone—which chimed as he pulled it from his pocket. He stared at the screen, blank and baffled. How had his father known to call? At this hour, it couldn't be coincidence.

It didn't matter. Whatever Isen was calling about couldn't matter as much as what Rule had to tell him. "Father," he said. "Two of *her* people came here somehow. They took Toby. They've got him."

A long, long silence. Then Isen's voice, pitched so low it sounded as much as a growl as words. "They've got Ryder, too."

"SCARED" was too small a word. Toby huddled up against the boulder where he'd been dumped and told to *stay put* and did not cry.

Almost everything here was rocks—big rocks, little rocks, gray rocks, reddish rocks. Black rock in that hill on his left. Speckled rock in a band cutting through the black. Pretty rocks like the one by his foot that was an unlikely shade of yellow. Chalk-colored rock jutting up on his left like someone giving the finger to the sky. Pink rock in the boulder he leaned against.

Rocks and dead stuff. Mostly dead vegetation—bare twigs, withered or rotting plants. But there were bones, too, here and there. Bones that hadn't come from any kind of animal he had ever heard of. And he might not know much about geology, but he was pretty sure all those different kinds of rocks weren't supposed to be all mixed up together. Not on Earth anyway.

This wasn't Earth.

The sky glowering down on them wasn't blue with day or black with night. It looked like metal, like those old brass candlesticks in Grandpa's bedroom, the ones he said had come down to him from a Nokolai Rho who lived hundreds of years ago. It glowed, that sky, though it held no sun.

He knew where he was. He knew, because his dad had been here. So had Lily, but she wouldn't talk about it. Bad things had happened here and it hurt her to talk about it.

Dad had told him some stuff, though. Enough for Toby to understand where he'd been taken.

He was in hell, and hell was full of monsters.

They came in all sizes and colors, like the rocks. The second-biggest one, the frog-demon whose warty skin reminded him of camo, must be about eight feet tall. She— he knew the monster was female because none of them wore clothes—had more muscles than Benedict. Her arms looked human, but her legs were more like a kangaroo's, with meaty haunches and big feet—built for hopping, not walking. She had a thick tail like a kangaroo, too. But she came closer to human than most of the others.

The warty monster was in charge now that his human kidnappers were gone.

He thought they were humans anyway. They'd looked human and spoken English, and they didn't smell like the monsters—a smell that somehow made him think of pumpkin pie, like someone had sprinkled them with spices. But his sense of smell was no better than a human's. He couldn't be sure.

Toby had never wished so badly to be on the other side of First Change. If he could turn wolf, he'd have Changed and ripped out the man's throat when he hurt Dirty Harry. Maybe the woman's, too, but he wasn't sure about that. It made his insides hurt to think of hurting a woman, even if she was evil. But he was sure he could kill the man.

At least, he could have if he'd been able to Change. The desire to do that burned inside him, a red-hot creature pacing and pacing inside the cage of his flesh. It wanted out. He'd never felt his wolf like this before. If his dad were here, he could ask what it meant. If his dad were here . . .

Tears burned his eyes. He blinked fast.

The bundle in his lap stirred and whimpered. "Shh," he said, stroking the baby's back. "Go back to sleep, sweetheart."

She didn't. She added fist-gnawing to whimpers. He held

her up to his shoulder and patted and murmured at her, but Ryder wasn't having any of it. Part of that was explained by the pungent aroma she gave off. She let go with a good, loud wail of distress.

Warty glared at him. "You keep her quiet."

She didn't really say that. She used some grunting kind of language, but Toby knew what she meant. Dad had said that in Dis—which was the other name for hell—the world followed The Rules instead of natural laws. The Rules were whatever the prince in charge of the region said they were, but one Rule they all used was that meanings were clear even if the words weren't.

Toby looked the monster right in the eye and said, "She's hungry, she needs her diaper changed, and she wants her mama. She won't be quiet."

Warty scowled. She seemed to be thinking, because she just kept scowling and didn't say anything for a long moment. Maybe thinking hurt. Finally she spoke again. Her voice sounded the way a giant bullfrog might. "You need food, too?"

"Yes." He wasn't hungry, but it was a good idea to eat if food was offered because he might not get a chance later. Besides, he wanted to see what they would do. Just before the man and woman left, the man had told Warty to take good care of "our prizes"—meaning him and Ryder. Taking care ought to mean feeding them. "I don't eat bugs," Toby added quickly, because *they* did. A bunch of the monsters had gone chasing after some flying bugs—the first life Toby had seen here, other than their captors—until Warty yelled and made them come back.

Warty grimaced. "You eat dead food."

"I need water, too."

Warty turned to another monster, one of the little ones. It was about three feet long, green, and looked like someone had smashed together a beetle and a slug, only the slug had tentacles and teeth. Warty grunted and the beetle-slug chittered, but though they weren't speaking the same language, they understood each other. That was The Rule about meanings again.

Toby understood them, too. Warty wanted the beetle-slug and its (companions? siblings?) to go get the baby-thing, a container of water, and one of the dead-food-things. Beetle-slug wanted to know which dead-food-thing. Not the lords' food, stupid, said Warty. The other stuff. The beetle-slug and three of its companions or siblings—they looked alike anyway—scampered off, heading for the only creature there that was bigger than Warty.

A lot bigger. It was undoubtedly a demon, too. Everything that lived here was some kind of demon, but this one was beautiful. Weird, but beautiful. It looked like an enormous, shaggy caterpillar with a whole rainbow's worth of silky fur striping it from one end to the other. It had a zillion legs, no head that he could tell, and was as tall as a grown man and longer than two cars, end-to-end. The others used it to carry stuff. They'd strapped all sorts of things on its long back.

They'd strapped Toby there, too, until he persuaded the woman to let him take care of Ryder. She hadn't been hard to persuade. She hadn't wanted to "mess with the squirmy little thing."

The beetle-slugs swarmed up the giant caterpillar's body, veering around a pile of mysterious parcels to detach something Toby couldn't see. A moment later, an object sailed around the parcels and fell to the ground. A diaper bag. Ryder's diaper bag.

"Hey!" Toby cried. "Be careful. You might break stuff inside it, and where will you get more?"

Warty glanced at him. "Shut up." Casually she twitched her tail—then slapped him with it.

It was like getting clubbed with a meaty baseball bat. He toppled over. He managed not to drop Ryder or land on top of her, but she let out a frightened wail. "It's okay, sweetheart," he told her, cuddling her close . . . unable to see her clearly because his stupid eyes were blurred by tears. That *hurt*. "You're okay, aren't you?"

Gradually Ryder quieted, her wails fading into heart-breaking little sobs as he sat up again—winced, and kept murmuring to her. The whole side of his face throbbed. He blinked away the wetness and saw that the diaper bag had been left in front of him. So had a bottle of water and a sandwich wrapped in cellophane with a bar code on its label.

He scooted closer to the diaper bag so he could dig inside it with one hand, keeping Ryder propped up with the other. The bag was pretty full—a change of clothes, a thin blanket, a little bitty stuffed dog, diapers, a two-handled cup . . . good, she'd need that. And there was what he was looking for: her pacifier.

Ryder latched on to the pacifier with desperate eagerness. Maybe it would soothe her long enough for him to get her diaper changed. But what to feed her?

Ah. One pocket held her little spoon in its case and two jars of that special baby food Cynna bought. Organic stuff. He took out a jar of apricot-oatmeal, a diaper, and the baby wipes. Then he set about removing the full diaper and cleaning up her little bottom.

There were six diapers in the bag. Lots of baby wipes, but only six diapers. And only two jars of food. He fastened one of the diapers on Ryder and looked up at Warty. His heart pounded. Maybe the monster would hit him again for talking, but he needed to know. "How long does this stuff need to last?"

Warty stared at him for a long moment, then blinked like a reptile, with the bottom lid lifting to cover her bulgy eyes. Then she smiled. It was not a nice smile.

She came over and squatted down close enough for him to smell her. Pumpkin pie, he thought again. "It's funny to watch you take care of the human larva. Or is it a nymph?

It does look something like a grown human . . . do you know what we do with our young, little boy?" She leaned closer. "We eat them."

He recoiled.

She giggled. It was an eerie, girlish sound coming from a monster with a voice like a bullfrog. "We eat them," she repeated, and giggled some more as she stood, enjoying her joke. "Stupid boy. There is more food for the larva. The lord has a use for it. For you, too."

Toby licked dry lips. "What use?"

Warty grinned, showing teeth. Pointy yellow teeth. "Maybe he will eat you."

Toby thought that was one of the monster's little jokes. He hoped it was. But he was glad when Ryder started fussing again. It gave him a reason to look away from that toothy grin.

"Scared" was not a big enough word.

Fear could get so large that it swallowed you. Toby knew that. He and his dad had talked about fear lots of times. But this was different. As vast as his fear was, it couldn't swallow all of him. It couldn't touch the red-hot creature pacing and pacing inside him, waiting for its time.

But not patiently. Not patiently at all.

TWELVE

LILY ducked into the downstairs bathroom so she could pull on her jeans. Lupi might not care if she was only half-dressed, but she did. She used the facilities, washed her hands, and splashed water on her face, hoping to trick her nearly-three-in-the-morning brain into alertness, and *did not think* about how Toby was supposed to be upstairs right now, asleep in his bed. Safe.

At least he was wearing his pj's—the blue ones she'd given him last Christmas, which were already too short. Half the time he didn't. He'd been raised to wear pajamas to bed, but lupi didn't bother with that sort of thing, so half the time—

Shut up, she told herself and stood there, face dripping, eyes shut tight. She wanted her cat. She wanted to hold Dirty Harry's warm, purring body, wanted him back, safe and whole. She wanted Toby to be still asleep in his bed. Wanted Ryder to be held safe in her mama's arms.

God. Dear God. How was she going to do this? Cynna must be going crazy. Lily wanted to go to Clanhome, both to be with her friend and to question her, but Rule couldn't stand to leave the place where Toby was supposed to be.

Cullen, of course, would fly back here immediately, which meant that no one who knew anything about the workings of magic or the existence of the Great Enemy would be investigating the bombing. Oh, Ruben would do what he could, but the Bureau was being run by an ass-wipe who'd block him for the sake of covering his own sorry ass. Meanwhile, Unit 12 was leaderless, adrift . . . and Rule hung on the edge of a precipice. If he didn't fall off and start killing people, it would be a wonder.

Lily felt achingly, horribly alone in spite of the fact that she'd had to duck into the bathroom to be alone. She just kept thinking about how much she wanted Harry back, as if restoring him would restore everything and everyone else. It was irrational as hell.

The emotion is irrational, a cold voice agreed, *but your conclusion that the cat's life is both morally and tactically important is sound. I am landing now. I will first examine the place from which the boy was stolen.*

"**WHAT** kind of deal did you make to get him to come?" Rule asked.

They stood together, watching the dragon who'd inserted his head in the brand-new hole in the wall of their house. The window in Toby's bedroom had been too small, so Sam had removed it, along with a bite or two of the wall. The black dragon's version of examination involved lots of up-close staring.

"I didn't."

"Not that it matters. We need . . . you didn't?"

Rule was a couple steps back from the edge now. Not calm, no, but his control no longer seemed a glassy thing, ready to shatter. Trying to put his foot through Mateo's chest may have helped, or he may have simply outlasted that first, hysterical rage. "He thinks this may be connected to Weng, which makes this his business or his responsibility or something. It involves him anyway, so there's no debt for his help tonight."

They watched some more.

"I need to do something," Rule said. "There's nothing I can do that will help, not yet. But I need to do something."

"We can go talk to Cynna. To your father. Sam will probably want to examine Ryder's room, too. And Dirty Harry is there. Sam will need to examine him, too." If he was still alive.

CYNNA was pale beneath her ink, but calm. Horribly calm. Eye-of-the-hurricane calm. She folded a pair of jeans and placed them on top of one of the three piles on her bed, then regarded it with a frown. "What am I forgetting?"

"I don't know what you're packing for," Lily said.

"I'm not sure, either."

Cynna and Cullen's little house was crowded. Arjenie, Lily, and Cynna were in the master bedroom; Isen and two more lupi were in the living room; Benedict was on the front porch with yet more lupi; Rule was in the nursery. Ryder's nursery. As soon as they arrived, Rule had Changed so he could compare the scents he found there to what he'd smelled in Toby's room. Were they dealing with the same kidnappers in both places, or had there been two teams?

"That's her cold-weather pile," Arjenie said helpfully. "In case it isn't Dis, or if Dis has gotten cold since you were there."

Lily had gotten most of Cynna's story from Isen. The moment Cynna realized Ryder was gone, she'd cast a Find for her baby. With people and objects she knew well, she didn't have to stop to take a pattern—she could cast the

Find right away. But what her Gift returned had been oddly blurred, even though it had seemed to show that Ryder was quite close, less than five miles away. At that distance, she should have had a crisp, perfect Find.

She'd experienced that odd blurriness in a Find once before. The possibility that this was the same sort of problem had scared her. She'd cast another Find, this time using a baby gift from their friend Max. She'd added Ryder's birthing name to her Find.

Max wasn't just short, ugly, and obnoxious. He was a half-gnome, and birthing names were a gnome thing. They weren't true names, but they were powerful. Max had said the name was in case the baby "gets in trouble—sick or badly hurt." It would let Ryder draw on Max's strength, if necessary. Cynna had hoped the name would also sharpen her Find. It did. It did more; it let her feel what Ryder felt— not emotionally, but physically. The sensations were dim, but enough for her to know that Ryder was alive. She was a bit chilly, a bit wet down below, but she didn't hurt anywhere.

She'd called Isen. Badly as she wanted to rush to her baby herself, she wasn't an idiot. Others could get there faster, others who were better than her at a quiet stalk, if one was needed. She'd told Isen exactly where Ryder was— three miles to the north-northwest, which put her on the slope of one of the foothills that were part of Nokolai Clanhome. Isen had already known something was wrong; he'd felt *her*, he said. The Great Bitch's magic had intruded into Clanhome, but he hadn't been able to tell exactly where.

Isen had sent Benedict and a full squad racing toward Ryder, then he and a second squad had picked Cynna up in a Jeep and headed there, too. They'd arrived only a few minutes behind the four-footed crowd . . . but Ryder hadn't been there. Cynna's Gift insisted that her baby was right *there*—some ten feet belowground, moving along at a brisk pace. She was almost certainly the most powerful Finder in the nation, and she trusted her Gift, but what it told her made no sense . . . if Ryder had still been in this realm.

The realm that was easiest to reach from Earth—the one most physically congruent—was Dis. Otherwise known as hell, because that's where demons came from.

"What else do I need?" Cynna asked. "What am I missing?"

"If it's Dis?" Lily said. "Medical supplies. Food. Weapons. Ammo. Cynna, I'm trying to pin down the timing. What I know is all thirdhand. Could you—"

"They took her diaper bag." Cynna turned blind eyes on Lily. "So they plan to keep her alive. They wouldn't need it if they . . . but I can't remember what all is in it, so I'm not sure what to take. Only two jars of baby food, though. I'm pretty sure there were only two jars in the diaper bag, so I need more food, but how much?"

The largest pile on the bed was baby things. Food, diapers, wipes, clothes, toys.

"We don't know enough yet," Lily said, helpless. "Maybe you could figure what she'd need for a week, and when we learn more we can fine-tune it. Cynna—"

"It may not be Dis. I don't know. I don't know how to find out."

Lily didn't, either. She just knew she really, deeply did not want Toby and Ryder to be in Dis. "We'll need weapons no matter what realm it is. Cynna, a while back you told me Dis was now time-congruent with Earth as well as physically congruent. Are you sure of that?"

"As sure as I can be without opening a hellgate." She didn't look away from the pile of Ryder's things. "Time there and time here used to only match up sporadically, but the Turning seems to have dragged the two realms into full congruency."

"How can you tell?"

"Demons. I don't summon them anymore, but it's possible to, uh, chat with one without—"

Rule spoke suddenly from the doorway. "They're the same. The same two scents I found in Toby's room. I feel as if I should know one of them, but I can't place it."

He'd remembered to pull his jeans on after Changing back to two legs, probably because this was Cynna's home and nudity would be rude. Lily wasn't sure Cynna would have noticed. At the moment, Cynna might not notice if he'd painted himself blue. Lily nodded. "So we've got two perps, not a multitude. Good. What else can you tell from their scents?"

"Both are human or predominantly human. One's male. The other one, the one that seems familiar, is female. There's an odd note to her scent, which may be why I can't identify her. It reminds me of Friar."

That jolted her. "He's in Dis." That's what they'd concluded, anyway, after Cynna exorcised him. Friar wasn't a demon, but he seemed to have acquired enough demon tricks—specifically, the ability to go *dashtu*—to be vulnerable to exorcism.

Rule nodded, his expression grim. "So we've thought. It doesn't smell like him, but it reminds me of him. I wish I had something of his to smell so I could compare the two scents. Cynna, can you do that Find for Toby now?"

"Yes. Yes, I can do that. Do you have something of his? I could probably Find him without a pattern, but I can cast a stronger Find if—yeah, that's good," she said when Lily handed her Toby's toothbrush. She'd brought it along, knowing the sort of things Cynna used to get a pattern. Cynna headed for the hall as if glad to be in motion. "They're probably together. I hadn't thought of that. Toby's with her. That's good." She stopped abruptly, looking at Rule. "I don't mean it's good Toby was taken. I mean—"

"That he'll take care of her," Rule finished, laying a

hand on her shoulder. "If it's at all possible, Toby will look out for Ryder. You know he will."

"Yes. That's what I meant. Do you know why? Do you have any idea why they've been taken?"

"Only guesses."

None of Lily's guesses were comforting. She changed the subject. "Cynna, I've heard from Isen about what happened, but that's second-hand. If you're up to, it I'd like to hear it from you."

"There's not much to hear." Cynna's voice was crisp again. She had herself back under control. "Follow, and I'll tell you."

Lily did, assuming her friend was headed outside. For a strong Find, Cynna liked to build her focus with a stamp-dance ritual performed outdoors.

"I'd stayed up late, hoping to hear something about Martin or . . . just something, you know? Cullen texted me when his plane landed, and I decided I'd better turn in. I knew Ryder—" Her voice caught briefly. "I knew she was going to wake up early. She always does. So after I heard from Cullen, I turned in. I fell asleep pretty quickly. I don't know what woke me. I don't remember hearing anything and the wards weren't triggered, but something woke me. I got up. I don't know why. I didn't feel a premonition, nothing like that. I just felt restless, so I got up to get a drink of water. I looked in Ryder's room. That was automatic. I looked in, and she wasn't there."

"Do you know what time that was?"

"No. I didn't look. At first I couldn't believe she was really gone. She had to be there. Only she wasn't. I did a quick Find. That's when I knew it was real, that she was really gone. But it was blurry, so I did another one. I used her birth name. That made it so clear, like crystal . . . did Isen tell you about that? I have to focus hard, but I can feel her. She's all right. Physically, anyway, she's all right."

"That's a big comfort. And after you did that Find, you called Isen?"

"Yes." Cynna moved through the living room as if no one were there. One of the men stepped quickly out of her way.

"Isen said you called him at two nineteen. What time did you go to bed? Did you check on Ryder then?"

"Of course. She was fine. Sound asleep."

"What time was that?"

"I don't . . ." She paused in the doorway, frowning. "My phone. Cullen's text will have a time stamp. Does it matter? I don't see why it matters."

"We don't know yet what matters. Do you know where your phone is?"

"The bedroom. It's in there someplace, I think." Cynna stepped out on the front porch. Rule followed. So did Arjenie.

Lily didn't. She wanted to get Cynna's phone.

"Lily." Isen took her arm, speaking low. "Do you know what Cynna plans to do?"

"Go after Ryder somehow. You're sure about what time she called you?"

"Yes. Cynna intends to summon the other Rhejes. She wants them to open a gate, as they did once before. That could turn out very badly."

Lily tucked away her preoccupation with timing. Isen thought this was important. She'd better listen. "Because they may have set a trap?"

He waved that aside. "Of course they will. We have to assume they'll expect us to follow, if we can. My immediate concern is about summoning the Rhejes, gathering them together. Our Enemy has shown that she can acquire formidable weaponry—missiles, even a nuclear bomb."

And with the Rhejes all in one spot . . . Lily shivered. The Rhos might run the clans, but the Rhejes were their heart, their link to the past and to the Lady. Also to some really potent spells. "That could be bad, all right. I—"

Outside, Cynna called, "I Found him. He's with Ryder. They're not moving now. Earlier Ryder was moving. She was moving away from me at about ten miles an hour at first, but she stopped moving about twenty minutes ago. She and Toby are both staying put now. They're between thirteen and fourteen miles north-northwest of here."

Lily's brow furrowed. She kept her voice down. "I don't see what I could do. There's no way of stopping Cynna, even if I wanted to. I don't. We have to go after Toby and Ryder."

"Yes. We need to find a way to do that without collecting every Rhej in one spot."

We will deal with that.

Lily's eyes rounded. Isen's narrowed.

"With what?" Rule asked from the front porch.

Apparently Sam was addressing all of them. Lily added another question. "When you say 'we,' do you mean dragons, jointly?"

I mean that dragons will arrange for a gate, if one is needed. Cynna Weaver is correct in her surmise that your stolen young were taken to another realm, but we do not know which one. Determining that will be difficult and time consuming. The traces I found are faint. They are sufficient for me to be certain no gate was involved and are consistent with what I would expect if a crosser shifted there, but insufficient for me to tell what realm was involved.

"A crosser?" Lily repeated.

So the elves name those able to travel between realms without a gate.

"Like Gan."

"And my father," Arjenie said, coming back inside.

And a sprinkling of others among the low sidhe, Sam

agreed coldly, *as well as some of the middle and wild sidhe and all of the high sidhe. None of which is relevant, for none of them were involved.*

"How do you know?" Cynna demanded, following Arjenie into the living room.

My conclusion derives from multiple sources. You are aware of one. Rule Turner stated that the two intruders smell human. Rule Turner, Isen Turner, I request your permission to invite another of my kind to join me in your respective territories—specifically, to the sites where your young were stolen. His assistance will increase the probability that I can determine where your young were taken.

"Leidolf grants permission, as stated," Rule said.

"Nokolai grants permission, for the purpose stated," Isen said.

He requests that you refer to him as Reno. He will arrive in twenty-one minutes. I have retrieved a memory sequence from the cat you call Dirty Harry. I will—

"Is he all right?" Lily broke in. Harry had suffered a depressed skull fracture. She'd spoken with José, who'd gotten that diagnosis from Nettie, so she knew that much. A depressed skull fracture was not good news, but it was something a healer could deal with. Usually. Sometimes. Though if he'd suffered brain damage before Nettie started working—

He is alive and your healer seems competent. He stands a decent chance of remaining alive. Do not interrupt again. I have made a tentative identification of one of the intruders, based on a comparison of Dirty Harry's memory with data I have obtained in the past two months. He was the man you know as Tom Weng.

Rule growled.

"Weng?" Lily repeated, startled. "Are you—no, of course you're sure. Sam, Cynna doesn't know about Weng—what he really is. I have to tell her."

I did not extract a promise of silence when I spoke to you about Tom Weng's heritage. I ask that you employ discretion in speaking of it. I was not able to identify the other intruder, whose scent Rule Turner finds familiar. I will place Dirty Harry's memory in your minds; perhaps one of you will be able to identify her. You may experience some disorientation.

Blank.

Dark . . .

WARM. *Sprawled in comfort across favorite softness, warmth radiating up from my bed/nest, the warmth and scent of my (smell/boy/mine/TOBY). Pleasurable vibration in my throat. Drowsy, eyes closed, limp . . . self and world saturated with scents, the house-sounds normal, my whiskers tasting the slightest movement of air. All peaceful.*

I contemplate a memory: tension, curiosity. A new man-wolf comes today; talk-talk (smell/wolf-lion/RULE) talk-talk DIRTY HARRY . . . New man-wolf my enemy? Complex sifting of sensations, scents, memories . . . conclusion: new man-wolf enemy of (smell/wolf-lion/RULE), yes. (Smell/wolf-lion/RULE) not mine. His enemies not mine?

Uncertainty.

Enemies of (smell/she-tends-me/beloved/LILY) my enemies. Yes. Watch new man-wolf tomorrow and more tomorrows. Learn if he is my enemy or enemy of (smell/she-tends-me/beloved/LILY). Now (smell/she-tends-me/beloved/LILY) home good (smell/boy/mine/TOBY) sleeps good yes all good . . .

Warm. Sleepy.

Air moves. Moves wrong. Eyes snap open to gray-green-pale world of night and my muscles clench—intruders! Magic-stink! Wrong-scum-humans here, bad. Two of them, male and female. They grip each other and move oddly. My ears pin back as I crouch and cry death to them.

*Female scum-intruder lets go of male and drops lower. He reaches out swiftly—reaches for me or for (smell/boy/ mine/*TOBY). *I attack—*

LILY came back to herself. She was sitting on the floor— sitting normally, not like a cat, which was reassuring. When she opened her mouth, she half expected to growl instead of speaking. "Well, that was weird."

Rule knelt beside her, his hand on her back. He looked pale, but he hadn't collapsed to the floor the way she must have. "Are you all right?"

"Fine. It was more than a little disorienting, but I'm fine." She got to her feet.

You did not recognize the intruders.

"*I* wasn't present. I was Dirty Harry, and he doesn't— didn't—know them." Cats live in the present. She'd always heard that, but experiencing it was different. So was the way Harry thought, in a blend of sensory images with very few words. Like the way he named Toby—by his scent, first; a sort of an abbreviation that combined the concepts of young, male, and human, which Lily translated as "boy"; Harry's sense of possession; and what Harry considered the boy's sound-name: scent + boy + mine + TOBY.

It had all made sense at the time. It didn't now.

Rule's frown stopped a hair short of a scowl. "I didn't feel like I was Dirty Harry. I saw what he'd seen, smelled what he'd smelled. I wasn't him."

You do not possess any aspect of mind magic, Sam said. *Lily Yu does. When I inserted the memory, she activated and strengthened her link with the cat, causing her to experience the memory as Dirty Harry. Lily Yu. Do not do this again without my supervision. Such immersion in another being's consciousness is unsafe for one at your level of training.*

"What are you talking about?" she said. "What link?"

The link formed by the cat you refer to as Dirty Harry.

Lily blinked.

Cats are not universally telepathic. Their ability to, in your vernacular, "read minds" depends largely although not entirely upon the formation of a particular type of mental link. Kittens instinctively form such links with their mother and siblings. Not all retain the ability in adulthood, but those who do often establish links with other beings with whom they've formed an emotional bond. Such links are generally inaccessible to any but the cat. Your ability to access it, however inadvertently, interests me. I will wish to investigate this at a later point, assuming we survive.

That was a disquieting way to put it.

We approach a particularly dangerous cusp. Rule Turner, you recognized one of the intruders.

"Yes." Rule's frown hadn't abated much. "Or I thought I did. Dirty Harry's vision is quite different from mine in either form, however. If Lily didn't recognize her, I'm probably wrong."

"Don't go by me," Lily said. "I wasn't paying attention to faces. Or rather, Dirty Harry wasn't paying attention and I wasn't present, so I couldn't. What I remember . . ." She tried to summon the memory, but it was fragmented now. "I remember how they smelled—which is weird—and how big they looked and the way they moved. That was important, how they moved, and their faces weren't, so Harry barely noticed them—but, ah . . . I think they were green." She frowned. "Could they be green?"

Arjenie nodded. "To a cat, yes. Cats' eyes have the same color receptors as ours, but they have a lot more rod cells and fewer cone cells. Rod cells give them excellent night vision, but without ample cone cells, they don't distinguish colors as easily as we do. Most experts think they see blues and greens a lot better than reds and oranges."

Lily shook her head. "How do you know these things?"

"Never mind that," Cynna said in a tight, hard voice. "I didn't recognize either of them. Rule? Who did you think the woman was?"

"Ginger. Ginger Harris."

THIRTEEN

‎〜

GINGER Harris. Thirty-two—no, thirty-three now. Five-seven, one twenty-eight. Caucasian with red hair and brown eyes set deep in a triangular face. An intriguingly pointed face, like a Siamese cat's. And alive, apparently. That had been in question.

The last time Lily had seen that face, Ginger had been making a play for Rule, or possibly for her. Ginger had suggested a threesome, anyway, and it was impossible to say if the offer had been genuine, intended to distract, or simply part of her passion for the outrageous.

The time before that, Ginger had been trying to get Rule framed for murder.

The time before that . . . many years before that . . .

It was neither fair nor accurate to say that all of Lily's memories of Ginger Harris were bad, but nightmares weigh so much more than happy memories. She carried the weight of her oldest nightmare with her as she set off for Nettie's place.

She also carried her newest weapon—an M4A1. That might seem unnecessary, given the three lupi guards spread out before and behind them, invisible in the darkness, but none of the guards carried an assault rifle. She'd retrieved hers from the trunk of the car before setting off, though she'd left the grenade launcher attachment in the trunk. That was a recent purchase, not government-issue, and she'd had too little practice to be confident using it.

Nettie Two Horses lived in a small stucco cottage only five minutes from Isen's house. The clinic next to it was small, too, but well equipped to provide basic care for her patients. For human or lupi patients, that is. Nettie was not a vet. A physician, a healer, and a shaman, but not a vet. Still, this wasn't the first time she'd used her Gift to help a sick or injured animal. Probably the first time her patient had been a cat, but she'd healed dogs before. Lupi liked dogs, and once hierarchy had been established, most dogs were fine around lupi.

Cats, not so much. Lily trudged up the road and thought about how it had felt to be Dirty Harry, who was alive. Who might stay alive, according to Sam. That wasn't as awful as the other directions her thoughts wanted to take.

"Why the M4A1?" Arjenie asked.

Lily glanced at her. Trust Arjenie to ID it properly. "Did you recognize it because of Benedict or because you once saw a photo of one?"

"I know what an M4 looks like. They're carried by armed forces in fifty-two countries, including ours. I guessed that this was the fully automatic version because I knew you'd been wanting a machine gun—which this isn't, in spite of its rate of fire, because it uses magazines with . . . is it thirty rounds?"

Lily nodded, fascinated. It wasn't as if Arjenie loved weapons. She loved facts. In times of stress, they comforted her.

"So it has to be reloaded, while a machine gun generally is fed continuously, so the M4A1 is considered an assault rifle rather than a machine gun. In spite of that, it's banned under Title II of the National Firearms Act, which outlaws machine guns, because of its barrel length and capability for fully automatic fire. I assume you're allowed to have one because you're FBI?"

"It took some finagling on Ruben's part, but yes."

Arjenie nodded. "Okay. So why are you carrying it now?"

"Most weapons don't do more than annoy a demon. This should be able to take one out. Maybe not one of the really big ones, but even then it stands a better chance than my nine millimeter. It might even kill a dworg."

"Um . . . you're expecting demons or dworg?"

"Not expecting, but we can't rule them out. Especially demons. With Tom Weng and Ginger popping back and forth between realms, who's to say they won't bring a red-eye demon along next time they drop in?"

"I see. Who's Ginger Harris?"

Lily kept her voice steady. "The sister of a grade school friend of mine. Ginger tried to frame Rule for murder a couple years ago. She was working with the Azá—maybe voluntarily, maybe not. Their leader—Harlowe—had that staff, the one that messed with people's minds. She might have been influenced or compelled by it. Shortly before we shut down that hellgate they were trying to open, Ginger disappeared."

"The Azá worshipped the Great Enemy. Did Ginger worship her, too?"

"Not noticeably, but that doesn't mean anything. Ginger majored in flippant with a minor in sarcasm. If she worshipped anything, she kept it to herself."

"And she vanished."

"Yeah." Lily trudged on in silence a moment before adding, "There was a good chance she'd been killed. Harlowe's crowd liked to keep potential witnesses to a minimum, and whether or not she was a voluntary ally, she was definitely a potential witness." Hindsight said they should've looked for Ginger harder, longer. Hindsight was a bitch. There had been so much to deal with . . . she and Rule had just been hit with the mate bond. She'd been kicked out of the San Diego PD and joined the Unit. At the fight at the hellgate, Rule had lost his second-oldest brother, Lily had been injured, and she'd killed for the first time . . .

"Your school friend never knew what happened to her sister?"

"Sarah died a long time ago." At the hands of a pedophile who'd snatched her and Lily off the beach. The nightmare pressed down hard. "I don't like to talk about that. It's not a secret exactly, but I don't like to talk about it."

"Okay."

A question popped out of Lily's mouth without her having decided to ask it. "Why did you come with me? I'm glad you did," she added hastily. "Just surprised, because . . ." Her voice trailed off. She didn't know how to say the rest.

"They didn't need me for planning. Why do you ask?"

Rule, Benedict, Isen, and Cynna were planning the assault on hell, or wherever they would have to go—though "planning" wasn't the word Lily would have used. Brainstorming, maybe, since they didn't know enough to make a real plan. But brainstorming now might save time later, and at the very least it gave them something to do. Lily understood that need. "I guess I thought you'd stay with Cynna."

"Cynna has a lot of people with her, and I thought you might need a friend."

Something lurched inside Lily—something awkward and painful. After a moment she said, "I do. Thank you."

"You're in a difficult place, aren't you? Everyone's worried about Cynna. About Rule. And we should be, because they're caught in a nightmare and need everyone's support, but you're Toby's parent, too. A stepparent is just another kind of parent."

Taken from his bed, in his pj's . . . "It's not the same."

"It doesn't have to be the same to be horrible."

. . . where he was supposed to be safe. The awkward thing inside her cracked open. "I can't—" Her voice cracked, too. "I can't do what I have to unless I'm the cop right now. I can't be the parent. I have to be the cop."

"It's okay to fall apart, you know."

It wasn't. It wasn't okay at all, not for her. Arjenie did it—collapsed into tears, then pulled herself back together and did what she needed to. Lily didn't know how to do that. The chasm inside her was too big. If she fell in, she might not climb out again. And she didn't know how to say all that, either, so she just shook her head and kept moving.

". . . STOPPED the bleeding and began taking down the swelling, which was dangerously high. I couldn't have lifted the depressed skull fragment, though, if your dragon hadn't decided to help." Nettie walked as briskly as she spoke, crossing the fifteen feet between her house and the clinic. She opened the door. "That takes too much power. Very odd sensation, being fed power by a dragon. It doesn't feel at all like clan magic, but I had no trouble using it."

Lily wasn't sure Sam would appreciate being referred to as her dragon, but she let that pass. "And you think Harry will be okay now?"

"I'd give him a better than fifty percent chance. He's a fighter. That much is obvious, even to someone like me who doesn't know much about cats. He's in sleep now." Nettie crouched to check on her patient, who lay on the clinic's floor. The blanket beneath him had been folded so his head and shoulders were slightly elevated. "I'll keep him that way until late morning, then see how he's doing. We may need to move him to a veterinary surgical clinic. Among other things, they can place an IV to keep him hydrated, which I can't do. Even if I were qualified, I lack the proper equipment. Nothing I have is the right size."

"Cats dehydrate quickly." Lily unslung her rifle and set it on the floor as she knelt beside the too-still body. "Is he running a fever? Can you tell?"

"A slight one. Not worrisome."

Lily stroked the orange fur, careful not to touch Harry's head. Equally carefully, she unfurled her mindsense. She didn't want to accidentally trip whatever switch activated the mental link Sam claimed existed.

The cat's mind was all smooth and shiny, with no texture for her to "speak" to. That's what she'd experienced when she tried using her new sense with him yesterday—God, only yesterday!—after they returned home, but she'd hoped that this time would be different. That, after somehow using that mysterious link, she'd find his mind receptive. She wanted to tell him she was here. That he was being cared for.

Mindspeech was about words, though, wasn't it? And Harry didn't think in words. Maybe . . . gently she stroked his mind with her mindsense while her hand stroked his body. Maybe he could feel that, maybe he couldn't, but it was worth a try. Those with mind magic could sometimes feel this kind of mental touch, and Harry did have some kind of mind magic or he wouldn't have been able to establish a mental link. And that was weird, because she'd never felt any magic when she petted him. Maybe his fur kept her from feeling it?

Suddenly she knew what he needed. "Do you have a shirt I could borrow?"

"Sure, but you and I are not exactly the same size," Nettie said.

"It doesn't matter. I want to leave my shirt with him. It will smell like me."

"Ah. Good idea." She turned away to rummage in a drawer. "There ought to be some scrubs that . . . here they are."

Suddenly Lily's mindsense nearly yanked itself away, out of her conscious control. Up. It wanted to go up and check out . . . "Reno's here," she said. And how did she know it was the other dragon, not Sam? Yet somehow she did. Just as she somehow knew where his mind was even though she hadn't let her mindsense go hurtling toward him.

And who was Reno anyway? None of the dragons used that call-name. Could he be the New York dragon, who hadn't deigned to tell humans what they were to call him?

"Reno?" Nettie repeated. "Who's that?"

Arjenie—who had probably been quiet for as long as she was able—launched into an explanation of who and what Reno was and what they hoped he'd be able to help Sam do. Nettie listened closely, asked some questions, and handed Lily a cotton top that would undoubtedly dwarf her. Nettie was five-ten with wide shoulders and full breasts.

Lily stayed beside Harry, touching him gently with her hand and her mindsense, knowing she needed to leave. To go back to Isen's and add whatever she could to the brainstorming or planning or whatever you wanted to call it. They were all assuming the dragons would be able to figure out where they should go. They had to. There was no Plan B.

Yet still she sat and petted her cat.

Beloved. That was part of Harry's name for her. She blinked away the sudden dampness and pulled off her T-shirt.

LILY and Arjenie didn't talk much on the way back to Isen's. Lily didn't know what Arjenie was thinking about, but she was brooding over timetables.

Thanks to Dirty Harry, she knew when Toby had been

taken: 2:20 A.M. She knew that because she'd glanced at the clock when the cat's howl woke her—a reflex apparently too ingrained to be aborted by emergency. Lily had found Cynna's phone and checked the time stamp on the text from Cullen. That had come at 1:33. Cynna had called Isen at 2:19. Lily mentally added a few minutes to the first time for Cynna to read the text, respond, brush her teeth, and get in bed. She subtracted a couple minutes from the other number for Cynna to perform the two Finds. That left her with Ryder being snatched between 1:37 and 2:17. Toby had been taken at 2:20. At most, forty-three minutes had elapsed between the two kidnappings.

Dis was physically congruent with Earth, but it wasn't geographically identical. For example, the low mountains here at Clanhome correlated to an area of Dis that was mostly plains with a few rocky hills. That's why Cynna had felt as if Ryder were ten feet belowground—wherever Ryder was, ground level was ten feet lower than it was on Earth at that spot. But while the topography of the two realms didn't always match, the distances did. According to Cynna, the time should, too.

There were eighteen miles between Cynna and Cullen's house and Lily and Rule's place. Same should be true in Dis, which meant that Ginger and Weng would have had to travel eighteen miles after snatching Ryder in order to grab Toby at 2:20. So if time passed the same there as here, at the max they'd had forty-three minutes to cover those seventeen miles. Lupi could do that. Humans couldn't, not without a vehicle.

Maybe they weren't in Dis.

Lily wanted that to be true. She wanted it badly enough that she didn't trust her reasoning, so she kept poking at her assumptions.

Cynna said that Ryder had been moving until roughly 3:00 A.M. She'd estimated the speed at between six and ten miles an hour. Cynna also thought Ryder had been lying down while she moved, possibly asleep because she wasn't moving her arms or legs. Wherever Ryder was, then, something capable of traveling six to ten miles an hour seemed to be carrying her. A demon of some sort, probably.

At ten miles an hour, it would take almost two hours to go eighteen miles—way over the forty-three minutes that had actually passed. Therefore, either: (a) ten miles an hour wasn't their transport's top pace; (b) Ginger and Weng had used some other way to travel between the two houses; or (c) they weren't in Dis.

Lily couldn't see any way of determining the top pace of a completely unknown means of transport, so she considered Door Number 2. How else could they have traveled those eighteen miles?

A car seemed highly unlikely. She didn't think one could be taken to Dis without a gate, and even if it could, she wasn't sure it would work. Dis was a fairly high-magic realm, and magic wasn't kind to technology. Maybe if they had a really low-tech vehicle, one that magic wouldn't mess with too much . . . but were there any roads in Dis? She hadn't seen any . . . wait. What if they used a vehicle intended to operate off-road? A dirt bike like the one Cynna was so enamored of, for example. Or an ATV, or a pair of them. Were ATVs or motorcycles low-tech enough to function in a high-magic realm?

She didn't know. She made a mental note to ask Cullen about that when he got here.

If vehicles wouldn't operate in Dis, that suggested the answer was behind Door Number 3: they weren't in Dis. The time just didn't . . . wait a minute. What if Ginger and Weng had gone back and forth between Dis and Earth?

Say they started in Dis, entered Earth just long enough to grab Ryder, and popped back into Dis. There they walked or ran until they were outside the area in Dis that corresponded to Clanhome. She knew they'd traveled at

least that far in Dis because Isen would have felt the distur-
bance if they crossed back into Earth while still in Nokolai
territory. He hadn't.

So they cross back to Earth outside Nokolai Clanhome,
where they've got a car waiting. Drive to Lily and Rule's,
leave the car, and hurry to the spot that correlates to Toby's
room. Cross back to Earth, grab Toby, then back to Dis.

Could they do all that in forty-three minutes?

She considered the road between Clanhome and home
and the distance from Cynna and Cullen's to the borders of
Clanhome—specifically, to the road leading into it. Yes,
she decided. It was just possible, if they ran instead of
walking and drove like hell while in the car. They'd have
had to be both fast and fit, but it was possible. "How much
power does it take to cross realms?" she asked suddenly.

"I don't know," Arjenie said. "Why?"

Lily explained her reasoning. "That would mean they
were popping back and forth between the realms a lot. It
would be good to know if that's even possible."

Arjenie spread her hands. "I'm no help. I don't think my
father ever talked about that. He was limited in how much
mass he could take with him when he crossed, but I don't
know if the limit was imposed by the amount of power it
took to cross or by other variables. You think they're
in Dis?"

"I don't know. The timing is really tight if that's where
they are, but the other realms all belong to the sidhe, right?
The Two Queens would not make the Great Bitch welcome.
She'd have to work through agents there, just like she does
here. Dis is different. No one claims it but demons, and we
know the GB can enter Dis using an avatar."

"Her avatar got eaten, though, didn't she?"

"Sure, by a demon prince, but that doesn't necessarily
mean *she's* gone. It might mean the GB's new avatar is a
demon prince."

Arjenie grimaced. "That is not a happy thought. And

Dis is probably where Friar is, plus it's the realm closest to Earth . . . though 'close' is the wrong word. The realms are separated, but distance isn't a factor in that separation. But I'm told that Dis is the easiest realm to access from Earth."

"Do you know why?"

"I *think* it's connected to the fact that they're highly congruent. Not topographically identical, from what you've told me, but congruent. Oh, and that's something I was wondering about. Toby's room is on the second floor, right?"

Lily nodded.

"So how did Tom Weng and Ginger Harris get there? It would be a huge coincidence if the spot in Dis—or wherever—that corresponds to that spot here just happened to be exactly one floor higher."

"Oh. Right. I hadn't thought about it." So she did. "My memory from Harry . . . he thought they moved oddly. I think they were floating. Levitating. Tom Weng can levitate, and he and Ginger were holding on to each other. I'd guess he carried her up with him."

"That's really not good news."

Lily glanced at her, puzzled. "Nothing today has been good news, but I don't see how that makes things worse."

"Well . . . it means they've got a Finder, doesn't it? Or an unusually good Finding spell so they can locate their targets very precisely. But I guess you'd already thought of that. They knew which rooms held Ryder and Toby, after all."

She hadn't thought of that. She hadn't once thought of it, and the realization hit her in the pit of her stomach. If she could miss something that obvious, what else was she missing?

LILY knew something had happened the moment she and Arjenie stepped into Isen's house. It was quiet. Too quiet.

She exchanged a look with Arjenie, then they hurried to the great room at the back. Cynna stood stock still near the big table, her fists clenched. Isen was on the phone, the house line. Rule was nearby, his phone in his hand.

She looked at him. "What?"

His eyes were dark with worry. He kept his voice low. "Isen just heard from Czøs. Lucas's younger son is missing."

Lucas was the Lu Nuncio for Czøs clan. His son would be the heir's son . . . just like Toby. "When? Do they know when he was taken?"

"Very broadly. Sandy—the boy's name is Alexander, but they call him Sandy—lives with his mother, who is on good terms with Lucas but doesn't live with him. She called him about three hours ago and accused him of having stolen Sandy. He went to her house, where he discovered much the same situation we have—a missing child and the scents of two strangers, apparently human. Scent trails that come from nowhere and lead nowhere." He paused. "Sandy is four years old."

Shit, shit, shit. "Czøs Clanhome is in Minnesota. Is that where Sandy and his mom live? In Minnesota?"

"Yes."

"That's hundreds of miles from here."

"Closer to thousands," Arjenie put in. "Two thousand, to be specific, depending on what part of Minnesota we're talking about."

"But it's too far! Ginger and Weng couldn't get there that fast. Even if they came back to Earth and took a plane, they couldn't get there that quickly. We must be talking about a different realm, not Dis—one where a point in Minnesota corresponds to a spot much closer to us—"

"We don't know what we're talking about," Rule said flatly. "We don't have a clue. Cynna says that Toby and Ryder haven't moved from the place they were an hour ago."

"Multiple teams after all, maybe?"

"Maybe. Isen, Lucas, and I have split the list of the other clans between them. Sam is too busy to pass word his way, so we're calling. Their children—especially the children of the heirs—may be in danger."

FOURTEEN

~

LILY woke up slowly, the nightmare reluctant to let her go. The horror of it clung like a spiderweb as she groped her way through the sticky remnants . . . she'd been eight years old again, locked up in the trunk of the car with Sarah. That part was familiar and drawn from memory. The next part, though, the bit with the knife—that had never happened. In the dream, her back had started hurting, and when she felt around, she found a knife stuck in it. It had been terribly painful to pull the knife out, but she'd managed.

Then the monster who'd kidnapped her and Sarah had opened the trunk, but this time she'd been ready for him. She'd jumped out and stabbed him over and over. But while she was killing the monster, she'd become an adult, and somehow it wasn't Sarah who was with her, but Toby. Only when she looked around, Toby wasn't there anymore. Neither was the car. And the body at her feet, the one she'd killed, wasn't the monster. It was Dirty Harry. She was alone with the bloody remnants of her victim's body . . . and she was in hell.

She shuddered, sat up, and scrubbed her face with both

hands. Stupid bloody subconscious. Nothing subtle about it. "I get it," she muttered. Toby was a little older than she'd been when she was kidnapped, but close enough to wake that old nightmare, especially since it was Sarah's sister who was playing the monster in today's version of Horror R Us. The dream hadn't just been a recap, though. It had been set in Dis, the place where she'd died . . . part of her had, at least, and if that part had eventually been reunited with the rest, that meant she could remember dying. Dis was not a place she wanted to go.

And Dirty Harry? Why had she dreamed about killing him? She glanced at the empty bed beside her. Sometimes Rule understood the coded messages from her subconscious better than she did, but he was gone now—gone from the bed, the house, and Clanhome, according to her mate sense. They'd lain down together for a nap in the room that had been his back when he lived with his father.

She sighed. Probably the Dirty Harry part of the nightmare meant she'd better be damn sure she knew who the monsters were. Ginger Harris and Tom Weng were sure as hell acting like monsters, though. Did her stupid bloody subconscious disagree? Why would it?

No answers floated up from the uncooperative dark places in her mind. She ran her fingers through her hair, trying to wake a few brain cells. She felt heavy, logy, as if someone had stuffed her with ten pounds of cotton while she slept, most of it in her head.

Coffee. Coffee was good at clearing out the cotton. Coffee and a shower, she amended, in that order, because she hated pulling dirty clothes back on after a shower, and she didn't have . . . her eyes fell on a familiar backpack sitting on the floor beside the closed door, with her boots next to it. Draped atop it were jeans, undies, a T-shirt, and the leather jacket Rule had given her for Christmas last year. She'd only worn it a few times; leather wasn't comfortable in San Diego.

Apparently she did have clean clothes.

She'd made a list of what she wanted to take during their last planning session. Looked like Rule had sent someone to the house to fill the order . . . or rather, she thought, checking more closely with her mate sense, Rule had gone to their house and sent someone back here with her stuff.

But he'd stayed there. Why? She frowned, shoved the sheet back, and got up. She grabbed her weapon, clothes, and phone and went to get clean. It was maybe a tiny bit paranoid to take her weapon with her when she was at Clanhome surrounded by lupi. She had no problem with that. Better a bit paranoid than separated from her Glock if she needed it.

No dworg attacked her while she stood under the hot water, however. She went ahead and washed her hair, wondering how long it might be before she could do that again. And thought about Rule, Toby, and hell.

Rule had urged her to nap, but he hadn't intended to. She'd persuaded him to try and sleep on the grounds that needing less sleep did not mean needing no sleep, and there was nothing pressing for him to do. They were in waiting mode now. Waiting for Cullen to return; waiting for the dragons to tell them where they should go; waiting for gnomes to come build a gate to that destination . . . gnomes being the premier gate-builders, according to Sam.

Before napping, they'd held another planning session, one Lily had taken part in. Their preparations were based broadly on two assumptions. First, that the dragons would learn where the children had been taken. Second, that Weng and Ginger would know they were coming—and would have a trap or ambush ready and waiting.

And that, of course, was bad. You didn't want to do the very thing your enemies expected. But they had no choice. Gates could only be opened on nodes. Tom Weng was a sorcerer; he'd know where the nodes were and would either have them watched on his side—whatever realm that lay in—or would set some kind of magical boobytrap. Or both. What they really needed was a way to surprise the bad guys, but none of them had come up with a way to do that.

Lily sighed and shut off the shower. How long had she slept? What time was it?

She dried herself quickly and grabbed her phone to find out. She learned it was past four in the afternoon of a very long day—and that she'd received two texts and three voice mails during her nap. She scowled. She hadn't slept so hard that her phone wouldn't have woken her. A quick check explained why it hadn't. The sound was off.

No doubt Rule had wanted to make sure she wasn't disturbed. That was not his decision to make, dammit. Quickly Lily skimmed the texts. Pete's confirmed that the backpack held the things she'd asked for—socks, undies, ammo, and her first aid kit, among others. Her sister Beth wanted to know what was going on. And the text from Rule didn't tell her a damn thing about what he was up to—just that he'd sent her assault rifle to the spot at the foot of Little Sister where they were staging some of the supplies.

Food and water and first aid stuff they had in abundance, so two sets of that had been assembled, with one set left at each of Clanhome's two accessible nodes. They didn't know which node would be used for the gate, so they were trying to be ready to leave from either one. The staging spot at the bottom of Little Sister was as close as they could readily come to a halfway point.

Lily pulled on her clothes and brushed her wet hair, then braided it quickly while listening to the first voice mail, the one from her father. He loved her; he was sure they'd get Toby back; he and her mother stood ready to help in any way possible. The next voice mail was from the Air Force colonel she was supposed to be working with. He wanted her to call him.

She wasn't going to. She'd called Ackleford earlier and

handed that particular investigation over to The Big A. She'd called Ida, too, since she lacked any more authoritative contact for Unit 12. Someone needed to know that the only investigation Lily would be handling right now involved the kidnapping of children using magical means.

Five children taken—at least that had been the count when she'd lain down—and all of them except Ryder the son or descendent of a Rho. Toby, at ten, was the oldest, followed by Diego, the eight-year-old grandson of Ybirra's Rho; four-year-old Sandy of Czøs; Ryder; and a three-month-old baby named Noah, whose grandfather had been the Etorri Rho until his death nine years ago. They'd been taken from Canada, California, New Mexico, and Minnesota. All over the bloody continent, in other words.

Ryder was the only girl the kidnappers had taken. Since she was the only female lupus ever born, that wasn't surprising. She was also the only one who'd been living in a clanhome. Clanhomes were in some nebulous way imbued with a clan's magic, which repelled the Great Bitch's magic. Her agents were able to physically enter a clanhome, but crossing into a clanhome using *her* power would alert the Rho, as it had Isen, and would probably take a lot more power.

They'd spent that extra power in order to grab Ryder, hadn't they? That had to be significant. Unfortunately, Lily didn't know why.

The continent-wide kidnapping spree might mean that Ginger and Weng weren't the only ones kidnapping kids, which would not be good news. Multiple perps capable of crossing realms on a whim—and taking others with them—was not a happy thought. The alternative was that they weren't operating out of Dis, after all. If Ginger and Weng were the only crossers, they'd have to have been crossing to and from a realm that wasn't physically congruent with Earth, so that a point there which aligned with western Canada was right next to a point that aligned with Arizona.

If so, that left them with no idea where to go. Not unless the dragons came up with a destination . . . which they obviously hadn't, Lily thought. Not yet anyway, or someone would have woken her.

Isen had sent lupi to the other three crime scenes to see if the scents left behind matched those of the intruders here. He should have heard back from the one headed to New Mexico by now. Lily twitched with the need to go find out. First, though, she sent Ackleford a quick text telling him to call Colonel Abram. Only then did she listen to the last voice mail. The one from Ida. Dread and hope mingled in her gut. This was surely about Croft . . .

"Lily, this is Ida. Martin is doing better than expected. He's not out of the woods, but he's holding steady. I hope you are, too, in this difficult time. However, that is not the primary reason I called. Perhaps you've seen the e-mail announcing the appointment of Stephen Marsh as the acting head of Unit Twelve. Mr. Marsh wants you to call immediately. Use the office number."

Who the hell was Stephen Marsh? Lily frowned at the phone in her hand and strapped on her shoulder harness, then went in search of the second item on her wake-up list. One bonus from grabbing a nap at Isen's house: someone had probably made coffee. Stephen Marsh could wait long enough for her to get some caffeine in her system.

Isen was in the great room, talking with Pete, Benedict's second. Lily paused on her way to the kitchen. "Any more kidnappings?"

"No. Our warning may have made a difference. The clans have been gathering those with founders' blood into their clanhomes."

"And the guy you sent to New Mexico?"

"He reported thirty minutes ago. The scents left behind there are the same."

Did that rule Dis out as their enemies' base? Lily was trying to work out the timing as she headed for the kitchen, where Isen's houseman was cutting up a large roast. "Stew," Carl told her in his laconic fashion. "Supper at seven thirty. Coffee's fresh. Cookies in the jar." She blessed him, poured a cup, refused a second offer of cookies, and went to find out what else had happened while she slept.

Pete had left. Isen stood near the fireplace, looking tired. "Any other news?" she asked him.

"Nothing major," he said. "Frank's picking Cullen up at the airport. They should be back soon. Your theory seems to be holding up. Pete just told me they've finished the detailed check outside our perimeter. No traces of the invaders' scents except in one spot next to the highway, on the far side of the last curve. The guards wouldn't have been able to see the intruders there."

She nodded. "What's Rule doing? Did he say?"

"Only that he had Leidolf business to attend to."

Leidolf business? Now? "Not that damn Challenge," she said, half in certainty, half in protest.

"He didn't say. He took Leidolf guards with him."

Lily's hand twitched with the urge to call Rule immediately and ask what the hell he was up to. She restrained herself. "Is Cynna still asleep?"

"She woke up about an hour ago. She's working on the charms she started earlier."

Lily frowned. Around noon, Cynna had started constructing some kind of charms which had to be built in stages. The first stage had left her pale, shaky, and exhausted enough that she'd accepted Nettie's offer to put her in sleep. "That's not much rest, considering how drained she was."

"I mentioned that," Isen said dryly.

"I was in sleep, not just asleep," Cynna said as she stepped in the open French doors. "You know it works faster."

Lily frowned. Cynna didn't look rested. She looked hard. Hard and angry. "Cynna, do you know anything about Stephen Marsh? Apparently he's the new head of Unit 12, but

I've never even heard his name. Makes me think he's not Unit. Until now, that is. I'm supposed to call him."

"That dickhead? Don't. Isen—"

"Don't?" Lily repeated, eyebrows climbing.

"Save yourself the grief," Cynna snapped. "You won't like anything he has to say. Marsh was an MCD hotshot back when MCD was registering lupi, only he called them 'vermin' and thought extermination would be a better policy. Ruben finally got him promoted."

"Why would Ruben—"

"Because Marsh may be a dickhead, but he's competent, plus he knows which asses to kiss. The only way to get him out of MCD was to kick him upstairs. Isen, I need that Devil's Dung."

"So you told me. Jason's on his way back with it. The first source you suggested wasn't home, so per your instructions, he didn't try to collect it himself but proceeded to the next one on your list. Mrs. Rogers was reluctant at first. She was concerned that he wanted the rhizome for, ah, evil purposes."

"Yeah, it can be used in some nasty spells. The one I'm constructing, for example. But she gave in? Did he tell her it was for me? Or for Cullen, rather? She wouldn't know my name, but she knows Cullen."

"She wasn't convinced Cullen's motives would be pure," Isen said dryly. "However, Jason called me. When I explained that my grandson and four other babes and children had been taken by a sorcerer, she accepted that as a valid reason to use a spell involving Devil's Dung."

"What in the world is Devil's Dung?" Lily asked.

"The common name for asafoetida," Cynna answered. "It's necessary for the last stage of the spell. The powder is easy to find—it's used in Indian cooking sometimes—but for this I need the whole plant, root and all. It has to be fresh, and it has to be dug by someone with a Gift who can chant the *manušikane* or something similar."

"The man-you-see-what?"

"A Romany chant. It preserves the integrity of a plant's magical structure for a time."

"What are these charms for?"

Cynna's mouth curved in a hard smile. "Blowing up other spells."

"And that's nasty?"

"It can be. Once activated, they trigger a sort of magical explosion that unwinds shaped magic. But it also disrupts innate magic, sometimes with deadly effects."

"They are very powerful charms," Isen murmured. "She's been drawing heavily on the clan's magic."

Cynna gave him a flat look. "I will spend every one of you, if that's what it takes."

"No," said a new voice. "You won't." Cullen stepped into the room.

Cynna didn't exactly welcome her husband. Her eyes narrowed. "Don't tell me what—"

"You won't, because I won't let you."

"You can't stop me."

"I damn sure can." He moved toward her like she was prey. "It wasn't your fault, Cynna."

"I know that."

"It wasn't your fault."

A tremor shook her. "Shut up. Damn you, just shut up. I don't need—"

He reached her, grabbed her shoulders, and shook her. "Listen to me! It was not your fault!"

She punched him in the gut—and collapsed into sobs. Cullen gathered her close and they clung to each other.

"Good," Isen murmured. "Good. Come on." His glance collected Lily as he headed outside.

"Asshole," she heard Cynna say in a quavery voice.

"Bitch." Cullen said that the way another man might say, "Sweetheart." "You hit me."

"A love tap . . ."

Then Lily was on the rear deck, too far for those soft voices to reach. Isen stood at the edge of the lower deck, looking solid and strong and hairy. Rather like an old-time mountain man, she thought, with a dense thicket of hair and beard surrounding his face, the rusty brown salted with gray. His hair was long enough to tie back now, though he seldom bothered.

Isen had started growing his hair out a couple—three months ago. When Lily asked why, he'd smiled faintly. "A whim." She'd snorted, but dropped the subject. Isen lied well. If his answer was unconvincing, it meant he didn't intend to talk about his real reasons.

"Is that what she needed?" Lily asked quietly when she reached him. "To hear that it wasn't her fault Ryder was snatched?"

Isen nodded. "But not from me. Not from you, either, so stop looking guilty for not saying the magic words. She wouldn't have heard them. Cullen's the only one who could get through that hard shell she's been busily encasing herself in."

Lily's eyes narrowed in sudden suspicion. "Did you call Cullen? Did you tell him what he needed to do?"

Isen just smiled.

She shook her head. "How do you do that? How do you know . . . it's not mind magic. It's just you. You know what everyone needs, even though you must be half-crazy with worry yourself. And none of us can do that for you. We don't know—*I* don't know—what you need."

For a long moment he looked back at her, his face unnaturally still. When he spoke, his voice was almost normal. Almost. "I need two things. First and most, I need what we all do—to get Toby and Ryder back, safe and well. I can't do what the rest of you can. I'm not the warrior my older son is, nor a master strategist like Rule. I can't sling fire and spells with Cynna and Cullen, nor can I assemble a puzzle with most of the pieces missing the way you do. I won't be part of the team who leaves to rescue Toby and Ryder. I could be. If I removed the heir's portion of the mantle from Rule and placed it in Benedict, I could go, but that would be unforgivably self-indulgent. You will need Benedict's skills far more than mine. So I do what I am good at. I help the rest of you keep your heads clear so you can do what I cannot. I help you, but I also use you. It is," he finished bleakly, "what I'm good at."

It was Lily's turn to be silent. "And the second thing?" she said at last. "You said you needed two things."

"Well." He grinned at her—or perhaps just bared his teeth. He didn't look like a mountain man now. Not like a man at all, though he still stood on two feet. He looked like what he was—the alpha wolf, the one all the other wolves obeyed—primordial, potent, and deadly. "I also need to sink my teeth into my enemies' throats and feel their life-blood spurt, hot and salty, into my mouth. It's unlikely I will be able to do so, but you can help me deal with this unmet need, Lily. If you are the one who kills them, either of them, tell me about it. Let me share vicariously in that joy."

FIFTEEN

~

BENEATH a sky with neither sun nor moon, clouds or stars, monsters were playing. A few of them sat the game out, making sullen lumps on the landscape with their backs to the rest, delegated to keep watch. One—the one that looked like an enormous caterpillar striped in rainbows—might have been asleep. It wasn't moving, but since it lacked visible eyes, it was hard to know if that meant sleep. The game the rest played resembled football in some ways, though without a ball; it involved a single goal (a rock), lots of running, shoving, kicking—each other, not the nonexistent ball—biting, and a great deal of confusion about who was on which team.

Three boys sat on sandy ground twenty feet from the caterpillar monster. All three were dark-haired, barefoot, and in pajamas. One had coppery skin; the other two were Anglo. One was much younger than the other two. And crying.

"Diego," Toby said, "see what you can do for Sandy."

"I can punch him if he doesn't shut up," the other boy muttered. "How's that?"

Toby looked up from his own task—fastening a diaper on a tiny little bottom. Sandy had probably had a bad dream. He'd been napping, like Ryder, then all of a sudden he'd sat up, his eyes wide. And started crying. "C'mon, Diego. He's only four. Hug him. Play with him."

Diego shot Toby an angry look. "How can I play with him if he won't stop crying? He's going to wake up the other one, and then she'll start crying, too."

Anger flashed through Toby. He tried to stuff it back down, but it didn't want to go. Diego was only two years younger than him, old enough to help instead of making things harder. "The 'other one' is named Ryder, and you're not worried about her crying. You're afraid you will."

The younger boy flinched. "Am not."

Toby's lip curled. "If you're going to lie, at least do it better than that."

Diego didn't respond. He didn't do what he'd been told, either. Just looked down at his feet and started picking at his toenails. Again.

"Sandy." Toby made his voice soft, but it was hard to do when he was so mad. "I need you to do something."

The little boy looked up, eyes wet and nose running. "Wh-what?"

"Take the used diaper to the trash pit."

Sandy sniffed, wiped his nose on his sleeve, and looked over his shoulder at the narrow crevasse where they'd been dumping trash—it was well away from the monsters—and nodded. He padded over and picked up the wad of stinky diaper.

"Thank you." At least that had worked. Toby had tried to give Diego things to do, too, to keep his mind off his fear, but Diego wasn't cooperating.

He wasn't *obeying*. Anger flared up again, hotter than ever.

Toby took a deep breath the way his dad sometimes did and fastened the new diaper in place in spite of the tiny little legs kicking. He had to get a grip on his temper. He was the oldest, which meant he was in charge, which meant he couldn't just yell at the younger boy. Which he probably shouldn't do anyway. Toby knew what Diego's problem was. He was scared all the way down, so scared he was afraid of his own fear, and it was making him mean. Toby's dad always said that everyone gets scared, but fear doesn't have to control you. *When you're scared*, Dad said, *it's best to step right up into the fear. Then take the next step. And the next.*

Toby had been doing that. For hours he'd been stepping up into his fear, taking the next step. Well, the next step now was to get Diego pried loose from his toenails. And his fear.

Sandy returned and stood in front of him. "Toby?"

"Yeah?" What did his dad do when people he was in charge of were scared? He'd tried keeping Diego busy, but that hadn't worked. What else?

"My dad says it's okay to cry."

"My dad says that, too." But Dad didn't do it. Didn't cry, that is. Not when people were depending on him, because when you were in charge, you had to look and sound calm. In control. At least, Toby thought, he didn't have to worry about smell. He probably stank of fear, but the noses around him were no better than human. "But if you cry too much, your nose gets all stopped up. I don't like it when that happens."

"Me, neither." A pause. "I'm hungry."

The demons had given them stuff for the babies, including a bunch of bottled water. No food for them, though. He'd have to ask Warty for that, and Warty wouldn't want to interrupt his stupid game. Toby grimaced and corralled one of the little kicking legs and got the foot into the leg of the sleeper. The baby jammed his tiny fist into his mouth, but that wasn't what he wanted. His face scrunched up and he started making fussy sounds. Toby gently stuffed the other little foot where it belonged. "Noah's hungry, too." He looked up and found a smile. "Babies first, right?"

Sandy nodded, though he didn't look altogether sure of that. "I'm thirsty, too."

"Diego. Get Sandy some water, okay? And Noah needs a bottle."

"Already? He just ate."

"It's been a couple hours, and babies this little have to eat real often." It had taken a while for Noah to accept that he was getting a bottle, not a breast, for his dinner, but eventually he'd gotten the idea. "He needs a bottle."

Diego made a face, but he stood and headed for the small heap of stuff the monsters had gotten down from the caterpillar demon. They had a whole bunch of the little bottles. They were already filled with formula, so all you had to do was unscrew the lid and screw on a nipple. They only had a few nipples and no way to wash the used ones, but Warty had said that there'd probably be "soap and stuff" where they were going.

That's how Toby had learned they had a destination. When he asked where they were going, Warty had told him to shut up, but at least he knew they'd be going someplace. "Sandy," he said softly, "I need you to do one more thing. You can sit here with me, but I need to talk to Diego, and I need you to be quiet while I do that."

Sandy frowned. "I don't like Diego."

"He's okay." At least Toby hoped so. "He doesn't like being scared, so he gets mad instead. That's what I need to talk to him about."

Sandy bit his lip but sat. A moment later Diego was back. He handed Sandy a bottle of water—he'd taken the lid off already, Toby noted—then held out the bottle of formula. He'd put the nipple on. "Here."

Toby stood up, the fussy baby in his arms. "You're going to feed him this time."

Panic flashed across the boy's face. "I can't! I don't know how! I didn't grow up on a clanhome like you, so I'm not used to taking care of babies, and he's so little—"

"I didn't grow up on a clanhome, either. I've lived with my dad for the last year, but until then I lived with my grandmother. Hold your arms out."

Automatically, the boy started to do just that—realized what he'd done, and whipped them away. "I'll play with Sandy. I shouldn't have—but you keep telling me what to do." His chin set stubbornly. "I don't like it."

"You agreed. We talked about it, and you agreed I was in charge."

"I didn't know you'd be so bossy! You pretend like you're a grown-up, but you aren't! You're just a kid like me, and I—I—" Diego clamped his lips together. He swallowed.

"It's okay to cry," Sandy informed him.

Diego flashed him an evil look.

"I wish we had a grown-up here, too," Toby said. "But we don't, so I'm all you've got, which is why you agreed I'd be in charge." Mostly, Toby thought, Diego had agreed because the in-charge person had to talk to the demons. Also to the two humans, when they showed up. Diego was more scared of them than the demons, which proved that the boy wasn't stupid. "You're what I've got, too, so you're going to learn how to feed this baby. How to take care of him, and of Ryder, too. You have to, Diego. What if something happens to me?"

Diego stared at him. "It won't. They—they didn't kill us, so they want us for something. Ransom, I guess."

Or death magic. Toby wasn't going to explain about that, though. "Probably, but we can't count on it. We both have to be able to take care of the babies, Diego. They need us.

Sandy needs us, too. Now, stop acting like a silly human, getting mad because the one in charge tells you what to do. How does that make sense?"

Diego flushed heavily enough for it to show beneath his dark skin. He looked down.

Oh. He'd been doing that all along. Looking down, looking away. Giving a subordinate message and then arguing—and that's why he made Toby so mad. Diego's body language said one thing, but his actions said another. But at eight, Diego was a lot like a human boy, with just hints of a lupus. He gave confused signals because he was confused, not because he was trying to lie. His wolf must be sound asleep.

And Toby's wasn't. He hadn't known the wolf felt like this, all hot and angry. He wanted—needed—to ask his dad about that, if this was how he was supposed to feel . . .

"What is it?" Diego asked. "What's wrong?"

"My wolf," Toby said gruffly. "He's . . . been stirring, sort of."

Now Diego's eyes were wide, too. "You're only ten."

"I know," Toby snapped. Ten was too young for First Change. "I didn't say I was about to Change, just that my wolf is . . . It makes me edgy." He meant that as an apology, but it didn't come out that way, so he made himself smile. "C'mon, Diego. Sit down, and I'll show you how to take care of Noah."

"Me, too," Sandy said. "I can help, too."

"Sure you can."

Toby told the two boys about supporting Noah's head and how to burp him. Diego had never held a baby. He wasn't around little kids much because his mom didn't let him go to his clanhome very often and his cousins on his mom's side were all older than him.

Just as Toby shifted Noah to Diego's lap, Ryder stirred. Inspiration struck. "Diego," Toby said very seriously, "I'm putting you in charge of Noah."

Diego's eyes were big. "You mean really in charge? The lupi kind, where you're responsible for them?"

"That's right. I'm still in charge of all of us, but Noah is yours to take care of."

Diego nodded, looking very serious. Toby handed him the bottle. "I'm going to check on Ryder now. Remember that being in charge doesn't mean you know everything. Ask questions if you need to."

As Toby moved away, Sandy piped up, "Can I hold his bottle?"

"Maybe in a minute," Diego said. "I need to learn how first."

Ryder was up and moving—crawling off in the wrong direction, lickety-split. As Toby trotted quickly after her, he heard Diego add softly, "I'm sorry I said that about punching you. I wouldn't really do that."

Toby smiled and scooped Ryder up, swinging her in a big circle to make her laugh. He'd gotten it right this time. Diego was a dominant. He hadn't realized that at first because of those mixed signals the boy kept sending. A dominant should've automatically tried to help Sandy when the little boy woke up crying, but Diego wasn't used to being around little kids or babies. He hadn't known what to do. That made him feel bad, which made him mad, which made him resent Toby for knowing what to do. But that was also the answer for how to handle him: give him someone to take care of. Because that's what dominants do. They take care of others.

Ryder felt big and solid after holding Noah. She patted his cheeks with both hands and babbled away at him, her expression intent. She couldn't talk yet, but she didn't know that, so he listened and nodded and told her he didn't know what she was saying, but it sounded important. That made her chortle and grab his hair.

Which then tried to stand straight up, especially on the nape of his neck.

He knew that feeling. So did the other kids—at least he thought Ryder did from the way she acted, and Diego and Sandy had said they felt it, too. He turned slowly.

One moment the demons were playing their rough game. The next, two humans stood in the middle of them. Arguing.

". . . how you think it's my fault, I do not know."

"Don't be so sensitive, darling. Just because I called you a lazy bitch—"

The woman froze. When she spoke again, it wasn't her voice that came out. This voice was *big*, as if a mountain had decided to talk. A female mountain. "Tom."

The demons had all stopped moving the instant the two humans appeared. At the sound of *that voice*, they all flattened themselves on the ground.

The man didn't drop to the ground. When he replied, his own voice was polite. "Yes, Great One?"

"That word is not allowed."

He inclined his head. "My apologies. I misunderstood the nature of the prohibition."

"You understand now?"

"I believe so."

"Excellent." The woman patted his cheek as if he'd been a child and she his doting aunt. "She dislikes you very much already, you know. You needn't try so hard. Now, everyone needs to eat, then get ready to move out. No more little excursions. Clearly my enemies are on the alert. You won't be able to take any more children."

"We agreed on seven."

"If possible, Tom. It is not going to be possible . . . yet."

The way she stood, Toby couldn't see her face. He wasn't sure he wanted to. Had it changed the way her voice had? His insides felt funny, like they'd turned to water.

After a pause the man—Tom—nodded. "You are correct."

"How good of you to notice." The girlish giggle sounded obscene in that mountain voice.

Ryder must have thought so, too. She whimpered and turned her face into Toby's chest. Automatically he patted her back.

The woman turned toward them. She looked just like she had every other time he'd seen her. Ordinary. Pretty enough, he supposed, and maybe a little older than Lily, but he wasn't good at guessing grown-ups' ages. Her hair was red and short, and her face was pointed, like a Siamese cat. She wore ordinary clothes, too— jeans and a girly T-shirt, bright pink with lacy stuff.

She'd worn a thin blue sweater and a flowered skirt the last time he saw her, when she and the man brought Noah back with them. The time before that, when the two of them showed up with Diego, she'd been wearing a dress that didn't look like anything he'd ever seen before—long and wispy and green, kind of see-through. When they delivered Sandy, she'd been in jeans and a yellow shirt. But she had worn the same thing twice in a row—when she and the man kidnapped Toby and again when they brought Ryder back, she'd been wearing black slacks and a tight, lacy black shirt.

The woman clapped her hands once. "You heard the boss," she called. "Get busy now, everyone. Get everything packed up." Her voice was hers again, not the mountain's. Then she looked right at Toby and started for him.

He glanced quickly at the others. Diego cuddled Noah in one arm with his other arm around Sandy, who stood as frozen and terrified as a baby rabbit under the gaze of a predator. Toby swallowed and patted Ryder and watched the woman walk right up to him. The man, as usual, acted like Toby and the other kids didn't exist. He was pointing at the ground, his lips moving. Some kind of spell?

The woman smiled at him. It wasn't a nice smile, though it pretended to be. "Have you guessed my name yet, little boy?"

That was her game. When they first brought him here, he'd asked who they were. The man had ignored him, but the woman had told him to guess. Every time she and the man showed up with another stolen child, she asked for his guesses. "Mary Ann," he said. "Like on that old show. *Gilligan's Island.*"

When she laughed, it sounded nothing like the mountain's horrible giggle. "It's been a long time since anyone's mistaken me for the girl next door. She was sexy, though, wasn't she? I always figured she was screwing the professor. The millionaire, too. A girl can't afford to be too picky, and when they finally got off the island, he'd be the one she wanted to—shall we say—keep in touch with. But I never was sure if she and Ginger had a thing going on as well. What do you think?"

"I think you weren't able to steal any lupi kids this time."

"No, they'd moved the son of the Kyffin heir. On the bright side, it did piss Tom off, but it also meant I'd wasted *my* time." She pursed her lips. "I think your father has been tattling. Oh, it's possible one of the others spread the warning, but I prefer to blame your father." She smiled again, a happy smile this time, and bent down and purred, "What do you think, little boy? Is it your father's fault we can't get any more children yet?"

Toby wanted to look away—or run away—or maybe pee his pants. He didn't know why this woman scared him so bad, but she did. Even before he heard her talk in that mountain voice, she'd scared him. "What do you mean by *yet?*"

"We will get them. Some of them anyway. Those who survive the coming difficulties." Her smile widened. "Don't worry. You and your fellow prisoners should survive your parts in our little war. Your father, now . . . do you think he'll come after you, Toby?"

Startled into honesty by the question and the use of his name, he blurted out, "Yes."

"I do hope you're right," she said. And giggled. And even though it wasn't the mountain's voice this time, it was *her* giggle—sweet and high and quite mad.

SIXTEEN

~⟋

"**ALL** right, but get back to me about it stat," Special Agent Derwin Ackleford told the man who might have thought orders ought to move in the other direction, given that he was Derwin's boss.

Crowley wasn't a bad sort, though, Derwin thought as he reached across the car seat to grab the pack of cigarettes he'd tossed next to a bunch of carnations dyed an improbably bright pink. Mostly he was a pretty good boss. Mostly he left Derwin the fuck alone. So he let Crowley tell him again why he couldn't have what he needed right away, then ended the conversation on a friendly note. "Yeah, yeah. In the meantime, try not to get yourself shot."

He disconnected, pulled out a cigarette, and remembered he was trying to cut back. He scowled and slid it back in the pack. Dammit, he needed the deep background on Colonel Marcus Abrams. There was something off about the sonofabitch. He couldn't put his finger on what, but his instincts had been screaming ever since he talked to the guy. And yes, dammit, he knew nothing was getting done like usual. Not with Headquarters blown up. Not with every-fucking-thing-else that was going on. Two hours ago, an agent at the Boston office had gone goddamn nuts and opened fire on everyone in the place. Killed seven, injured six more. One of the dead was the shooter, killed by return fire, so they wouldn't be asking him what the fuck he'd thought he was doing.

And now another shooting, this one in Georgetown. Crowley had just told him about that one, which hadn't even hit the national news yet. That was probably because the newshounds were so busy with all the other fucking disasters. Aside from Ackleford's own case, the Headquarters bombing, and the Boston shooting, North Korea was having itself a meltdown, China was a fucking mess after that nuclear bomb, and for no fucking reason anyone could figure out, Paris had decided to hold a riot. A really big one.

On a slower news day, the shooting in Georgetown would have drawn a mention by now. Three FBI agents involved in the investigation of the bombing of Headquarters had grabbed a late lunch at a Georgetown restaurant. As they were leaving, a man on the sidewalk called out one of their names, got a response, and opened fire with a handgun.

Crowley hadn't known what the weapon was—he was passing on shit he'd heard unofficially—but it must have been a semi-automatic of some kind, judging by the results: five injured, one dead. Three of the injured had been nearby civilians. Of the FBI agents, one was dead, the other two injured, including the man who'd stopped the shooter. Ruben Brooks had jumped the motherfucker after the man put a couple slugs in him.

Ruben Brooks was lupi. Lupi were hard to discourage. Brooks had kept the perp alive, too, proving he wasn't an idiot. Maybe they'd learn something.

They sure as hell needed to. The world had been going

to hell for as long as Derwin could remember, but all of a sudden it was like someone had stamped on the accelerator.

He stopped at the light, drummed his fingers on the wheel, and thought about the cigarette he wasn't smoking. Then he thought about calling Karin. Why the hell hadn't she answered the text he'd sent her three fucking hours ago? It would piss her off if she realized he was worried about her, but he didn't mind pissing her off. And dammit, this was about work, not their personal lives—at least the text had been about work, even if the personal shit was creeping in. He hesitated to interrupt her, though. She was an agent, too—Unit 12, not regular like him—and part of the team working on the bombing.

But someone was going after FBI agents, dammit, and maybe with an emphasis on those connected to the bombing investigation. Someone was going after the whole damn Bureau. Someone with major mojo. He was fucking damn sure of that. Whoever had bombed Headquarters had used magic, and he sure as hell did not believe random people were randomly going crazy and shooting random fucking FBI personnel without some kind of fucking magical brain-scrambling.

Which was how he'd ended up talking to Isen Turner, damn the man.

Derwin didn't know enough about magic. He needed help and had damn few options. He couldn't reach Karin. Yu wasn't available. Seabourne wouldn't be, either, it being his daughter who'd been snatched along with Yu's stepson. Derwin had some tact. He hadn't even asked the man. But he'd thought Arjenie Fox might be able to spare him a little time. She was FBI, wasn't she? Not an agent, but she worked for the damn Bureau.

Instead she'd told him apologetically that she really couldn't leave Clanhome right now, but she was glad he called, and could he hold on a moment? Then she'd passed the phone to Isen Turner, the lupi boss. Who wanted to send fucking *bodyguards* to watch out over Derwin.

Derwin brooded over the insult as he checked the rearview mirror again. A while back he'd thought there was a Toyota trailing him, but he hadn't seen a sign of it for the last twelve blocks. Pity. Someone trailing him would mean he was on the right trail himself, or close enough to get their attention. Whoever *they* might be.

He pulled into the parking lot of a small strip mall. Maybe this meet—if the guy showed up—would hand him a clue. He could sure as hell use one.

He'd gotten a tip. The Bureau got tips all the fucking time, of course, and most of them were useless. But this one had been worth following up. The text had come to Derwin's cell phone, for one thing, and that number wasn't widely known. Someone wanted to meet in person to tell Derwin about "funny stuff" happening at the Air Force base, but refused to say who he was. Refused to meet with anyone else, either. It had to be Ackleford. The clincher was that the texts had come from the phone of an airman at the base: Airman First Class Rodney Klepper.

At least, Derwin thought as he grabbed his cigarettes and the damn bouquet, some things still worked. They could still track a fucking phone number. He got out of the car and immediately lit the cigarette. Klepper might not have anything more substantial than a grudge—he clearly wasn't the brightest bulb, or he'd realize Derwin could ID him from his phone number. But someone from that base had used an Air Force jet to fire goddamn missiles at California's goddamn dragon. That might not rate as high as blowing up Headquarters, but on a less calamitous day, it would look pretty damn major. This Klepper just might know something worth listening to.

Or he might have something else entirely in mind for their meeting. Someone was killing FBI agents, after all.

Derwin couldn't see any reason this mysterious "they" would spend resources on him, but he had no fucking idea what their goal was, so who knew? If so . . . well, depending on how it went down, that might turn out to be even more informative.

The strip mall was typical for this neighborhood—neither upscale nor down. A taqueria held down one end, a convenience store the other. The middle was filled by a dry cleaner, a tax place, a donut shop, some store called Fantastic Worlds—comic books maybe?—and a liquor store, with the liquor store the largest. Everything except the tax shop was still open and it was getting on toward supper, so there were a fair number of cars in the lot and people coming and going.

The taco joint smelled good, Derwin thought, drawing smoke deep into his lungs. Maybe he'd have tacos afterward. He checked his watch. Nearly time. Better get in place. Klepper wanted him to stand in front of the convenience store holding a bunch of stupid flowers so the idiot would know who to approach.

Civilians. Ackleford snorted and took a last drag from his cigarette, seeing no irony in thinking of the airman that way. Civilians all watched too much TV and thought they knew all kinds of stupid shit. This particular idiot could have found out what Ackleford looked like by visiting the office's website. Policy was for the Special Agent in Charge to have his damn photo on the damn home page. Not that the pic looked much like Ackleford—they'd insisted he smile, for one thing. But it would have given the idiot some idea who he was meeting.

Ackleford hadn't pointed that out. Better if Klepper felt clever and in control. For now.

He stuck the flowers under his arm and walked over to the convenience store and went inside. Several people were in the store: a youngish woman, pretty and obviously pregnant, probably Mexican-American; a scruffy guy in his early twenties, also Mexican-American, with a thin little mustache; a business type in a wrinkled white shirt, bald, black, wearing sunglasses; another woman with a little kid, a girl about four. The clerk was in his twenties, pale, with a wild fluff of ginger-colored hair and rimless glasses. Ackleford bought a pack of cigarettes from him and went back outside.

Because he wasn't an idiot, he knew the bouquet might identify him only too well. He parked himself up against the ice machine. The way it was situated, it mostly blocked him from the street. A really good shooter might get a head shot, but from a moving car? Not damn likely. He lit another cigarette and waited, watching.

The pumps were busy. Two pickups, a dinged-up Volkswagen, a Subaru, a Toyota . . . shit. Ackleford stiffened. Was that the Toyota that had been behind him earlier? There were a zillion white Camrys on the road, and the one he'd watched had been too far back for him to get the plates or even a good look at the occupants. They'd been male, though. He was sure of that much.

The guy filling the tank of the Camry could have been one of the two he'd seen. Impossible to be sure. Under six feet; one-seventy, all of it muscle; brown hair that needed a cut; between twenty-five and thirty; western-cut jeans and boots; white T-shirt. No visible weapons, and it would be damned hard to hide much, the way he was dressed. Derwin relaxed slightly as the man finished and hooked the nozzle back on its hook, but the guy didn't get back in his car. Instead he headed for the convenience store.

Probably going after smokes, candy, or a Coke. Derwin kept track of him anyway, even as he kept part of his attention on everything else. You had to stay a bit out of focus, trust your instincts to alert you to anything—

Derwin never even saw the guy move. One second he was tracking the man. The next, all one hundred and seventy pounds slammed into him, taking him down to the concrete. At the same instant he heard the unmistakable roar of a gun—the crash of glass smashing—someone screaming.

"Charlie!" his assailant called as Derwin tried to slam the heel of his palm into the guy's chin, but got his own hand caught and held.

"Got him!" someone called back.

"Whoa, now, whoa," his assailant said, grabbing Derwin's other hand and holding both of them away from his body. The motherfucker was *strong.* "You don't want to shoot me. I just saved your life." He grinned like an idiot.

"Listen, asshole, I'm—"

"Special Agent Derwin Ackleford. We know. Isen sent us."

Derwin quit struggling. Wasn't doing any damn good. "Let me the fuck up, you idiot. I've got to—"

"Go arrest that woman who shot at you. Sure." The idiot— the *werewolf* idiot who'd assaulted him, and Derwin understood now why he hadn't seen the man move—bounced to his feet. "Charlie's holding her for you."

Derwin got to his feet a lot more slowly. Broken glass shimmered in the sunlight all around them. "Her?" he said slowly, knowing he was an idiot, after all. He hadn't thought about someone shooting out through the window. Just about a drive-by or a walk-up.

"Yeah." The young man sobered. "Weird, huh? I saw her pull the gun and signaled Charlie, then I took you down."

He sure as hell had. Isen-Fucking-Turner had been right. Derwin gritted his teeth but got it said. "You cut by that glass?"

"Nothing worth mentioning."

He turned to look through the busted window. The scruffy guy with the mustache had pinned the arms of the pretty young pregnant woman behind her. She was crying.

He pulled his weapon with his right hand, his shield with his left, and went back into the store. "FBI!" he called loudly. "Is anyone hurt?" To the hundred-seventy-pound assailant who'd followed him he added, "There's a mom with a little girl in here. I don't see her. See if you—"

He was too slow. He had his damn gun out, but he was too slow. The bald guy stood with his left side to Derwin, so he didn't see the man's right hand move. The instant he saw the gun in it, though, he fired—too damn fucking late.

The two gunshots sounded almost simultaneous.

They learned later that the bullet had gone right through the pregnant woman to hit Charlie. Charlie, being lupus, lived. The woman and her unborn baby did not. Neither did the murdering bastard who killed them, but that was no consolation at all.

SEVENTEEN

~⫘~

DESPITE Cynna's advice, Lily did call Stephen Marsh. But it was five o'clock by then, which meant it was eight in D.C. Her call went to voice mail.

So did the next call she made, this one to Rule. She scowled at her phone and told herself she wasn't hurt, that he didn't mean to shut her out. That's what he was doing, but not on purpose. Next she called Mike. Voice mail again. Two more calls to other Leidolf clan members got the same result. Whatever Rule was doing seemed to involve every Leidolf in the area. She could not believe he'd decided this was a great time to go fight to the death in a stupid Challenge, but if that wasn't it, what in the world was he up to?

Maybe it wasn't what he was doing, but what someone else had done. If they'd been attacked—

Her heartbeat lurched into third gear, her mouth dried out, and automatically she touched Rule with the mate sense, assuring herself he was alive. If only the damn mate sense told her more than . . . shit. She was an idiot.

Rule was less than twenty miles away. With someone else—anyone other than a dragon or another sensitive—that would've been too far. Her mindsense was malleable; she could disperse it in what she thought of as a mind-mist and pick up a general, 360-degree map of nearby minds. She had to focus it into a probe to speak to one of those minds, however, and she couldn't keep it focused over such a distance. Not unless the mind she sought belonged to a dragon or another sensitive.

With Rule, though, she had a handy cheat. She sent her mindsense zipping along the mate sense. *You okay?*

Fine, she got back. *But busy.*

Not fighting demons, dworg, or Mateo?

No. Explanations later.

Okay. She laid that word in his mind and let her sense coil back up in her middle. Time to . . . Her phone chimed. She pulled it out, saw the number, and frowned. Better get it over with. "This is Special Agent Yu."

"Special Agent, I'm Unit Twelve Director Stephen Marsh," her caller said.

RULE sat in the backseat of his car, drumming his fingers on his thigh and feeling . . . odd. He had no other way to describe the sensation; it was neither good nor bad, pleasant nor unpleasant. It was, he decided, rather like having a missing tooth and being unable to stop poking at the odd empty spot with his tongue. There was a gap where before all had been solid.

The sensation was distracting in its newness. He was glad of that. It gave him something to focus on. Something other than fear and rage.

He should have gone ahead and Changed and run the seventeen miles between his new home and the old one. He'd thought about it, but he wasn't sure of his control. And that was a damnable thing, but it did no good to pretend otherwise. He was on a hair trigger, wound so tight that for the first time in his adult life, he feared falling into the fury.

His wolf should have been able to help. The man was susceptible to that berserker rage, but the wolf was not. His wolf was unavailable. When he reached for that part of himself, all he felt was rage. The man's rage, or the wolf's? He didn't know, but it felt like rejection. As if that part of himself raged not just at his enemies, but at the man—who'd failed to keep Toby safe.

Being with Lily would help. It always did. But that was a damnable thing, too, because he dreaded seeing her. She was not going to like what he needed to tell her. He'd already delayed too long. Yet even that dread was better than . . .

Deep inside, the volcano rumbled.

No. He would not, could not, think about his son and what might even now be happening to him. He would *by damn* hang on to his control. He had to.

His father dealt with danger to those he loved by simply believing they would survive. Lily did much the same. Creative denial, she called it. As long as there was some chance, however slim, the person she feared for would survive, she'd believe in that chance. Why not? She couldn't grieve faster by getting an early start.

He wished to God he could do that. For him, though, the odds mattered. He couldn't hang his hope on whichever peg suited him. Normally he could lean on his wolf when anxiety mounted, but his wolf was no help to him now.

When he reached Clanhome, he'd speak to Cynna first, ask her to check her Find on his son. He needed to know Toby was alive. Then he would tell Lily that he couldn't handle one more fear. He couldn't let her go with him. If he feared for her as well as Toby, his control would shatter.

She'd resist. He knew that. She'd be angry. In the end,

though, she would understand. She had to. He could not have his attention divided. His son's life was at stake.

They pulled up in front of his father's house. He got out and took a moment just to breathe, to fully see and smell the world around him. The sun had dipped beneath the low mountains that cradled Clanhome and the air was warm and golden, smelling of creosote and wolves and home. There were more guards around his father's house than usual. It was oddly quiet; when he focused, he caught the soft voices of those inside the house. Carl, speaking of supper. His father, asking a question.

Then he stopped heeding the rest of the world, because Lily rounded the corner of the house, heading for him. She wore jeans, a dark T-shirt, the boots he'd sent to her, and her shoulder harness.

He didn't run to her. He didn't run away, either. He walked like a goddamned adult.

"Hey," she said, then stopped, studying him, a little frown tucked between her brows. "You look like you need a run."

"Not now."

"Soon, then. What in the world have you been up to? You were gone a long time."

Automatically he reached out, brushing his thumb across that frown line. "Arranging matters so I'm free to go when the time comes."

"What does that mean?"

"It means Leidolf now has an heir."

"What? You installed the heir's portion of the mantle in—in who? And how could you—"

"The ritual is simple enough. Not easy," he admitted, "not with such a thin blood-tie between us, but simple. That didn't take long, but I stayed to brief him on various matters he'll need to know if he inherits the full mantle. It's an odd sensation," he added, "having part of the mantle lodged elsewhere."

"He who? Dammit, Rule, who did you make your heir? I didn't think any of the guards had founder's blood."

"They don't. Mateo Ortez does."

She stared. "You made the man who wants to kill you your heir."

"It's temporary, as I warned him, but it's a tidy solution. I almost wonder if he didn't arrive at the Lady's prompting as he believes, if not for the reason he believes."

"I can see why you wanted Leidolf to have an heir, but—" She broke off and shook her head.

"Where's Cynna?"

"Out back. She and Cullen were going to finish those charms she's been working on—she wanted Cullen's eyes for the last part—then make something Cullen dreamed up. He calls it a demon bomb. Rule, why didn't you send for someone else with founder's blood?"

"Because that would take time. I will not *wait*, Lily. Not one minute longer than I have to. Best to ensure the safety of the mantle first so I don't endanger all of Leidolf, because . . ." He took a slow breath and reversed the order in which he'd planned to tackle things. Cynna wasn't available now, so he'd move straight into the part he dreaded. "Because the threat this time is too great. We're going to our enemies' territory, and they will be ready for us. Which is why—"

"Rule!" The voice was deep and gruff and came from the side of the house. "Don't talk to them yet! Gotta talk to you first."

Temper at the interruption washed over Rule. He shoved it down. He'd hadn't realized Max was here, though he'd known Max was coming. He'd called him earlier. Max was tough and smart and he loved explosives. He collected them the way other people collected stamps or guns. He was also the only one other than Cynna who could use Ryder's birth name to find her. "Talk to who?" he called back.

Max's reply was not in English. Fortunately, Lily's was. "I think he means the gnome gate-builders. They just arrived and immediately went around back to look over the node under the deck. The one tied to the clan."

Rule's heartbeat quickened. He knew little about the building of gates, save that it had to take place on a node. "Is that where they'll build it? And do they know where we need to go?"

"The answer to both questions is that they don't know yet. At least that's what Max said. The gnomes won't talk to me. I wanted to ask them some questions about the gate and what we can take through it, but according to Max they can't speak to any of us until they've followed some kind of protocol."

"Max is with them?"

"He brought them here." She paused. "All of them. In his car. It's around back now."

"Ah—how many would that be?" Rule was picturing Max's car—an ancient VW Bug with a yellow hood and one red fender accenting its fluorescent green paint job.

"Twelve. Apparently that's the optimum number for creating a gate."

"They must have"—looked like the clown car at the circus as they climbed out, one after another after another. Gnomes were small, but not that small—"been quite crowded."

"Yes." She did not let her lips twitch. Good control. "They would have been here faster, I'm told, but had to wait for three of their number to arrive from other realms."

Rule's eyebrows shot up. "The gnomes from our realm can't build a gate?"

"Sure they can," Max said, puffing as he rounded the corner of the house, "but nowhere near as quick. Probably couldn't make it big enough, either. Those three are what you might call heavy hitters." He shook his head in admiration. "Old Jenerder was all excited at hosting them, especially Byuset. Don't think there's a being in all the realms who's Byuset's equal with gates, and I include the Queens in that. Oh, Mabron and Third Councillor are good," he said, coming to a halt to grin up at Rule. Max's grin always reminded Rule of one of the less friendly gargoyles. Maybe it was the teeth. "But Byuset knows more about gates than the rest of 'em combined. I'd like to know what kind of deal the dragons made to get *him* here. I've got my suspicions, but I'd sure as hell like to know if I'm right."

"Mmm." Rule was trying to think of how to get Lily aside so he could finish the conversation Max had interrupted. Not that he wanted to, but . . . "And this Byuset came from another realm? Wouldn't he need a gate for that?"

"We don't talk about that," Max said. "I need to take you to meet them, but there's some protocol you have to learn first."

"I've dealt with gnomes, Max. I'm aware of the need for courtesy."

"You haven't dealt with these guys. First thing to know—I can't introduce you because they can't acknowledge me."

Lily frowned at him. "That's what you told Isen, but I got a phone call and didn't hear your explanation. What do you mean?"

"They can't acknowledge me because they can't speak to me, not in Ggilek—what you'd call gnomish."

"Those stuck-up, bigoted—"

"Stuff it," Max said. "Fact is, I'm not full-blood and I've never taken the *tvortish,* so I've got no status, so they can't talk to me."

Rule tried to explain. "He's being literal, Lily. Status is built into their language. I don't understand all the ways it affects their speech, but I know there are thirteen verb tenses for the thirteen statuses. A gnome can't use the correct tense to address someone of no status because there isn't such a tense."

"They could speak English," Lily snapped. "Problem solved."

Max rolled his eyes. "Guess what? The three from out-realm don't speak English, and the rest can't talk to Rule until those three have acknowledged him. It would be rude."

"Can't they use translator disks?" Rule suggested, thinking of what he'd been told about Edge, where such disks were common.

"Sure, but later. You can't do the protocols in English, and you have to do the protocols."

"This never came up before," Lily said. "And from what I've heard of Cynna and Cullen's time in Edge, where they were surrounded by gnomes, they didn't have to jump through a bunch of hoops to talk to someone."

"Because no one expects humans to get the courtesies right, so mostly gnomes ignore 'em when dealing with humans. Or with lupi, for that matter. And it's okay to do that when everyone's of the same *hitsuche*, which has been true for all the gnomes you ever met—Earth's gnomes are all Hragash and Edge's gnomes are all Harazeed. But these gnomes are a mix of three *hitsuche*: Hragash, Hirmon, and Harazeed."

"A *hitsuche* is like a clan, right?"

"You don't have a word for it. A *hitsuche* has a council, but it isn't a government. It's not a religion, either, not the way you people do religion, and it isn't a family the way you do families. It's about tradition and balance and . . ." He frowned, scraggly eyebrows drawing together over his long drip of a nose, then shrugged. "It's where you fit. When you get gnomes of more than one *hitsuche* together, you have to use the formal protocols because they don't all fit together. That's how we keep from going to war."

Rule's eyebrows lifted. "I thought gnomes despised war."

"Duh. That's why they use the formal protocols. They're complicated, so listen up. You'll be speaking as the second eldest in your clan—and never mind how old you are. That's your status. The eldest—that would be Isen—shouldn't speak to them until you introduce him. I told him that, so he won't."

"Rule," Lily broke in, "that's Grandmother's car."

He followed her gaze to the car heading toward them at

a sedate pace. "So it is. I wonder if she knows something we don't. Max, excuse me a moment. I—"

"Not now!" Max exclaimed. "Rule, this is important. You have to pay attention!"

"I'll find out." Lily squeezed his arm once and moved away.

Damn gnomish notions of courtesy. Rule forced his temper down and dragged his gaze back to Max. "I'm listening. My father won't speak to these gnomes until I introduce him."

Max heaved a gusty sigh. "That's right. And you speak as Nokolai Lu Nuncio, not as Leidolf Rho, not until you can be introduced in that role. We'll deal with that later. Now, Isen's been named Hragash-friend, but you aren't, so you'll speak as the outsider second eldest of an allied warrior power. That's less respectable than a trading power, but it doesn't pay to offend warrior powers, so you'll be treated as fourth status, second degree. None of the gnomes are representing their *hitsuche*, so they'll be accorded their personal status, which makes Byuset the one you introduce yourself to. His personal standing to an outsider is third status, first degree, so he's higher status than you."

"I can't say I agree with that." Madame Yu's aging Buick pulled to a stop behind Rule's car. Her companion, Li Qin, was driving. One of the Nokolai guards hurried up to the car to open the door for Li Qin; Lily was getting Madame Yu's door.

"You don't have to agree. It's like that guy over there opening the door for the old lady. She could get the damn door herself, couldn't she? But he opens it to show her courtesy because that's how it's done."

Lily and her grandmother were speaking, voices low—speaking Chinese, which was annoying. Rule didn't understand Chinese. He tore his gaze away from them. "It's strange to hear you harping on courtesy, Max."

Max snorted. "Why d'you think I've never taken the *tvortish*? I hate that crap. Now shut up and let me finish. You'll speak first, and in Ggilek—I'll teach you what to say—and bow low. Ninety-degree angle, Rule. That's important. You hold the bow until—"

"No. A low bow is an act of submission."

"It doesn't mean that to gnomes, so it doesn't matter."

Rule showed Max his teeth. "You have it exactly backwards. It doesn't matter what the gnomes think. To me and my people, it is submission."

"Dammit, Rule, it doesn't have to be! And even if it were, this is why the second eldest makes the initial contact—so all that bullshit won't apply to the clan as a whole. Get off your high horse and—"

"If I am acting as my father's second, what I do affects all of Nokolai."

Max gargled out a couple words in what must be Ggilek. Swear words probably.

"The gnomes' deal is with the dragons," Rule said flatly. "Let them talk to the dragons."

"You *have* to talk with them, Rule," Max said frantically. "You have to greet them, offer them hospitality. If you don't, you're according them no status! You don't understand what that would—"

"Do not worry," Grandmother said, breaking off her conversation with Lily to stride toward them. "I will arrange matters."

"You!" Max hooted.

She looked him over with the haughty disdain only she and cats could achieve. Then she gargled at him.

Max scowled and gargled back. She answered in what had to be gnomish; it involved sounds the human throat should not be able to produce. Max's eyebrows shot up in comic surprise, and his response sounded uncharacteristically tentative. She answered and they went back and forth briefly before he exclaimed, "That'll do it! Come on. They're out back."

"One moment." Madame Yu looked at Rule. "Do I have

your permission to offer these gnomes the hospitality of your clan?"

"Ah . . . yes."

"Good." Then she did something unusual. She reached up and cupped his cheek. "Rule. We will get Toby back. We will bring all the children back." With that, she turned and followed Max.

"Hank," Rule said.

The guard who'd opened Madame Yu's door responded. "Yes?"

"You heard that? Madame Yu will speak with my voice when she offers the gnomes Nokolai's hospitality. Make sure the others know."

"Got it." Hank loped off.

Lily was watching her grandmother's erect figure as it vanished around the side of the house. "She speaks gnomish. I didn't know she spoke gnomish. Half the time she barely speaks English—that's on purpose, of course, but still . . ." She shook her head.

"Your grandmother is an amazing woman, but how is she going to 'arrange matters'?" Rule asked.

"She said she can speak for Sam in this, which makes her first status, second degree. Apparently a first-status sovereign power can do pretty much whatever the hell she wants as long as she's polite about it. Not that Grandmother put it that way, but that's what she meant. She's going with us, you know."

"I didn't." And he wasn't sure it was a good idea. Madame Yu was tough and powerful in her way, but . . . never mind. He'd deal with that later. He could not let himself be distracted again. "Lily—"

"There's something I need to tell you."

Hearing the words he'd been about to utter come out of her mouth startled him into silence.

"You know the Unit has a new head," she went on. "A guy named Stephen Marsh. He's regular Bureau now, but he used to be MCD. Cynna says he's an asshole. I tend to agree. He called me."

"He's going to be a problem?"

"You could say that. He wants me in D.C. on the double to be part of the investigation there. And by 'part of,' he means he wants me to confirm Cullen's findings by touching God knows how much rubble. I told him," she said, simmering. "I told him about Toby, but he already knew. He knows my stepson has been kidnapped and he still wants me to drop everything, leave you here—he doesn't know about the mate bond, so he thinks I could do that— and start running my fingers over crumbled walls and desks and shit, when Cullen has already checked most of it! He said I could not be left in charge of the investigation here anyway, it being so personal. That would be against Bureau policy."

"I can see why that would be so. What did you say?"

She snorted. "I asked him who the hell else was going to handle it, then? Because as far as I know, none of the other Unit agents has a relationship with the black dragon, whose assistance is absolutely essential to recovering the children. Do you know what he said?"

"No. Lily—"

"Neither do I. I hung up on him. So I may or may not be a Unit 12 agent at the moment. I thought you should know."

She'd refused her superior's direct order. Humans didn't punish that sort of thing as harshly as his people did, but this Stephen Marsh wasn't likely to overlook it. Which meant he was too late. If he'd gone ahead and had the argument about whether she would accompany him, she wouldn't have hung up on the man. "Perhaps you should call him back."

Her brows drew together. She didn't respond.

"I've been trying to tell you. Not trying hard enough, but my own head wasn't clear on the subject at first, and . . ." He stopped and rested his hands on her shoulders. "Lily, this isn't like other times we've gone up against strong opponents. Our enemies are expecting us, and they've shown themselves to be powerful and resourceful. We're going into their territory, and we're going almost blind, without knowing what resources they have. It's unlikely that all of us who leave on this mission will come back."

"And?" she said in a dangerously low voice.

"I want you to stay here."

"We don't always get what we want, do we?"

"Lily, I can't do this! I can't handle you being in such danger when Toby is . . . I'm barely keeping it together now. I'll be risking so many people I love on this. I can't risk you, too. I need—"

"What about what I need?" She stepped back, letting his hands fall away. "Have you thought about that?"

The volcano shuddered inside him. "Be careful. I'm not safe right now. Don't raise your voice at me."

"I'll damn well yell if I want to! Has it even once crossed your mind—dammit, Rule, I haven't tried to stop you from going, no matter how insanely dangerous it is. I won't. I don't have the goddamn right to do that, and you don't, either!"

"He's my son!" Rule bellowed.

"I know that! And maybe this stupid-ass attitude of yours is partly my fault. Maybe I've been too careful. You're the parent with the hands-on experience and he's been yours all along while I'm new to this, plus you're lupi and so's Toby, so I've held back, but—but dammit, Rule, he's *mine, too!*"

His control tore right down the middle. He flung back his head and screamed. Screamed with all the rage in him until his voice tore, too.

He came back to himself slowly. It was very quiet.

"Is that why you never yell when we argue?"

He looked at his *nadia*. She stood exactly where she had before, her head tipped slightly to one side, dark eyes steady on him. He would have answered, but when he tried, nothing came out.

The effort hurt. He put a hand to his throat and looked around.

Ten feet away, a wolf cowered on the ground. Behind him was another wolf, also flat on the ground. He saw two more prostrate Nokolai off to his left, but they were farther away and had remained men. And just behind Lily . . .

"You'll do now, boy," his father said, and gave him a nod.

If you have finished challenging the sky, said a cold, clear mental voice, *you may wish to know that Reno and I have completed our task. Your stolen young were taken to Dis.*

EIGHTEEN

DIS. The hell-realm. The place where demons walked . . . and flew, and swam. The realm without a moon.

Technically, Sam didn't order them to join him near Cullen and Cynna's house. He called that a "strong suggestion," adding that he would not elaborate until he and Reno finished discussing technical matters with the gnomes. He would then provide additional information to those who chose to assemble near him and Reno.

Additional information had better mean answering a few questions, Rule thought, then sending them on their way. Too damn much time had passed already.

Lily must have thought something similar, because she rushed inside to grab her backpack and jacket before they set off on foot for Cullen and Cynna's place. Walking was the default at Clanhome, and why rush there in a car when Sam wouldn't talk to them yet? Isen tactfully chose to wait for Madame Yu, Cynna, and Cullen to join him before setting off, which allowed Rule and Lily a degree of privacy.

"How can it be Dis?" Lily muttered. "I don't see how it can be Dis."

He shook his head, frustrated. Whatever damage he'd done would heal, but it hadn't yet. His throat felt like raw meat. He reached for the backpack she carried by one strap.

"I can carry . . . oh, all right, if it makes you feel better."

It did. He slid her backpack onto his own shoulder. His was at the staging spot.

"Still can't talk? Well, if that's what you have to expect if you start yelling, I can understand why you always fight cold, not hot. It would suck to lose a fight because you couldn't speak."

His mouth quirked, charmed in spite of himself by her notion of what constituted a fight. They never fought. They disagreed, they argued, but they did not fight. He would never fight Lily.

Which was, perhaps, why his voice was broken. Or half the reason.

It was not what he'd expected to happen. When his control snapped, he'd been sure he'd be sucked into the Change—or worse, into the fury. But his Chosen had been standing in front of him and it *was not possible* to harm her. That was not a choice, not a decision, but a simple fact of existence. With her in front of him, he could not fall into the fury.

Which did not explain why he'd screamed instead of Changing. He didn't understand that. He'd simply done so, pouring his rage into a scream that damaged his vocal cords, pulled four nearby lupi into the Change, and caused every Nokolai clansman within hearing to abase himself. In the process, he'd alarmed their gnome guests and caused his father to race out to see what was attacking them this time.

He wondered if he would be embarrassed about that at some point. Gods, he hoped so. He hoped he survived long enough that life would smooth out and he could spare attention for such minor pangs.

Toby was in Dis.

Toby. He'd failed his son. Failed—

No. Don't think of that.

Toby was in Dis. So was Ryder, an even smaller baby, and two more children.

Lily intended to go there with him. He didn't know how to stop her.

Their enemies would be waiting—backed by the Great Enemy, who could probably act more directly in Dis than she could here. The odds were high that even if he survived this mission, others would not. He could not handle losing Lily.

Toby was in hell . . .

Lily believed he didn't see her as Toby's parent.

She was right.

She was his *nadia*, his Chosen, his wife. She was not the mother of his son, and he had no model for "stepmother," no understanding of that role. In a society where no one marries, there are no stepmothers. He had, he admitted, little enough understanding of "mother." His own had been entirely absent.

Not that he'd missed out on mothering as a boy. The sisters and daughters of his clan had watched out for him, tended scraped knees, scolded or praised, lectured or listened. And that, he supposed, was the role he'd assigned Lily where Toby was concerned. She cared for his son, yes, just as many women had showered affection on him as a boy.

But the women of Clanhome hadn't claimed him. He'd never been theirs the way he was his father's.

Lily had claimed Toby.

Did that mean the same to her it as did to him? Did she know what it meant to him? Claiming was different from simply loving. Affection could wax or wane. Bonds of love, loyalty, or enmity might strengthen over the years or be sundered. But claiming was for always. Once you claimed someone as yours, you could not unclaim them.

Human adoptions were for life, weren't they? And hadn't she spoken up for Dirty Harry, who was hers?

She'd claimed Toby. He stopped.

She got a pace ahead, turned, and looked at him. "What?"

He set her backpack down on the road and put his hands on her shoulders the way he had before. This time he spoke different words, and in a hoarse rasp. "Of course he's yours, too."

They were still wrapped in each other's arms a few minutes later when an eye-poppingly bright green Volkswagen with a yellow hood, a red fender, and a shitload of gnomes shot past.

THE adobe bungalow where Cynna and Cullen lived was the oldest intact structure on Clanhome. When Isen's father sank so much of the clan's money into purchasing the land for Clanhome well over a century ago, little had been left for building homes. But adobe was cheap, and the clan had had plenty of willing hands if not, at first, a great deal of expertise. Their first attempts hadn't survived, but this one—built last, and with the addition of cement to stabilize the adobe bricks—might well make it another century or two.

Somewhere along the line, the house had been stuccoed. In Rule's lifetime it had been white, sandy beige, and once—briefly—bright yellow; it was currently chocolate brown. About fifty years ago, Claude Cheveaux, who was then Isen's second, had added a second box to the first, creating a long covered porch as well as a second bedroom and bath plus a small "whatever room." Claude had kept his weapons collection in the whatever room. The man who lived there next had used the little room as an office; the one after him, for storage.

It was currently a nursery. An open-air nursery. The little bungalow had suffered the same deconstruction by dragon as Rule's house. He could see the gaping hole from a hundred yards away and wondered if the house could be restored properly. Wondering if it would matter. If they didn't get Ryder back . . .

They would. They had to.

"Do you think they darken with age?" Lily asked. "The babies are such bright colors. So's Mika, and she's the youngest of them."

"What?" He dragged his gaze from the wounded house to look straight ahead, where Sam lay on the road, sunlight striking iridescent sparks from his midnight scales. Not that he fit the road; his coils lapped over onto the earth on either side. Reno was coiled in the meeting field about twenty yards from Sam. "I don't know. You could ask. That probably isn't a close-held secret."

"Which doesn't mean they'll answer."

That was sure as hell true. Neither Sam nor Reno had spoken yet, though everyone but the fighters who'd accompany them was present, including Max. Not his gnome squad, however. The oppressively bright Volkswagen sat empty just up the road, near the foot of the path that led up Little Sister. Twelve gnomes were currently tromping up that path. Rule glanced that way. He could just make out a few of the small figures, though most were hidden in the scruffy growth on the mountain's slope. They'd almost reached the node.

Arjenie's voice drew his attention back to ground level. "It's weird to see two dragons so close together, isn't it?"

"It is, rather." There were sixty feet between the two dragons—not close in human or lupi terms, but sixty feet might be a dragon's notion of personal space. Dragons were largely solitary beings. Rule knew they gathered occasionally for what Lily called their singalongs, but he had no idea if those were social occasions or some communal project, song being the way dragons worked magic.

Reno was not, it turned out, the New York dragon. They'd known that as soon as they saw him, for the New York dragon was the color of autumn leaves seen through dark glasses. Reno was green—almost black on his legs, wet moss green on his belly and sides, bright chartreuse along his spine. In startling contrast, his frill was bright orange. There were several green dragons, but according to both Lily and Arjenie, only one with an orange frill. Reno was the dragon the Spanish called El Draco, after the constellation. He laired outside Madrid . . . just under six thousand miles away.

Rule had that figure from Arjenie, who'd apologized because it was such a rough approximation, but she'd never had occasion to look up that particular distance. Still, she thought it a decent estimate, based on what she knew was the distance between San Diego and Paris—5,680 miles, which she had looked up once—when Rule and Lily flew there for their honeymoon, to be specific. She had, she assured Rule, allowed for Madrid's being farther south and west than Paris, and for the greater girth of the earth as you moved closer to the equator. She'd added that it would take a jet eleven or twelve hours to cover that distance, then gone into a breakdown of the rate of travel of intercontinental ballistic missiles, which reached their peak speed of six to seven kilometers per second after ten minutes of acceleration . . .

Rule had tuned out the rest. The gist was that Reno seemed to have flown here faster than a jet, but slower than an ICBM.

Cullen's current theory was that when dragons went invisible, they entered *dashtu* or a similar state. *Dashtu* was a demon trick that put them out of phase with the rest of the world . . . whatever that meant. Maybe being out of phase allowed them to reach absurd speeds.

Or maybe it was just magic. Since they shouldn't be able to fly in the first place, Rule considered that as good an explanation as any.

"Quit that," Cullen said sharply, followed by, "Very clearly."

Rule looked over his shoulder at his friend. "Is Sam talking to you?"

"Reno. He was poking at my shields. I've dropped the one that blocks mindspeech, so there wasn't any reason for him to . . ." Cullen paused. "He says he wanted to test them. I don't know why. Given the nature of dragon spawn, we don't have to worry about Weng using mind magic . . ." Another pause. "All right, I get it."

"We don't," Cynna said.

"Sam pointed out that Tom Weng is not our only opponent. He's right. We don't know what Gifts the Great Bitch might have bestowed on Ginger Harris."

"Or how directly *she* might be able to act in Dis," Rule added grimly.

"Yes," Madame Yu said crisply. "Here the Enemy must use agents. In Dis she can employ an avatar. She has done so before."

"The one that was eaten by a demon prince," Max said.

Madame sniffed. "We would be unforgivably foolish to assume that means she lacks an avatar."

"Yeah," Lily said. "Maybe that same demon prince."

"That is unlikely."

"Why?" Lily demanded. "I want that to be true, but why? Using a demon prince as avatar would let her control that lord's territory. That's a huge advantage."

Max snorted. "Yeah, but she'd be stuck there. Demon princes can't move out of their territories."

Madame Yu nodded. "Also, unwilling avatars are less useful than willing ones. Attention and power must be spent on control—a great deal of attention and power with a demon prince. *She* is capable of this, but Sam considers it unlikely she would keep such an avatar for long. She has had time to find a willing vessel."

"In Dis?" Cynna said dubiously. "Demons will make deals to let someone ride them sometimes, but that isn't the same thing as becoming avatar."

"She would not choose a demon." Madame Yu clucked her tongue and looked at her granddaughter. "Ginger Harris disappeared shortly before the Azá attempted to open the hellgate, did she not?"

"Yes, but . . . oh. Shit. Hell. You think she's . . . that would be bad."

Rule's jaw clenched. Was Ginger Harris the Great Bitch's avatar? There was a difference—a huge and terrible difference—between one of the Great Bitch's agents and a true avatar. His son was in Ginger Harris's hands . . . "The hellgate was never opened. Wouldn't Ginger have had to go to Dis to be made *her* avatar?"

"I do not know, but it matters little. Your Robert Friar was given Gifts while in this realm, was he not? I think this Ginger was given a Gift also—that of crossing realms. She then went to Dis and became the Enemy's avatar."

"It took a sidhe lord to conduct the ritual that gave Friar his Gifts."

Madame shrugged. "We do not know how this was done, but it was done. Clearly either Ginger Harris or Tom Weng has the ability to cross realms. We know this, and there are reasons to believe it is not Tom Weng."

"Such as?" Lily asked.

"If it is not Ginger, why is she needed for these kidnappings?"

Rule scowled. That made too damn much sense. Still— "If it's Ginger who's doing the crossing, then why is Tom Weng needed?"

Lily answered that one. "For attack or defense, if they're spotted. Maybe to Find the children. Someone has to be locating them magically."

Benedict spoke in his slow, thoughtful way. "I don't see why Ginger would need magical help from Weng if she's the Great Bitch's avatar."

Ginger Harris can enter this realm, said a cold, familiar mental voice. *The Enemy cannot. If indeed Ginger Harris holds a portion of the Enemy, when she enters Earth, she is only herself, and thus is limited to whatever actual Gifts the Enemy has bestowed upon her. For technical reasons I will not go into, it is unlikely that Ginger Harris possesses any Gift other than the ability to cross between realms.*

"A portion of the Enemy?" Rule frowned. "I thought avatars held the entire consciousness of the, ah, the power inhabiting them." Some might refer to the Great Bitch as a goddess. His people did not.

Mortal flesh cannot contain the entirety of an immortal Old One. Moreover, Ginger Harris would be a new avatar, having served as vessel for between twenty-one months and eleven years, according to my estimate. Such a new avatar—

"Wait a minute," Lily said. "Eleven years? No way. I touched Ginger when I was investigating the Fuentes murder. That was less than two years ago, and she didn't have any magic then, so she couldn't have been carrying the GB around."

You know that the realms are not all time-congruent. You have either forgotten this or failed to give the fact even casual attention.

"What does that have to do with it?" Max asked, scowling mightily. The scowl was probably intended to mask other feelings. Max was not comfortable around dragons.

If Ginger Harris is able to cross realms, she has not been restricted to Earth or Dis. While those in this realm lived twenty-one months, she may have lived as much as eleven years in another realm or realms. Eleven is the ceiling due to theoretical limits on the amount of temporal discontinuity possible between realms which are otherwise sufficiently congruent for contact. By "contact," I do not mean crossing directly from one realm to another, but reachable through—

"That's how they did it!" Lily burst out. "That's how they were able to do everything in such a short time—zigzagging all over North America in one night. They didn't stay in Dis! They went to a realm where time passes faster than it does here."

Relative time flow is not that straightforward, but in essence you are correct. They would have crossed into multiple realms, not just one, using both temporal and physical discontinuities in a sophisticated manner to travel what are, here, large distances in a single night. The power expended and the technical mastery required for such an outcome vastly increases the likelihood that Ginger Harris is an avatar for the Enemy, as it is nearly impossible that she could do so without guidance.

"You don't think Weng is the crosser," Cullen observed. "Or the one providing guidance?"

Such guidance needs to be mind-to-mind, as language cannot convey what is largely unquantifiable. That alone eliminates the mind-dark Weng, but in addition, neither dragons nor dragon spawn can cross realms this way, just as we cannot build gates. I do not explain. Yes, Cullen Seabourne, the matter you contemplate is connected, and I would like to know how you acquired such a weighty secret.

"I wasn't thinking at you," Cullen protested. "I was just thinking."

Clearly you were "thinking at me," or I would not have heard you with your other shields raised. I require an explanation for your knowledge.

There was a long pause, then: *And the wording of that vow? I see. No, this is not a revelation to myself or to Reno, but had Lily Yu been open to mindspeech at that moment, you would be forsworn. I accept your intention to guard this secret, but doubt your ability to do so without training. Learn to think without any of your thoughts leaking into mindspeech. Lily Yu will be able to assist you in this, should you both survive the next few days. If you survive and she does not, come to me. I doubt I will be able to undertake your training myself due to the escalation of the war, but I will arrange for it.*

"Escalation?" Isen said sharply. "Are you talking about something more than the destruction of FBI Headquarters and the nuclear bomb that killed Fa Deng?"

Those were the opening rounds in what I believe is a major assault.

"What?" Rule exclaimed. He wasn't the only one.

You should know that I have brought Ruben Brooks into our discussion, as what I say next is of great import to the Shadow Unit. He will hear what I say, but I will only pass on to him those of your comments and questions I deem pertinent.

Originally I had planned to depart Earth in order to determine the origin of Tom Weng. That is now out of the question. The Enemy has been muddling the patterns for some time, making them extremely difficult to read. However, the level of turmoil in the patterns increased abruptly when she stole your young. That turmoil now surpasses her ability to fully mask her presence and plans.

Although much remains unclear, I can state three things with a fair degree of certainty. Note that I base this on what I see in the patterns here. With rare exceptions, I cannot reliably read the patterns in other realms. First, Lily Yu, Cynna Weaver, and Li Lei must be part of the party which transits to Dis. You had decided on this already; I merely confirm its wisdom. Second, the assault which I perceive in the patterns is ongoing, consisting of multiple strategic strikes and culminating in a major magical assault and an invasion. The nature of both the magical assault and the invasion remains murky, but the timing is reasonably clear. They will commence between eight hours and three days from now. Third, if I am not in this realm during this period, the United States and some portion of the rest of the continent will fall to the Enemy.

NINETEEN

~

IN the stunned silence that fell, Rule's thoughts caromed and collided noisily like out-of-control billiard balls.

A major assault. That's what Sam was talking about.

Smack!

The Great Bitch was not simply expecting them in Dis. She wanted them to come, had planned this to draw as many of them as she could away from Earth when she attacked.

Smack!

He would go anyway. His father would have to fight the war without him. His father, Ruben, and so many others.

And *smack*: Lily might be in as much danger here as she would be in Dis. There was no point to his crazy fear . . . and it was crazy, because he'd been trying to do the impossible: to protect himself from the possibility of her dying. And he couldn't. It didn't matter how much he needed her to live. It didn't matter if her death would break him. If he broke, then he broke. He couldn't prevent that, either.

A strange peace settled over him. Not *certa*, for there

was no battle. Not yet. Fatalism? Deep inside, his wolf snorted at his need to find a word tag for everything.

His wolf. His wolf was *present* once more.

It was Lily who broke the silence—unsurprisingly, with a question. "What does Ruben say? Has he had a hunch?"

He is currently experiencing a vision. I judge it best not to interrupt.

"Well, hell." That was Cynna.

Ruben seldom had visions. When he did, it meant major events were about to occur. World-changing events. Yet Rule's newfound calm held. "Open warfare. That's what you're expecting, I think?"

I expect both overt and covert attacks to be part of the upcoming assault. I will confer now with Isen Turner, Arjenie Fox, and Ruben Brooks regarding preparations for the assault. The rest of you should not consider your mission to rescue your young as being apart from the war. The vast increase in the turmoil of the patterns suggests their capture is important to the Enemy's plans. You should now speak with Reno about your objective. He goes with you.

Startled, Rule turned to look at the green dragon. What had compelled the dragon to volunteer? He was welcome—well, mostly welcome. A dragon was unlikely to place himself under Rule's authority, but otherwise—

I no more place myself under your authority than you place yourself under mine, Rule Turner. That mental voice was as cold as Sam's and sharp enough to slice glass—and somehow unmistakably not Sam's. *My reasons for making this transit are not your affair.*

"You are wrong." Madame Yu's voice was very nearly as cold as the dragon's. "I correct this. Reno comes because he was the mother of the last botched hatching. The one which led to the creation of dragon spawn."

The green dragon's reaction was sudden and alarming. His head shot forward, the great jaws gaping, then snapping—and while he was too far for those jaws to close on Madame, there was no mistaking the threat. For a long moment the old woman and the dragon stared at each other across forty feet, Madame Yu indomitably erect and smaller than the head of the beast she confronted. Finally she sniffed. "Had I not thought it necessary, I would not have done so," she said, adding after a moment: "Tell them yourself."

Surprisingly, he did. *Parenthood is a private matter for dragons. It is extremely offensive for it to be spoken of openly. Do not assume that because I did not punish Li Lei that anyone else will be permitted a similar offense. I suggest that those of you who will accompany me approach more closely. Humans have difficulty heeding multiple conversations, and those who will remain here will be vocalizing their responses to the one you call Sam.*

Rule glanced at Madame, a question in his raised brows.

"The one now calling himself Reno has a complicated attitude towards humans," she told him. "Not a flattering attitude, on the whole, but we are not presently in danger from him." With that, she started toward the green dragon.

Where she led, the rest of them must follow—though Benedict delayed briefly to say good-bye to his mate. Arjenie could not go with them, not when she was carrying new life. She understood this, but the way she clung to Benedict and he to her . . . understanding doesn't erase pain.

Dragons smelled like hot metal and spice—warm spices like cinnamon and clove, black pepper and turmeric. They also smelled meaty, like the predators they were. As Rule drew near the small mountain of scaled coils that was Reno, the smell of a huge carnivore filled his nostrils and hit his hind brain, making his wolf snarl inside him. Sam's scent no longer affected him this way, but Reno did not smell like Sam. His scent was new and Rule's wolf did not like it.

He stopped ten feet from the nearest coil. Reno's head was about as long as Rule was tall and more than two body lengths above him. Rule looked up at that head, but not at the eyes. Dragons ensorcelled with their gaze.

Lily stopped beside him, her head tilted back. "You've been poking at me. I don't like it."

I am taking preliminary measurements to pass on to Byuset. The first node he examined is not suitable for a gate to Dis. The second one is. The topographical disruption is very slight and is in our favor coming from this side. Before he begins construction, however, he requires data on how much power and living mass will be transiting.

"There will be twenty-five of us," Rule said. "Three squads under Benedict's command plus Cullen, Cynna, Lilly, Max, Madame Yu, and myself. Benedict has been keeping track of the estimated weight of our supplies and equipment."

Unless you plan to bring several tons of inert mass, weight will not be an issue. Simple mass is not a major determinant for a gate builder of Byuset's skill. However, you will probably not be able to transit twenty-five beings in addition to myself. I explain further. None of you other than Li Lei know how to lock your power down so it will not interact with the gate, and power must be included in the calculations which determine the gate's safe transit limits. Therefore—

"You're doing the assume thing," Cullen said, shaking his head. "I would've thought a being your age would know better."

Do you claim to possess the ability to lock down your power?

"Not me. Not reliably anyway." He looked at Cynna.

Cynna didn't reply out loud, but a few seconds later Reno responded as if she'd spoken. *Cynna Weaver, that technique should work if you are certain you can maintain it for at least thirty seconds.*

"I can."

Very well. I will subject all of you except Lily Yu to fur-ther testing in order to quantify your power in the manner used by the gnomes.

"Everyone but me?" Lily said, eyebrows raised.

As you suspect, the nature of your power renders it impossible to measure. Sam has supplied the gnomes with an estimate which he is confident will prove adequate for their purposes. I will now discuss mass. All living beings possess both simple mass and living mass, that which demons call üther. *Living mass or* üther *is more difficult both to contain and to calculate. As none of us are able to perceive* üther *directly in the manner used by demons and the cat is unconscious—*

"The cat?" Lily repeated, startled.

Do not interrupt. The cat is unavailable, so it will be necessary to approximate the living mass of each of you based on—

"Hold on a minute," Cynna said. "None of this measur-ing was necessary when we opened a hellgate before. We couldn't send many people through it, but that was a matter of what you call simple mass and of time. It was a small gate and couldn't be held open long."

I repeat: do not interrupt. It slows us down. It also annoys me.

Madame Yu spoke in rapid-fire Chinese.

This is why I dislike interacting with humans. Very well, I explain further. You did not transit with a dragon when you opened that hellgate. My presence in this gate will induce instability, which limits the amount of additional mass and power which can pass through the gate.

"We transited with a dragon when we returned," Lily said. "With twenty-four of you, in fact."

The Eldest sang us home. You have no more understand-ing of what that means than an infant, in falling to the ground, grasps the nature of gravity. You are aware of the bare fact that he did so, however. I perceive in some of your minds the idea that it would be easier to make this transit without me. You are correct. However, I do not consider this option worth consideration. First, it will almost certainly be necessary to kill the spawn, and you are unlikely to succeed in this. If you did, the results would be unfortunate. Dragons do not cosset our young in the manner of humans, but we strongly dislike any who kill them.

"He took my son," Rule said, his voice almost a growl. "And Cynna's daughter. And three more of our children."

These circumstances would render it a less-than-mortal offense, but it would remain an offense. Some of us might find it difficult to continue to ally with you, and the alliance between us is critical to defeating the Enemy. My second reason for rejecting the option of your proceeding without me is that you would be unlikely to survive. Certainly none of you can live for long without air.

"Without air?" Benedict repeated, scowling.

It is likely that the Enemy used the demon prince called Xitil as avatar for a brief period. It is unlikely Xitil survived having been avatar. It is highly unlikely that the death of that demon means that the region currently lacks a prince. Whoever that prince may be, the Enemy must have some agreement with him, her, or it which allows her avatar and agents to operate there. That agreement may include the new demon prince's active opposition when we arrive. It is possible for such princes to remove the air from a small area of their demesne, such as that around a node. This is not easily done, but it is possible, as are several other manipulations you are unlikely to survive.

Benedict was still scowling. "It would have been good to know that a few hours ago, when we were making our plans."

Reno ignored that. *I can interfere with such manipulations. Without my assistance, you are unlikely to survive them.*

"What about opening two gates, one after the other?" Cullen said suddenly. "One for you, then one for us."

The instability I referred to lies within the node itself. After the gate we use collapses, another gate cannot be constructed until the node regains stability, a process which is impossible to predict. It will probably take more than three days and less than three years for the node to stabilize, but even that broad estimate is not certain.

"How do we return, then?" Cynna demanded.

Obviously, the gate used to return will have to be constructed at another node. However, there will be a time lag before it can be built. Opening a gate is extremely draining. Byuset will probably be unconscious and thus unable to direct the construction of the second gate. Without his participation, the second gate will be smaller than the first. This should not be an issue. I shall not return with you. This will provide sufficient time for Byuset to recover, at which point he can construct a third gate which I may use.

"You'll stay behind?" Lily exclaimed. "In Dis?" Even for a dragon, that was dangerous verging on deadly.

If, as I assume, you wish to transit the largest party the gnomes' gate can accommodate, once you retrieve your young, your party will be too large to return through any gate the gnomes can construct.

Lily felt stupid. How had she not thought of that?

You could, of course, leave several of your party behind while the remainder returns with your young. Those left behind would almost certainly perish. I, however, can survive a brief stay there. It is logical for me to remain until a third gate can be constructed. Be aware that the second gate will not be opened immediately upon the collapse of the first gate. I am told it will take between five and fifteen hours for the gnomes to recover sufficiently to construct it. I will signal them which node to use.

In other words, they were going to be stuck in hell for hours—maybe a lot of hours—after they rescued the children. Lily exchanged a glance with Rule.

"How will you signal?" Benedict asked at the same

moment that Cullen said, "You don't have a node picked out for the second gate yet?"

We do not know where we will be when we wish to return. The gnomes will inspect nearby nodes for suitability while we are away, testing them for power and accessibility from the Dis side.

"You mean like knowing if a node that's on the surface here is buried in rock in Dis?" Lily asked. "They can do that?"

Yes.

"How will you signal the gnomes?" Benedict repeated.

"Can you mindspeak across realms?" Lily asked. "Talk to Sam, at least? The Great Bitch did that, though she had to have a telepath on the other end." Helen Whitehead had been a telepath. She'd also been a psychopathic bitch who'd put out Cullen's eyes, framed Rule for murder, and tried her damnedest to collect Lily so the Great Bitch could use Lily's wiped-clean brain to store a backup of the Codex Arcana. Lily had put an end to those plans by killing Helen.

No.

"Why not? You and Sam are both telepaths, so—"

I am not an Old One. Reno sounded miffed. *I will communicate by sending a pulse through the node which will be picked up by the gnomes' jabak. Jabak are the devices with which they communicate across realms. Shaped pulses of a particular nature are sent into a node and can be read by jabak at all nodes which share congruence with that one.*

"Cynna and I have seen them used," Cullen put in. "They're a bit like telegraphs."

They are very little like telegraphs. Rule Turner, Byuset informs me that, based on my preliminary estimates, it will not be possible to transit myself and twenty-five others unless he builds a permanent gate, which would take considerably longer and create an unacceptable security breach. He believes it possible to construct a temporary gate which will transit between ten and fourteen beings in addition to myself—quite a remarkable achievement. The

*precise number of beings will depend on the final measure-
ments I provide. I have finished measuring the power of
those present and now need to approximate your living
mass. This will take longer. You may experience a brief
sensation of pressure, or you may feel nothing.*

Rule waited, frowning. Nothing happened. Nothing went
on happening until Cynna burst out, "They're moving!"

Rule looked at her. The lacy ink on her face stood out in
stark contrast to her sudden pallor. "Ryder and Toby?"

"Yes. Away from us. They're moving away from us."

Suddenly Sam rejoined the conversation. *How quickly
and in what direction?* Cynna didn't reply out loud. Sam
must have plucked the information directly from her mind,
for he continued with the barest pause. *In that case, you
must hurry. I suspect they do not intend to remain in Dis.*

Rule spun to face his brother. "Benedict. Get everything
up to that node, fast. And the men."

Reno spoke. *I must complete the measurements. We do
not yet know how many can—*

"Go ahead and measure," Rule snapped. "We'll assemble. Anything and anyone over the limit, we'll leave behind.
Tell Byuset to start building the gate—ah, that's a strong
suggestion, not an order. Lily—"

A small orange being with bright blue hair and absurdly
large breasts popped into existence next to one big, clawed
foot. She shrieked and jumped—literally jumped, landing
five or six feet away from the dragon. That wasn't enough,
apparently, for she scooted toward them quickly.

"Gan?" Lily said in a disbelieving voice.

The newcomer stopped and beamed. "Hi, Lily Yu! Hi,
Cynna Weaver! Hi, Cullen Seabourne and Rule Turner! It's
not tomorrow yet, is it?"

"Not—" Lily shook her head. "Never mind. Are you
here to . . . why are you here?"

"I'm going with you, of course. Didn't they tell you?

Dragons." She shook her head. "They never tell you the important stuff."

"But how did you get here?" Lily cried. "How did you know to come here at all?"

"The black dragon told me."

That is not— Then Reno did a very un-dragon-like thing. He paused.

Was Sam talking to him? Explaining how he'd done what Reno had just said was impossible? Lily wanted badly to eavesdrop on that conversation.

Gan burbled on, oblivious. "It all arrived in a burst! Everything exploded in my head and I passed out and when I woke up I knew you needed me and where and when I should come. I had to go through four realms to get to here and now, but I made it!"

You arrive in time to assist me, Reno said.

Gan cast the dragon a suspicious look. She was wearing the most amazing costume. It seemed to be made out of pockets. Khaki pockets, to be specific. The only pocket-free zones were her head, hands, and boots. Even her leather belt had pockets. So did the small backpack. "Are you hungry, dragon?"

No. I am using the call-name of Reno. Refer to me that way. I need to measure the üther *of those who would use the gate. You need only observe them. I will take what you perceive and convert it into terms the gnomes can use.*

"Oh. Okay." She began looking them over, her gaze snagging briefly on Grandmother. "Wow! Did you know she—"

I know. Continue.

Gan did. It didn't take long. "Are you done? Lily Yu, this is going to be so much fun! If we don't get eaten, that is."

Lily dropped to one knee to look the former demon— her friend—in the eye. "Gan, are you sure about this? It's going to be very dangerous."

"Well, duh! It's Dis! That's why you need me. Don't

worry—if something tries to eat me, I'll leave. I've got tons of power, so I can pop in and out all day and—oh, hi, Max! I didn't see you at first. Maybe we can fuck later."

"Is that all the measuring?" Cullen demanded. "Good. Gan, we're leaving now, and we're in a hurry." He crouched with his back to the former demon, now the most powerful person in the realm of Edge. "We're glad to have you, Chancellor. Climb aboard."

TWENTY

‿

THE sun squatted on the rim of the hills to the west, red and baleful like Sauron's eye. A fretful breeze tugged at a strand of Lily's hair that hadn't been properly caught up in her braid. She was too hot in her leather jacket, though she'd left it unzipped, both for coolness and so she'd have access to the Glock in her shoulder harness. She adjusted the strap of her M4A1, her heart beating a steady *go, go, go*, and thought about a ten-year-old boy, a nine-month-old baby, and how life was more of a loop-the-loop than a straight line. Here she was, ready to set off on a rescue mission to hell. Again.

This time Rule was with her, though. And this time they'd be traveling a lot faster—fast and light. On motorcycles. Five dirt bikes and three dual-sports or adventure bikes, to be specific. And God knew that the enthusiasts among them were determined to be specific. Most of their supplies were not coming with them. Ammo had taken priority over medical supplies, which ended up being mostly superglue and a couple rolls of gauze. They'd packed lots of jerky, but water was heavy and cumbersome. They'd cut that to the bare minimum.

As for people, eleven had ended up being the magic number. Eleven of them could transit the gate before it collapsed. That didn't include Gan, who didn't need a gate to cross, but while the former demon might be a valuable asset, she couldn't be considered part of the fighting force. It was a long way short of the three squads they'd planned to take, but they hadn't planned for a dragon, had they? Surely Reno would make up the difference when it came time to fight.

Currently the green dragon was flying in tight circles overhead. The clearing which held the node was barely large enough for him to land. It wouldn't hold him and the gnomes, much less everyone else, so "everyone else" was parked along the trail above the node. They'd need to enter the gate from this side.

". . . unfortunately, I'm the only one who can use it," Cullen finished.

Rule's eyebrows lifted. "Not even Cynna? You said it was based on her spell."

Cullen shook his head. "It's a sadly jury-rigged contraption. Doesn't even have a proper trigger. I'll have to, ah . . . you might think of it as hot-wiring a car. You need the Sight to grab the right 'wires' and connect 'em."

"How many demons will it kill?"

"Somewhere between twenty and a hundred, I think, if there are that many in the blast zone. It depends on the demon. Some are more resistant to magic than others. Those it doesn't kill outright should be incapacitated for a time."

"I guess we'll find out," Rule said. "You'd probably best get in position."

"Right. See you in hell." He turned and headed back to his bike.

Rule had been asking Cullen about his demon bomb, which was based on a spell Cynna knew that killed demons and only demons. The spell did this one at a time. Cullen's bomb did it wholesale.

At least he thought it would. He hadn't exactly had a chance to test it.

Rule looked at Lily, frowned, and fiddled with her helmet strap, tightening it. "Remember to pancake me. Follow my motions exactly."

"I've ridden on the back of a bike before." Not since she was nineteen and she'd only dated the guy for a couple months, but still. It wasn't that complicated.

He was grim as he tightened the strap. "Not on back of a dirt bike."

"I thought we had one of the dual-sport types."

"Are you arguing just to be arguing?"

"Pretty much." She wanted to kiss him for luck. Or just because. His helmet and hers were in the way, so she settled for stroking his jaw. "I'll stay up against your back and lean as you do."

One corner of his mouth turned up, but his eyes remained intent. As if he was memorizing her. He kissed his fingers and brushed them across her lips. "Glasses," he reminded her.

Obediently she slipped on the wraparound shades she'd borrowed and the world darkened. Rule's helmet had a visor; hers didn't. She was just glad they'd found one that fit, having seen what can happen to a helmetless rider's head. He swung his leg over the borrowed Triumph and settled into the seat. She climbed on behind him, adjusted the hang of the assault rifle on her back, and put her feet on the foot pegs.

They didn't know if motorcycles would prove immune to the disruptive effect of high ambient magic, but the bikes didn't have to work for all that long. Plus they'd have a dragon with them, soaking up magic—if Reno stayed close, that is, instead of flying way overhead. Reno refused to commit to doing so, nor would he venture an opinion on the

bikes' functioning in Dis. Ambient magic levels there varied too much to make any estimate meaningful, he said,
though he did say that the bike Lily rode was unlikely to
malfunction. She took that to mean that while she didn't
soak up as much magic as he did, she'd soak up enough.

They were proceeding as if Sam was right and their enemies intended to leave Dis for yet another realm. If he was
wrong . . . Lily couldn't remember a time Sam had been
wrong, except for the one she'd learned about only two days
ago. That whole creating-dragon-spawn thing had been a
huge mistake. Which was why he and the other dragons
were helping so much now.

Loop-the-loops. Her thoughts, like her life, kept getting
caught up in them.

Assuming Sam was right, though, they really needed the
bikes to work. Toby and Ryder were currently over fifteen
miles from the node, moving northwest at between six and
eight miles an hour. If they could average thirty miles an
hour on the bikes, they'd catch up in about thirty minutes.
They hoped to go faster, of course, but the terrain might not
let them. According to the dragons, the part of Dis that corresponded to Clanhome wasn't mountainous, but neither
was it uniformly level.

"Explain to me again why the kidnappers need to go
somewhere else before crossing," Lily said to the small
orange being perched on a rock overhead.

"Sure," Gan said. "When you cross, you go to whatever
spot in the other realm matches up with where you are.
Some realms match up all crooked, though. I could get to
Dis from pretty much any spot in this realm, but if I wanted
to go to, say, Tzaizo, I'd have to go . . ." She cocked her head,
checking some internal metric. "Well, there isn't a spot
nearby that touches Tzaizo except for the one down below,
but that one opens into solid rock, so I wouldn't use it."

"You can tell that? If there's rock or whatever on the
other side of where you cross?"

Gan preened. She loved being the expert. "*I* can, but a lot of crossers can't, so mostly they die before they figure it out. It helps if you can go *dashtu* while you're learning."

Lily nodded. "*Dashtu* means you aren't material, so it doesn't kill you if you cross into rock or under the ocean?"

"No, you're still made of matter, but your matter isn't talking to the other matter."

Lily decided not to ask what that meant. Gan would try to tell her, and then she'd really be confused. "So you think Ginger and Weng have to travel to reach a spot that correlates with the realm they want to cross to? One that doesn't open up underwater or inside rock?"

"Sure. That's what the black dragon thinks, too. I don't know what the other one—Reno—thinks. I don't talk to him 'cause I don't like him."

"Why not?"

"I dunno. How come none of the wolves are going as wolves?"

Rule answered that. "I'd wanted some to go four-legged, but there won't be enough of us for that to work. Wolves can't carry children."

Or use weapons or ride motorcycles. And Dis had no moon. No moon meant no Change, so whatever form the lupi were in when they entered the hell realm, that's how they'd stay until they left.

"No," Grandmother said firmly. "I thank you, but I will not wear that."

Lily looked over her shoulder. The rest of their party was lined up on the path: Cullen on his dirt bike, then Cynna's bike—she wasn't on it at the moment—followed by Benedict and his passenger on a dual-sport Suzuki, then Mason and Max on the last adventure-style bike. Behind them were Carlos, Daniel, and Jude on dirt bikes.

Benedict had room for a passenger because his Uzi—a nice little Vector Arms, full auto—was holstered under his arm. His extra clips were in a custom-made ammo belt he wore commando-style across his chest. He did sheath his machete on his back, but his passenger had assured him she could manage.

His passenger was Grandmother. In full biker gear.

Li Lei Yu wore the jeans Lily had seen her in at Sam's lair with her own shoes, as they hadn't been able to find boots to fit her. But her jacket, on loan from a young Nokolai still at *terra tradis*, was the real deal—black leather with zippers. With it she wore wraparound sunglasses and the boy's helmet—black also, but with flames. Grandmother loved it.

Cynna had been handing out necklaces with charms attached. Lily wasn't wearing one because she couldn't use charms—her magic ate theirs—but everyone else was. Everyone but Max, who insisted he couldn't be affected by mind magic. And indeed, his mind was as slick as oil to Lily. Max—and Grandmother.

"Take it," Cynna urged. "You may be able to protect yourself from mind magic, but why spend that power if you don't have to?"

"You do not understand the nature of my protection or my power. I do not explain. I will not wear the charm."

"But the other one, the sleep charm—"

Grandmother snorted. "If I cannot put someone to sleep without a charm, that bit of metal will not help."

"I'll take it!" Gan piped up. "I've got shields, but a little extra protection won't hurt. How do they work?"

Cynna grimaced and looked up at Gan. "The first one shields against mental attack. It doesn't work on passive magic, but it's aces on blocking active attacks. I'll activate it when I put it on you. You have to activate the sleep charm yourself. You do that by licking it, then you hold it against the skin of the person—or being—you want to put to sleep. You can't take your hand away or they'll wake up."

"Huh." Gan wrinkled her nose. "I don't want to be close enough to anything we meet in Dis to touch them."

"It can also be used to keep someone who's wounded asleep so they don't suffer."

"It would be better if we didn't get wounded. Demons like to eat the wounded ones. They shouldn't eat you, and lupi are like humans, so they shouldn't eat them, either, because of it making them go crazy, but with Xitil dead the rules won't be working, so some of the stupid ones will—"

"We won't let them eat our wounded. Do you want the damn charms or not?"

"Yes!" Gan held out both hands. "Throw me the necklace."

It is now time for silence. The gate builders commence.

Quickly Cynna tossed the necklace up at Gan, who caught it. Then she hurried to her bike, which was leaning against a handy bit of rock. Apparently real dirt bikes, as opposed to the type of hybrid Lily was on, didn't have kickstands.

Lily peered around Rule's shoulder to watch the clearing below.

Twice she'd seen a gate opened. The first time it had been three Rhejes and Cullen doing the opening; they'd used chanting and candles, though Cullen had also done something with his athame. The second time a gnome had drawn an elaborate pattern involving runes.

Runes and gnomes seemed to go together. This time, ten of the gnomes squatted in a circle, each with a rune laid into the dirt in front of him or her. The runes were as slick and dark as if they'd been ink-drawn on smooth paper rather than rough ground, but she hadn't seen how they'd been formed. Gnome Number 11 stood at the southernmost point of the circle holding a small, glowing globe. If she was doing anything with that globe, it was nothing Lily's eyes could see. Byuset made a slow circuit of the runes, pausing now and then to make some tiny adjustment with a long, thin blade.

Go, go, go.

Lily thought about Toby and wished desperately she could reach into that other realm with her mindsense—how in the world had Sam done that with Gan?—and tell him they were coming.

Byuset moved to the center of the circle. He made a gesture with his blade. Slowly the runes lifted from the dirt . . . and began to rotate, moving clockwise—and inward, she realized as their movement quickened, guided by Byuset's oversize athame. They were spiraling toward the center, moving ever faster. Any moment they'd smack into each other.

She felt Reno's sudden descent before she saw him—felt his mind plummet toward them. Rule shifted and kicked their motorcycle to life and she leaned into him the way she'd been told, arms around his waist. The roar from their engine was quickly joined by those behind them even as they were buffeted by wind and debris from dragon wings— and then she couldn't see anything but dragon. Reno landed with his wings held high, his wingspan being wider than the clearing, furling them along his back as the rush of his landing carried him forward on four feet—straight for an almost invisible shimmer that suddenly loomed in the air, tall as a house, which made it just big enough for Reno when he lowered his head.

As he hit that shimmer, he vanished—head gone, then neck, shoulders, belly, and tail—as if someone had scrubbed a reality eraser along the whole, enormous length of him. Then the tip of that tail reappeared, flicked once, and vanished again. That was the signal.

Rule opened the throttle. Dirt flew from their passage, too, as they aimed for that shimmer. Her heart in her mouth—*go, go, go!*—Lily leaned forward with her mate and went roaring into hell. The shimmer *shook* her as they passed through, as if every cell in her body shuddered at once in a somatic scream, but quick as a thought, they were through. And the world changed.

This world was slightly lower than the one they'd left. Their bike sailed through empty air to land with a jolt. Rule held them upright and accelerated. Around them, dirt and rocks—a rolling land, mounded here, dipping there. And empty. No plants, no grass, no demons, no—wait, were those trees? Lily caught only a glimpse as their bike growled up one of those low mounds half a football field away from where they'd entered. And stopped, the motor idling.

It was cooler here. Not cold, but maybe ten degrees cooler. Overhead, an eerie sky glowed, devoid of sun, moon, or stars. Off to the right—the east, that should be—the trees she'd glimpsed. Only now she saw they were but the stripped skeletons of trees, dead black spears ranked along the rolling ground. Everywhere dirt and rocks. Off to the right, distant mountains were ghostly blue shadows against the glowing sky. Ahead the land was deceptively open. The gentle swells of earth could conceal any number of attackers, so she nudged the coiled-up sense in her gut and sent it out to check. And found nothing.

"Where's Reno?" Rule said as Cullen stopped beside them, with Cynna's bike right behind. Lily looked over her shoulder and saw Benedict and Grandmother heading toward them. Farther back, a shimmer in the air winked at her and gave birth to Mason and Max on a battered black motorcycle.

"Overhead," she said automatically.

The air winked again and Carlos shot out.

There was plenty of air, too, wasn't there? It smelled dusty and dead, tinged with the exhausts from their bikes, but they had no trouble breathing it. Nor was there a firestorm. No demon hordes or demon princes . . . at least none she could see.

Cynna pulled up beside Cullen; Benedict's bike climbed

to a stop on Rule's right, and Carlos opened his throttle to catch up. Behind him the shimmering air birthed Jude, then Daniel . . . and stopped winking.

"No minds nearby," Lily said, "other than ours, not for thirty yards or so . . . shit. What's he doing?"

"What?"

"Reno. He just shot off to the north. Northeast," she corrected herself. "He's in a hurry, too." She quit fighting the pull, and immediately her mindsense shot out after him in a way that felt tactile to her, like reaching out a hand on an arm that stretched and stretched. Just before it connected, she made that hand into a fist—probably Sam would call that a metaphor, but it felt like a fist—and used her knuckles to rap on the icy crags of a mind mostly hidden. Cold on top, that mind, like Sam's, but with her mindsense clenched in a fist, she couldn't sense anything else about it . . . which was the point.

This was how she'd gotten Sam's attention without opening up mindspeech herself—use a fist, not fingers. Her physical fingers took in magic. Her mental fingers did, too, though it was only mind magic they absorbed. She'd decided her mental knuckles lacked the sensitivity of fingertips, that touching with them would not draw her into that rapt, trapped fascination.

It had worked with Sam. It worked with Reno, too, but he didn't answer her knock. She drew her mindsense back. "Reno's ignoring me. Unless he mindspoke one of you instead—"

"No, but—he went northeast?" Cynna pointed. "That way? That's where Ryder is. Maybe he sensed something. Maybe he went to stop them—Weng and whatshername. Ginger."

Lily frowned. "That's the right direction, but why—"

"Wow," said a new voice off to the left. Gan. The former demon had arrived in her own way and stood about ten feet away, looking around. "This place sure went downhill after I left."

"Looks like bloody Mordor," Jude said, "only instead of a cute little hobbit, we got Gan."

"I'm better than a hobbit," Gan assured him, then added, "What's a hobbit?"

"Come on, Frodo. Better climb aboard." Jude held out a hand.

"Okay." Gan scampered to him and let him pull her aboard the bike.

"There's no magic," Cullen said suddenly. "We're right next to a node. I should see sorcéri all over the damn place, and I don't. A ley line, sure, a big one, but . . ." He frowned at the ground as if it had offended him. "Odd. Damned odd."

Lily frowned. "No magic, no big, bad demon prince trying to smother us or fry us . . . is this what a territory in Dis looks like when it doesn't have a demon prince?"

"No," Gan piped up. "At least, I don't know what it would look like without a prince, but somebody's claimed this territory. They're just doing a lousy job."

"What do you mean? How can you tell?"

"There's rules. They feel different than they used to. Sort of slippery, 'cause some of them don't apply to me now that I'm growing a soul." She sounded smug about that. "But there wouldn't be any rules if there weren't a prince."

"We need to go," Cynna said. "Now."

They did.

TWENTY-ONE

~⁓

ROCK and dirt, eerily glowing sky. No sun and no moon, and the loss of the Lady's song made Rule's stomach quiver, but he'd survived that loss before. He kept his gaze out front and his ears tuned, although not much could penetrate the roar of the noise cloud they moved in. Air whipped by, smelling of dirt and exhaust; Lily stayed flat against his back as she'd promised. The warmth of her comforted him . . . and made his wolf quite smug.

Of course his mate was with him. Why did he keep having to learn that lesson?

We're coming, he told his son. *Hang on. We're coming.*

Of all of the lupi present, he was likely the least skilled at off-roading. Earlier he'd taken this bike for a spin to remind his body what to do. The dance of throttle, clutch, and shift had come back to him, but he was rusty. He hadn't been on a bike of any sort since before Toby was born. Because he was probably the slowest, it made sense for him to take the lead, set the pace. He did not set the direction, however. That was Cynna's job, and she rode at his right.

There was another reason for him to take point: his passenger would sense the minds of any who lurked ahead in ambush. They'd agreed on that in advance. So far, Lily had issued no warnings. The land seemed as empty to the mind as it was to the eye and nose.

We're coming, Toby.

At any moment, the kidnappers might take his son and the others beyond reach. Rule wanted desperately to open the throttle and find out how fast the bike could fly, a need held in check by the thin rein of reason—thin, but made strong by memory. He'd crashed a bike once. When he was young and stupid, he'd let himself be pushed off the road by a semi whose driver had probably never even seen him.

A human wouldn't have survived that crash. Lily wouldn't have survived.

Rule kept his speed within reason and his gaze ahead. The land swelled and dipped, pocked by rocks large and small and by twiggy revenants of what had been plants and bushes. What manner of death had swept this land? Nothing moved. Nothing grew. Had there been a fire?

No fire now. No firestorm upon their entry, either. No attack from demons. No demon prince standing gravity on its head or sucking out all the air. No demons at all, so far. Reno had been wrong.

And where was Reno? Why had the dragon flown off without a word? Reno didn't like talking to humans and seemed to make no distinction between humans and lupi. Had he flown ahead so he wouldn't have to talk with them? Did he think he could single-handedly destroy the kidnappers without harming the children?

Maybe he could.

Had it been Sam with them, Rule wouldn't have worried, but he was uneasily aware of how little he knew about the green dragon. Did Reno care about the children, or only about catching up with the dragon spawn?

Ahead, the ground rose sharply in a jumble of dirt and rock and dead vegetation. The ridge curved on their left, growing into mounded boulders. On the right was dense growth, which would be hard to get a bike through, especially without leathers; it blended into the dead forest. He went straight, gunning the engine to pick up speed. He couldn't stand on the pegs, not with a passenger, so he gripped the gas tank firmly with his thighs and leaned into the climb. The slope was rough and bumpy, but they crested the ridge without major problems, and—

Rule did not lock up the front wheel. Quite. He braked hard, but let up almost immediately, skewing the bike to the left as they skidded to a stop.

What had been a slight rise on one side was much greater on the other. More abrupt, too. You might call it a cliff.

"That was exciting," Lily said, breathless.

He snorted in unplanned amusement. A quick glance told him Cynna had safely come to a stop, too, though she'd veered right instead of left. He looked out . . . movement. Shit. In the distance, but still—"Cynna, get back down. We're too visible." He made a gesture that told the others to stop. "Lily. Get off and get flat."

She slid off. He shut off his engine and wheeled the bike back down the slope far enough for it to be out of sight, put down the kickstand, and crept back to the top of the ridge, which was about ten feet wide here.

Lily lay flat looking out. He joined her. A glance told him more than he wanted to know. They were about a hundred feet up on this side—and the drop-off could readily be called a cliff. Below, the dead forest spilled out over the plain, though to the left there seemed to be a path . . . a dry streambed, he thought. And on the horizon, the lower half of a mountain squatted, black against the sullen glow of the sky. Given their elevated vantage point, Rule guessed that oddly singular peak must be four or five miles off. "Getting down will be even more exciting."

"Can we?"

"Not here. Cynna—is that where we're headed? That weird peak?"

"Yes," Cynna said tersely. "The children are there . . . no, not quite there, but they're really close to it. Is that movement near the base of the peak, by those boulders?"

"Yes." *Too late.* The words, the knowledge, beat at Rule. They were up here; the children were down there and four or five miles away. Surely the caldera was their enemies' goal—and Rule still had to figure out how to get down. He looked around. Cullen had flattened himself next to Cynna; everyone else had stopped their bikes in place partway up the hill. "Benedict, bring me the binoculars. Carlos, Daniel, leave your bikes and look for a way down, preferably one fit for the bikes." He didn't want to abandon them. If they did, the lupi would have to run ahead, leaving the women to catch up as best they could. He hated that idea. Hated it fiercely. But they were running out of time . . . "But we have to get down, with or without the bikes. Carlos, head to my left. Daniel, go right."

"Shit!" Cullen half raised himself from his prone position. "It's all going there. The magic. I can't imagine how they did it, but all the magic is being drained from the land into that caldera. That's why everything's dead."

"A caldera?" Lily said. "That's like a dead volcano, isn't it?"

"More like the bloody eye of Sauron," Jude muttered under his breath.

"That's where Xitil's court was," Gan piped up from the back of Jude's's bike. "In a dead volcano. Mostly dead. Sometimes she stirred it up."

"Is this it?" Rule asked. "Come look." As Gan hopped down from the motorcycle, he went on, "Lily, where's Reno?"

"At the caldera. Flying over it." She frowned. "Should I try to contact him again? I'm not . . . on the way here, it occurred to me it might be possible for someone to sense my probe."

"I didn't know that was possible."

"Maybe it isn't. I'm just guessing, but it seems like someone who was really good at mind magic could spin a net sort of the same way I create a mind-mist to see if there are any minds nearby. It would take a godawful amount of power, though, to set a net that big."

The Great Bitch had a god-awful amount of power. "And maybe catch you in that net?"

"I don't know. I don't know what's possible and what isn't."

"Better not risk it."

Benedict tapped Rule's leg. "Here. You won't get much detail from this far. Don't forget to turn them on."

Turn them—oh, right. These were the new ones, with image stabilization. Rule located the power button. "Lily, are you able to keep watch around us without tripping this hypothetical mind-net?" All he saw through the lenses was fuzz. He adjusted the focus.

"I don't know, but we need for me to keep watch. I'm pretty sure I'd know it if I did trip something."

"Hmm." He messed with the focus some more . . . now he could make out what he saw. Stone. Blocks of stone, some oddly regular, strewn around the ground surrounding the caldera as if a giant's hand had swiped his block castle, landing the pieces in tumbled piles.

"That's it," Gan sang out. "That's Xitil's old palace. I wonder if she's dead? I don't think we should go there, Rule. It's bound to be dangerous."

"It's where the children are," Lily reminded her with

more patience than Rule could summon. "The children are why we're here."

What was that? A wildly colorful creature of some sort, long and sinuous. Rule couldn't make out any details before it vanished behind one of the huge stone blocks. Whatever it was, it was gone now. He turned the binoculars on the dead forest, hoping to trace that dry streambed, see if it led where they wanted to go. "Gan, can you see *üther* from this far away?"

"See it where?"

"At the caldera."

"No one can see *üther* through rock, but even if the rock wasn't there, it's too far, except maybe for Xitil's pets. They probably could, if any of them are still alive."

"Xitil's pets?"

"You know—those great big flying demons. They were fighting with the dragons when we were here last time."

Oh. Those. Rule remembered them with great clarity.

"They're probably gone. They eat a lot, and there's nothing here to eat."

Rule couldn't follow the dry streambed all the way through the trees, but it did seem to be headed in the right direction. Where were Carlos and Daniel? They had to get moving, get down there . . .

"We're too late." Cynna's voice was as flat and harsh as the dead land around them. "We can't get there in time."

"Don't assume," Lily said coolly. "Sam thought they meant to cross to another realm, but that's a guess, not a fact. He didn't know about the magic being drained from the land, channeled to that caldera. Whatever they're up to there, Sam didn't know anything about it, so we can't assume he was right about them crossing. Maybe that caldera is their goal. Clearly they're doing something major there."

Cullen gave a nod. "Reno's there. Surely he'll do something

if they try to take the children elsewhere, but we need to hurry."

Rule's heart hurt. "No."

Everyone turned to stare at him. "Haste made sense earlier, when we hoped to catch up with them in the open. Not now. Either the children will be taken to another realm before we can reach them, or they'll be held in a highly defensible structure. I could see that much about it with just a quick look through the binoculars. Given that it used to belong to the demon prince of this region, I would guess it holds less visible surprises. Haste will just get us killed. It won't rescue the children."

"Shit!" Cullen said explosively. "Hellfire. You're right, damn you."

Cynna cursed, quietly and extensively. Benedict simply nodded. Lily grimaced.

Rule kept going because he had to. "Gan, you've been there? To Xitil's palace?"

"Sure! Well, only a couple times, but I remember it pretty well. Plus I know a lot of stuff about it from having eaten old Mevroax."

He blinked. "I need to talk to you about—"

"Rule!" Carlos didn't speak loudly, but voices carried well in this dead landscape. He was still out of sight amid the jumble of rock to their left, but by the sound of it was headed back. "There's a gully or maybe a dry streambed. Lots of loose rocks, but it switches back and forth, so it's not impossibly steep—at least the part I could see isn't. It'll be tricky, especially for those with passengers, but I think the bikes can take it."

"Daniel!" Rule called. "To me. We're moving out. Gan . . ." He looked at Lily and grimaced. "I need Gan to ride with me so I can question her about the caldera. Jude and I will swap bikes. I don't want you on the back of a motorcycle not made for passengers."

"That will not be necessary," Madame Yu announced.

"I chose to enter this place able to cast spells because we expected a magic-based attack. This did not happen. I think now the physical advantages of my other form will be helpful. Lily may ride with Benedict. I will Change."

"Very well," Rule said as Carlos jogged toward them and Daniel called out a response to his summons. Madame Yu moved away. Rule knew she preferred privacy for her Change, which was very different from the way lupi did it.

Toby, we're coming. Too damn slowly, but they were coming.

CARLOS'S notion of what constituted a bike trail turned out to be more expansive than Rule's. He laid his bike down twice before reaching the base of the cliff, and he wasn't the only one. Only Benedict and Cullen made it to the bottom without mishap, making Rule glad Lily was behind Benedict, not him. No injuries, however, so they kept going. Their path was a genuine gully at first, the banks over Rule's head; Madame Yu, now in her other form, took point. Rule hadn't asked it of her, but neither did he argue. He seldom argued with seven-foot Siberian tigers, and never with Madame Yu.

The forest grew dense around them. The dead trees looked much odder up close than they had at a distance. Most were shaped like a spear twenty or thirty feet high with sparse, delicate branches that reminded him of an umbrella's spokes. A few looked more normal, resembling oak or ash. They passed a thicket of what appeared to be oversize manzanita right down to the red bark and twisty branches, only with wicked thorns.

After a while the gully flattened out. The banks were only a foot or so above the streambed when Madame Yu reappeared and planted herself athwart their path. Rule braked and signaled the others to halt.

Behind him Lily called, "Grandmother says we're very close."

"Very well. We'll break for food, water, and planning."

They pulled the bikes out of the streambed—dry now, but who knew if it would remain so? Though the area seemed to be under severe drought. It bothered Rule that he'd neither seen nor smelled water since they emerged in hell. They'd been unable to pack in many supplies on the bikes, and water was bulky. They'd only brought four gallons, thinking they'd be able to find more if they were forced to linger here longer than planned. That might prove to be a mistake.

Rule asked Madame Yu to keep watch a little longer so they could all drink and eat—just jerky, but there was plenty of it. Carlos and Mason took their jerky with them to patrol a twenty-foot perimeter and Madame was able to have her share, though they had to jury-rig a drinking bowl for her by digging a hole and lining it with a bit of plastic. Rule opened the discussion. "Our first need is information. Lily, we need Reno's input. He's still up there?"

"Yes. Ah . . . two possible explanations for his silence have occurred to me. One, maybe for some reason it's dangerous to use mindspeech here and now. Two, maybe he's a prick."

Madame Yu snorted. She was stretched out near Lily—an impressive sight. Lily looked at her, her gaze unfocused. "Grandmother says reason one is correct, but doesn't eliminate reason two."

Rule drummed his fingers on his thigh. "Cynna, can you tell if the children are still in this realm?"

"Not for certain," Cynna said tensely. "I felt it the moment they—well, I think they were taken underground. My Finds are muffled. Hindered. Finding isn't Air magic, but it grows out of Air, and stone inhibits it. Shit, enough stone could block my Finds entirely if I hadn't already cast them. It feels like there's stone between me and them, but I don't know. If they were in another realm, one that isn't physically congruent to this one . . . I don't know how that would feel."

Lily frowned. "I'm going to try to locate Toby's mind with a really narrow probe, one that would be hard to spot if someone's watching for—"

That would be both dangerous and unsuccessful. The children are belowground. I doubt you could penetrate the rock and earth to reach him.

"Reno!"

"About fucking time!"

"Why haven't you—"

That should be obvious even to a human. The Great Enemy is, as we surmised, present in the form of her avatar, Ginger Harris. Using mindspeech is hazardous. I am currently shielding this conversation, but it is—

Lily broke in. "Wait a minute. What about the way I detect other minds? Not mindspeak them, but locate them. I make a sort of mind-mist and—"

I am aware. The technique you perceive as employing a mist is relatively safe, for it is almost impossible to sense or seize. What you think of as a probe is denser, easy to detect, and your protective magic is attenuated when you reach beyond your body. Do not attempt it. Do not interrupt again. I have examined the magical construct at the caldera. It is quite large, running from well below the surface to nearly one hundred feet above it. It is not precisely a gate, but can be used as one—albeit, I suspect, with greater temporal distortion than is normally acceptable. I will fly through it to leave this realm. When I do—

Furious, Rule broke in. "What do you mean? Because of you, I wasn't able to bring enough fighters! And now you're going to run off and—"

BE QUIET.

The mental shout *hurt.* The pain wasn't physical, but it was real. Pain did not stop Rule. He spoke as icily as the dragon. "Is this how dragons pay their debts—by abandoning their allies?"

You are a fool. The obligation is not to you personally, but to the alliance of beings fighting a common Enemy. I offer you such assistance as is reasonable, but my primary goal is to stop her.

Lily spoke with tightly held anger. "And how do we get back without you? None of us can signal Byuset."

Is this not obvious? Gan can cross back to Earth and inform the gnomes which node they should use. You waste time. I cannot shield this conversation indefinitely, so attempt to think rather than reacting with recriminations and petty questions.

"This question is not petty," Rule said coldly. "You said we were to leave the spawn—Tom Weng—to you. You won't be here to deal with him."

One of you partakes sufficiently of dragon that if she kills the spawn, it will be a matter of duty and not an offense. Why else do you think I allowed Li Lei to come?

Madame Yu snarled—at the supposition she'd needed Reno's permission, Rule supposed—then ostentatiously began to groom herself.

We are almost out of time. When I transit via this construct, it will create substantial instability in the construct itself, the ley lines feeding it, and the twin nodes beneath the caldera, leading to a massive explosion. The Enemy can shield her avatar from many ills, but not from such an explosion as this would be. It would kill her avatar along with everything else within fifty to a hundred miles, destroy the construct, and might well damage the interstitial region. This would seriously disrupt the Enemy's plans. She will therefore be forced to devote considerable power and time to stabilizing the construct, ley lines, and nodes. This will be difficult enough to require her full attention. I suggest you attack while she is thus engaged.

"You endanger the children!" Cynna cried. "If you're wrong about what the Great Bitch can or will do—"

I do not require your input. I inform you of what I will do that you may take advantage of it. Even humans should be able to see the wisdom in avoiding direct battle with one you are entirely incapable of defeating.

"What is this construct?" Benedict asked. "What's it for?"

The construct is currently channeling vast amounts of power away from this realm. Without examining the terminus of that power, I cannot definitively ascertain its purpose. I have determined that it possesses a cyclic nature. Between twenty and forty-five minutes from now, it will reach the apex of its cycle. I will depart then. I will not be visible to you; however, Cullen Seabourne will see the power flare caused by my departure. There may be effects visible to the rest of you as well.

I expect the Enemy to be fully occupied with stabilization for between two and twenty hours after my departure. Note that while she will be distracted, her forces and allies will not. However, they are less extensive than I expected; you have a chance of defeating them. I will now provide Rule Turner with information about those forces.

Abruptly, knowledge bloomed in Rule's mind like an unfolding fractal—unfolding in three dimensions, staggering his senses with the sudden imposition of data couched in inhuman terms. This tunnel, *here*—and these hot spots where demons of *this* sort waited—this spot marked as dangerous, but the meaning of that danger buried by alien thought-constructs . . .

Reno was still speaking—or speaking again? Rule's dazed mind could barely take in the dragon's words.

. . . this representation of the disposition of her forces to be largely accurate, but due to the haste with which it was compiled and the necessity of doing so without attracting

the Enemy's notice, it may be incomplete. Note that it does not include any passive traps within the structure. There was insufficient time to locate those. The spawn is currently with the children in the room I marked. I did not locate Ginger Harris, but the Enemy is well able to conceal her mind—and that of her avatar—from the sort of cursory examination I was forced to make to avoid detection. I will not risk speaking with you again, so I suggest you prepare yourselves for battle.

A moment's silence, then Lily asked, "And that's it? That's all you're saying?" Unsurprisingly, there was no answer. She twisted to look at Rule. "Did he give you that information?"

"Yes . . ." Rule shook his head sharply, trying to throw off his befuddlement. "Not in words, but as . . . it isn't the sort of mapping I'm used to, but it is a map. I don't see how he . . . Reno would have had to penetrate rock and dirt to locate the demons and the children. Mind magic isn't supposed to penetrate rock and dirt."

"Dragons do it, though. At least Sam does. I don't know how. Grandmother?" She looked at the tiger, who'd risen and padded closer. She put her hand on the huge head. "Grandmother says matter is not made entirely of matter, but of space as well. Power can flow through the spaces in rock, although only the older dragons can shape their power to do this. She also says this doesn't matter, for you ask the wrong question. You should ask if Reno can be trusted."

"I don't trust him."

"She does not, either, in some things." The cadence of the words was clearly Madame's, not Lily's. "In this, we probably can. It is unlikely he would go to the effort of destroying us through such complex misdirection when simply withholding information would have the same result." Lily scowled and added, sounding like herself, "You think he might want to destroy us?"

The tiger snorted.

"She says she does not predict Reno's goals, but he will not act to benefit our Enemy. She observes that if he did wish us dead—"

"I get the point. Max. Reno doesn't expect the demons fighting for *her* to be distracted. We should remedy that."

TWENTY-TWO

~

THE room was not entirely dark. Mage lights bobbed around near the ceiling, but not enough to make it really bright. But Toby didn't want to see any better. There were too many demons here.

Not monsters. Demons.

Toby couldn't put into words why some of the creatures in Dis made him think "monster" while others immediately made him think "demon." What was the difference? But there was a difference, even if he couldn't explain it, and these . . . these were demons.

There were two types in the big room. One type stood up on two legs and had red or pink skin and no hair. Their faces looked like gargoyles, only with more eyes—two in front and two in back—and they had little horns on top of their heads and long, clever tails almost like a cartoon devil, only without the arrowhead at the tip. Instead they had a bony ridge that looked sharp enough to cut you open. Like all the other demons Toby had seen, they were naked, so he knew some were male, some female, but the females didn't have breasts. There wasn't room for breasts because that's where the smaller pair of arms grew, right out of their chests. Those arms were short and ended in hands that looked almost ordinary. The upper arms were long and thick with muscle like an ape's and grew out of powerful shoulders. Those arms ended in claws like the ones on their big feet.

The second type of demon were built like giant, hairless hyenas, with skin that ranged from dun to black. They only had two eyes, but those eyes were red and glowing. They had two short rear legs and two longer front legs, plus a pair of weird-looking arms with too many joints sprouted from their chests. Those arms ended in hands, but with claws so wicked long Toby didn't think they could use their hands for much.

The two kinds of demons didn't mix. The four-eyes stayed bunched up together near the entrance jabbering at each other, while the red-eyed hyena types wandered around the big room. Did that mean the red-eyed demons were higher status or nastier than the others? Maybe the two were the same thing with demons.

A ring of fire three feet high penned in Toby and the kids in the middle of the room. It was real fire, too, not the fake kind Cullen sometimes used. Toby was hot and sweaty from sitting near it, but he didn't have much choice. Their circle of floor wasn't very big. He wiped his forehead. Three of the hyena demons stopped just on the other side of the fire and stared at him with those glowing red eyes.

Their stares should have scared him. And they did, only not enough, because they made the hot, growling presence inside him angry. Made him want to stare back and force them to either back down or fight him. And that was about as stupid as any thought he'd ever had. Was his wolf crazy?

Ryder babbled something, sounding cranky, and pulled his hair. He switched her to his other shoulder. His arms ached, but he didn't dare put her down because of the fire.

She could move really fast when she wanted. He and Diego were sitting with their backs together, with Sandy cuddled up against them, dozing. Touching each other like this helped. At least it helped Toby. He hoped it did something for the others, too.

"I don't think your dad's coming." Diego's voice was tight with the effort of not crying.

"He'll come." Ryder squirmed and whimpered. Toby wanted to whimper, too. He was so *tired*. He didn't want to comfort her and change her and feed her and play with her and . . . he just wanted to sleep. He wanted to curl up in a ball and sleep and sleep until his dad showed up. Because he *would* show up. Toby knew that. He just didn't know when.

"Don't let her start crying again," Diego said. "She'll wake Noah up."

Diego had it easy. Newborn babies sleep a lot. They weigh a lot less than nine-month-old babies, too. Ryder was pulling his hair again, announcing, "Da! Da!" Which might mean all sorts of things, but added to her squirming, probably meant she wanted to be put down. Toby lowered Ryder to his lap. "Where's Toby?" he said, holding his hands in front of his face and trying for a happy voice. "Here's Toby!" He dropped his hands and made an astonished face.

A month ago, she'd found that hilarious. Not so much now. Cullen said Ryder was at the discovery stage, which meant crawling as fast as she could in exactly the wrong direction, finding objects she shouldn't have, then scattering them, destroying them, or trying to eat them, and screaming with rage when you took them away. The screaming-with-rage part was supposed to be optional, Cullen said, but Ryder considered it *de rigueur*. Toby thought *de rigueur* was probably French for "hardwired into her operating system."

Sure enough, she had no interest in playing peekaboo and oozed out of his lap like a chubby snake. "Stand up like a big girl," he urged before she could escape entirely, taking her hands. Standing up was a new enough skill to hold Ryder's attention awhile . . . he hoped.

THE ground was hard beneath a liberal covering of pebbles and dust. Lily and most of the others sat on that hard ground about halfway up the side of a slope. Most, not all; Max had already left on his mission and Cullen was about twenty feet away, lying flat at the top of that slope. Watching.

Quite a view from up there . . . if you liked rock. Rock in pebbles, chunks, slabs, and broken blocks littered the ground all around the dead volcano, the detritus of half a mountain tossed every which way when a demon prince ate something that didn't agree with her. Their spot was roughly midway between a jagged break in the caldera's walls— hidden from here by the jumble of rock—and another opening. One much smaller and hidden by more than rock.

Turned out that Rule's dragon-imparted map didn't just cover the tunnels beneath the caldera's surface, but also some of the land around it. That's how he'd been able to bring them here.

Lily shook her head, frustrated. "It's not working. I'm not getting any pulses back. You're not thinking words at me."

Rule had wanted Lily to try acquiring his implanted knowledge through mindspeech, but mindspeech was not telepathy. She only picked up thoughts framed in words, and not all of those—only the thoughts the sender considered speech. That suggested to Cullen that intention was part of the package, so Rule had tried *intending* to send Lily the knowledge he'd acquired from the dragon. No go.

Rule ran a hand through his hair. "Dammit. Why couldn't Reno have sent the info to everyone?"

"I don't see how he could send it at all, so I can't answer that."

He grimaced. "At least you'll have Gan with you."

Lily knew what was really bugging Rule. It bothered her, too.

Cynna shrugged. Lily hadn't been sure her friend was paying attention, but apparently she had. "I may not have dragon-implanted knowledge, but I'm a Finder. I can follow a damn map, even that pathetic excuse for one you sketched in the dirt. And I know where the children are."

"I've been known to follow a map, too," Benedict said dryly. "Though we can't rely on Reno's information too heavily. The physical features, maybe, but not the location of the demons. They won't necessarily stay where they were."

"No." Rule glanced at his watch. "Two minutes for questions, if anyone has them."

Rule had been forced to come up with a plan in a hurry. He'd pulled together a good one, Lily thought, even if she did hate part of it. The same part he hated. She would be in Benedict's party, not Rule's.

Splitting up was chancy when they were so few, but Rule's dragon-imparted knowledge of the underground ways made it a chance worth taking. That, plus Cullen's demon bomb and Gan's gastronomically acquired memories. The moment Cullen spotted the power flare marking Reno's departure, Rule would lead him, Carlos, Daniel, Mason, and Jude racing loudly into the caldera on dirt bikes. To make sure everyone noticed, they were taking the grenades.

That's when Max would contribute his bit by dropping explosives—something called military dynamite—down one of the ventilation shafts. That shaft was well away from where the children were, and right on top of a room that might or might not hold a dozen demons. It had when Reno mapped the place, but whether they were there now . . . anyway, while Max's boom and Rule's party drew all the attention, Benedict's party would descend into the tunnels

via a hidden entrance. Hidden didn't mean unguarded, but
Reno's information suggested a single sentry just inside a
small chamber. It might even be the same sentry Xitil had
used, which Gan described as a giant spider-shaped demon
with suckers on its legs.

Mason asked about the unused bikes—the ones Benedict's party wouldn't be riding, for their target was less than
half a mile away. An easy run. Just leave them, Rule said.
Daniel asked about the rendezvous point . . . "If we can't
reach the intended rendezvous, shouldn't we have a backup
spot?"

"If that happens," Rule said, "the situation will likely be
too fluid for plans we make now to be applicable. Lily and
I can always find each other."

Fluid meant chaotic and bloody. Lily was grimly aware
of how often and how radically plans changed the moment
you engaged the enemy. Assuming Benedict's party made
it past the door guards, though, reaching the children
should be fairly straightforward. Not easy, but straightforward. And they would, as Rule had noted, have Gan with
them. The former demon had once eaten one of Xitil's
councillors or courtiers or something—a being very familiar with the palace, anyway. When one demon ate another,
it consumed more than flesh. Gan possessed "old Mevroax's" memories.

Rule's party would do their damnedest to make it all the
way down to the chamber where the children were, but that
wasn't their only goal. They went in to kill demons. As
many as possible. Benedict's group didn't just have to reach
the kids. They had to get out again—carrying two babies
and a four-year-old and protecting the two older boys. Then
they had to get to a stable node and stay alive while Gan
went to tell Byuset and the other gnomes where to open the
gate, then wait for that gate to open. Best to kill as many
demons up front as possible.

Not that demons were all they'd have to deal with.

"And if *she* isn't as preoccupied as Reno thinks she will be?" Benedict asked.

"I'll answer that one. She will be." Cullen had spoken softly without taking his eyes off his view of the caldera. They weren't trying for dead silence; *she* knew they were here. The Great Bitch shouldn't be able to eavesdrop on them—her magic would be sufficiently repelled by that of Rule's mantles to disrupt clairaudience, which was one of the more delicate Gifts. But there were several other ways *she* might detect them, so they assumed she knew exactly where they were . . . and hadn't sent anyone to deal with them. Which meant this was a trap.

They still had to go. At least they would have the element of surprise in one important way: Reno. *She* didn't know about him, and his departure would alter the situation radically.

Something Lily hadn't felt since coming to this place drifted across her cheek. She shivered.

"What is it?" Rule asked sharply.

"Just a sorcéri."

"Are you sure? If it was some kind of probe—"

"It felt exactly like a sorcéri. It didn't feel like mind magic."

"I thought there wasn't any ambient magic here."

Cullen responded without looking at them. "Not in the surrounding land, but the caldera's bound to have sorcéri, with those twin nodes. I've seen a few drifting nearby. The wonder is that there aren't more. By all rights, the ley lines ought to be throwing them like crazy, and they aren't. I don't know how the hell *she* managed that. All the igneous rock helps, but doesn't explain . . . our Enemy's a tidy bitch, though."

"Back to my question," Benedict said. "What if you're wrong? What if *she* doesn't give her full attention to the instabilities?"

"That would mean we all died, making the point moot.

We're talking about hydrogen bomb amounts of power, Benedict, caught in mid-explosion. Multiple hydrogen bombs, because *she* will have to stabilize two nodes and the magical construct, plus the ley lines feeding it. And all of it chaotic as hell—no, worse than that. To some extent she'll be dealing directly with *chaos energy*. You don't know what that means. I barely do," he admitted, "but if you think of her task as hopping on one foot across a thin wire strung all the way across the Grand Canyon while juggling a dozen primed grenades . . . in a thunderstorm . . . while someone randomly yanks on your other foot, you'll have some idea."

A moment's silence. Rule spoke. "You're not reassuring me."

Cullen had shrugged. "We have to assume Reno's right and the Great Bitch can pull that off. Any other possibility renders our planning unnecessary."

"True. And while we will hope that Weng will focus on my group, we can't—Cynna. Pay attention."

Cynna snapped back into focus with a scowl. "I was checking on Ryder."

"So I guessed. If you check on her as often when you're belowground as you have been above, Tom Weng will have no trouble surprising you."

"Your bunch is supposed to draw his attention."

"If you rely on that and Weng doesn't take my bait, you make yourself and your party easy targets for him. You all die, and Ryder remains in his hands."

A muscle jumped in Cynna's jaw. She gave a short nod.

Tom Weng—dragon spawn and sorcerer. Probably a mage rather than a true adept, according to Sam, but "mage" was an extremely broad category, and they knew he was capable of complex and powerful spell-casting. Weng was the reason each party needed someone capable of slinging magic around: Cullen with Rule's party, Cynna with Benedict's. Grandmother would be with Benedict's party, too, but she'd be limited in what she could do magically. A tiger can't use the oral components necessary to cast most spells. Rule and Benedict had argued briefly about which form Grandmother should be in, but that was a waste of time, as Lily had pointed out. Whatever they decided, Grandmother would do it her way.

Her way turned out to be remaining on four feet. She'd informed Lily via mindspeech that it took a great deal of power to transform, and she preferred not to expend that much in a place where magic was in short supply. Also, without her, Benedict would be the only member of their party who stood a chance of fighting demons up close and personal. They'd do their best to avoid that, of course, but if they were rushed by enough demons, some might get past their weapon fire. Or drop from the ceiling. Or pop up from the floor. Or find some other way to throw a surprise party for their visitors.

Lily's ability should cut down on surprises, but her range would be limited underground. Plus she wasn't sure she'd notice a whole troop of demon minds if she were busy enough—say, trying to kill a red-eye or two.

She was really hoping there wouldn't be any red-eyes. Unfortunately, they didn't know. Rule couldn't decipher all the information Reno had sent. The map itself, yes, and the number and location of the demons, but not what kind of demons they were. Trying to decode those thought-tags was like trying to read hieroglyphics, he said. Parts of it almost made sense.

"All right," Rule said with another glance at his watch. "Time for talking is over. Lily."

He'd said her name in the same even, controlled voice he'd used all along. His eyes weren't the same. Not the same at all. She looked into them and got the falling-elevator feeling and thought, *Down is so much farther down than it used to be*, and she stood up and stepped into his arms. "No good-byes," she whispered fiercely, and he either agreed or obeyed, for he didn't say a word, just held her so tightly she couldn't breathe, didn't need to breathe . . .

Then he let go. He even smiled. It was a cracked, crooked sort of smile, but the courage of it lifted her heart and hurt it. "We're good," she told him.

He gave her a nod, still wordless, and moved away.

The motorcycles were propped against the slope leading up to the ridge. Rule's group headed for them, putting on helmets, checking weapons. Lily, like the rest in Benedict's group, stayed where they were. They wouldn't move until Rule's party went roaring off; by then, the Great Bitch should be too busy to notice that they'd split into two groups.

There had been some discussion—i.e., argument—over how many would be in Benedict's party. Benedict had won that one. He wanted all the lupi with Rule because Rule's party would be actively seeking demons to kill. They'd try to make it to the room where the children were, but they'd do it the hard way.

Which was why Lily was in Benedict's group. Oh, it was a good tactical decision. Cynna wasn't much of a shooter. They'd need Lily's weapon and her ability to sense nearby minds. But tactics were only part of the story. She was with Benedict because those with Rule were more likely to be injured or killed. Including him.

STANDING up was a big success. Of course, every time Ryder did it—with Toby's help—she went down again, mostly because she always tried to walk and she couldn't, not yet. Cynna called her a born overachiever. But falling on her butt didn't discourage Ryder one bit. She reached for his hand to do it again.

They'd gone through this routine about three thousand times when Ryder suddenly froze. Toby's gaze flicked up. Sure enough, the woman with two voices stood just on the other side of the fire, smiling at him. The man was there, too, slightly behind the woman, but Toby couldn't spare any attention for him. Not with *her* so close.

"Such a cute baby," the woman said in her ordinary voice. "Not that I care much about babies, but I don't object to them. And my other half—that's terribly inaccurate, by the way, but I've never been good at math. My other half positively dotes on babies. Especially girl babies. So pure . . ." She sighed in a dreamy way that sent ants crawling up Toby's spine. "You're right, you know."

Toby didn't speak. He wasn't sure he could. Even his wolf went still.

"Diego should have more faith in what you tell him. Your father is not only coming, he's here. Quite close, actually. But we can't make it too easy for him. Where would be the fun in that? Time to cut those traces Ryder's mommy is using to Find you two." She pointed at him. This time her voice rolled through him like thunder. "*Midello-sha!*"

Toby froze in anticipation of . . . but nothing happened.

"All right, Alice," she said sweetly, stepping aside to reveal a woman he'd never seen before. "They're all yours now."

"**STRETCH** out," Benedict said.

"But if—"

Benedict interrupted Lily without speaking a word. He just looked at her.

Lily sighed and pulled one leg up so she could hug her thigh to her chest. She stood stork-legged for a count of five, then switched legs.

She knew why Benedict wanted her to stretch. She was strung tight. She hated waiting. She especially hated it when she didn't know when it would end—in the next second, or not for another fifteen minutes. She hated being so close to Toby and Ryder and the other children and unable to act. She really hated knowing that any one of those around her might not live through that action. Maybe more than one. And that was assuming they didn't all get blown up in the massive explosion Reno expected to cause in another second or minute or fifteen minutes or whatever unless the Great Bitch stopped it like he thought she would—

Shut up, she told herself. She lifted her arm so her right elbow pointed at the sky, then pulled on that elbow with her other hand. Her rifle was in the way, but she managed.

"You look funny," Gan observed. "How come you're doing what he said?"

"Because he's in charge."

"How come he's in charge?"

"Because he's very, very good at this." She switched arms. "Gan, you need to obey Benedict, too, because he'll do a good job of keeping you alive. If he says duck, you duck. If he says for you to cross, you do that."

Gan gave the big man a doubtful look. "I don't have to wait to cross until he says."

"You don't have to, but you want to wait if you can. You wouldn't want to waste power crossing if you don't have to."

"I have lots of power now," Gan assured her. "And crossing around here is as easy as it gets. Pretty much everywhere I stand there's a realm bumping up against me. Twin nodes, you know."

"Actually, I don't."

Gan was astonished. "How could you not know about that? But maybe you've never seen twin nodes. They're really rare. They thin out"—she waved both pudgy hands vaguely—"stuff. Whatever separates the realms, it's thin here, lots thinner than with just one node. Makes it easy to fall through even if you aren't a crosser like me. That's why Xitil made her palace in the dead volcano, so she could soak up power from those nodes and grab anyone that fell into Dis from some other realm. Mostly she ate them," Gan added, "but sometimes she kept one around, if they were useful or interesting."

"Humans?" Benedict asked, looking mildly curious.

"Sometimes. She didn't eat them, of course, because of their souls, but mostly they died pretty fast anyway. Humans are really bad at healing."

Grandmother snorted. Cynna frowned. "So you can't cross just anywhere? If you wanted to cross right here, could you?"

"Oh, if I crossed here, I'd end up in the air." She squinted as if thinking. "I'm not sure how far up, but probably too far. Plus that realm isn't time-congruent at all. The more the time is out-of-whack, the harder it is to cross, and if you don't match the time closely enough, your mind gets all confused, and it takes a while for it to settle down. But if I hopped over a few feet, I could cross into a real nice realm. I don't know the name of it. It looked a lot like Earth, but it isn't Earth because there were a lot of elves, which is why I didn't stay there long. Elves hate demons. Do you think they'd hate me now that I'm not a demon anymore?"

"The elves in Edge don't hate you."

"Yes, but I'm important there. I wouldn't be important to elves in other places."

"Forget the elves," Benedict said. "You understand what to do when Seabourne signals?"

Gan rolled her eyes. "I'm not stupid. I get on your back and—"

"On my shoulders. The machete's on my back."

"So I get on your shoulders instead. I still think it would be more fun to ride the tiger, as long as she didn't eat me."

Grandmother nudged Lily with her nose. Obediently Lily put her hand on one big paw. Touch made mindspeech easier; it also meant she didn't have to send out a probe, which Reno said would attenuate her protection from mind magic.

Grandmother's mind was a marvel to Lily's new sense. Power blazed deep within, but the surface was darkly mysterious—like a comet or small asteroid, all crags and crevices. For some reason it wasn't compelling the way dragons' minds were. Instead, it felt . . . familiar.

Yes? she sent, and listened, then said aloud, "Gan, Grand-mother wants to know why this Xitil of yours wanted a side door which allowed people to sneak in on her."

"Oh, she had lots of side doors. Not always the same ones—she rearranged things all the time, so you never knew if a path in still worked or if it would drop you into a pit like this one does. Or like it did, but Rule said it still does, right? Though not right away."

"Yes, but why?"

"Well, she liked practical jokes, especially if they involved screaming, plus she had to give her courtiers something to do. They were always scheming and trying to kill each other or her, though not her very often because most of them weren't *that* stupid. So sometimes she made everyone enter court through a secret entry to see if they could, or else she watched to see who was meeting who secretly, or sometimes she created entertainments where someone she was annoyed with had to go through a trial. That's how I got to eat old Mevroax. She sent him into a real big maze and he made it out in spite of getting attacked a bunch of times—at least he thought he'd gotten out, but that was her tricking him, so when that big stalactite fell and pinned him, he was so weak that—"

"I get the idea. So you think—"

Cynna grunted and bent over, clutching her gut.

The sky over the caldera erupted in a geyser of rainbow light.

From the other group, ready on their bikes near the top of the ridge, Cullen cried out, "That's it!"

"Go!" Rule said, and engines caught.

Lily reached Cynna right after Benedict, who was help-ing her straighten. "What is it?"

"My Finds. They're gone, both of them." Cynna's face was pale and strained beneath the inky traceries. "I can't feel Ryder anymore. Or Toby."

Shock weakened Lily's knees. She couldn't speak. Couldn't put words to her fear.

Benedict could, though his voice came out harsh as a crow's call. "What does that mean? Have they been taken to another realm? Killed?"

"No! No, that's not—death would weaken the Finds, not cut them off like this. I incorporated a lot of physical patterns, so even if—if there were just bodies—" Cynna stopped. Gulped. "And I'd still Find them if they were in another realm. I did before, didn't I? No, someone cut the Finds. Both of them. I don't know how, but they did. I felt it. The power, the workings—it all slapped back into me, like rubber bands breaking."

Benedict grabbed Gan around the waist and flung her up on his shoulders. "Hold on. Can you run?" That was directed at Cynna.

"Yes. I can try recasting—"

"Good," he said, and shouted "Come!" to all of them. And he took off.

TWENTY-THRFF

~~

THEY ran—Benedict in the lead with Gan on his shoulders, Lily with a mist of mind-stuff pushed out around her. As she reached the top of the slope, she caught a glimpse of the last motorcycle vanishing between two huge rock pillars. The noise of the bikes stayed with her as she hurtled down the other side, where loose rocks and dirt turned her run into a skidding slippery slide. Grandmother bounded ahead and paused at the bottom, nose up and tail lashing.

As the ground leveled they turned left, away from the route the bikes had taken. A wide, shallow gully ran along the base of the caldera, and their goal was less than half a mile away. Rule hadn't been able to tell them what the entrance looked like, so they were depending on Gan to recognize a spot that might not look the way she remembered. Or the way old Mevroax remembered. Lily did not understand how one being could hold multiple sets of memories, but Gan didn't seem to have any trouble with it.

Explosions—one, two, three—went off some distance

away, their percussive fury muted by the caldera's rocky sides. Lily felt them in her feet. And kept running.

"Here!" Gan squeaked, and nearly fell off when Benedict stopped.

"Where?" Cynna demanded.

The caldera rose along their right, a stony mass unmarred by dead vegetation. There wasn't enough dirt for anything to have grown. In one tumble of rock Lily spotted a hole. An extremely uninviting hole it was, too, being dark and low. "You mean that crevice?" She pointed. "It's low. We'd have to crawl in one at a time."

"I don't see a crevice," Benedict said, reaching up to swing Gan off his shoulders and set her on the ground. "If you do . . . illusion?"

"Xitil couldn't do illusions," Gan said. "They're like lies, and besides, demons don't do mind magic."

"The Great Bitch can," Cynna said slowing. She was studying Benedict, not the jumble of rock. "But it's not one of her best things. It doesn't come easily, so she seldom bothers. Or at least she seldom did, back during the Great War. If . . ." She nodded sharply. "Benedict, your eyes keep flickering past one spot. I think it's a don't-see-me spell, not illusion. A strong one."

"Isn't that mind magic, too?" Lily asked dubiously. "Your charms—"

"Protect against mental attacks, not passive magic. I explained that. A don't-see-me spell placed on an object is passive."

If Cynna said so, Lily believed her. Even if she didn't get it. Better find out what was in that hole in the ground. Lily gently puffed at the mind-mist she'd been keeping around her, sending it into the hole . . . "One mind just inside," she reported. "Inside and up about ten feet, as if it's on a ledge or—Grandmother!"

The tiger had leaped toward the hole—flattened herself, and sprang inside.

Benedict sprinted after her—closed his eyes, and dove inside.

Lily reached the hole two paces ahead of Cynna, who panted, "I can't see it. I still can't notice the damn hole. Lily? Can you tell what's going on?"

She heard the sounds of battle beneath. No shouts or screams—no roar from a tiger—but thuds, motion . . . she yanked her attention to the mind-mist she'd already sent down there. "Three minds—Grandmother, yes, and Benedict, and the demon—its mind is slick to me. There's something odd about it, but I can't tell what with just the mist, and—oh. That one is fading." She'd never touched/seen a mind die, but she had no doubt that's what she sensed. "The demon's dead."

"I wish I could've seen that fight!" Gan was bouncing on her toes. "Killed the m'reelo just like that? Wow. Was it the tiger or the big man who killed it? How come the tiger doesn't have to wait for the big man's orders?"

"Madame is dragging the body out of the way," Benedict's voice came from below. "Come. The drop is about five feet. Toss the little one down first. I'll catch her. Lily, take the rear."

The rock chamber where Lily landed a few moments later was dark, the floor slick with blood. At least she guessed it was blood. She couldn't see worth shit, but she heard . . . "Grandmother. Ick."

"Sensible to eat her kill," Benedict said. "She has a lot of mass to maintain, and a few bites of jerky won't have filled her stomach. Cynna, some light, but keep it dim."

"She killed the m'reelo?" Gan asked, excited, as two mage lights popped into existence overhead. "All by herself?"

Lily unslung her rifle and looked around, able to see the chamber better now—only it wasn't a chamber. It was a broad tunnel, high-ceilinged and round, cut through rock as black as coal. The footing wasn't great. The floor wasn't as curved as the ceiling, but it wasn't flat, either.

"I helped," Benedict said dryly, sheathing his machete and pulling his Uzi from the holster. "Madame, we need to go. I'd like you to take rear this time. I'll take point. Lily, you're at my left and just behind me. Warn me if you sense any minds. Cynna and Gan, you're behind Lily. Remember the firing pattern."

"You first, then when you drop back to reload, I take over," Lily said. "Then you again while I drop back and reload."

Benedict nodded and started down the tunnel.

"M'reelo are pretty hard to kill," Gan told Lily chattily as they followed. The tunnel ran straight for about thirty feet in the direction they were headed, then curved left. "They're really fast and they grab you with those suckers and hold you so they can punch their venom in. I don't know what their venom does to humans, but it paralyzes demons. Most demons anyway, though for some it takes more than one bite, and a m'reelo can only bite once because it empties their venom sac. And it doesn't affect *khahlikka*, but nothing much hurts them, so—"

"Shut up, Gan," Benedict said. "This looks like a lava tube. Igneous rock. Ricochets will be a problem."

Gan must have thought "shut up" meant "lower your voice." She went on more softly, apparently addressing Grandmother. "I guess the m'reelo didn't punch any venom in you. Did your fur keep the suckers from grabbing hold?"

Grandmother made a low noise in her throat.

"How come I can't understand you? The rules should let me understand you. Unless you lose words when you're a tiger?"

"No," Lily said. "She doesn't. The rules don't work on me, either, remember? Gan, you need to be quiet."

"Okay," Gan said, dropping into a whisper. "I really like your grandmother's claws. I was going to grow claws, but then I stopped being a demon so I grew hair instead. Hair isn't much good to a demon. It doesn't kill anything so hardly any demons grow it, so it's hard to grow because you have to figure out *how*. I bet that's why she didn't get grabbed and venomed by the m'reelo—because she's hairy all over and the suckers didn't stick. I wonder why there was just one m'reelo? Do you think the rest all died when Xitil blew up the place?"

"The rest?" Benedict repeated sharply.

"Sure, m'reelo always hang out in herds, and there used to be—"

"Incoming!" Lily sang out, swinging her weapon to her shoulder and releasing the safety. "Lots!"

The glow from two little mage lights didn't reach far. At first all Lily saw was a squirming black mass rushing toward them from around the curve up ahead—a mass that covered the floor, ceiling, and walls of the tunnel. All at once a huge ball of light blazed and she saw bulbous black bodies, triangular heads with mandibles and glittering eyes and legs. Too many legs.

She hated spiders.

Benedict didn't bother to unclip the Uzi's stock and brace it against his shoulder. He held it out one-handed, Terminator style. Not the preferred method unless you were a lupus and had both the strength and the hours of practice needed to keep the muzzle from climbing.

The noise was deafening for about four seconds. It didn't take long to empty a clip at full auto. Black buggy arachnids splattered the rock with goo and body parts. Benedict stepped back. Lily, already sighted in, squeezed the trigger, controlling the recoil automatically. More enormous arachnids splattered—and then she was out of ammo and stepping back, one hand reaching for a new clip.

Instead of stepping forward, Benedict leaped straight up. She glimpsed that out of the corner of her eye but had no time for more—the m'reelo were still coming, scuttling over the bodies of their comrades, racing along the walls or ceiling as easily as the floor. She shoved the new clip home as Benedict's machete flashed over her head—and as she resumed firing on advancing uglies, a m'reelo fell on the floor, narrowly missing her. Its blood did not miss her. She didn't move, emptying her clip at giant spiders that were *way too close*. Ran out of ammo again, but she had the next clip ready—eject, slap the new one in, fire . . .

Then silence. Nothing moved. No, wait, a leg was twitching on that one. She should . . . not bother. Benedict had seen it, too, and moved past her. One quick stroke from his blade removed the head from the body.

Her hand shook as she lowered her weapon. Her ears rang. Carefully she sent her mind-mist out . . . "They're all dead. Those sons of bitches were linked somehow. Like a hive mind or something. I couldn't tell when I just sensed one, but when they all came at us . . . my eyes saw lots of creatures. My mindsense saw one mind with lots of moving parts. Weird."

Benedict nodded. "So the rest knew it when we killed the first one and came running. Makes sense. Any more of them?"

"No minds within my range except us."

"What's your range here?"

"Pretty much zero through the rock. About sixty feet if I follow the tunnel."

"You can look around the corner, then? Good." He sheathed his machete, but kept his Uzi in his right hand. Lily realized he must have killed the m'reelo over her head left-handed. He frowned. "Where's Gan?"

"She vanished the second you started shooting," Cynna said. She had her handgun out, but holstered it now. "She can't go *dashtu* here, so—"

"She can't?" Benedict's frown deepened. "You're sure?"

"Demons can only go *dashtu* in other realms, not in Dis. I don't know why. I'm dropping the bonus light now. Takes too much concentration."

As abruptly as it had arrived, the largest, brightest ball of light vanished.

Benedict scowled. "She must have crossed. Dammit, we need her, but I don't like standing around waiting for—"

"Whew." The high-pitched voice came from directly behind Lily. "That was loud. Did you kill them all? I want a machine gun."

"You're too small," Benedict said. "A mini-Uzi maybe, but we don't have one. Come on. Same order."

The floor of the tunnel was covered in spider bodies. They had to step on them. The carapaces cracked. The guts squished. Lily shuddered.

"You okay?" Cynna asked.

"I have spider blood on me."

"That's the girliest thing I've ever heard you say."

"Lots of people don't like spiders. It has nothing to do with who has ovaries and who has testicles."

"You're scared of spiders."

"Shut up, Cynna."

Gan piped up. "I'm scared of m'reelo. Most beings are. Not the *khahlikka*, I guess, because m'reelo venom doesn't work on them, and not Xitil's pets because they eat m'reelo, but a herd of m'reelo can pull down a pretty big demon, so even the big ones are scared of them. Aren't you scared of m'reelo, Cynna Weaver?"

"Not as long as Lily has plenty of ammo," Cynna said as they rounded the curve behind Benedict.

The tunnel slanted down steeply. Nothing ahead but lots of darkness—empty, as far as her mindsense could tell.

"Do you have lots of ammo, Lily Yu?" Gan asked.

"Plenty," she said, hoping that was true. She had seven more clips, which would seem like a lot if she hadn't just burned through three clips in under a minute. "Benedict, why did you use your machete instead of shooting that one over my head?"

"Bad angle. Ricochet. Everyone needs to shut up now."

Cynna snorted. "With all the gunfire, I don't think we need to worry about anyone hearing us."

"I want to hear *them*. I can't with all your chatter."

They shut up. Even Gan. Which left a lot of silence for Lily's imagination to fill.

She tried to focus on her mind-mist, not on what—or who—might be observing them this very moment. Probably nothing and no one, she told herself, but the back of her neck prickled. The Great Bitch ought to be far too busy to scan her domain clairvoyantly—if she could even use clairvoyance in this avatar. Lily did not know much about avatars, an omission she intended to remedy when she had time. Damn Reno for giving them so little time for questions. She hadn't been able to ask half of what she needed to.

She also tried not to think about what might be happening to Rule. At least she had the mate sense to tell her where he was, that he was alive. Cynna didn't. She wouldn't know if Cullen survived until they saw him again.

The tunnel continued to slope down, steeper in some places than others, twisting around more than it had at first. They'd passed two openings that led off who-knew-where— Rule had mentioned them—when the floor turned rough and the walls drew in closer. Lily was glad for her boots and worried about Grandmother's feet. Benedict paused and whispered something to Cynna. One of the mage lights winked out and the other seemed dimmer. They continued with Lily barely able to see her footing.

Had Cynna been able to recast her Finds for Ryder and Toby? There was a lot of rock between them and the children. Too much for a new Find? Lily wanted to ask, but the silence had taken on weight, as if it would require a physical effort to break it. Plus they must be getting close to the pit—that would be why Benedict had eliminated one of the mage lights. The pit was occupied. The cacophony of gunfire had surely alerted anything with ears, even this far away, but did demons know about guns? Would the resident of the pit understand what it had heard?

Benedict raised one hand to signal a stop. He turned to Lily, moved close, and bent to breathe in her ear almost too softly to be heard, "Pit should be a little ways past that crumbled bit. I'm going to try crossing it. Stay here. Stay quiet. I may be gone awhile. Can you pass this on in mind-speech?"

Lily nodded and reached for Cynna's hand. As she passed on Benedict's instructions, he moved off into gloom the dim glow from the mage ball didn't penetrate—not to her eyes anyway. He'd mentioned a crumbled bit that she didn't see, so she assumed his vision extended farther into the murk than hers. She took Gan's hand next. Gan's mind made her think of a walnut—not as easy to reach as some, but with enough texture that she could do it. Gan, of course, wanted to chat, but Lily cut her off and placed a hand on Grandmother's head and repeated everything.

Then they waited. The silence was profound. All she heard was the faint susurration of her own pulse in her ears.

Rule had described the pit that lay ahead. He couldn't tell them anything about its occupant—the information about it was in hieroglyphics, he said—but Gan was sure it was what she called the pit demon. Old Mevroax had heard of such a pit and its occupant, though he'd never seen it. There should be a rickety wooden bridge over the pit, she said. A few feet beneath that would be a dark, still pool.

The liquid in that pool wasn't water. It was acid—acid produced by the demon hiding beneath its surface. Acid which helped digest its prey. Impossible, according to Gan, to cross the bridge silently, for it was designed to creak . . . and the pit demon hunted by sound. Gan didn't think it had eyes, though a couple of stories Mevroax had heard made her think it was sensitive to light in some other way, but its hearing was excellent. It seized anyone who stepped onto that bridge and dragged him, her, or it into the acid pool.

Fortunately, the bridge wasn't the only way to cross the pit. A narrow ledge ran around the rock chamber. If you were very quiet, Gan said, you could make your way across on that ledge without the pit demon noticing. Probably.

That's what Benedict was doing now. Checking out the ledge, making sure it was passable. If it wasn't . . . well, it needed to be, that was all. If they absolutely had to, they could backtrack, take one of the tunnels they'd passed, but those were much more tortuous routes. Without Rule's mental map, they were likely to get lost. Likely to run into more demons, too. Maybe more than their small party could handle.

At last she saw Benedict's figure emerge from the gloom. He came up to her, took her hand, and breathed in her ear the way he had before, "Mindspeak me."

I'm listening, she sent.

Benedict's mental voice sounded exactly like his physical voice. *The ledge is crap, but intact. The walls are phosphorescent. Enough light for me, probably not for you and Cynna. Don't know about Gan. Ask her. Tell me what she says.*

Questions and responses passed between her, Benedict, and the others. Gan saw in the dark "as well as any gnome and better than some." And how well did gnomes see? "Better than humans. Better than dogs. Not as good as owls." Grandmother's night vision was at least as good as Benedict's, Lily assured him, and probably better. Her size, however, was a problem. The ledge was too narrow in places for a seven-foot tiger, however agile. Benedict wanted Grandmother to resume her human form. Grandmother asked how wide the pit was. Between fifteen and seventeen feet, he told her via Lily. That would not be a problem, she said. She would jump the pit, going last in case she made some small amount of noise in landing.

Benedict agreed to this and gave his orders. Cynna was to leave her mage light where it was. Not extinguish it—its dim glow at their backs would help for a time—but she shouldn't allow it to follow them. The tunnel continued to narrow, so they would go single file. About forty feet from here it was partly blocked; a chunk of the ceiling had fallen. After that, the tunnel crooked left and then right in a way no natural lava tube would. No doubt the volcano's deceased ruler had tinkered with it.

The pit came right after the second tight turn. Benedict would guide the two who wouldn't be able to see the ledge clearly, if at all: Cynna first; Gan second, on her own if she could see as well as she claimed; then Lily with Benedict; and last, Madame would leap across.

They set out.

By the time they reached the rubble blocking part of the tunnel, Lily could see the others only as vague shapes. Getting across the loose stone silently was impossible—for her anyway, and apparently for Gan and Cynna, too. Benedict and Grandmother managed it. Visibility was even worse on the other side, and Benedict had them link hands: him first, then Cynna, Gan, and Lily, with Grandmother pacing silently behind her. Gan's small hand was warm, her grip tight. When they turned the first sharp corner, real darkness descended like a blanket. Lily found herself breathing carefully, as if the blackness might truly smother her. She reminded herself that things did not *always* go to hell when she was underground, then had to stifle a hysterical giggle. She was already in hell.

So was Rule . . . several yards over her head and about half a mile *that* way. The contact, however limited, provided by the mate bond helped.

They proceeded slowly, with two of their number unable to see anything. Space became both constricted and unformed, as if dissolved by the blackness, and the need for silence pressed on Lily almost as grindingly as the darkness. The second turn was even tighter; she had to feel her way around it with her free hand. And then a glow appeared ahead. Faint, so faint she'd never have noticed if the darkness had been one shade less absolute, but welcome. Even if it did mean they'd almost reached the dwelling of the pit demon.

The slow crawl of their hand-linked line halted. After a pause, Gan tugged Lily forward. She obeyed, and in seven steps saw the source of the faint luminescence over the top of Gan's head. The chamber's walls glowed a faint, eerie green—not enough light to see by, not for her, but enough to restore definition to the space around her. Easy to see where the exit was in that wall, for it was utterly black. Large, too.

Leaning forward to peer over Gan's head, she saw luminescence splashed up three walls and caught and reflected by liquid below. On one wall, two dark forms. She couldn't see the ledge they moved along. To her eyes they seemed to be lizarding across the eerie green wall, visible only because their bodies blocked the glow. She watched, reminding herself to breathe, as the two forms reached the other side and promptly vanished once there was no phosphorescence to block.

The moment they did, Gan released Lily's hand and set off, a much smaller occlusion of the glow. Long moments later, she, too, was erased by the darkness of the exit.

One form started back toward Lily. The largest one. Benedict moved more quickly on his own than when acting as guide and soon stood in front of her, solid and reassuring. He took her hand, squeezed once, and tugged her to the left.

TWENTY-FOUR

"To me!" Rule yelled as he sprang from the ledge, twisting in midair so his feet hit what remained of the demon's face. The crunch was satisfying. So was the way the giant demon howled in outrage, even if it did hurt his ears.

Best of all was that it dropped Carlos to reach for Rule.

No time to find out if Carlos lived. The creature might be huge, but it wasn't slow. Rule hit the ground running, aiming for the juncture with the next tunnel.

Big, heavy feet followed him.

He reached the intersection and kept going. A burst of gunfire greeted his passage, shatteringly loud. Some instinct made Rule spin to see if—oh, shit, yes. He jumped again, getting out of the way. The behemoth was toppling.

A ton or so of monster hit the stone with a sullen thud. And didn't move.

Rule wiped blood and sweat from his face, looking around. Everyone was unhurt except Carlos, who was farther back in the tunnel. And, of course, Daniel, who had been injured in the first big fight and unable to keep up. They'd left him guarding the bikes. "Cullen. Check on Carlos, back down the tunnel. Jude, go with him. Mason, stand watch. Max—"

"I'm okay," wheezed his friend—but he didn't move from the spot where he'd fallen when the giant finally let go.

"Hang on," Rule told him. "I'll help in a minute. I want to be sure the son of a bitch is really dead this time."

They'd first encountered the enormous demon aboveground, but one of the grenades had seemed to lay waste to it. They hadn't taken time to check. In retrospect that looked like a mistake, but an understandable one. Most creatures didn't survive having some of their brains spill out of a broken skull.

This one had apparently only been stunned. It must have followed them down into the tunnel, catching up while they were distracted by a dozen smaller demons. In killing them—crablike things with nasty pincers—Rule's party had gotten split up. Rule had ended up on a ledge because it gave him a good range of fire. Jude, Mason, and Cullen had pursued some of the demons into an intersecting tunnel. Carlos had taken a deep wound in his leg, and Max had been wrapping it with gauze when the behemoth arrived and grabbed them both.

Rule had remembered what Gan said about demons and the wounded. When the creature started to lift Carlos toward its mouth, he'd acted. He hadn't been in position to shoot—Carlos and Max were in the way—so he'd jumped.

It had worked. That's what counted.

"Carlos will be okay," Cullen called. "Got knocked silly, but he's come around. I'm finishing with his leg now, and he could use some food to help with the healing drain."

"Feed him, then. Max?"

"Dislocated shoulder. If someone would pop it back in the socket, I'd be fine. Tell me that thing is dead."

"There's no pulse and not enough left of the head to

mention. Unless it carried its brains somewhere else . . ."
Rule bent to examine the remaining pulped bits of skull.

STEADY.

The voice was clear, intimate, and impossibly lovely.
Unmistakable. Awe froze Rule in place . . .

The mate bond snapped.

His vision blackened. He lost track of the world and his
place in it—lost track even of his body in the shock of that
loss.

Then the bond was back. Lily was back. Belowground
like him, only deeper, and *that* way . . .

"Rule!" Mason's voice, urgent. "Rule, what happened?"

"Stay on watch," he managed to croak, utterly unable to
answer the question. What the hell *had* happened? Other
than him toppling over onto his side, that is. He pushed
himself upright, then continued to his feet and found that
he *was* steady. Just as the Lady had commanded.

"Rule?" That was Cullen's voice, worried.

He looked over his shoulder. Cullen was helping Carlos
limp toward them. "I'm fine. Max needs his shoulder put
back in place."

"I'm glad you're fine. You're also blazing away like a nova."

"What?"

"Power." Cullen released Carlos with a pat on his arm
and came up to Rule. "You've suddenly got about twice
your usual load of magic."

He was oddly reluctant to speak of the experience, but
this was his friend. His closest friend. Rule lowered his
voice. "The mate bond snapped. Then it came back. Lily's
okay, but just before that—"

"Trouble," Mason called. And underlined his warning
with a burst of fire from his weapon.

WHEN Benedict had called the ledge crap, he hadn't been
kidding. Even at its widest Lily had to move sideways. Maybe

it was Benedict's solid, reassuring presence that left her feeling . . . not fearless, for she was supremely conscious of the emptiness at her back and the creature which lurked below. But capable. She could do this. Slow and careful, that was the thing, and when the ledge narrowed so much her feet didn't fully fit on it anymore, Benedict guided her hand to first one grip, then another. With those to balance her, she was able to creep along the worst spot on the balls of her feet.

Then—hallelujah!—it widened again, and she breathed more deeply as she sidled around a curve in the wall with the dark exit looming only a few feet away . . .

STEADY.

The voice was calm, clear, as implacable as it was beautiful. And familiar. Lily froze under the sheer immediacy of that voice.

And lost Rule.

And cried out—

Then he was *back*, the mate bond telling her as surely as ever that he was right *there*—alive! He was alive!—but that second of loss had loosened her grip on the world and her knees. She'd folded and was in the process of falling off the damn ledge when a sure, strong arm slid around her waist and hoisted her the rest of the way off. And flung her through the air.

She landed badly, with her legs sticking out over the air, but a hand—Cynna's hand—closed around her arm and helped her scramble the rest of the way to safety. Cynna released her. She realized her weapon wasn't on her shoulder. She patted around in alarm, hoping against hope it had slid off her shoulder when she landed, not while she was in flight.

"Oh, no!" Gan cried. "The big man—"

Light blazed, dazzling bright. And she saw Benedict still on the ledge—with a huge, corpse-colored tentacle wrapped around one leg. His machete flashed, but the angle was bad.

Blood dripped from a slash in the creature's putrid skin, reddish-purple blood, which was a surprise. All the demon blood she'd seen before had been as red as her own. But the tentacle remained wrapped around his leg.

"Hell, no, you don't!" Cynna cried out. She flung both hands in front of her and began chanting words that tumbled through Lily's mind without registering.

Now that she could *see*, it was easy to spot her weapon, right by the edge. She reached for it as the liquid in the pit began to bubble in a slow seethe. A second tentacle slid up from below the surface of the acid pool and reached for Benedict.

Already lying down, Lily shifted just enough to bring her weapon to her shoulder and fired, stitching a careful line across the second tentacle. Purple blood flew everywhere, along with gobbets of pallid flesh as the bullets cut the damn thing in bloody pieces.

Yet another tentacle shot up out of liquid that was now boiling madly, emitting fumes that burned Lily's eyes and nose. And another—but the one gripping Benedict went slack. Then the others did, too. A moment later, a pale, enormous body floated to the surface, bobbing in the bubbling liquid.

A tiger roared.

"Back up!" Lily rolled quickly, getting out of the way. A second later a tawny, black-striped body sailed seventeen feet over the frothing liquid to land with graceful ease on their side.

"Good shooting," a deep voice announced.

Lily sat up, blinking eyes watering from the fumes. Benedict didn't look any worse for wear, and *he* hadn't lost his weapon. Any of his weapons. He stood on the other side of Grandmother. "What happened?"

She swallowed. "The mate bond. It—it was gone. Then it came back. Rule's alive, but I thought . . ." Only she hadn't, not really. No thought could form in the vastness of that loss.

Benedict frowned. "That doesn't make sense."

"No." She should tell him about the voice. She knew she should, but somehow she couldn't. Or didn't. Wasn't supposed to? She shook her head and got to her feet, hitching her weapon on her shoulder. She was shaky. That was probably just the adrenaline, but her eyes were watering and her nose and throat burned. "I think we're breathing in acid vapor."

"Probably." Benedict looked at Cynna. "What did you do?"

"Heat," Cynna said, her voice hoarse. "I can't call fire the way Cullen does, but I've been practicing with heat. Easier for me."

"Is it going to keep boiling long?"

Cynna shrugged. "I was mad and in a hurry. I shoved in a lot of heat."

He gave the bubbling pool and its dead occupant a level glance. "Glad you hurried. Let's go. No need for silence. They know we're here. Same order."

"It may be icy," Cynna warned.

Benedict's eyebrows lifted.

"I had to get the heat from somewhere, didn't I? Benedict, I need a moment. I need to recast my Finds."

Benedict paused, then nodded. He turned to Lily. "Where's Rule?"

"That way." She pointed ahead and up. "About half a mile away in straight-ahead distance. God knows how far that would mean traveling these tunnels."

"Can you tell where—"

"I can't get to them!" Cynna's face twisted.

"Too much rock?" Lily asked.

"That's not it. I can Find Cullen even though there's a lot of rock between us."

Of course she could. Lily had forgotten that Cynna did

have a way of knowing if Cullen was alive. She felt foolish and relieved.

"But I can't Find either of the children. I've got Ryder's birth name, dammit, I've got the power, but . . . I think it's a ward. A strong enough ward could block a Find. I could get through eventually, but—"

"We don't have time," Benedict said. "We go now. Same order."

The temperature dropped about ten degrees when they stepped into the corridor that led from the pit demon's lair. It continued to drop as they advanced until there was ice in spots. The floor here was different than what they'd seen, being both level and made from a gritty, reddish rock. The walls and ceiling were still curved like a lava tube, but the black rock was slick enough to reflect the pale glow from the mage lights. This corridor was clearly fashioned, not just appropriated. Someone had made aesthetic choices.

According to Rule's map, this corridor should run straight to the room where the children were being held. They would not, of course, stay on it.

"Anything?" Benedict asked.

"No. Cullen could just look. Dammit, I need modifiers." Cynna was using her Gift to try to locate a secret door, but the pattern for "door" alone didn't seem to be sufficient. She'd said that there were so many spots that fit the door pattern, her Finds went to fuzz, trying to locate all of them at once. She needed something specific to that particular door to modify her search.

"It all looks the same," Gan said doubtfully. "Old Mevroax found it by looking for the dull spot, but everything's the same shiny."

Grandmother made a coughing noise. Lily turned. The tiger was sitting next to the wall about ten paces back, the tip of her tail twitching. "Grandmother? Did you find it?"

A regal inclination of her head.

Cynna started toward her. "It's spell-locked. I'll get it undone. It may take a while, but—"

The tiger leaned forward and coughed on the wall. A portion of it vanished.

"Or you can do it," Cynna finished.

TWENTY-FIVE

~~

THE secret door thought it was a window. At least that's what Cynna muttered as they entered the tunnel it revealed. She added that she could have located it if Gan had told her to Find a window instead of a door, even if it was still only one of many.

Lily learned that she—and possibly Grandmother—were the only ones who'd seen the window portion of the wall vanish. Everyone else still saw rock, which must have made stepping through the window unnerving. "I thought Xitil wasn't good at illusions," she said, looking at Gan.

"Maybe she got an elf to do it."

"Elves hate demons."

"Yeah, but they fall through sometimes, and then they really want to go home, so one of them might've made a deal with Xitil. Make her some illusions and the elf could go home."

"Falling through means accidentally crossing to another realm?"

Gan nodded. "The palace and the area around it is full of cracks."

"Cracks?" Cynna repeated.

"Places where it's easy to fall through. It's the twin nodes. They do something that makes cracks. There's lots of them here. Some of those realms you do not want to fall into. There's this one . . ." She shuddered. "I don't want to go there again."

"Keep it down," Benedict said. "If you have something to tell us, whisper."

Belowground windows didn't look out on gardens, of course. They looked into chambers in the rock. According to Gan, Xitil's former councillor had regularly used this tunnel to spy on her courtiers via those magical windows, which opened into various chambers . . . including the one where the children were held. In Xitil's time, it had been called the small audience hall. The main one had been destroyed when the mountain blew up.

This tunnel was much more cramped than the others they'd been in. Lily could walk upright, but Cynna and Benedict had to duck at first. Lily thought of Rule's claustrophobia and hoped Benedict didn't share it. At least they could use mage lights freely. They didn't have to be quite as carefully silent, either; small sounds would be buffered by the thick stone and, as they neared their goal, might not be a problem at all. The small audience hall used to be sound-proofed by a spell. Whether that spell still worked, they didn't know.

Getting there was the trick. Rule had described the tunnel as twisty; they soon discovered how accurate that was. Within thirty feet it had gone up, down, left, left again, down, right . . . it made like cooked spaghetti for all it was worth. Lily was thoroughly lost by the time Benedict signaled a stop and beckoned Gan.

The little former demon came forward and Benedict

rumbled in a low voice, "I'm having trouble matching this to Rule's depiction. You're going to be able to spot the place where the window into the audience hall is?"

"Sure," Gan whispered. "Or anyway, I can spot the windows. They're marked."

"Marked how?"

"Like that one." Gan pointed at a bit of rock that looked exactly like every other bit of rock.

"I don't see anything."

"It's right there, that bright dot of *urti*."

"What's *urti*?"

"I don't know the English word for . . . oh, that's right. Humans don't see *urti*. I guess lupi don't, either. It's the color your body glows in the dark."

Sounded like Gan was talking about infrared. Lily whispered, "Do all demons see *urti*?"

"In Xitil's territory they do. Xitil's bugs see *urti* and everyone eats the bugs, so even if you didn't grow up here, you end up seeing it, too. Not enough time has passed for that to change."

Benedict had Gan lead them after that. Gan didn't argue, which surprised Lily. The little one must feel pretty safe in this tunnel, cramped and twisty thing that it was. As they continued, the ceiling height varied. In a couple spots Benedict had to bend nearly double, and at one point everyone but Gan proceeded on hands and knees. The tight spaces didn't bother her. Being unable to mindspeak Rule did. She wanted, needed, to check on him, ask if he was injured, if anyone else was injured, to . . . just to hear him, really. At one point she was sure from the way he moved that he was fighting. He survived that fight. She knew that much.

It wasn't enough.

They paused three times to check the windows. The first time was to make sure the window spell still worked. "Be really quiet," Gan whispered sternly. "If anyone's in there, they'll hear you once I open the window."

"Why?" Cynna asked.

Gan rolled her eyes. "It's a window. Sound goes through an open window."

"Normally sight does, too."

"Not with this kind of window."

"What about scent?" Benedict asked.

Gan tipped her head. "I don't know. Mevroax never worried about scent, but maybe that's because demons don't smell as good as you do." Gan spoke the activating word and breathed on the wall. A large section of the rock wall vanished . . . leaving them unable to see a thing. The chamber on the other side was completely dark. Gan blew another puff of breath and the wall came back. "Works fine," she said, "but I'm not sure where I am. We'd better check some more windows."

The second chamber was dark, too.

The third chamber wasn't. It was occupied.

Three demons appeared to be humping a huge, pink mass of flesh covered in what looked like small mouths and . . . whoa. Were those what they looked like? Yes. Yes, they were. By the time Gan breathed on the window to close it again, Lily had counted six penises of different sizes poking out of the quivering pink mass.

"What in the hell," Benedict breathed, "was that?"

"A chur-chur. That's like . . . a sex toy? Or maybe you'd call it a sex object. Xitil kept several of them around for guests who weren't all that lethal. If you felt like fucking but it wasn't safe to fuck with anyone nearby, you could go fuck a chur-chur."

"On another subject," Lily said, "I can tell you that I can't sense anyone on the other side of the window when it's closed. When it's open, I can. The rock doesn't seem to be there anymore."

"It's *dashtu*," Gan informed them.

"The spell turns the rock *dashtu*?" Cynna exclaimed softly. "How could . . . that's only supposed to work for living things. And demons can't go *dashtu* in Dis, so how could Dis rock go out of phase that way?"

Gan rolled her eyes. "Xitil was a *prince*. You people don't seem to get what that means. Going *dashtu* someplace else is easy because your body already knows it doesn't belong there, but if you tell it to go *dashtu* here, it doesn't believe you. But a prince can do all kinds of stuff no one else can, plus Xitil was really good at rock and all kinds of Earth magic. One of her names was Earth Mover."

"Good to know," Benedict said. "I can add that smells move through an open window just fine. That chamber reeked. Gan? You know where we are yet?"

"The next window on the right should open on the audience chamber."

They travelled another fifty feet, but wound around so much it was hard to say how much distance they actually covered. Finally Gan stopped at a portion of tunnel that looked like every other part, except for the ceiling, which was a lot higher. Ten feet or so.

Gan whispered, "This is it. Everyone get real quiet before I—"

"Hold off on opening it." Benedict spoke softly and made a gesture that meant quiet. He didn't move for a long moment. "I don't hear anything. Either no one's there, they're all real quiet, or that spell you told us about is still working. You sense anything, Lily?" When she shook her head, he asked, "Where's Rule?"

"Not far," she said, low-voiced. "Less than half a mile. He's level with us, but he's barely moving. I'm guessing they've hit a barrier of some sort."

"Or demons."

"He's not fighting. Fighting is lots of small, quick movements, and he's moving really slowly. Listen, I've been thinking. You're hoping to wait for Rule's party to arrive and draw everyone's attention again before we enter the chamber, right?"

He nodded.

"It would be good for Rule to know we're here and waiting for him."

"No mindspeech." His decree was no less certain for being issued in a soft voice.

"The situation's changed," she said urgently. "I've been thinking about it." Thinking a lot, and arguing with herself about whether to tell Benedict, ask Benedict for permission, or just do it. "I see why a probe could be dangerous. Normally they'd be easier to detect, but right now *she* isn't looking for someone using mind magic. She's too busy keeping everything from blowing up, and even if a tiny bit of her attention isn't on that, it's different when I mindspeak Rule. Almost the same as when I touch someone, because I sort of send my probe along the mate bond. That's of the Lady, so the Great Bitch can't touch it, can't even sense it. I think the bond would keep *her* from sensing my probe, so I can mindspeak him fairly safely."

"Define 'fairly safely.'"

"I can't. I don't know enough about this shit. It's mostly a feeling," she admitted. A feeling that when the mate bond had returned, it came back stronger. As if the Lady had done something to it . . . and why was she so certain she shouldn't speak of that? "But it's a strong feeling."

He considered that briefly. "No. Benefits don't outweigh the risks."

"But—"

"No. How long before Rule's here?"

She struggled to keep her voice even. Benedict was wrong about the benefit-risk ratio. Or she thought he was wrong, but he was in charge and . . . and that was harder to accept than she'd expected. "An hour if he goes this slowly the whole time. That's if his path is fairly straight. If it's not straight, or if he runs or walks briskly or stops to fight demons . . ." She shrugged.

"I get the point. All right. We'll wait before opening the window—"

"We're running out of time," Cynna said tensely.

Benedict's expression didn't change. "We made it here in forty-four minutes. We've got a minimum of an hour and sixteen minutes left."

Lily blinked. Forty-four minutes? It had seemed longer. Much longer.

"That's if Reno's right," Cynna said. "And in that hour and sixteen minutes we have to get the kids and get out. Get to another node."

"We won't reach another node within the minimum safe period no matter what we do now. We do want to be out of the palace by then, if possible. We'll go in without Rule if we have to, but our chance of success is much greater with him and the others."

"Benedict," Lily said, "if Gan opens that window briefly, I can look for the kids. With my mindsense, I mean. We need to know where they are."

"Can you guarantee that you won't alert *her*, if she—her avatar—is in there?"

"Guarantee? No. I'm pretty sure she'd feel it if my sensing did brush against her mind," Lily admitted. "But if she's as distracted as Reno thought she'd be, she probably won't notice. And even if she did, she's already expecting us to come after the kids. I don't think it would make much difference."

"Do you have any reason to believe *she* knows about your mindsense?"

"I don't know." Lily had given that some thought earlier and come up blank. "I don't know what *she* knows, what she guesses."

"I want to keep your ability secret as long as we possibly

can. Anything *she* doesn't know is an advantage for us. No sensing the room yet." He looked at the others. "We're going to take a short break. Everyone should eat and drink. If you need to empty your bladder, do that. Go back around that crook in the tunnel. Even a demon can probably smell fresh urine. Gan, Cynna, I've a question for you."

Lily turned abruptly and, as Benedict asked something about the rock windows, headed for that crook in the tunnel. One of the mage lights went with her, for which she probably had Cynna to thank. Or maybe Grandmother.

Taking orders was easy when she agreed with them. This time she didn't. Not with either one, really, but especially the one about not contacting Rule. That didn't give her the right to ignore the order. But the need to reach out to Rule was so strong . . . which was one reason she'd decided she had to get Benedict's permission, wasn't it? She wanted that contact too much to trust her judgment.

She did what she had to and pulled her jeans up. Her hands were shaking. Her heart pounded hard. Too hard. She was so scared. Rule could die. Now, five minutes from now, in the next thirty minutes. He could die without her being with him. She should be with him, at least mentally. She needed . . .

Lily reminded herself that she was no precog. Just because she could imagine terrible things didn't mean they were going to happen. She didn't know what was going to happen, dammit, and she needed to pull herself together. This wasn't the first time she'd gone into action—into battle—and she knew better than to let fear take the lead.

No, taking the lead was Benedict's role, wasn't it?

She zipped up and headed back. She'd accepted having Benedict in charge of their party because it was clearly the right thing to do. He was incredibly good at this. Better than her. But if she'd been in charge, she'd have *had* to be calm instead of feeling like she was a couple breaths away from a panic attack.

Which Benedict undoubtedly knew. He must have been smelling the fear on her for a while now.

Gan was trotting toward her. "Hi, Lily Yu! You finished pissing? Come with me!"

She hesitated, but turned and went with Gan. She could keep watch.

"This is one human custom I like," Gan said as she undid her pants. "Though I do miss having a cock. It's easier to piss when you can aim it."

"I've often thought it would be," Lily responded solemnly. "What custom do you mean?"

"The one where the girls all go to the bathroom together. Gnomes don't do that. I told them they ought to, but gnomes don't like to try new things, plus they like to pretend they don't piss or shit. Isn't that funny? Humans pretend that, too, but they don't work at it as hard as gnomes do. Sometimes at a Council meeting I like to fart just to see if any of them . . ."

Gan chattered on. Lily half listened, half smiled, and tried to think her way past her fear. Gan didn't seem to be scared. Not for herself—probably because she could zip off into another realm if she did get scared—but not for the rest of them, either. Yet Lily knew she mattered to Gan. So did Cynna. She thought that Cullen and Rule did, too. Did it not occur to her they could die? Or was a former demon simply better at setting fear aside than Lily was?

". . . should have seen his face turn red! It was lots funnier than hitting him would have been, but I think he hates me more now than he would have if I'd just gone ahead and hit him. Does that mean I won?"

"Hmm." Lily dragged her attention back to what Gan had been saying . . . something about a prank she'd played on one of the Edge councillors. "I guess that depends on what your goal was. If you wanted to make him look stupid, you won. If you wanted to ever work with him again, you lost, Gan." She knelt so she could look Gan in the eye. "I haven't thanked you for coming. It means a lot to me that you did. Thank you."

A big smile lit that ugly-cute face. "I'm a good friend!"

"You are an excellent friend. A wonderful friend." Lily hugged her. Gan's body was warmer than hers and smaller and much tougher, though the last quality didn't show. "I've been wanting to ask about the medallion." One of the most potent artifacts ever made in any of the realms, the medallion worn by the Chancellor of Edge kept the small, odd realm inhabitable. "I don't see it. Did you bring it with you?"

"Of course! I couldn't take it off. That would be bad. Really bad. Oh. You're wondering about what happens to Edge when I'm not there? Don't worry. I can't take it off, but also it can't leave Edge, so even though I'm wearing it, it's still in Edge."

She blinked. "I don't understand."

"Me, neither. I didn't know it would be like this until I came to your wedding. After a while I realized that it was on me, but it was also back in Edge. Weird, huh? I really liked your wedding. I want to have one, too, except I don't want to be married. I haven't figured out how to have a wedding without being married."

Lily's lips twitched. "Maybe an open marriage?"

"Where you still get to fuck other people?" Gan considered that. "Maybe, but I'd still have to pick someone I wanted to hang out with. If you're married, you have to hang out together. I like girls better for hanging out, but I like guys better for sex because of their cocks, even though they don't have enough breasts. I like breasts, especially big ones. If I could find a hermaphrodite . . . but Edge doesn't seem to have any." She frowned in disapproval.

"It's a dilemma." Lily stood. "We'd better get back." Even though she didn't want to. Going back took her that much closer to the moment when . . . when what? She didn't know.

Gan wasn't scared, but Lily was scared for her and for everyone else . . . and those fears were small and insignificant compared to the terror that kept threatening to swamp her about Rule. Why? Why was this time different? She'd feared for him before. She'd never let it stop her. Dammit, just because she wasn't in charge didn't mean she had the luxury of indulging in terror. Every one of the people with her needed her to be focused, at her best. Toby needed that. Ryder did. So did two other kids and a baby even smaller than Ryder.

She was so damn scared.

When they returned, Grandmother was lapping water from a depression in the rock. Cynna gave Lily a nod and headed for the improvised latrine. And Benedict was as implacably calm as ever. "Here," he said, and handed her a piece of jerky.

Dutifully she took it, clamped her teeth on the tough strip of dried meat, and tore off a bite.

"It's not your fault, you know."

Her mouth full of jerky, she could only frown at him.

He bent his head toward hers and spoke in the softest possible voice. "You lost the mate bond. It came back, but the loss was real. I know what that's like. If a guy's heart stopped and it took them a few minutes to get it started again, he'd be alive—but he still would've been dead for a time. That would affect him. Your loss is affecting you."

Everything she'd been trying not to think, to feel, rushed in on her. The jerky in her mouth turned into a wad impossible to swallow. She closed her eyes. She thought about spitting out the jerky. About crying. Wailing. About how hard she'd been not-thinking about those brief, endless moments of loss even as she tried desperately to come up with a reason to contact Rule, to hear his voice in her mind and . . . after a moment she began grimly chewing. Eventually she managed to swallow the horrible mass in her mouth and open her eyes again. "What do I do about it?"

"No idea. But you'll do okay." He patted her shoulder. "You might feel like shit, but you'll do what's needed. And I need to go piss." He gave her a nod. "You're my second. You've got it while I'm gone."

TWENTY-SIX

~~

IT took Rule and Mason together to move the last boulder. They could have used another set of hands, but there wasn't room. Sweat ran down Rule's back and chest, stinging fiercely where it hit unhealed gouges. They didn't have to move it far, thank the Lady and all the gods. Another couple inches . . . and done. Rule inhaled deeply, wiped his forehead, and slipped sideways through the opening they'd made.

The tunnel ahead was empty. Of life anyway. There were plenty of rocks, debris from the fallen ceiling, but nothing they couldn't clamber over easily. "Hydrate," Rule said, and unsnapped his canteen. "Drink it all."

Only five of them now: him, Cullen, Max, Jude, and Mason. They'd left Carlos behind a couple tunnels back.

Carlos's leg hadn't finished healing from the wound dealt by the crablike demons when they were attacked again. His head might have still been bothering him, too, though he'd insisted he was fine. Whatever the reason, he'd been slow to react when the spider-things dropped on them from a crack in the ceiling. By the time the rest of them had killed the nasty creatures, he'd taken too many bites. Jude and Cullen had been bitten, too, but only once apiece. They'd both been sick and dizzy for several minutes. Carlos had been comatose.

They couldn't take him with them. They were already too few. Nor could Rule leave him there, unconscious and probably dying, to make an easy meal for any demons who happened by. He'd steeled himself to do what he must, and had already drawn his knife when Carlos stirred.

Rule had gotten him to drink some water, and his wits had returned enough to make the decision himself: a quick death at Rule's hands or the gift of Max's last grenade. Worst case, Rule had told him, was that he'd pass out again and get swarmed by demons before he could use either his gun or the grenade. A bad way to die, that. Best case, though, he wouldn't need the grenade. He'd recover enough to make it out of the tunnels and back to where Daniel waited by the bikes.

To Rule's relief, he'd chosen the grenade.

Carlos was still so weak when they left that he could barely sit up, even leaning against the tunnel wall. Rule doubted he could use his weapon, which was why he'd given him the grenade. Even a sick man could pull out the pin. But Carlos's healing was slowly clearing out the venom. They didn't know how long that would take, but if the demons left Carlos alone long enough, his healing would clear the venom from his system. Making it back to the bikes—where Daniel might or might not still be alive— might be a long shot, but he had a chance.

Rule hooked his empty canteen back on his belt. If they lived, there was more water back at the bikes. Their jerky was gone, unfortunately. They were hungry. Healing burned calories like crazy, and they'd all been injured at some point. More than once, for most of them. Rule's side still oozed from the deepest gouge the last batch of nasties had inflicted. "Jude. How's the arm?"

"Not usable yet, but the bleeding's stopped."

"Good. Everyone, how much ammo do you have?"

As they checked and reported, he consulted his inner map again. It had proved accurate. Even the blockage they'd just finished digging through had been marked. Unfortunately, Rule hadn't been able to decipher the marking until they saw the rocks blocking them.

Automatically he checked on Lily's location, too. Close now . . . and jerked his mind away. He couldn't think about her. Couldn't let himself wonder about her. He was too frightened for her. Too easily distracted by his need to see her, touch her, hear her voice . . . "All right," he said, his voice as crisp as ever. He was good at sounding competent, no matter how he felt. "We're close. Ten minutes away or less, if we don't encounter more opposition. Cullen, is there anything you need to do to get your bomb ready?"

"Not until I'm about to throw it."

"All right. Max, we'll probably need your skills to get through the door, if it's intact. There were fifty-nine demons in that room when Sam mapped it. That's too many. Let's keep Cullen in one piece so he can set off that bomb of his." In an enclosed space it would have a blast radius of about a hundred feet. It might not kill every demon in that radius, but it should reduce the odds against them substantially.

If it worked. "Same order, but at a lope now," he ordered. "Let's go."

ALL of the windows they'd checked had been roughly four feet wide. None of them started right at the floor; there was a "sill" of about a foot that you had to step over, and a second sill a foot down from the ceiling. But the ceiling height varied a lot in this tunnel, so the height of the windows varied.

This window was nearly nine feet high. On the other side of the barrier that was no barrier at all were red-eyes. Four of them, backed up to what they thought was a solid wall, blocking her view. Red-eyes were built like huge hyenas with a touch of centaur, except a lot uglier. Their skin was thick, rubbery, and varied from black to a tawny gray. They were hard to kill, and some of them carried a particularly nasty venom. Lily couldn't see the faces of these four, but she had a great view of their butts. Demons didn't use toilet paper.

Beyond them was the small audience hall, which wasn't small at all—probably ninety feet long, according to Gan, and shaped like an L, with the short leg of the L at the far end of the room. Lily couldn't see that portion, and not much of the long part of the L directly in front of her, either. The damn red-eyes blocked her view. She saw one of the pillars Gan had mentioned—black and carved into a fantastical, vaguely obscene shape. She caught glimpses of another type of demon moving around the room. These were about eight feet tall and bipedal. Red or pink skin. Too many eyes. Huge claws at the end of four of their limbs, and a slicing weapon on the end of their muscular tails.

Lily had part of that description from Gan, who called them Claws. She'd shivered when she spoke of them. They'd been some of the deadliest of Xitil's foot soldiers.

There was a buzz of conversation in the room, or Lily supposed it was conversation. Noise anyway. One of the red-eyes growled something. None of the four moved.

The window closed. The wall was a wall again.

Lily let out her breath. "I guess the rest of you understood what it said?" The rules were supposed to translate, but the rules used magic. Lily had just heard growls and squeals and mutters.

"It was complaining about the food," Gan said.

"Why did those bastards have to pick this wall to hang out at? They don't know about the window or they wouldn't keep their backs to it." Three times now they'd opened the window for a few seconds, taking quick peeks because they didn't want to risk some small sound or scent alerting the demons standing so close. Every time the damn red-eyes had been there, blocking their view.

"Luck of the draw," Benedict said. "Cynna?"

She shook her head, every inch of her taut. "Nothing. It doesn't matter if the window's open or shut, my Finds don't work. That has to be one hell of a strong ward around the kids."

Benedict nodded. "Wards can be set with fire, can't they?"

"Sure. If you're fire-Gifted, it's the quickest way. Not so quick for others, but possible if your Gift isn't unfriendly to Fire. Why?"

"Pretty sure I glimpsed flame near the center of the room this time."

Lily frowned. She hadn't seen that, but her attention was divided. Part of it stayed with Rule. That was orders, not self-indulgence. "Will we have to take the ward down to get to the kids? Can you do that, Cynna?"

"Probably not. Not safely, at least. Best if we leave that to Cullen. I'm thinking—"

Grandmother butted Lily, who sent a quick probe . . . "Grandmother says she's good with wards."

"All right," Cynna said curtly. "Madame Yu or Cullen can deal with the ward. Benedict, there are a hell of a lot of demons in that room. Maybe that's because this is supposed to be a trap, so our enemies gathered some of the toughest demons in one spot to kill us when we show up. But maybe it also means that Ginger's there. She'd want her avatar protected, wouldn't she? By a shitload of demons and by that ward."

"Good point. Not proven, but possible. Timing, Lily?"

"Rule's still not moving." He'd moved quickly for a while, then stopped. Hiding maybe? Avoiding a patrol? Not injured. She had no reason to think he was badly injured, unable to move. "If Ginger is there, do we have an obligation to try to take her out? It wouldn't kill the Great Bitch, but it would damn sure—oh, wait. Shit, that was stupid. The last thing we want to do is kill Ginger Harris. Ka-boom."

Benedict was silent a moment. "Gunfire was problematical anyway until we located the children, but we'd better locate Ginger Harris as well before opening fire. Or determine that she isn't present. If we—"

"Rule's running again," Lily said suddenly. "Fast. He'll be at the entry in a couple minutes at this pace."

"Form up," Benedict said crisply.

LILY waited, barely breathing. Benedict stood up front with Grandmother, who'd opened the window with a puff of breath. Those two were by far the best suited to clear a path—and to survive doing it. Lily stood right behind Grandmother; Cynna was beside her. Gan sat on a narrow ledge several feet away, looking unhappy. She wouldn't be going in with them.

Lily's shortest, orangest friend wasn't upset at being left out. She had no intention of charging into a room full of Claws and *khahlikka*—her word for the demons Lily called red-eyes. But it had finally occurred to her that her friends might be killed. She didn't like the idea.

The red-eyes were exactly where they had been the last time they checked. If they'd moved at all, she couldn't tell. The others, the Claws, continued to move around the room. Lily still couldn't see the fire Benedict had glimpsed, but surely it was there, hidden by the way-too-fucking-many demons, and the children were behind it.

Lily didn't believe in God, but she didn't exactly disbelieve, either. Mostly she tried not to think about it. Life after death was real. She knew that much, having died once. Some kind of Deity might exist, too, however unlikely it seemed. With every carefully silent breath she prayed to Whoever or Whatever might be out there that the children were here and okay—and that Cullen's demon bomb worked.

Couldn't hurt. Might help.

The explosion wasn't all that loud as explosions go. Not much louder than the whomp that followed. Something large, hard, and heavy had hit the floor on the other side of the room.

All four red-eyes took off at a run. They were as fast as Lily remembered. Every other demon in the place seemed to have the same idea, to get to the place where the noise had come from.

Benedict didn't move. Didn't let them move. Lily did not have a great view of what happened next, but she caught a glimpse of a single figure sailing through the air over the heads of the charging demons. A flash of memory: Cullen sailing through the air just like that, hurled there during one of the battle dances the lupi practiced over and over. At the crest of his flight, he threw something—then fell right into the massed demons below.

Red light flashed, blanketing the chamber for an instant. Demons began collapsing.

Benedict charged out into the room. Grandmother followed in a sinuous orange-and-black leap. Then Cynna and Lily.

She had a confused impression of bodies, demon bodies, everywhere. And magic. Her face tingled with the constant brush of sorcéri. The bodies were thickest on the other side of the room, where Cullen had gone down. Benedict and Grandmother raced that way—and yes, there was a circle of fire, higher than her head, in the middle of the room, centered on one of the black pillars. And Rule. She saw him just inside the huge, arched entry on that side of the room, his shirt bloody and tattered. And Jude and Mason and Max. And two red-eyes racing toward them.

Movement at the edge of her peripheral vision. She spun, weapon ready. A very-much-alive Claw raced toward her. She squeezed the trigger.

It took an ungodly amount of time for the thing to stop. It—he—didn't collapse until he was nearly on top of her. She jumped to one side to avoid his toppling body.

"Jude, we've got it," Rule called out. "Go to Cullen."

Which was just stupid—two lupi and a half-gnome weren't enough to kill a pair of red-eyes, not when they were in man-form and couldn't shoot because of the children—but someone should see about Cullen, who must be buried beneath the largest pile of dead demons.

Grandmother had stopped at the fire circle. She wasn't doing anything visible, just staring at it. Benedict hadn't made it that far, being stopped by an enormous Claw, easily nine feet tall, who stood between him and the burning ward. As she watched, Benedict danced away from a slash from one of the creature's long arms and drew his machete. He and the blade looked small next to that Claw.

Where was Cynna? She didn't see—oh, there she was, running past the fire circle. Headed for the pile of demon bodies? Yes, looking for Cullen, Lily realized, as Cynna started tugging one of the bodies off. As she did, a Claw rose out of that unholy pile, shook its head as if dazed, saw Cynna, and grinned. Jude was approaching at a run, but one of his arms was in a sling.

Lily called a warning and sprinted to her left to get an angle she could shoot from.

The lights went out. Mage lights and fire-ward both. Cynna called out a string of syllables Lily had heard before. Someone else cried out, but that word wasn't familiar.

Lily tripped over a demon body and went down. She rolled, coming up in a crouch, her assault rifle still clutched in her arms, straining to hear anything approaching . . . *not your ears, dummy*, she told herself, and unfurled her mind-sense, sending it out as a mist.

Benedict wanted to keep her ability a secret, but the element of surprise wouldn't do them much good if she was dead. As long as she kept it away from the center of the room . . .

No minds close, but two over there, faint but slick, obviously demons . . . and there and there and oh shit. A lot of the demons who looked dead weren't. Some of the minds she found were dim, almost extinguished. A few flickered and might yet go out. But they weren't dead yet. She sent her mist along the wall to her left—or where she thought the wall was—and stopped, staring. What was that?

A faint iridescence stretched from floor to what was probably ceiling. It was barely discernible, more like the wan memory of light than an actual glow. Phosphorescence, like in the pit demon's lair? No, there was a hint of movement, like gossamer veils shifting in the breeze. The magical construct? Could that be it? It's dragon-induced instability might have made it visible to ordinary vision. But it wasn't much more than a foot wide. Reno couldn't have flown through—

"Freeze." The voice was loud and incongruously bored. "Everyone. Or I slit his throat."

Three mage lights popped into being above the spot that had been circled by fire, illuminating three people, a black pillar, and a demon: Tom Weng, Ginger Harris, a looming Claw . . . and Toby.

Weng was looking extremely Chinese, if a touch anachronistic. He wore a scarlet silk *shenyi*, the long wraparound robe with enormous sleeves favored by the nobility of various Han dynasties, heavily embroidered and trimmed in black. Ginger Harris, too, wore a *shenyi*. Hers was spotlessly white, practically glowing in its purity. She sat on the floor, her eyes open and unseeing. The Claw was naked. He stood at Weng's back, towering over him. Toby wore the same blue pajamas he'd gone to bed in two nights ago. They were still too short and much dirtier than they had been.

The knife Weng held to Toby's throat looked quite modern.

"I'd rather not kill him," Weng went on. He had an armlock on Toby. Weng was not a tall man and Toby had been growing a lot lately. The top of Toby's head was right at Weng's chin. "I went to a great deal of trouble to acquire him. But I will if necessary. Put down your weapons."

Rule stood frozen twenty feet from Weng and Toby. How

had he managed to get that far in pitch blackness without making a sound? Behind him, Mason, Max, and the two red-eyes all stood motionless. Jude had almost reached Cynna, but he'd stopped as ordered. The Claw who'd been about to attack her was nowhere in sight—downed, maybe by the spell Lily had heard Cynna calling out. The Claw at Benedict's feet wasn't moving, either, but that was probably because its head was half-severed from its neck. Grandmother, the closest to Weng, crouched low, motionless but for the tip of her tail. It twitched.

"Weapons," Weng repeated, and did something with Toby's arm. Toby yelped.

Slowly Lily set her M4 on the floor. She scanned the rest of the room quickly. Still no sign of Cullen . . . or, she realized, of Daniel. Or Carlos. An icy stab of fear made her stiffen. Killed?

"What are you?" Weng said, looking at Grandmother. "I suppose you can't answer. Not a tiger, however. Or not merely a tiger. I require all of you lupi and humans to sit down. The tiger creature should lie down on its side. Do I need to specify what I will do to the boy if—ah, I see that I don't," he said as, one by one, they complied. "Lily Yu." He turned his head to smile at her. "How interesting to meet you here."

Toby stood so still, staring straight ahead, eyes wide with fear. Lily fought to keep emotion out of her voice. "But not surprising, surely."

"Oh, but I didn't think you'd come. None of the children is yours, after all, and you do not have happy memories of this realm. My associate was convinced you would, however. She's quite pleased about it."

"Do you mean Ginger Harris?" Who looked as motionless and unaware as a statue. Lily couldn't tell if she was breathing.

"More or less. By the way, what did you do to destabilize

the nodes? She will not be in a good mood when she finishes tidying up the mess you made."

He didn't know about Reno. "I didn't do it."

"Who did?"

Cynna broke in. "Where's my daughter?"

"Are you Cynna?" Weng asked. "Silly me. Of course you are. She's with the other children, Cynna. Were you aware there are cells next to this audience hall? I believe the previous ruler liked having them nearby so she could amuse herself with her prisoners from time to time."

Lily frowned. He hadn't said Ryder was in those cells. He'd implied it, but he hadn't said so. "Why are your demons standing around so peacefully? Those of them who survived, that is."

"Because I told them to. Whose idea was that little bomb? Yours, Cynna?" He turned a nasty version of the smile on her. "You dabble in demonology, I believe. It has inconvenienced me considerably, that bomb."

"You're just trying to cheer me up," Cynna said.

Would a dragon spawn avoid speaking an outright lie? The sidhe did, Lily knew. They'd twist themselves in knots to avoid lying. It had something to do with the way their magic worked. Did dragons—or their offspring—have to avoid lies as well, or was she reading way too much into his phrasing?

"What's wrong with my son?" Rule demanded.

"I'm keeping the boy quiet so he doesn't startle me. None of you want to startle me, do you? Stay very calm and quiet while I have a little chat with Lily." He turned that smile on her again. "Stand up, Lily."

She did, feeling the worst sort of conspicuous.

"Come to me."

"Why would I do that?"

"Because I'll release the boy once I have you."

"And why would you do that?"

He just smiled and did something again with the hand
she couldn't see. Toby yelped in pain, just like before.

Exactly like before, in fact. And he still didn't look at her.
He hadn't once looked at his father. That wasn't right. Lily
took a deep breath and a slow step forward and disregarded
orders again. She nudged her mind-mist toward Weng,
keeping it away from the motionless Ginger.

"What is that tiger creature?" he asked. "Keep moving,
Lily, and answer me truthfully. If I don't believe you, I
might decide to cut off some small portion of the boy."

Lily took another step and offered him the smallest truth
she thought he'd accept. He had the Sight, so he'd see
Grandmother's magic. "A shape changer."

"Oh?" He studied Grandmother a moment. "I believe you
spoke the truth. How interesting. Shape changers are rare.
Now tell me who destabilized the nodes and how he or she
did it."

"Cullen Seabourne. I think your demons killed him."

"And how did he do it?"

"I don't know." Weng wasn't there. Not to her mindsense.
And Toby . . . what the hell? Her slow advance paused.
Quickly she formed the smallest, thinnest probe she could
manage. She had to know . . . "You'll let Toby go in exchange
for me?"

"I have said the boy will be freed once you are in my
hands. Keep moving."

"Just one problem."

"Oh?"

"That isn't Toby." She drew her Glock and fired, double-
tapping the huge Claw.

Toby melted, splashing at Wang's feet.

Doppelgänger. Just as she'd thought. Quickly Lily aimed
at Weng's head and fired again.

The bullets fucking *bounced*. She knew that because
one ricochet zipped right past her, sounding like an angry
wasp. The flame-ward had shot up again.

She spun and sprinted for her weapon. Dammit, she'd been almost sure the fake Toby was a doppelgänger. Not sure enough to risk trying for Weng first, though, not with the fake Toby's head so close to his—but she should have. Should've trusted what her mindsense told her instead of her eyes. There'd been a blank spot where Toby stood, plus a thin cable of mind-stuff connecting the simulacrum to the tall Claw, who must have been operating it.

Behind her, a tiger roared.

So did Rule.

Weng's voice boomed out, amplified somehow: "Take Lily Yu alive. Also the tiger. Kill the rest."

The tiger? What the hell?

Lily skidded to a stop, swiped her M4 off the floor, and tried to pay attention to what her mind-mist told her, but noticing it took effort when her other senses were flooded with urgent information. Like Cynna chanting loudly and Rule's shouted command to *get to Lily!* and the goddamn tail that shot out of nowhere, aimed at her gut.

She dropped, rolled, and fired while lying on her back at the big Claw that was almost upon her. She hit it, too, in the head, even though she hadn't gotten the M4 seated against her shoulder, so it bucked like an angry bull, the muzzle climbing so badly that the last of her round killed the ceiling.

But the Claw's mind flickered and went out. One down. "They're not all dead!" she shouted, ejecting the spent clip and grabbing a new one. Shit, not that many left. She switched from full-auto to burst to conserve ammo. "A bunch of the ones who look dead aren't!" She shoved to her feet, looking with both eyes and with mindsense, and realized she'd been late with that announcement. A goddamn swarm of demons erupted from the short part of the L-shaped room. Others were rising from where they'd lain.

Like the three red-eyes headed her way.

The tiger leaped on one. Benedict took on another, his machete flashing.

Lily started to aim at the third, but it was between her and the fire. Her bullets would bounce off and the ricochets might hit Grandmother or Benedict. It took two precious seconds to shift to her right and fire.

Hit him, too, but in the chest, which was not enough to discourage him. He kept coming, and those red-eyes were *fast*. She tried to leap aside, but too late. The red-eye piled into her. She landed hard, with the demon on top and—

Grandmother landed on the red-eye's back. A few hundred pounds of tiger and demon pressed the air out of Lily's lungs. That lasted long enough for black to flicker at the edges of her vision, long enough to scare the shit out of her. Then the weight was gone and she was dragging air into her lungs. Shakily she sat, then pushed to her feet.

Grandmother was more red than orange. Red and wet. These demons bled crimson, unlike the pit demon. The demon beside her lacked a head. Lily wasn't sure where it was. "Thanks." Her voice was hoarse and almost as shaky as she felt.

"Lily!" Rule yelled, his voice urgent.

"I'm good!" But he wasn't—or wouldn't be for long. The demon swarm—a bunch of red-eyes and at least three Claws—was pushing him, Mason, and Max back. A burst of gunfire announced that at least they weren't out of ammo— but only one burst suggested they might be low. And Cynna and Jude needed help. They had three demons attacking— two red-eyes and a Claw. Cynna tossed something invisible at one of them and—oh, good, Benedict finished with his demon and took off to help Cynna and Jude.

Grandmother nudged Lily with her head. Lily didn't need to use her mindsense to know what that meant. *Go.*

She did, veering to the right—and tripping when a tail shot out and gripped her ankle.

One of those damn not-so-dead Claws lay on its side, propped up on one elbow. It hadn't recovered enough to get to its feet, but its tail seemed lively enough. Lily took careful aim—at the head this time, no point in shooting anywhere else. One quick burst got rid of the problem.

Grandmother growled. And shoved at Lily. She got to her feet, but her ankle twinged. Dammit, if she'd wrenched it—

The right-hand wall was about ten feet away. A big chunk of it shimmered. And vanished.

The terror-stricken screams that erupted in the audience hall came from the goddamn demons.

TWENTY-SEVEN

~~~

THE creature revealed by the vanished section of wall was pink, deep rose pink shading into soft baby pink. And huge. It—no, she—was roughly the size of an African elephant, though shaped very differently. Like the red-eyes, she had an upright torso melded to a legged section, but she looked like someone had blended slug with centaur instead of hyena. Her legged section was low to the ground and carried her on myriad legs like a centipede's. Blue eyes circled her round head like a headband, and her mouth went halfway around her head. She had six breasts, four arms distributed with a disturbing lack of symmetry, and a tail like a scorpion's curling up over her back.

Something that large shouldn't be able to move as fast as she did. One second she was inside a dimly lit room little bigger than her body. The next she'd zipped out and grabbed the closest demon. A red-eye. She lifted it off the floor and bit off one of its legs.

Lily realized she was backing up. Limping, but her ankle was holding her, so she kept doing it.

Weng's voice came from everywhere and nowhere. "Xitil was such a bad girl. Hosts should not eat their guests and allies. She's been punished for that, of course, but she's quite mad. I'm afraid she hasn't learned as much as we might wish from her punishment, which has left her hungry. Very hungry."

Xitil, demon prince—former? current?—was not entirely naked. She wore a harness of some sort, with dull red jewels affixed in places. She took another bite of her red-eye. An arm this time. Blood spurted. She licked her lipless mouth with relish. Her tongue was long and red. The red-eye's three remaining legs kicked, but feebly. It had stopped screaming.

Cynna started chanting.

"Xitil," Weng said, adding something in a guttural language.

The pink monster turned to face Lily. And smiled. And pulled off another leg, but she tossed this one on the floor and bit into the red-eye's gut. Disgusting goo oozed up around her mouth.

"Surrender, Lily," Weng said with great cheer, "and I may be able to stop her from killing everyone. She has some respect for the device she wears."

"I thought you wanted me alive," Lily said as she continued to retreat. Grandmother kept pace beside her.

"Oh, Xitil won't kill you. She may not have learned all her lessons, but she knows my colleague wants you alive, and she will not disobey too badly."

"Your colleague is busy," Lily noted. "And you can't control Xitil directly the way *she* can."

"Precisely." He didn't sound at all put out by her observation. "She might play with you a bit. She'd turn you over to me eventually, but she knows so many unpleasant things to do to a human which fall short of fatal. If I were you, I'd ask nicely to be allowed behind this ward."

All around the room, demons were retreating, just like

Lily. Taking careful steps away from the monster that haunted their dreams the way they haunted those of humans.

Cynna stopped chanting. Lily's gaze flicked that way just in time to see her throw something at the demon prince—a charm. Small, silvery, it sailed straight at three or four tons of pink flesh.

It hit. Every inch of pink flesh quivered. Muscles jerked. All of the blue eyes rolled back in their sockets. The dull red gems on her harness flashed bright crimson, and there was a sound almost like firecrackers going off.

The harness fell away.

"What have you done?" Weng screamed. "You fool, you've freed her!" He switched to yelling in the guttural language.

Xitil paid no attention. She smiled slowly and turned to face Cynna. And shot off on all those short, absurdly fast legs.

Lily launched into a run, too, still limping and without much idea of what she could do. Distract the pink monstrosity somehow. Grandmother shot past her. Lily saw others running, too—Benedict, who was closer, and Rule, and that had to be Max, and for a second she thought she glimpsed something small and orange darting between pillars. Couldn't be—

But none of them were as quick as Xitil. She reached the pile of bodies and reared up, half her centipede legs lifting off the floor to lift her head to the room's high ceiling, high above the blond woman with skin covered in inky traceries.

Behind Cynna, another figure rose. This one was covered in gore and wobbled as if uncertain of his footing in the carrion heap. He tilted his head back, looking up at the monster towering over him and his lady, and flung out one hand. "Burn, bitch."

Black fire streamed from his fingers. Mage fire, hugely dangerous to call, capable of burning anything. Lily had seen it consume an ancient artifact that had been crafted by an Old One. It struck the pink flesh . . . and splashed off.

Xitil laughed. High and bright, like a girl presented with a new puppy.

"Well, shit," Cullen said, his body wavering in the non-existent breeze. And fainted.

The fire he'd called did not all wink out with him. Little black flames licked along the floor where it had splashed off Xitil. Even rock burned for mage fire.

Xitil lowered herself, reaching for Cynna with one long arm ending in a taloned hand. Cynna dived beneath that hand just as Benedict reached the other end of the demon. Lily couldn't see what he did—Xitil's body blocked her—but she saw that scorpion tail uncurl and strike with devastating speed even as Rule raced toward the place where his brother had been. She set her weapon to her shoulder, centered the sites on that large, round head, and squeezed the trigger—and the earth rumbled and moved, knocking her to her knees. She tried to get up, but the shaking continued, so she gave up and got ready to shoot from her knees.

Someone beat her to it, firing a steady burst. Bullets thunked into that rubbery flesh of Xitil's head and neck—and vanished, leaving no visible wounds. Xitil tilted her head as if considering, then scuttled with shattering speed toward one of the black pillars.

Max raced out from behind it, an Uzi in one arm.

Lily sent a burst at the demon's head, hoping to distract her. Smoke was beginning to build up. The fire Cullen had lit was growing, creating more fire, normal fire that licked its way along the nearest bodies in that morbid heap. Oh, shit, Cullen was there and unconscious. The ground still vibrated as if ready to explode, but it wasn't rocking as badly. Lily pushed to her feet and limped quickly toward the mortuary pile, where Cynna was pulling on an arm. Cullen's arm.

Jude got there first. He bent to get Cullen in a fireman's carry—not easy when he had only one usable arm, but with Cynna's help he managed it. They didn't need Lily, so she paused, trying to think. How do you stop a demon prince? She had no bloody idea. Xitil was impervious to mage fire, for God's sake. Cynna's charm, designed to disrupt ordered magic, had only acted to free her from whatever that harness did to control her. Bullets sank into her flesh as if absorbed. She was, apparently, capable of shaking the very ground they stood on.

Never mind. They weren't here to stop Xitil. They were here to get the children and *get out*. Weng had mentioned cells. He might have been lying, but—oh, there was Grandmother, sniffing along the wall where the now-empty cell was, the one that had held Xitil. She'd had the same idea, no doubt. Her nose might tell her where to look, and she could open all kinds of things, so—

A stifled cry made her spin. That had sounded like Cynna—but she didn't see her. Jude, yes, with Cullen's body draped across his shoulders, but no Cynna.

No Xitil, either, dammit, so where— The smoke was getting thick enough to make visibility poor, but not enough to hide anything that big. The fire was spreading faster now. They had to hurry, but—there was Xitil, and oh shit, there was Rule standing over his brother's body—please God, his unconscious body, not dead!—preparing to defend both of them against a giggling demon prince.

He had a knife. A bloody damn knife against a mountain of demon.

Lily slapped her weapon back up to her shoulder and fired a burst. Xitil swatted the air as if annoyed by gnats. Lily squeezed the trigger again . . . empty. Shit. She released the old clip, reached for a new one—

"There you are." Weng loomed up out of the gathering smoke a few feet away. He wasn't smiling anymore. His beautiful *shenyi* was smutted with ashes on one long sleeve. And two enormous Claws accompanied him.

No time to load. Lily turned and ran.

"Get her!"

The fire was directly ahead. So was one of the black pillars. She slapped a hand on the pillar, meaning to use it to skid through a turn without slowing down—but the floor was slick with blood. Her skid turned into a slip, wrenching her bad ankle, making her lurch sideways. Her head struck the pillar in a white sizzle of pain, dizzying her. *No time. No time.* She fumbled the clip into her weapon as she turned—

"Lily Yu!" a squeaky voice called from very close by. "Hold still!"

The Claws loomed up out of the smoke. Her arms shook as she raised her weapon. One of them swatted it out of her hands with contemptuous ease. The other reached for her with both arms.

Two more arms—much smaller arms—circled her thigh and held on tightly. A lightning bolt shot down out of nowhere, splitting her sore skull in half, and shot her out into darkness.

SOMEWHERE, deep in the darkness, Lily knew she should wake. But she felt safe here, in this muffled place. Out there was . . . pain.

The thought dragged the reality in with it. A dull pounding . . . in her head. And with that, she had a head again. And a body. A body that ached. Groaning, she opened her eyes. And squeezed them closed again as brightness sent a fresh stab of pain.

After a moment she opened them again, squinting this time. The sky was a bright, cloudless blue. That didn't seem right. Why . . .

Memory tumbled in, all in pieces. The rocky bleakness

of Dis. Red-eyes. Fire. Rule facing off against some monster with only a knife. Dirt bikes. Tom Weng in a red *shenyi*. Spider demons charging in a black mass. A sharp crack on her skull. Cullen throwing black fire. Screams. Grandmother's fur covered in blood. Rule calling her name. An enormous pink monstrosity . . .

Xitil. She felt a burst of satisfaction at identifying that memory shard. She'd been in Dis and she'd seen the demon prince. But surely Xitil was dead? No . . . they'd been wrong about that. She remembered the wall vanishing and what it revealed. Xitil had been in a cell next to the palace's small audience hall . . . the cells. Toby. Ryder. The children.

All this worked through her brain with the slow drip of molasses until she jarred up against the last thought. The children! Where were they? Where was Rule? Automatically she reached out with the mate sense, but the answer it returned was so fuzzy . . . could he be that far away? The mate bond had never let them be separated by that much distance before.

He wasn't close, though. That much was certain. He wasn't with her.

Where was she?

Her head was not working right, but her arms did as they were told, shifting to push her up. The movement hurt her head. The light did, too, but she made herself look around.

Green. That's the first thing that struck her. She was surrounded by green . . . a bank of trees fronted by all sorts of greenery. The giant frilled leaves of a gunnera caught her eye, and the ferns growing under it, and shy lavender flowers she thought might be some kind of anemone. And those were hostas. No gardener could fail to recognize hostas. Lily hadn't had good luck with them in San Diego's climate, but she hadn't given up.

If only her head worked better . . . she'd hit it, hadn't she? Knocked it against that black pillar because her foot slipped when those Claws were chasing her. Must have hit it harder than she'd realized to leave her this muzzy.

She turned her thick, heavy head. The bank of trees went all the way around, interrupted by a couple of paths. Somewhere nearby, water gurgled. She didn't see it, but she heard it. She was sitting in an open area, surrounded by trees and plants. Sitting on grass. Soft, mowed grass.

She was in someone's garden? Or a park? How had she gotten here, for God's sake?

The Claws had caught up with her. Two of them. A bolt of remembered terror shot through her. One had knocked her weapon out of her hands, and . . . and someone else had grabbed her thigh. Someone small who called her Lily Yu.

After that, pain and blackness.

Gan. Gan had brought her here. She wasn't in Dis anymore because Gan had crossed to this place and brought Lily along. Oh, God, she'd done this before, hadn't she? Been yanked into another realm by Gan, who could bring someone else with her when she crossed if she had enough power. She'd said several times that she had lots of power now. From the medallion, no doubt.

Last time this happened, Rule had been with her—with one of her anyway. This time he wasn't anywhere close. He'd been facing off with Xitil with a goddamned knife the last she saw him, and the damnably blurry mate bond made her think he was still there, still in Dis fighting for his life against—

Shut up, she told herself. Rule was alive. The bond might be fuzzy, but she knew that much. He was alive and so was she. Start from there and build on it.

A deep, shaky breath. Think, dammit. The other time she'd crossed with Gan she'd blacked out and woken up hurting. She was pretty sure her headache was worse this time, but she'd hit her head, after all. She'd been confused that other time, too, even worse than now because she'd had her memories stripped. She'd been split in fucking two.

That hadn't happened this time, she told her suddenly frantic heartbeat. This time she knew who she was. She remembered everything. At least she thought she did. Gan had risked the roomful of demons and Xitil herself to save Lily from the Claws, who would have turned her over to Weng. Whose "colleague" wanted Lily alive.

Two years ago, the Great Bitch had wanted to capture Lily alive so she could use Lily's clean-wiped brain to store a copy of the Codex Arcana, the legendary Book of All Magic. God. Lily scrubbed her face with both hands. Was that what *she* wanted Lily for now? But she'd tried to kill Lily several times in the intervening two years. What had changed to make her revert to capturing Lily?

Never mind that for now. Gan had brought her here . . . but where was here, dammit? And where was Gan?

Lily looked around as if she might have overlooked three feet of khaki-clad orange topped by bright blue hair. She even looked up.

High in the blue sky, a shape soared. The color was indistinguishable against that brightness, but the shape was unmistakable. A dragon.

Reno! Could Gan have brought Lily to the same realm Reno had flown off into through the construct? Gan hadn't said she could tell where the dragon went, but maybe it hadn't occurred to her. Sometimes Gan had a poor grasp on what facts were important. Quickly Lily unfurled her mind-sense and sent it out and up and up . . . but she had to push to reach that soaring figure. There was no sudden eagerness to connect with the dragon's mind, no easy draw.

There was no dragon mind there to contact.

"There you are," said a female voice.

Startled, Lily swiveled on her butt. And saw a dead woman.

She was tiny, no more than five feet tall, with the twiggy bones of a bird. Her forehead was high and round; her chin was small and round; her skin was very pale and bore a delicate tracery of wrinkles around the eyes. She wore loose black trousers and a pale blue top with a mandarin collar. Her neatly pinned-up hair was the pale uncolor of a blond who's gone mostly silver.

The last time Lily had seen that hair, it had been wet with blood. The hood to the woman's robe had slipped off her head while Lily was slamming her head against the rough stone floor. "Helen?" she whispered.

TWENTY-EIGHT

～

ON a stretch of sandy beach lay a man's body. He was sprawled on his stomach, one arm out-flung, the other by his side. His jeans were ripped and bloody. The sand beneath his body was pink with watery blood.

A wave washed in, tickling the fingers of the out-flung hand. He didn't react.

The beach was deserted save for the gulls. Most of them soared overhead, calling out suggestions or complaints to each other—*eee-yi-yi-yi-yi*. A couple of them hopped along the sand, turning over bits of seaweed or shells washed up by the waves.

One gull landed near the man. It cocked its head, studying him with a bright, black eye. After a moment it hopped closer and tugged at his hair with its beak.

He didn't react. The gull, however, did, launching itself skyward in a flurry of hasty wings. So did its two compatriots on the beach. The reason for their departure slunk closer, ten feet of orange and black lethality. A seagull would have barely made a bite for such a beast, but why take chances?

A smaller being trotted alongside the beast, her skin almost the same shade of orange as parts of the tiger's fur. She stopped a few paces back, frowning fiercely. The tiger continued until it could sniff the man from head to toe, then snorted softly. The big head gently nudged the man's side.

Rule groaned.

Keep reading for a sneak peek of
the next Lupi novel by Eileen Wilks

DRAGON BLOOD

Coming soon from Berkley Sensation!

PAIN comes in many varieties. There's the crushed outrage of a smashed thumb and the *oh shit* rip of a twisted ankle. A bad tooth throbs, a headache pounds, and when a bone breaks the bright shock of it shorts out the whole system, as intense as a climax.

There is also pain that swallows the entire world, admitting no presence beyond itself. Pain that goes on and on.

Rule woke to pain.

In the first few seconds or eons there was no place to put the pain, nothing to assign it to, no sense it was lodged in this or that part of his body. Pain was entire, complete . . . until it wasn't. He grew aware of a voice. Not words, for the pain-universe allowed him no space to sort sound into words, but he knew this particular sound was a voice.

He was not alone.

Some instinct rose from a place so deep inside the pain could not shut it out. An instinct that said *quiet*. That said *listen*. He was hurt, badly hurt, and he was not alone.

Not-alone was dangerous. His nostrils flared. He did not smell clan or Lily. He smelled . . .

". . . did you stop?" the voice was saying. It sounded scared. "It's not enough to get him out of the water. We've got to get to cover. One of them could swoop down at any moment and . . ."

The word for what he smelled eluded Rule, but he knew the scent. No, two scents. The one that went with the voice was not-trusted. The other . . .

"Hey, why did you—what are you—eeep!"

The other was very dangerous.

"Oh, right. The sleep charm. I forgot about that. I can put him in sleep and then he won't scream anymore. Okay. You can back off now. Please back off."

Very dangerous, but also . . . his. His, and trusted. Rule made a huge effort and opened his eyes.

The glare made his eyes blur, or maybe they'd already been wet. He panted, open-mouthed, as pain threatened to white-out his other senses. He blinked to clear his vision. All he saw was blue. After a moment he caught the word for all that blue: sky. Then a large head loomed over him, furred in orange and black with white above the eyes and on the ruff.

Tiger. That was the word for the one with the dangerous-but-mine scent.

The tiger licked the side of his head with a huge, rough tongue. And purred.

The tiger had a name. Madame Yu. Yes. He was safe. He did not need to defend himself with Madame Yu here. His eyes closed in exhausted relief.

"How did Cynna say it worked?" the voice asked. "I hold it on him, but there was something else."

Memories flickered through Rule and landed on a name. Gan. The voice belonged to Gan, who used to be a demon and an enemy but was now a friend. She was not-trusted because her judgement was unreliable, not because she wished him ill.

"No, don't lick me! Lick him if you want, but I don't—oh, I get what you mean. I'm supposed to lick the charm to activate it."

Madame Yu was here. Gan was here. Where was his mate? Automatically Rule reached for Lily through the bond. Panic flickered, a hot little flame amid the larger pain. So far. She was so far away—

Something damp and metallic pressed against his cheek. Sleep swept in, soft and comforting as a blanket, and separated him from both thought and pain.

WHEN Rule woke again, pain was not the entire universe—more like a tidal sea that waned and waxed with each breath. He floated on that terrible sea and reached again for Lily through the mate bond.

Alive. She was alive, but how could she be so far away?

Madame Yu was nearby. She wasn't a tiger now, according to his nose. She must not be expecting immediate attack, or she wouldn't have returned to her weaker form. He smelled smoke and cooking meat . . . a campfire? Yes. He did not smell Gan except for a faint, lingering scent that seemed to come from his own body, as if the former demon had handled him while he was unconscious. But Gan was not close now.

The ocean was. That mélange of scents soothed him with its familiarity and timeless indifference. He hadn't noticed it the first time he woke, but only the wolf had roused then. Good thing Madame Yu had been with him. He might have killed himself trying to kill Gan or to escape. Lupi had been known to wake in the operating room . . . at least, their wolves had woken up, often with unfortunate results for the surgeon. To an injured wolf, almost everyone was an enemy.

That assumed he could have moved. He was badly hurt this time. It wasn't just the pain, though that spoke convincingly, but the weakness, the woozy, out-of-control feeling . . . from blood loss? Probably, though his aching head suggested a concussion might be contributing.

The pain in his head didn't worry him. Neither did that in his leg—a deep wound, but he hadn't bled out, so it would heal if he lived to heal it. He might not. The worst pain came from his gut.

Even lupi had trouble healing gut wounds without medical care. Surgery was usually required, assuming there was someone to hold the patient in sleep. Units of blood helped. An IV to replace fluids. Nettie, he remembered, had given his father antibiotics when Isen had lost part of his duodenum to a Leidolf attacker a couple years ago. Normally lupi shrugged off unfriendly microbes, but gut wounds were particularly nasty. And why, Nettie had asked, should Isen spend resources healing an infection if he didn't have to?

None of that seemed to be available here . . . wherever "here" was.

Not Dis. Not with the blue sky he remembered seeing. Earth? Had he somehow been returned to Earth? What had happened to him?

With the question, a jumble of memory poured in. Fire. His brother's body, bloody and motionless. Lily on the other side of the cavern, nearly hidden in the smoke. No sign of Toby or the other children, and Cullen either unconscious or dead. Cynna trying to rescue Cullen. A mountain of pink flesh looming over Rule, giggling. Rule gripping his knife firmly as he faced Xitil, the mad demon prince, who had turned out to be insufficiently dead. She'd been about to kill him when . . . what? He couldn't think, couldn't remember—but he remembered enough to know that the only medical supplies he'd had were a roll of gauze and a tube of superglue.

No, he'd used the gauze on Daniel—who was still in Dis, he supposed, if he was still alive. But the others—what had happened to them?

Troubled out of the privacy of pain, he opened his eyes.

Directly overhead was rock, but he was not underground, he saw with relief. Beyond the rock was a dark violet sky, alight with stars. It was not quite full night, but nearly. He turned his head and saw a campfire and a naked woman.

She squatted by the fire, her back to him. A black-and-silver braid hung down the lovely curve of her spine, tied at the end with a scrap of cloth. She was not young, though he saw muscle in her slim shoulders; her skin held a hint of the crepe of age. Perhaps she felt him looking. She looked over her shoulder and spoke crisply. "You're awake. Good."

He blinked. The naked woman was Madame Yu. This should, of course, have been obvious. His brain wasn't working well.

"You need water," she said, and set something down—a stick with what might have been half a rabbit impaled on it. The source of the cooking-meat smell.

Rule lacked the human prejudice against nudity, but for Madame Yu to be unclothed . . . that was just wrong. But she'd been a tiger, hadn't she? She didn't have her clothes with her, hadn't been able to bring them along when they . . . came here? Were brought here? "Where?" he croaked, meaning *where are we.* "The others. What—"

"Water now, then explaining." She unscrewed the cap on a collapsible canteen. "I will lift your head. Do not try to help."

Abruptly he was horribly thirsty. "I'll leak." He pictured the water sliding down his throat only to spill out onto the ground when it reached the hole where his guts should be.

"I have glued you back together." She slid one hand beneath his head and lifted.

She'd superglued his gut? Did she know what to attach to what? "Did—"

"Gan held you in sleep while I glued. You will not leak. Drink." She held the plastic bladder to his lips, giving him little choice.

The water was warm and tasted of dirt. He gulped it down eagerly.

She moved the canteen away before he was ready. "Not too fast, I think."

"How bad . . . am I hurt?" Enough that talking was painful. It forced him to breathe more deeply.

"Most of the damage was to the ropy part of your intestines. I removed the worst mess and glued together what remained. I trust your healing can regrow what was lost." The last sounded like a parent's no-nonsense instruction: *brush your teeth, wash your face, regrow your intestines.* "There was also damage to the . . . bah. What is the word? The knobby intestine. *Jiécháng.* It was not severed, however. I glued it closed. I did not see damage to your other organs, but I was in a hurry. We were in the open. Drink again."

He did. The knobby intestine . . . the colon? Rule knew a little anatomy, enough for the kind of rough battlefield medicine he might have to use on one of his men. By "the ropy part" she must mean his small intestine. Apparently he would have to regrow a lot of that.

"You also have a deep wound in your thigh. I used the last of the glue there after Gan and I moved you to this spot. I did not have enough glue to seal it fully, but it is not bleeding anymore." She withdrew the canteen again.

He licked his lips, dizzy. "Gan?"

"She has gone to steal some things. She can go *dashtu* here, so this should not be difficult."

"Steal from . . . who?"

"There is a village."

"Humans?"

"Yes. This is not one of the sidhe realms."

Was that good or bad? He couldn't think. "How did we get here?"

"Gan brought me and also Cynna and Lily. You, I believe, were brought here by Lily."

He started to shake his head and winced. Definitely a concussion. "Lily can't do that. And she is . . . far away." Much too far for his piece of mind or for her to have somehow brought him here, wherever "here" was. Madame still hadn't answered that one. Maybe she didn't know.

"You did not arrive in the same place as Lily because you did not leave from the same place in Dis."

"Lily can't cross realms."

"Tch. Gan did not bring you, and who else could? She did bring Lily. You must have been pulled here with her by the mate bond."

That . . . made sense, actually. He vividly remembered the Lady's voice saying *steady*. Even more vividly he remembered what had followed. The mate bond had vanished, then returned, supercharged. At least that's what Cullen had said—that Rule was suddenly glowing with twice as much magic as usual. "The Lady," he said slowly. "She arranged it."

"Very likely. You are muddled from your wounds. This is not surprising. You were nearly dead. Is your memory bad?"

"I remember most of it. I don't remember receiving this." His hand lifted two inches to indicate his stomach. The tiny effort exhausted him.

"I think Xitil did that, but I was busy and did not see it happen. Do you remember Xitil?"

"Yes." A mountain of pink flesh towering over him. A band of blue eyes circling a round head. A mad giggle.

"Do you also remember that the children were not in the audience hall, as we had thought?"

He remembered the doppelgänger that he'd thought was his son and how it had felt to watch it *melt*. "He . . . they . . . the children must be in the cells." He ran out of breath and drew in air slowly. Carefully. There were cells off the audience hall where they'd fought demons, a demon prince, and a dragon spawn. He'd seen Xitil emerge from one. "Couldn't get to them. Cells sealed by rock."

"Not exactly rock. When the false Toby melted, Gan thought to look for the children with her *üther* sense. It is very hard to hide *üther* from one who can perceive it. Rock blocks this perception, but Gan tells me the cells were sealed with something like the window we stepped through—ah, but you did not see the window. You may think of it as part-time rock. Part of the time it is rock, part of the time it is not. Gan discovered that, to her *üther* sense, this part-time rock flickers. When it does, she can perceive beyond it. She did not notice this earlier because the flicker does not happen often. Also, she was not looking in the right way." Madame shook her head, disapproval blending with forgiveness. "She is very young."

Rule had the impression the former demon was at least twice his age. But as an ensouled being . . . yes, in that sense Gan was very young. "The children? She found them?"

"The cells were empty."

All the air left the world. For long, terrible seconds Rule was pinned in a dark, airless void before his chest remembered its job and lifted, letting in air and sending pain ribboning through his gut.

"This does not mean they are dead," Madame informed him sternly. "You are not to think so. It is likely they were taken through a gate. Drink again."

He let her lift his head—hell, he probably couldn't have stopped her. But he wanted answers, not water. "Why likely?"

"Gan says there was a gate. A permanent gate, but closed at the time. She is certain of it. To her, a gate feels like a wind that bubbles instead of blowing. This has little meaning to me, but much for her. Drink," she repeated, and this time gave him no choice but to swallow or let her dribble water over his closed mouth. She had pity on him, though, and continued talking as she administered measured sips. "Gan found this closed gate when she came out into the hall. She could tell what realm the gate opened into. It was, she says, very bubbly. This means to her that it had been used very recently."

She moved the canteen away, letting him catch his breath. Absurd that drinking water could run him out of breath, but it had. "She thinks this means the children were brought here through the gate. I think this, also."

His heart thudded sharply. "They're here?"

"Not yet. I explain." She tipped the canteen to his lips again. "At the time Gan found the gate she believed we would all be killed. I do not say she was wrong; matters were not going well. She wished to live. She wished also for her friends to live. Cynna was closest, so first she brought Cynna here. She returned to the audience hall and grabbed Lily and crossed with her. She returned again and grabbed me—not because she counts me as a friend, but I was close. Also, she was impressed when I killed a m'reelo. She could not bring anyone else here because she cannot return to the audience hall from this point, not at any of the critical moments. She is already in all the other times she might have crossed to."

He managed one last swallow and turned his head slightly. "That makes no sense."

"Obviously there cannot be two of her in Dis at the same instant. You have drunk it all? Good." She took the canteen away.

"How could there be two of her at the same time?"

Grandmother gave that disapproving *tch* again. "I have just said that could not be. You are not thinking well."

"Tired."

"Too much talking. Rest. I will get more water." She stood.

Madame looked even more naked when standing, though her dignity was unimpaired by the lack of clothing, just as her spine was unaffected by the tiredness he could see in her face.

"Wait. You said . . . the children are not here yet."

"Ah. Yes. Do you remember that many realms do not match with each other in time, even when they touch in place? It is so, and time is very crooked between Dis and this place. This let Gan choose, a little, what time she crossed to. She had to bring each of us to a different time because she could not be here twice at the same moment, and she was in haste, so she is not sure what time she brought us to. But she believes we all arrived here before we left Dis."

He was too exhausted and hurting to make much sense of that, but he thought he got the important part. "The children aren't here yet."

"No. We have some time—between one and three weeks. They will not arrive in this portion of the realm, however. We must travel when you are able. No more talk now. I will be gone ten or fifteen minutes. There is a seep. It is not far, but it is necessary to be cautious here when crossing open ground."

"Why? he asked. Then, more sensibly—for there were many reasons the open might be dangerous—he asked once more, "Where are we?"

"*Lóng Jia*." Her black eyes were remote, as if she looked out on some private vista, one that held great meaning. Then her gaze sharpened and flicked to him. "In English, you would call it Dragonhome."

Want to connect with fellow science fiction and fantasy fans?

For news on all your favorite Ace and Roc authors, sneak peeks into the newest releases, book giveaways, and much more—

"Like" and Follow Ace and Roc Books!

facebook.com/AceRocBooks
twitter.com/AceRocBooks

FROM *NEW YORK TIMES* BESTSELLING AUTHOR

EILEEN WILKS

RITUAL
MAGIC

A NOVEL OF THE LUPI

When Lily's mother suddenly loses all her memories after age twelve, Lily knows that she is under the influence of something even stronger than magic. And when she learns that others have fallen victim to the same fate, she must discover what dark force connects them...

PRAISE FOR EILEEN WILKS

"Grabs you on the first page and never lets go."
—Patricia Briggs, #1 *New York Times* bestselling author

"One of the best Were series I have ever read."
—Fresh Fiction

eileenwilks.com
facebook.com/eileenwilks
penguin.com

Penguin
Random
House
BERKLEY

M1460T0715

Connect with Berkley Publishing Online!

For sneak peeks into the newest releases, news on all your favorite authors, book giveaways, and a central place to connect with fellow fans—

"Like" and follow Berkley Publishing!

facebook.com/BerkleyPub
twitter.com/BerkleyPub
instagram.com/BerkleyPub

BERKLEY | Penguin Random House